DELIVERING THE COMMONWEALTH

Delivering
the Commonwealth

MARK SCHAEFER

RESOURCE *Publications* · Eugene, Oregon

DELIVERING THE COMMONWEALTH

Resource Publications
An Imprint of Wipf and Stock Publishers
199 W. 8th Ave., Suite 3
Eugene, OR 97401

www.wipfandstock.com

PAPERBACK ISBN: 978-1-5326-7858-5
HARDCOVER ISBN: 978-1-5326-7859-2
EBOOK ISBN: 978-1-5326-7860-8

06/19/24

For Renata and Joaquin

May no frontier ever stop you from going boldly after your dreams.

CONTENTS

CONTENTS

A NOTE ON LANGUAGE

LANGUAGE PLAYS A ROLE in this narrative, mainly to show how language might change over time and the challenges that such changes would present for peoples who have not communicated in a long time.

The convention in this book is that Modern English stands in for the contemporary language of our main characters, the Anglic of the twenty-eighth century. Slightly older versions of that future language are represented by slightly older versions of our contemporary language, even though the older version of a future language would still be a future version to us.

By doing this, I hope to give the reader a sense of the different language changes without having to figure out what twenty-fourth-century and twenty-eighth-century English would be like and writing the entire novel in those.

PROLOG

"BLOWN RIGHT OUT INTO vacuum. All of them."

Jareth Killian lifted his head from his beer glass to see who'd said that. He'd been sitting at the bar, nursing his drink—another in a long line of them—staring ahead and tuning out the inane chatter and the pickup lines surrounding him. But this was different.

"God, that's terrible. All of them?" asked a second voice responding to the first.

"Well, all from that one ship."

Jareth turned toward the voices. A middle-aged man was excitedly relaying this information to a woman of the same age. They had that look that couples on a first date have when they're happy to have a topic to discuss that gives them enough fodder for things to say.

Jareth tried to shake the haze of his foggy thinking and followed their gazes up toward the screens on the wall behind the bar. There, in the center of the image, was a destroyer—cut in half like some kind of cutaway diagram with debris and bodies radiating away from the wreckage. The ship had several additional gaping holes through which more crew and equipment were venting into space. The chyron across the bottom of the screen read, "Fleet destroyed."

Jareth willed himself to focus—today was not a day to indulge his listlessness and lethargy. Something was happening. Something big. He turned to the couple.

"What's going on?"

If they were surprised by his question, they didn't show it. Whatever was going on was news to everyone.

"Remember those unidentified objects at the edge of the Kittim system?" the man said.

"Yeah," Jareth replied. Three weeks ago, Long Radar on Farmark spotted what appeared to be a fleet of vessels moving from the edge of the system. Hyperspace relays and perimeter sensors had not recorded any drop out of hyperspace—whatever they were, they had crossed the great void between stars at sub-light speeds. Authorities in the Kittim system made several attempts to communicate with the fleet but had been unsuccessful.

"Last I'd heard," Jareth continued, "the ISG was escorting a diplomatic delegation out to meet them."

"Hostiles," the man said, showing a keen gift for understatement.

Jareth's mind raced, woken from its slumber. Who were they? Where had they come from?

No one from the League had ever colonized the systems beyond, but research drones had visited them; there weren't any inhabited systems within a dozen light-years.

Jareth turned back to the bar and stared at the drink in front of him. "It figures," he said, picking up the glass and downing the remainder.

"You say something, Jare?" asked the bartender, working his way toward Jareth.

"What's that, Stepha? Oh, I was just thinking that we've been out here all this time, cut off from the rest of human civilization without so much as a word from any other systems. And now, out of nowhere, the first vessels from outside the League to appear in our space bring nothing but death and destruction. It figures."

"Yeah, it does, doesn't it? You want another?"

Jareth turned back toward the bar and regarded his empty glass. It was early—only around twenty-two o'clock, still three hours until midnight—but he was done. "Nah, I'll settle up." He waved his handheld at the bar to pay his tab and got up to leave.

"See ya again tomorrow?" Stepha said.

"Yeah, likely." But Jareth wasn't so sure.

He looked around. Everyone was staring at the screens or their handhelds. Nobody was talking. Someone or something had reached down out of the cold depths of interstellar space and gotten their attention. They'd undeniably gotten his.

On the train ride home, he did something he hadn't done in a long time—he took out his handheld and began scrolling through news feeds, passing up his usual fare of mind-numbing vids and cheap entertainment. On his screen were images of battered hulls of League ships coming in from Farmark. Each vessel seemed to have gaping holes where tons of equipment and hundreds of crewmembers had been flushed out into the vacuum of deep space. He paused at an image of a cruiser with the proud emblem of the League of Four Worlds scorched by fusion fire and particle beam. He lingered on a photo of a shell-shocked fleet officer being taken aboard a medical frigate. He scrolled through a steady stream of images of nothing short of a catastrophe but could not look away.

Jareth nearly missed his stop but was jostled by a fellow passenger at just the right time to snap him out of his doom-scrolling. He exited the train and walked the half-kilometer to his apartment complex. Through the windows of his neighbors' homes, he could see screens displaying newsfeeds, interviews with military specialists, and analysts trying to make sense of it all.

He entered his apartment and turned on the screen to one of the larger news feeds. There was a panel discussion—a couple of pundits, their usual security reporter, and a fleet captain in the Intersystem Guard. One of the pundits was in the middle of speaking.

"—just doesn't make sense how the ISG could suffer such a major setback against such a primitive enemy."

The other pundit jumped in. "Clearly, they're *not* primitive. They may not have FTL capability, but that doesn't seem to have been a setback for them. Isn't that right, Fleet Captain?"

The ISG fleet captain, whom the chyron on the screen identified as Fleet Captain Leyna Schneider-Yu, nodded. "That is correct, Kaden. Our sensors have not detected any hyperspace ability in these vessels. Nevertheless, their weapons technology is potent, and we were unable to do any damage to their hulls."

The political correspondent jumped in. "Fleet Captain, as tragic as what happened in Kittim is, does the ISG believe that Fairhaven, Pherat, and New Sydney are at risk? If the Invaders don't have hyperspace—"

"The Invaders don't have hyperspace engines, but judging from the fact that they made it to Kittim in the first place, and based on observations our vessels made during the engagement, they have engines capable of a sustained point-five gee acceleration. That would get them to Fairhaven in five and a half years, four if they can muster one gee acceleration."

Jareth sat back in stunned disbelief. Even without hyperdrive, they could be at Fairhaven in five years? The distance between Fairhaven and New Sydney was shorter than that between Farmark and Fairhaven—did that mean they could be in the Sharon system in only three years after that?

He changed the screen to another feed. Yet more pundits, yet more doom and gloom, yet more ISG officials expressing skepticism that the fleet could ever be ready to face the Invaders again, let alone in the time frames they were expecting. Jareth watched until well after twenty-five when fatigue began to overtake him.

He turned off the feed and fell unceremoniously onto his bed without even bothering to undress. He could feel the exhaustion from the shock of the day and the unrelenting coverage on the feeds. But as he closed his eyes to visions of shattered starship hulls and terrorized fleet personnel, he felt more awake in that moment than he had in years.

✦

THREE WEEKS WENT BY, and the news wasn't getting any better. Jareth found himself constantly absorbed in reports, scientific observations, and anything that could shed some light on what was happening and how the government would respond.

"Killian, put that damned thing down!"

The jocular voice of Lu Buhari-Singh snapped Jareth out of his doom-scrolling stupor. "You're going to give yourself a health condition overdosing on that stuff. And trust me, the plant doesn't have the best workers' compensation coverage."

Jareth had to laugh. Lu had a way of being disarming, effective, and ridiculous at the same time. He turned off his handheld and put it in his coverall pocket.

"I'm sorry, Lu. I just can't get my head around everything that's happened. I keep hoping that I'll open up the feeds, and there will be an announcement about an armada or a new superweapon we've developed. It feels like we're not doing anything."

"Yeah, I get it. You know all my family's from Farmark, yeah? These things take time, especially if you want to do them right. Right now, the ISG's focused on getting people out of the system."

"Yeah, I know. I guess part of it is that I feel like *I* can't do anything about it at all."

"Why don't you join up? The ISG's definitely recruiting."

"I don't know that that's for me."

"You were in the Merchant Marine, yeah? Security, right? Same skills that the fleet would want. Hell, the security work you do for me would look good on your record. And you've already got space legs."

"I'm no combat officer," Jareth said, and there, deep in the pit of his stomach, was that feeling of dread at even the thought of combat. He would have liked to have believed it was fear; that would have at least been honorable after a fashion. But he knew it was something else.

As if to spare him from further introspection, his handheld pinged. Everyone's handheld pinged. He and Lu exchanged a look and grabbed their devices.

"Chancellor's gonna give an address tonight," Lu read. "There's your news, Killian."

Jareth kept rereading the ping notification to see if there were any details. There weren't.

"Tell you what, I'll come meet you at your usual watering hole after work. We can watch it together and raise a glass."

"Yeah, I guess so," said Jareth. He hadn't been back to the *Infanta de Castilla* since the night the first reports came through. Given everything that'd happened, it'd lost its allure. Still, it would be nice to be surrounded by people when the Chancellor announced whatever new catastrophe she was going to announce.

"Great!" said Lu. "I'll meet you there after shift."

A couple of hours later, Jareth walked into the *Infanta* and made his way toward his usual spot at the bar. Someone else was sitting in "his" seat. Before he could decide whether to be miffed or not, he heard his name. "Killian!" He turned and saw Lu sitting at a table along the wall.

"Place is crowded," Lu said as Jareth walked over. "Looks like everyone's got the same idea."

"Looks that way. Have you ordered already?" Jareth took out his handheld and logged into the bar's service portal.

"Yeah, got something coming."

Jareth sat and placed his own order through his device. A minute or two later, a server showed up carrying a tray with their drinks.

"Well, look who it is!" she said. "Haven't seen you in a while!"

"Yeah. Been busy," Jareth replied as Lu raised his eyebrows in mild astonishment.

Almost on cue, everyone hushed as the screens around the bar, regardless of what feed they'd been following, now displayed the seal of the Office of the Chancellor of the Four Worlds. After a moment, the seal was replaced by the face of Aditi Parvat-Singh, the Chancellor of the League. She began to speak in her usual soft manner, flavored with a mild Farmark accent.

"My fellow citizens. An unspeakable tragedy has befallen our worlds. Our siblings on Farmark have suffered a cataclysm like no other in human history. What should have been a joyous day for all of us—the first human encounter with intelligent alien life—has become a day of sorrow and lamentations. The planets of the Kittim system have been devastated, and a hostile intelligence has taken up a position in the system designed to establish its control over worlds that had until recently been the homes to hundreds of millions.

"At this moment, ISG forces are conducting rescue and recovery missions in the Kittim system and attempting to find and save as many refugees as possible. Many residents of the system have fled in craft not meant for interstellar travel. Our fleet is doing the best it can to track down such vessels in the space beyond the Kittim system and deliver their passengers safely to Fairhaven. League Marines are also engaged in targeted rescue missions on the surface of Farmark itself, although these missions have proven to have high casualty rates. It is likely that such operations will be suspended in the near future."

"Crike," said Lu. "Imagine pulling that duty."

Jareth just shook his head slowly. The Chancellor continued.

"Our scientists and strategic analysts in the ISG have determined that if the invading forces attempt to reach Fairhaven next, they could be within that system in just over five standard years." There was a murmur now rumbling through the establishment. This was not a new number to hear—pundits and commentators had been putting this figure out for weeks—but this was the first time the government had said as much.

"And I wish to be forthright with you, my fellow citizens. Given the damage the ISG has taken from the Invaders and our utter inability to cause any significant damage to their vessels, the ISG does not believe we can be victorious in another engagement, even five years hence. Efforts at communicating with the Invaders have proven fruitless."

The rumble throughout the bar was building as more and more people began to digest what the Chancellor was saying. Jareth could feel his own growing sense of dread. On the screen, Chancellor Parvat-Singh paused, almost as if she knew her audience would react to what she'd said. Then, she took a deep breath and continued.

"In our darkest hour, we must reach out to that source of light that had burned the brightest in all of human civilization. Unable to repel or reason with the Invaders ourselves, we have no choice but to try to establish contact with the Commonwealth and enlist its aid."

There was pandemonium in the *Infanta de Castilla*. Jareth leapt to his feet and joined with others shouting nearby. Whatever the Chancellor said next was drowned out by the cheering patrons. No one cared; they'd watch the rest of it on replay later.

Jareth returned to the table where Lu was sitting and flopped down in his chair.

"The Commonwealth, Lu! The Commonwealth!"

Lu was happy, to be sure, but he looked more thoughtful than anything—not nearly as celebratory as Jareth and the rest of the patrons.

"What's on your mind, Lu?"

"It's amazing, for sure. One way or the other, we'll find out what happened to them. Why we've never heard from them in four hundred years."

That was an understatement, thought Jareth. Every Leaguer wrestled with the mystery of why the Commonwealth had never followed their expedition to establish trade and communications. Finding out what had become of them was like finally scratching a psychic itch that had been plaguing the Four Worlds for centuries.

"Yeah," Jareth said. "I imagine the gambling markets are going to start laying odds on the answers."

Lu leaned forward and adopted a posture that Jareth couldn't help but interpret as serious. Jareth leaned in attentively.

"Look, for the Chancellor to say, 'We have no choice but to try to establish contact with the Commonwealth and enlist its aid,' tugs on emotional strings that no Leaguer is without, yeah? It stirs in us that old sense of mystery, wonder, desire to know what had happened, and longing to be reconnected to the rest of humanity."

"Yeah, of course."

"See, Killian, the Chancellor's a politician. She has no idea whether the Commonwealth even exists, and neither do the rest of us. And even if it does, no one knows whether they'll be willing to help. And if they're willing, are they able to help? Who knows? But here's the thing: just talking about the Commonwealth has given us hope, yeah? When was the last time you'd seen anyone who looked like they were feeling something other than terror or hopelessness?" He gestured around the bar, and Jareth had to agree.

"I suppose there are worse things a politician could give her people."

"There's another thing," Lu said and gestured toward one of the screens on the wall. By this time, the screen was populated with talking heads dissecting and analyzing what the Chancellor had said. But Lu pointed to the chyron at the bottom of the screen: *Chancellor Announces Expedition to the Commonwealth: ISG Seeks Civilian Enlistees for Voyage.*

Jareth sat back in his chair. He couldn't quite name the feeling forming in the pit of his stomach, but he knew it wasn't dread.

"I need to go on that expedition," he said at last.

"You need to go on that expedition," agreed Lu. "You were looking for a way to contribute, and there it is, yeah? I'd go, too. Sadly, I'm too old, but you're not. You're a good man, good at supply, good at security, and you might be able to do something. So go, get us some help, and tell 'em to come back here with you and frag those bastards who toasted Farmark, yeah? I've got some friends in the ISG. I'll make sure you get an enlistment interview."

Jareth nodded slowly. Lu was right: they didn't know whether the Commonwealth existed or whether anyone there would be able to help. But in that moment, he knew he wanted to be a part of the effort to find out.

WHO WERE THE PIONEERS?

The Pioneers (pie-uh-NEERZ) were the brave men, women, and folx who founded our planets. They left other planets very far away on very big ships to look for a new home. They brought with them a lot of supplies, food, and even animals to build a new life!

The Pioneers had to choose how they were going to find a new place to live. There are two ways to find a new planet to live on. First, you can find a planet where there is no life and *terraform* (TARE-uh-form) it so that life can grow. Second, you can find a planet where there is already life and where people can live.

The Pioneers found some planets they could terraform but decided to keep going. They wanted to find planets where they could live right away without having to wait. They traveled a long, long way before they came to our planets.

HOW MANY PLANETS DO PEOPLE LIVE ON?

In our League, people live on four planets—that's why it's called the "League of Four Worlds." There are New Sydney and Pherat around the star we call Sharon, Fairhaven around Roger's Star, and Farmark around Kittim. Together, these four planets and three stars make up our League!

You may know that there are many more planets that people live on—more than 200! Those are the planets the Pioneers came from, but those planets are very far away. They are so far away that light or radio signals from us would take 700 years to get there! That's a long time to wait for the next episode of *Captain Defender*!

—From *A Child's Guide to the League of Four Worlds*

1 | KILLIAN | ENLISTMENT

JARETH WAS UP EARLY the following day. He checked his handheld; there was an unread message from Lu. "You've got an interview appointment at fourteen o'clock at the ISG recruiting station downtown. Don't worry about your job—it'll still be here when you get back." Jareth took a deep breath—this was really happening.

He packed a kit bag and took just the essentials. It didn't make any sense to take any more than that—if he were accepted, the ISG would give him anything he needed, and if he were rejected, he wouldn't be gone long enough to need anything more than what he had with him.

He locked the apartment and put the house computer on vacation mode so that the plants would get watered. It was only ten o'clock; he'd have enough time to stop by his parents' place on the way to the maglev station. He couldn't decide whether that was a good thing.

Jareth walked the kilometer to his parents' modest dwelling at the end of a quiet street in a New Kalgoorlie suburb and let himself in.

"Anyone home?"

His mother came running out from the study. "Jareth! What day is it? Shouldn't you be at work? It's lovely to see you."

"I have today off, Ma."

"Oh, that's lovely. Are you here for lunch?"

"No, Ma. Just swinging by on my way downtown."

"What's downtown?" said his father walking into the room from the opposite direction his mother had come. Jareth assumed he'd been puttering away in the shop again or whatever retirees did with their free time.

"The ISG recruitment office," Jareth replied. Both of his parents stopped in their tracks.

"Jareth," his mother began, barely concealing the instantaneous worry overtaking her. "You're not going to—"

"No, Ma. I'm not going to Farmark or Fairhaven," he said. He saw his mother's body relax in an instant from the tension that had just as suddenly overtaken it. "I'm applying to go on the expedition to the Commonwealth."

"The expedition! Oh, Jare, that's wonderful! Oh, I'm so proud of you, my brave son."

"I haven't gotten in *yet*, Ma. They might not take me."

"Why wouldn't they? You're perfect for this. You're smart, and you have all that good experience in the Merchant Marine. Oh, this is wonderful."

Jareth couldn't help but notice that his father was decidedly less enthusiastic.

"Jareth, that's all well and good. But the ISG isn't like any other job. You can't just bail like you did with the Merchant Marine because you decided you didn't like it."

"I didn't quit the Merch because I didn't like it, Dad. It just wasn't the thing."

"The thing?"

"Yeah, the thing. Like how you knew urban planning was for you ever since you were a kid playing city-building sims. Or how mom knew she wanted to work in social services because of her experiences as a teen when Grandpa lost his job. You both found work that was meaningful for you. I'm just trying to do the same thing."

"Well, I think it's just wonderful," his mother chimed in. "Padraig Killian would be proud."

"You know me, Ma—always looking to follow in the footsteps of the Pioneers," Jareth rejoined with mock seriousness.

"You're no Pioneer, Jareth," his father said in true seriousness. Jareth faltered at the unanticipated attack and was momentarily disoriented. He regarded his father for a moment, but his father's expression bore no clues as to what he'd meant by that.

"Look, Mom, Dad. There's no guarantee that I'll get in. I have an appointment this afternoon; that's all. I could be back tonight. But I know that if I didn't try to help, I'd regret it the rest of my life."

His mother was practically beaming. "Do you need anything for the road? Can I send you with anything to eat?"

"Ma!" Jareth laughed. "I'm going downtown, not into deep space!"

"Alright, alright. I'll let you be. Just want to make sure you're okay."

"I'm fine. I should go."

"I'll walk you out," his father said. Jareth kissed his mother goodbye and stepped out the front door, his father in tow.

"'You're no Pioneer,' Dad? Really?" Jareth said, turning to face his father.

"Look, Jare. I didn't want to say anything inside in front of your mother. It's obvious that your decision means a lot to her, her side of the family being all fleet veterans and everything. But we both know why this isn't a good idea for you."

"And why is that, Dad?" Jareth snapped.

"We both know that you didn't leave the Merchant Marine because you wanted to."

Jareth froze. What did his father know? *How* could his father know? "I'm not sure what you mean," was all he could muster.

"I think you do. Look, you're a grown man. You're capable of making your own decisions. I can't stop you, and it's not my place anymore to try to talk you out of anything. Perhaps this is the right course of action; perhaps not. But for your own sake, I'm asking you to rethink the direction your life is going, Jare. Really rethink it before heading off on this expedition."

"I've thought about it plenty," Jareth responded after a moment. "This is the right thing for me. Trust me, Dad. I know what I'm doing."

His father looked carefully at him and then nodded. "As you say."

Jareth was about to protest his father's barely concealed judgment when the latter stuck out his hand.

"Good luck, Jareth. Let us know how it turns out today."

"Thank you, Dad. I will," he replied, taking his father's hand. His father shook his hand firmly, then nodded again and returned to the house.

Jareth stood for a moment, watching him walk back inside. He saw his mother looking from the window and gave her another wave. He was glad that one of his parents understood what he was trying to do. He drew himself up, turned back toward the street, and walked the rest of the way to the maglev station.

THE MAGLEV TRAIN ENTERED New Kalgoorlie on a scenic bridge over the Crookit River and arrived at Bundt Station, a familiar and impressive structure he had passed through all the time when he was in the Merchant Marine. From Bundt Station, it was just a short block's walk to the Naval Recruitment Office in the League Building on Market Street.

A queue of people snaked around the block, but because of Lu's connections, Jareth skipped the line and took the elevator to the 29th floor. As the doors opened, he was greeted by a stunningly beautiful woman, immediately flustering the lizard and mammalian parts of his brain, nearly causing him to stammer. Fortunately, his higher brain functions wrangled that impulse; to do otherwise would have earned him a ticket right back downstairs and a spot at the back of the line. Because there were no sex or gender distinctions in the ISG, the fleet did not have a lot of tolerance for anyone demonstrating that they couldn't interact professionally with other sexes and genders. It was an absolute requirement when you were in close-quarters cohabitation for months on end.

"Jareth Killian, reporting for enlistment interview," he said.

She smiled slightly and checked a datapad she was holding. "You're with me, as it turns out, Mr. Killian. Follow me." She turned and walked toward a small office off to one side. It had a remarkable view of the Crookit River and Pioneer Square—no doubt an intentionally presented vista designed to stir up sentimental patriotic feelings and make you want to sign up to risk your life for the League.

Once Jareth entered the room, she extended her hand. "Lt. Marya Tavares," she said. "Please have a seat." Jareth sat in the client chair as Tavares sat behind the desk. She began scrolling through some information on her datapad. After a few moments, something caught her eye, and she looked up. "Says here you have experience in cargo and security, Mr. Killian."

"Yes, Lieutenant. I was cargo master on a freighter in the Merchant Marine."

"How was it that you became security chief?"

"Our security chief got killed in a freak accident. The captain tapped me for the job because I had done a lot of work with the chief securing and guarding some of our more sensitive cargo."

"What kind of cargo was it?"

"Injector nozzles for antimatter containment bottles, deuterium shielding, hyperspatial rudders, Long Radar arrays—that kind of thing."

"That's some pretty impressive cargo, Mr. Killian," she said. "It says here that you had only one security breach in seven years."

"That's right, Lieutenant. Just the one." Jareth braced—here it was. Here was the moment his hopes of getting back into space were dashed. He could feel his blood pressure rising and his hands becoming clammy. He hoped to Abe's God that he wasn't sweating and that his face still had some color.

"A laudable feat for cargo so prone to theft for the black market."

"Yes, sir," he replied tentatively. Had he just been spared? "We had a good crew."

"Perhaps it was good leadership. You certainly have recommendations to that effect from Captains Mfese and Bloch in your file. They seemed to think rather highly of you."

"I was just trying to do my job," Jareth said, desperately trying not to show too much pleasure or surprise. Mfese and Bloch were the best captains he had ever served under, and their praise meant a great deal to him—Mfese's in particular.

✚

THE LAST TIME HE'D seen Idris Mfese, it'd been in the latter's office aboard the *Cantankerous Vixen*.

"Killian, this is partially my fault," he'd said. "You'd been my security chief for so long that I forgot you never had the training I would normally require for the position. When Amara was killed, you did such a good job stepping up in the moment that it seemed like the right decision just to keep you where you were."

Jareth had just stared at the deck, too ashamed to raise his eyes to meet his captain's gaze. "I appreciate you saying that, Captain, but it's my fault. I froze."

"You did," he said. "But it's not every day we get raided by pirates, and you were never trained to repel boarding actions. It's understandable that you would not have taken point in the ship's defense."

That was a generous way of putting it. When the pirates breached the hull and stormed the hold, Jareth had been in an adjoining compartment. He could hear the atmospheric depressurization alarms going off in the corridor until the vented air could no longer carry the sound. Still, the thuds of the pirates' magnetic boots on the decking could be felt through the floor, and the occasional ricochet of a round off the bulkhead could be heard in his hideout. He knew that his crewmates were in trouble and that the ship's cargo was about to be seized—and he did nothing.

He would remember standing there as if watching someone else, with part of him screaming *Go do something, you fool!* But that part wasn't loud or persuasive enough. It was only once no more vibrations came through the deck plating that he dared to emerge from his refuge. By the time it was over, twenty-three million credits' worth of cargo was gone, Tallmadge, the cargo master, had been spaced, and a crew'man—Kian Lee-Chowdhury— was in sickbay with mortal injuries that would later claim his life.

"It's understandable, Killian. But we both know what has to happen next."

"I understand, sir. I'll save you the trouble. I'll have my resignation to you before the end of the watch." Jareth stood up, "Permission to be dismissed, sir."

"I need you to know that if it were up to me, this would be an opportunity to learn. I think you can be redeemed, and this tragedy could only make you a better officer. But twenty-three million credits' worth of cargo looted—there's no way that the shipper is going to allow the status quo after something like that." *Of course, it was the twenty-three million and not Tall-madge or Crew'man Lee-Chowdhury,* Jareth thought—*flegging corporations.*

"No, sir. I suppose not."

"Jareth," Mfese said, rising from behind his desk. "This feels like the end of the world, I'm sure. It won't be forever; you'll be back."

Jareth nodded, still unable to make direct eye contact.

"Dismissed."

That was the last time he saw Mfese. Jareth transmitted his resignation electronically, and not long after, he was on a shuttle headed to the Fairhaven relay station and home. Until his enlistment interview, he'd never known what Mfese had put in his file. Evidently, he'd simply written, "Discharged, 2781-09-17 (STD)." A final grace from his captain.

LT. TAVARES MADE SOME adjustments to her datapad and passed it to him. It now displayed an enlistment contract. "On behalf of the Intersystem Guard, I am granting you a commission of the rank of Lieutenant, Junior Grade. As you have already served with the Merchant Marine, you are eligible for abbreviated basic training to take place at the fleet facility at Novaroma, after which you will be assigned to a vessel in the Expeditionary Fleet. Given your experience and the great need we have for talented people, I would expect you'll be assigned to the command of Captain Kavanagh, but that is for others to decide." She rose quickly, and Jareth followed. He gave her a crisp salute, and she returned it. "Report to Ensign Stein on the 18th floor, and he'll give you your travel orders for Novaroma. Good luck, Lieutenant."

Jareth left her office stunned. A *lieutenant?* He had made no assumptions that he'd be accepted for the Expedition, and he was still processing the fact that Captain Mfese had not included his failure as part of his record. Perhaps Mfese had been serious when he said he'd have treated the incident as a learning experience. It was a kindness, for sure, but Jareth couldn't help but feel that he'd pulled one over on the ISG. How long would it take them to discover he didn't merit their faith in him?

Even if he had had nothing in his past to worry about, he would have expected only a non-commissioned rank at best. But an officer? He concluded the ISG must be nervous about sending too many of its current officer corps on this expedition, with the alien fleet still out there and showing no signs of relenting.

Ensign Stein was an agreeable fellow who gave Jareth his travel orders—yet another surprise: a ticket for a commercial sub-orbital. He would be at Novaroma in a few hours instead of the day's travel it would otherwise take on cheaper transport. The government was sparing no expense to make this expedition happen—why then, he wondered, were they okay with discount officers in their officer corps?

BULLETIN
Via LeagueNet 11020664983@112300.00.01
Unencrypted; Public Distribution Requested

Intersystem Guard Travel Restrictions
Date: 10 October 2790 (Std)
Destination: Kittim Star System
Warning: System Restricted Due to Invasion

Details: The Intersystem Guard has engaged hostile alien forces in the Kittim Star System. Alien forces are presently occupying several planets in the system and engaging in aggressive actions against incoming spacecraft. The Antimatter Production Facility on Triton, Moon of Falstaff (Kittim VII), has been scuttled by ISG personnel. Possible radiation hazard.

Recommendation: All travel to the Kittim Star System is prohibited until further notice. Only those civilian craft authorized by the ISG to participate in refugee rescue are permitted to travel to Kittim and must do so with ISG escort. Those currently in the Kittim Star System are advised to evacuate immediately and report to the nearest ISG outpost for assistance. Limited recovery and rescue operations are taking place on Farmark.

Further Information: Please monitor Intersystem Guard communications channels and official announcements for updates and additional information.

/END BULLETIN

2 | MAKINDI | ITHANGA ELIDE, FARMARK

BENJAMIN MAKINDI HAD ONLY once before been to Farmark—a family vacation when he was eight years old—to visit relatives for a wedding. He now wished he'd retained a better memory of it because the Farmark he could see now was a desolate nightmare.

Three klicks ahead of him, ostensibly, was the city of Ukunqoba, but where once gleaming ceramo-metallic skyscrapers had stood, now lay only piles of ash and columns of smoke.

"Abe's God, Master Gunnery Sergeant," came the voice of his lance corporal, Jonah Mehta-Valdez, behind him. "What are they doing?"

"They're burning the rats out of the fields," Benjamin replied.

"You really think we're gonna find anyone here?"

"ISG says they received a survivor signal from just outside Ukunqoba, about a klick ahead of where we are now." Benjamin surveyed the arid, dusty landscape before him, using his helmet's heads-up display to look for life-sign readings or signals received.

"What about *them*? Do you think we're going to see any of them?"

"Lance Corporal, if I never see one of them, that will be fine with me."

"I've heard they're creepy as—" Mehta-Valdez was silenced by Benjamin's suddenly outstretched arm. That same arm gestured for him to take cover, which he and the rest of the squad did at once.

"Movement at one o'clock," Benjamin said, crouching low to the ground. "Does anyone have eyes up?"

"Have a drone up now, Master Gunny," responded a specialist named Van Ness.

"Feed it to me, Specialist."

"Aye, sir."

Benjamin keyed a switch in his helmet's display settings and was given a bird's-eye view of the terrain before them. He could see the squad and the surrounding area, with a graphic overlay indicating elevations and wind conditions and highlighting anything moving. All was still; it must have been a trick of the light he'd seen.

He switched to infrared to make sure. It wouldn't be as helpful in the hot southern Farmark summer sun, but it might—he gasped. The display was covered with five-legged, starfish-like shapes.

He flicked off the display and looked around. *What the hell?* There was nothing there. He turned the display back on and scanned for distortion suggesting the presence of a cloaking device, but nothing showed up. That was when he noticed the elevation annotations on the display and leapt to his feet.

"Run!" he screamed. "Back to the lander!" For a moment, his marines looked at him in baffled confusion. "They're in the ground!"

The earth erupted around them as living nightmares emerged from the dusty soil. Each of the Invaders was about two and a half meters high. As far as Benjamin could see, there was no visible body, just a hub where its five muscular, cricket-like legs came together. At the end of each of its legs were eight tentacles. The creature in front of him reared up on three legs, holding a device in one of its "feet," which it braced with the fifth leg.

Benjamin dropped and rolled to his right, bringing his weapon to bear and firing round after round into the creature. He poured fire into the alien but couldn't figure out where to aim. Without any obvious brain center, how were you supposed to kill this thing?

All around him were the screams of his squad and the sound of constant gunfire punctuated by concussive sounds that he couldn't identify. The creature turned its weapon toward him as he dodged once again to his left. The Invader's weapon missed him by fifty centimeters but tore a hole in the ground, firing a round that surely would have gutted him had it found its mark.

"RPGs!" Benjamin shouted into the commlink, but all he could hear by way of acknowledgment were his marines' screams. He dodged another salvo and scrambled behind a boulder, praying for just a couple of seconds to act. He switched his XR-90 from Gauss rounds to rocket-propelled grenades. This model only carried a magazine of three such rounds. Hopefully, he wouldn't need more than that.

He rolled out from behind cover and fired an RPG at the Invader. The creature was rearing up once again to bring its weapon to bear on Benjamin, and the master gunnery sergeant's RPG struck it right at the nexus of its legs and detonated. The creature was blown apart, thick green fluid spraying everywhere.

Benjamin burst forward and ran through the settling dust where the alien had been. To his left, he saw another of the creatures pick up Lance Corporal Mehta-Valdez with three of its legs, each on a different limb, and pull the screaming corporal apart, his right leg landing about two meters in front of Benjamin. The master gunnery sergeant dropped and fired another RPG at the creature that had just murdered his corporal, blowing two of its five limbs apart. He didn't know if that was a mortal wound for these creatures, but he wasn't about to wait around to find out. He ran past the body of another marine—an alien slug had blown a hole through the marine's chest armor; a second one had taken the marine's head off. Benjamin grieved that he couldn't even tell which of his marines it had been.

"Echo Squad, on me! Fall back! Fall back!" He ran as hard as he could toward the lander, the servos in his armor straining to give him as much speed as possible. He had run about half a kilometer before he noticed no one was following him. He turned to look back. "Echo Squad! Report!"

The coms were filled with nothing but silence. He turned and continued running toward the lander, switching his comm settings. "IAC-17, do you copy?" he panted. "This is Makindi. We've been ambushed; squad is taking heavy casualties. We need evac now! IAC-17, do you copy? This is Ma—"

Something slammed into him, knocking him two meters forward into the dust. Seemingly, every alarm in his armor went off simultaneously: suit breach, severe bodily injury, concussion warning, sudden blood pressure drop, and a couple of others he couldn't identify. He tried to get back up, but he could only manage to roll over onto his back. He looked down and saw that the right flank of his suit had been blown off. Typically, a mere suit breach would be cause enough for alarm, but he was on Farmark—there was still an atmosphere he could breathe. From this angle, he couldn't tell how much of him the alien's round had carried off with the missing suit armor, but he could see a growing pool of blood staining the dusty ground beside him.

His vision began to blur, and the edges of his sight started to go dark. *So, this is it*, he thought. *This is a worthy death for a marine.* He tried to lift his head and could just make out the skittering form of one of the aliens racing across the arid terrain toward him. He was at the edge of consciousness when he saw the creature rearing back on three legs, aiming its weapon for the kill.

Something else slammed into him. He rallied long enough to look and see one of the alien's legs on top of him, its green blood spattered across his helmet visor. He sank into a dreamlike state, imagining he could hear voices shouting around him as he floated off the ground. He dreamed that he floated into the presence of a giant, who promptly placed his enormous foot on Benjamin's chest and pressed down, trying to suffocate him. He surrendered, and everything went dark.

✙

SOMEWHERE, OFF IN THE distance, something was beeping. *Go away; I'm trying to sleep*, he thought. The beeping seemed to get closer until it was right over his head.

He opened his eyes and then squinted. In the sterile bright light, he could make out an instrument panel that was the apparent source of the beeping.

A door opened, and he heard footsteps approaching. A young woman in a medical corps uniform leaned into his field of vision.

"You're awake!" she said. "Please, don't strain yourself. You've been through a lot, and your body still has a lot of healing to do. Are you feeling any pain?"

"I, uh, I," was all he could muster.

"You're on some pretty strong painkillers, so do let us know if you are in any discomfort. I'm going to go get the doctor." Benjamin heard her footsteps receding and the door closing behind her.

I guess I'm not dead, he thought. Then, the memory of what had just happened came rushing back to him. Mehta-Valdez, Van Ness, Singh, Chesnokov, all of them—they were all dead, weren't they? *I should be with them*, he thought. *It's not right. It's not right.*

The door slid open, and the nurse returned, followed by a man and a woman—a physician and someone in a fleet uniform. He was not quite coherent enough to discern the rank.

"Master Gunnery Sergeant Makindi," said the doctor. "I'm Doctor Gonzalez, your attending physician. Can you hear me all right?"

"Aye, sir," Benjamin rasped.

"No need to call me 'sir,'" the doctor said amiably. Your wounds are healing well, and vital tissues are regenerating nicely, but I want to make sure that you're not in too much pain. You left quite a decent-sized chunk of yourself on Farmark. If you hadn't been in battle armor with artificial blood stores and tourniquet mesh, you probably wouldn't have made it off the surface, let alone survived the acceleration during the escape."

The giant's foot, Benjamin thought. "No, I'm not in any pain. I do have a strange feeling that ants are crawling all over my right side, trying to tickle me."

"Those are the nanoprobes rebuilding your oblique muscles. They don't hurt?"

"No, they don't even really itch. Just sort of tickle."

"Good, good. Look, I won't lie—it was touch and go for a long time. You're lucky to be here, but you're through the worst of it."

"Where am I?" Benjamin finally thought to ask.

The woman in the ISG uniform stepped forward. "You're at the fleet command center over Fairhaven."

"Fairhaven?" he said, sitting up and rallying himself into a higher state of alertness. "How long have I been out?"

The officer and the physician exchanged a brief look. "It's been three weeks since you were extracted from Farmark," Dr. Gonzalez said.

"My squad—"

"You're the only one we recovered," the officer said.

Benjamin closed his eyes and laid his head back.

The officer turned to Gonzalez. "Doctor, may we have the room, please?"

Gonzalez looked at his patient and quickly scanned the readouts. "Yes, of course. Master Gunnery Sergeant, if your pain increases or you need anything, you can press the call button or use the voice response system."

"Thank you, Doctor," Benjamin whispered, eyes remaining closed.

"Thank you, Doctor," said the officer as Gonzalez nodded and turned to go.

"Master Gunnery Sergeant," the officer said after Gonzalez had gone. "I am Fleet Captain Asha Silva-O'Connor, Naval Intelligence. I am truly sorry about the loss of Echo Squad."

"Sorry enough to delay this interrogation?" Benjamin replied, opening his eyes and looking toward the ceiling.

"I'm afraid not, Master Gunnery Sergeant. You're the first survivor of a direct encounter with the enemy that we've had."

"There's not much that I can tell you that you couldn't get from my suit cams. Were they damaged?"

"No, but I'm not here to get the combat details. Your suit and the drone footage captured that well enough. I want to know what they were *like*."

Benjamin sat forward as much as his healing wounds would allow and looked Silva-O'Connor in the eyes. "What they were *like*!?"

"Yes, Master Gunnery Sergeant. As I said, you're the only one who has survived a direct encounter with the enemy. Statistically speaking, it's unlikely that our recon missions should have such a low survival rate when they come into contact with the Invaders. From what we can glean, their weapons are powerful but nothing that should tilt the balance so much in open combat. It stands to reason that they must have some other more . . . *intangible* advantage. We need to know what that is if we're going to properly equip our forces."

Benjamin looked down at his right hand. He felt a phantom sensation of desperately squeezing his XR-90's trigger until every last round was spent.

"They're monsters," he said at last. "They move wrong. They look wrong. They sound wrong. They're hard to kill. And they have little trouble killing us." Benjamin's vision was filled with images of Mehta-Valdez being ripped apart and of the headless, nameless marine staining the sands of southern Farmark with their blood and viscera. He looked down and saw his entire right flank soaked in blood and the room floor covered with body parts. His vision started to swim, and the giant stood on his chest again. And there was that beeping.

The door slid open, and the nurse ran in. "What happened?"

"I think he's having a panic attack," Silva-O'Connor replied. The nurse went to Benjamin, took a hypospray out of her scrubs pocket, dialed a setting, and pressed it against his neck. The hypo hissed as it dosed Benjamin with a sedative, and he collapsed back onto the bed, breathing normally.

When he woke again, Silva-O'Connor was still there, sitting in a chair at his bedside. On the other side of his bed was Dr. Gonzalez, holding a scanner and examining its readings.

"What—" he managed.

"You're okay. You're safe," Gonzalez said. "We had to sedate you, but you're going to be okay. You're safe."

Benjamin turned to Silva-O'Connor. "I should be dead, too. But for the IAC, I would be. It's not right that I survived when—"

"Master Gunny," Silva-O'Connor said, addressing him now not as an officer in Naval Intelligence but as a fellow service member. "I can't speak to the cosmic significance of why you survived when others didn't. I can only tell you that I am grateful that you did; your experience, however limited, can still give us a better idea of what we're up against."

Benjamin sat for a moment, then nodded. "Doctor, how long will it be before I can return to duty?"

Gonzalez and Silva-O'Connor exchanged a look. "The nanoprobes will have finished their work in a few days. You still have some other wounds that need to heal, and, of course, you'll need some physical therapy to get back up to fighting condition."

"Master Gunny," Silva-O'Connor interjected. "The ISG is suspending all operations in Kittim. No one's going back until we figure out how to fight them more effectively. That could be years."

"No. No. No. That's no good. I need to go back. I need to—"

"You need to heal," Dr. Gonzalez interrupted. "Rushing this won't do anyone any good."

"Besides," added Silva-O'Connor, "if you're looking for a way to contribute, I think I have an opportunity for you. It's not combat, but if successful, it could help us win the war."

3 | KILLIAN | NOVAROMA, NEW SYDNEY

NEWLY COMMISSIONED LIEUTENANT Jareth Killian made it through abbreviated basic training without incident. His idiot bunkmate, who'd vaped himself with a thermal grenade during a live-fire exercise, could not say the same.

The morning after basic was over, he received his orders to report to the LSS *Deliverance* for duty. The name struck him as an unlikely coincidence. The ship was either new or had been rechristened. Either way, he was looking forward to seeing it. He had been on a naval vessel a few times, but they had usually been cutters or something small. This vessel was bound to be at least a frigate, making it the largest spaceship he would ever have been on.

Jareth opened up the wardrobe in his barracks. Hanging there was his officer's uniform and his duty fatigues. He packed the fatigues into his travel case and dressed in the Class A uniform, following the protocol for reporting to a new vessel. He was proud to be wearing the uniform of the ISG, particularly an officer's uniform with its classic black jacket on black trousers, the gold stripe-and-a-half on the sleeve, and a crisp white hat. He put on the uniform, regarded himself in the mirror, and smiled: Jareth Killian, Lieutenant, Junior Grade, of the Intersystem Guard, ready to set sail to save the only worlds he had ever known. Much to his surprise, he looked the part.

He was scheduled to leave on an orbital shuttle at 1645 to take him to the harbor—he had almost an entire afternoon to kill in Novaroma.

Novaroma was an old city on New Sydney, having served as a major spaceport and navy base since the days of the Pioneers. Its kilometers and kilometers of salt flats, with dry weather that would not impede spacecraft launches, made it perfect for its purpose. In the middle of that broad salt flat was Novaroma—a city barely holding on to that designation since everyone knew that if it weren't for the spaceport, there wouldn't be any reason for anyone to be here. Novaroma was full of mercantile offices, cargo warehouses, hotels, bars, and sex workers. Pretty much anyone who catered to the needs of travelers, businesspeople, or the military. Jareth had some time to kill, and while he thought that it would be nice to have a woman's company before heading out on a mission from which he might never return, he also didn't want his last experience with sex to be something he'd had to pay for. The bar seemed like a better bet.

There was a bar just across from the sub-orbital passenger terminal. It had been called *Vincenzo's* when Jareth was in the Merchant Marine. Now, it was named *Dominic's*, and but for the name, the bar had not changed that much. There were a few improvements to the décor—a new game in the corner and different sex workers—but otherwise, it was the same place. He sat down at the bar, and when the bartender approached, he just pointed at the taps. "Give me a draft," he said. "Doesn't matter what."

"Nice to have selective clientele in my establishment," the bartender quipped.

"Well, to tell you the truth, I'm from outside of New Kalgoorlie. Don't remember what brands you have available here. I'll trust you."

The bartender shrugged, grabbed a glass, pulled a tap, and drew him a beer. Then, glancing at Jareth's uniform as he put the beer down in front of him, he said, "Where you off to?" That was a much weightier question these days, and Jareth wondered how many people who were off to recon or rescue in the Kittim system or off to Fairhaven to shore up the defenses had come through.

"I'm going on the Expedition," he said. Even in his head, the word had a capital letter.

The bartender paused and looked at him. It made Jareth wonder if he'd been the first one the bartender had met who'd said that.

"It's a waste of time," someone further down the bar said.

"What's that?" Jareth replied, turning in his direction.

"Frakkin' waste of time," the man replied. "They're all dead. Every last one of 'em." Judging by the number of empty bottles in front of him, this man had been going at it for a while.

"Easy there, Chollie," the bartender said. "You got no way o' knowin' that."

"Sure, I do," said Chollie. "Look, we been out here what, four hundred years, and they ain't never come lookin' for us. It's not like they didn't know how. It's not like they didn't have the money. It's not like they didn't have the ambition, yeah? Always a buck to be made in trade, yeah? So, why ain't they come? It's because there ain't no one *to* come. They're all toast, that's why. Frakked. Dead."

The bartender sighed. Jareth could tell that he'd heard this all before. The bartender gave him a look that said *you can try arguing with him, but I'm tired of it*. Well, hell, he did come here to kill some time.

"So, what killed them?" Jareth asked. The bartender gave him another look that said *Don't say I didn't warn you*.

"Them."

"Them?"

"Them same bastards what wiped out Farmark. They're just now getting to us to finish the job."

"But," Jareth began—he could see the bartender watching, waiting to see which argument he would use—"these guys came from the wrong direction. They came from the opposite direction of the Commonwealth."

"Chorg that," Chollie said. Jareth had no idea what *chorg* meant, but he could guess. He was still trying to figure out where the man's accent was from. Was that a Farmark accent? Could that be it? Lu didn't talk like that; neither did the Chancellor, but there was likely more than one accent on Farmark.

"Then how do you figure the aliens wiped out an entire civilization, hundreds of light years wide, then traveled over seven hundred light years to get here, skipped our systems, and went right to Farmark, all without any evidence of faster than light drive?"

"Well, if it wasna them, it was somebody goddam like 'em! Either way, the Commonwealth is frakked, and we're frakked, too. Just like Farmark. Just like Farmark . . . ." He downed the contents of his bottle and slapped his hand on the bar. "'Nother."

"C'mon, Chollie, you've had plenty," the bartender said. "You want I should lose my license?" But Chollie kept slapping the bar until the bartender finally relented and pushed another bottle over his way.

In the meantime, Jareth sipped his beer—it was good; he had been right to trust the bartender. When the bartender came over after a few minutes to see if he needed another, Jareth tilted his head toward Chollie at the end of the bar and said, "What's his story? From Farmark?"

"Yeah," said the bartender. "He was here on business when it all went down. Was headed back to a commercial liner in orbit when the ISG shut down all civilian use of the port and started mustering. By the time the emergency was over and he could leave, there was nowhere for him to go. He's been in the hotel here ever since. The government is paying his bill as part of the Refugee Act. I think he's spending the rest of his money here. Poor bastard—his entire family was on Farmark, and he hasn't heard if they made it off in the general evacuation. That's why he stays close to the spaceport. Just in case they should get off one of those shuttles someday and call him. They could be in a slowboat or, worse, left on the surface. So, he just sits here and waits. And drinks."

The beer was enjoyable, and the place was alright, but Jareth didn't feel like drinking anymore. He looked at his handheld: he still had a few hours to kill. Jareth figured he could do it at a public net terminal; he had been putting off writing his goodbyes to a lot of folks, including his parents. He should probably write the letter to his parents first; it was going to be the hardest.

He got up, put his thumbprint on the payment pad before him, and then pressed it again to add more credits. "Tell him next round's on me."

The bartender confirmed the payment and nodded. He pulled out another bottle of whatever Chollie was drinking and put it in front of him, telling him it was from Jareth. Chollie looked up at him.

"We're going to get them," Jareth said. "We'll bring them back. And when they come back with us, we'll avenge Farmark."

"You do that, delivery boy," Chollie said. "You run out and bring back those ghosts." He turned back toward his bottle, shoulders slumping.

Jareth nodded to the bartender. "Thanks for the hospitality."

He turned and pushed the door open onto the street and stood outside for a minute, collecting himself. He turned to head to the net terminal. As he turned, he caught his reflection in the front glass of Dominic's: Jareth Killian, Lieutenant, Junior Grade, a damned fool, ready to set sail on a pointless mission that wouldn't be able to save the only worlds he had ever known. Much to his chagrin, he looked the part.

AT SIXTEEN-THIRTY, JARETH TOOK his seat on the orbital shuttle in the second row, right behind the pilots. He had a view out of the forward and side windows. The crew made the usual announcements about safety protocols; he just stared at the view. The landscape around Novaroma was stark but beautiful in its own way. And in any event, it was New Sydney. Home. He wondered if he'd ever see it again—if the League could keep it safe. If Chollie's grief would become everyone's grief until there was nowhere left to go. He looked around the cabin—everyone was looking out the window. Maybe everyone felt the same way.

Crike, what was he doing? Why was he so down on a mission that hadn't even begun? Chollie's cynicism had gotten to him more than he was comfortable admitting.

He looked out the window at all the vessels coming and going from Novaroma. He shook his head, disappointed in himself. *This is the Intersystem Guard we're talking about,* he told himself. *We're not talking about some freighter in the Merchant Marine, staffed by a handful of competent officers and a bunch of crew just looking for a way to earn a living. The ISG knows what it's doing. They wouldn't mount this expedition if they didn't think it could work.* What was he so worried about?

At 1644, the gangway retracted, and the shuttle tipped up. Jareth could hear himself and all his fellow passengers breathing in deeply for calm. He'd never gotten used to the fact that an orbital shuttle launch was essentially sitting atop a fusion reactor, riding a missile into space. A deep rumbling began as the engines fired, followed by a shriek as the primary ignition took hold. Then, it was as if he'd been smacked backward into his seat as the engines kicked in and launched the shuttle upward.

In only a few minutes, the orbital was outside the atmosphere. A couple of people got sick when the vessel entered free fall—a shuttle like this didn't have gravitic plating, and some passengers weren't used to the sensation. Jareth noted that you could always tell the inexperienced ones—they instinctively looked for a handhold. As a veteran of the Merchant Marine, he was used to it and trusted in his harness, enjoying the feeling.

After a few moments, the shuttle turned and matched orbits with a higher-up structure. Jareth looked out his window and could make out the distant form of the naval harbor and the starship dry dock high in orbit. A starship was within its walls; he assumed it was the *Deliverance.*

The *Deliverance* was much larger than he had expected; it was nearly two-thirds longer than even the largest cruiser. As the shuttle approached the dry dock, he got a better view. His eyes scanned the length of the vessel from the bow sensor cone to the donut-ring-shaped Sheridan drive just behind the bow to the long, tapered cylinder of a hull toward the aft sensor tower. That was when he realized that the ship wasn't unusually long; it was towing two large cargo containers at the stern. He turned to the shuttle pilot. "Any idea what's in those cargo containers?"

"Antimatter fuel," she said matter-of-factly, although with a tinge of something else.

"That much?" he asked.

"Yes. I wonder if you've left any for the rest of the fleet while you go off on this wild goose chase." Jareth winced a little at the pilot's tone, even as he understood it. Antimatter wasn't cheap, but a starship couldn't generate the energies necessary for interstellar travel without it. It occurred to him that compared to the commandeering of all the available antimatter in the

League for this expedition, the cost of his suborbital ride to Novaroma had been a drop in the bucket.

"I heard that the Merchant Marine is scaling back its operations by 35 percent," the co-pilot added.

"Crike," responded the pilot. "So much for being able to afford good Fairhaven beer."

"Yeah, and even the handful of people who take interstellar trips are going to have to confine themselves to in-system travel unless they want to pay through the nose," the co-pilot replied. "Especially since we're down a production facility."

"Ugh. I completely forgot that the Triton Facility was in the Kittim system."

"Yeah, and they produced like a third of all the antimatter we use."

The pilot kept her eyes forward but turned her head to speak to Jareth over her shoulder. "After you all have taken all that starship fuel with you, you had better find someone at the end of this trip. Otherwise, you'll have hobbled the rest of us for nothing."

"We will," he said, not quite as confidently as he would have liked. Between his conversations with Chollie and now this pilot, he felt like he'd taken a one-two punch to his confidence in what he was doing.

The shuttle pulled alongside the *Deliverance* and docked. Jareth removed his restraints and started floating toward the hatch. It opened into a standard docking collar, and he floated through. At the end of the tube was another hatch with a blinking green arrow pointing down—the gravity warning. He spun himself around feet first, grabbed the grips, and eased himself through. As he crossed the threshold into the ship, his feet sank, and he was pulled into a standing upright posture.

Once on the deck, he and the other new arrivals were greeted by a petty officer who led them down three levels to a briefing room. As they followed her, Jareth considered the ship—it was new—and he wondered why the ISG was sending a new ship when the best ships would be needed in the League.

"Drive efficiency," the petty officer replied.

"Sorry?" he said, a little embarrassed that he'd been musing aloud.

"Yeah, drive efficiency. The newer ships have a better light-hour-to-gram-of-antimatter ratio than older ships. If the fleet is giving us most of its antimatter to get back to Commonwealth space, they want to ensure it's used efficiently. They'll want whatever's left for the war effort when we get back."

He thanked her, and she nodded. She was career, and he hoped that her impression of him as an officer had not been overly diminished; he should have known that answer. But, if her opinion had been reduced, she gave no sign of it as she stopped, gestured, and showed them into the briefing room.

The room had rows of chairs, like a theater or lecture hall, with a podium up front. The walls were tactical screens showing mission status, duty rosters, and other mission-related data. Jareth and his fellow recruits took their seats and waited.

Eventually, an average-height man of medium complexion wearing commander's stripes on his sleeves came in. Everyone leapt to their feet. "As you were," he said in a thick northern Fairhaven accent.

"My name is Husayn Delacruz, Executive Officer of the *Deliverance*. I am here to give you a mission briefing and answer any questions you might have. Lights." At his word, the lights dimmed in the room, and the center display showed a star chart—the League of Four Worlds.

"You are *here*," whispered some guy behind Jareth before being elbowed in the ribs by his neighbor. Delacruz continued.

"For the last four hundred years, no League starship has ventured beyond the boundaries of these three systems. Our mission and that of the *Brunswick*, which will be traveling with us, is to travel back to the last known boundaries of the Commonwealth and make contact as quickly as possible with any authority present. This will not be an easy task."

The screen shifted, and the scale of the map changed radically. The three bright stars representing the League retracted until they were almost a single point of light on the chart. Now visible on the display was a much more expansive collection of dots, ringed by a blue border. There was a murmur throughout the room. Jareth imagined that others were having the same reaction he was. It wasn't the size of the Commonwealth that made an impression—everyone knew how big it was supposed to be—it was the size of the void between that expanse and their little dot of a League.

"The colony ships that brought our ancestors here were equipped for such a journey. They were well-funded and had antimatter stores that could be used for long-range interstellar travel, and the reserves would be used to establish the colonies. Because the Pioneer generation decided to use significant portions of their reserves to continue scouting for habitable planets, their stores were seriously depleted by the time they reached the Sharon system and found a habitation-ready world. They had barely enough fuel to scout Roger's Star and Kittim before they were forced to cease regular interstellar travel. The original colony ship was landed on New Sydney, where it became the barracks and base camp for colonization.

"I tell you this so that you understand just how unprecedented this mission is. We have not had the means for such a trip since that first colony vessel left Commonwealth space. We have strung together storage canisters to house sufficient antimatter reserves for a round trip. This has necessitated the commandeering of all available military and civilian supplies. As you can see, the distance between our space and theirs is vast. If we reach Commonwealth space and find the first system uninhabited, we have enough reserves to explore another few systems inward. At a certain point, we will be forced to choose between turning around or making a one-way trip for one or both ships in the expedition."

Another murmur made its way around the room, and Jareth began to consider the genuine possibility that he'd signed up for an all-or-nothing kind of trip.

"I'll take your questions."

"Sir," said a voice from the back of the room. "How many jumps will we need to make to reach Commonwealth space?"

"Our engineers figure that with current engine design, only about sixty."

This time, the murmur was more than a murmur, and Jareth heard people distinctly gasping, "Sixty!"

"Sir, that's, what, twelve light-years a jump?" the questioner followed up. "What is the jump range of this vessel?"

"If this were standard fleet operation, the jump range would be limited to ten light-years on one fueling, which would be more than enough since the longest jump we ever take is seven light-years from Sharon to Kittim. However, this is a newer vessel with a better engine that has been rated as high as thirteen light-years per standard deuterium–antideuterium load."

People in the room shifted nervously. This expedition would push the limits of the Sheridan drive—a chilling thought for anyone who worried at all about the risks of hyperspace engine failure. Jareth had long desired to have as many different experiences in space as possible—turning into a big shiny ball of plasma as your vessel was ripped out of hyperspace by a failing engine was not one of them.

A young ensign sitting a few seats down from Jareth raised her hand next. "Commander, if we're traveling in twelve-light-year jumps, then we're not aiming for systems, are we?"

"That is correct, Ensign. We are taking a straight-line route to the extent possible. That means most of our refueling will be done in interstellar space."

"Sir," piped up another voice. "What system are we aiming for?"

"According to our records, the first Commonwealth system we should reach will be Sigma Librae and New St. Louis. That is, of course, assuming the Commonwealth has not expanded in four hundred years. In our best-case scenarios, we'll encounter Commonwealth settlement before then."

"Is there a worst-case scenario?"

"Yes," Delacruz responded soberly. "We get deep into Commonwealth space without finding anyone, having exhausted our supplies and our fuel."

"What do we do then?" Jareth asked. "Is there a plan for that contingency?"

"It might surprise you to know, Lt. Killian," Delacruz responded, demonstrating that he'd done his homework getting to know his crew, "that Command has planned for every contingency. If we wind up deep in Commonwealth space, not having made contact and unable to return, we are ordered to find the closest inhabitable planet and establish a colony. It is hoped that the two crews have enough genetic diversity to sustain a viable settlement. Both the *Brunswick* and the *Deliverance* are carrying frozen embryos for additional population support."

"And then what?" Jareth followed up, though he was sure he knew the answer.

"Then, Mr. Killian," Delacruz replied, "we do our best to build a thriving human society that will one day be capable of generating enough materiel and antimatter fuel to make the return trip to League space."

"If there's anyone left alive to return *to*," Jareth said, perhaps a little more glibly than a junior officer should in front of his XO.

"The likelihood that we may be on a colony world longer than the League has left to fight the Invaders has already been contemplated. It's why the first priority in the event we run out of fuel is not our return but the establishment of a thriving settlement."

Abe's God, thought Jareth. This was actually the fallback plan from ISG Command: in the event of mission failure, start a new colony and become humanity's new home. If they could come back, great. If not . . . . This mission had always felt like an extraordinary venture, but now it felt more like an irresponsible gamble without any real expectation of success. What had he gotten himself into?

After the briefing, Jareth was shown to his quarters—a small cabin, but at least it was his own. It was outfitted with hi-res flexdisplay walls that would give him a view of whatever he wanted to look at—New Sydney rainforests, Pherat desert canyons, the stars outside, even a vid—to provide some aesthetics and combat the claustrophobic nature of shipboard life.

He unpacked his bag, undressed, and took a quick shower. After changing for sleep, he grabbed his handheld and synced it to ship time. He wanted to be on time for his first duty shift at 0800.

The device chimed, announcing that it was now set to display that strange twenty-four-hour clock that naval vessels used instead of the New Sydney standard twenty-five-hour one. Its lock screen displayed the current time—2035. It was still early, but the day had taken a lot out of him. Perhaps with enough sleep, he'd feel better about the mission, or at least he would be able to feign feeling better about it when he met the captain on the bridge tomorrow. He hoped eleven hours would be enough.

He climbed into bed and was asleep before deciding what view to set his wall to.

4 | KAVANAGH | THE DELIVERANCE, NEW SYDNEY ORBIT

THE VIEW OF NEW SYDNEY from the Admiralty Offices on the Nova-roma Orbital Facility was one of Juliana Kavanagh's favorites. To be fair, almost any view of New Sydney from orbit was beautiful, but one of the virtues of a geostationary facility was that it experienced whole days right along with the planet. It was 0700 fleet time; today, that hour coincided with orbital dawn.

Juliana sat at one end of the conference room table and closed her eyes, letting the warmth of Sharon's sunlight bathe her face as it rose over New Sydney's eastern horizon. Her light complexion glowed, and her shoulder-length chestnut hair revealed its auburn highlights as the sun's light played across her features.

Her brief reverie was interrupted by the opening of the conference room door behind her. She rose immediately as Admiral Marak Turner-Li and Fleet Captain Asha Silva-O'Connor entered the room.

"As you were," said Admiral Turner-Li, taking a seat on the opposite end of the table, with Silva-O'Connor to his right.

Juliana sat back down but at attention with her back straight and hands folded neatly on the table before her.

"Captain Kavanagh," Turner-Li began. "On behalf of ISG Command, I want to say how very proud we are that you are commanding this mission. We believe there is no finer officer to represent the League's interests and advocate for us with the Commonwealth."

"Thank you, Admiral," Juliana replied. "That is very kind of you to say."

"You know, I knew your father and even did a tour aboard one of his ships. On a personal note, I am very glad that we have a Kavanagh taking the conn. That's a pedigree that anyone would want to have associated with their mission."

Well, that didn't take very long, Juliana thought. She took a surreptitious glance at her handheld on the table beside her. The chronometer read 0702—a grand total of two minutes into the meeting before someone had brought up the Old Admiral.

"Our family has served in the fleet for generations, Admiral. We take pride in our service and don't ever wish to earn any special treatment based on our . . . family history." She almost said "pedigree" to see if, on second hearing, he'd realize that he'd compared her to a racehorse or a prize show dog.

"Of course not, Captain. Your record alone merits you this command; that you're a Kavanagh is just icing on the cake for us."

Juliana was sure it was the other way around. The ISG really wanted to project images of competence and authority with this mission. Appointing the daughter of the legendary Gaius Kavanagh—the captain who had negotiated the release of thirty hostages and the surrender of their captors during the Iskander Mining Colony Rebellion and had later smashed the infamous Red Blade pirate syndicate—would accomplish that just fine. The fact that she was a highly skilled starship captain in her own right was the icing on the cake.

Fleet Captain Silva-O'Connor gave Juliana a reprieve from enduring the latest chapter meeting of the Gaius Kavanagh Fan Club.

"Captain Kavanagh, if I may address a few points pertaining to the mission?"

"Of course, Fleet Captain."

"I take it you have read the reports on my debriefing of Master Gunnery Sergeant Benjamin Makindi."

"I have. He paints a vivid picture of what we're up against."

"He does, indeed. It's a picture that we believe can be very effective in swaying sympathy to our cause."

"That was precisely the reason I made sure to study the report thoroughly."

"Excellent, Captain. Fleet Intelligence believes that having a first-hand account available to you, either for your own reference or for the benefit of any Commonwealth authorities you encounter, would aid your cause."

"A first-hand account, Fleet Captain?"

"Command has authorized the transfer of Master Gunnery Sergeant Makindi to the *Deliverance* as part of your vessel's marine platoon."

Juliana turned her head slightly and regarded the Fleet Captain with a sidelong glance. "Are you sure that's such a good idea? The poor man suffered a traumatic event and witnessed the wholesale slaughter of his squad. Is Command confident that returning to active duty so soon is in Master Gunnery Sergeant Makindi's best interests?"

"The master gunnery sergeant has expressed a desire to return to active duty, and Fleet Psychiatric has cleared him for some active service—obviously, combat is out. But as yours is primarily a diplomatic mission, it should provide the right mix of active military service without any triggering stimuli as the master gunnery sergeant makes his recovery. Besides, the story he can tell should be a very effective tool in your persuasion toolkit."

"Understood. I will let Major Li, my Marine Detachment Commander, know at the earliest opportunity." *What's one more crew member in need of healing?* Juliana thought.

"Thank you, Captain," Silva-O'Connor said, nodding her gratitude.

"Well!" interjected Admiral Turner-Li, smacking his hands on the table and rising from his seat. Juliana and Silva-O'Connor followed his lead. "We certainly don't want to keep you, Captain. You've got a busy day ahead of you." He walked around the table to Juliana and stuck out his hand. "Godspeed, Captain. The hopes and prayers of billions are riding with you."

"We will take good care of them, Admiral. You have my word."

Turner-Li pumped her hand one more time before letting go, turning on his heel, and exiting the room. Silva O'Connor paused a moment to nod in Juliana's direction before following him out, and then she, too, was gone.

Juliana stood for a few minutes, watching the terminator move slowly westward across the face of New Sydney. *You've earned this, Juliana,* she thought to herself. *The* Deliverance *is yours because of your own merit, no one else's. She has been given to you to command—you, Juliana, daughter of Gaius, Carrier of Messages, and Caretaker of the Broken.*

Her handheld chimed—a message from her XO: *How'd the meeting go?* She took one last good look out the window at the blue-green planet below, took a deep breath, and turned and exited the room. *I'll just tell him in person.*

JULIANA TOOK THE LIFT down the five decks from the main docking port to the command deck on deck twenty-eight. A marine was standing outside the hatch to the bridge.

The marine—Lance Corporal Okafor-Srinivas—snapped to attention. "Captain, sir!"

"At ease, Lance Corporal."

The marine nodded and turned to the control panel behind her. She pressed a button, and the hatch door was pulled inward before sliding to the right, clearing the hatch. "Mind your step, sir."

Juliana stepped over the coaming, through the hatch, and onto the bridge.

"Captain on the bridge!" called the ship's operations officer, Lt. Commander Lu Hannover.

"As you were," she said, moving forward to the center of the command deck. The bridge was the circular design that ship designers had favored for centuries. On the far bulkhead, opposite the entry hatch, was a massive display showing the view from the ship's bow. At the moment, that view contained a portion of the nightside of New Sydney as the *Deliverance* sat in dry-dock high above the planet in geostationary orbit.

The workstations were arrayed in two semicircles around the center facing inward. On the bulkhead behind each station was a flexdisplay that could become an instrument readout, a data interface, or even a viewscreen. Sometimes, in port, a bridge would set all of its bulkheads to viewscreen mode to give the crew a panoramic view of the planet they were orbiting and the space around them. At the moment, only the front display had a view outside, with the rest displaying various readouts and checklists in anticipation of launch.

Toward the front of the inner circle made by the workstations was the helm and navigation station, where the helm officer sat behind a large console. Behind that console was an empty area used for tactical holographic three-dee projections. Behind that were two chairs, each with an attached arm display and control panel, that could swivel to see all the stations on the bridge. Her Executive Officer, Commander Delacruz, was in his customary starboard-side chair. She took her place to his left.

"So, how'd it go?" he asked conspiratorially.

"About like you'd expect: a few minutes of talking about the Old Admiral before asking us to take on a traumatized marine for our security detail."

"Makindi," said Delacruz. "I read his file. An impressive marine. I don't think he'll be any trouble and will likely benefit us a lot."

"I agree. And you know me, I like taking on rehabilitation projects. If they'd put his record before me, I would likely have picked him myself. My problem was more the implications of why they were transferring him to us: nothing's going to happen on your voyage, so it'll be a safe place for recovery."

"Are you hoping for something other than a smooth, event-free journey, Captain?" Delacruz asked in a tone that made Juliana think he was mocking her ever so slightly.

"No, of course not. But I would have liked to have been sent off with a little more appreciation for the gravity of what we're trying to do rather than a celebration of the PR victory they get by having a Kavanagh on the bridge."

"I understand. I never had the problem of a too-impressive father. My father was so unimpressed with himself that he ditched his family name and took my mother's. Didn't even want to hyphenate. He said, 'Of all the Pioneers, Tem Fox was the least useful and sired a line of useless heirs. It's time to put the Fox name to rest.'"

Juliana smiled. Delacruz always had a way of knowing how to distract her from her petty gripes. It usually involved some kind of self-deprecating story, but she knew it was a mistake to underestimate the self-confidence of her XO.

The hatch opened again, and she overheard Okafor-Srinivas saying, "This way, Lieutenant."

"That'll be our new security chief," she said to Delacruz as she rose and turned toward the hatch. A tall, thin, but not wiry man with a light complexion and a mop of brown hair walked onto the bridge.

"Mr. Killian," Juliana said to the new arrival, who was clearly trying to get his bearings without *looking* like he was trying to get his bearings.

"Captain," he responded, saluting.

Juliana made a gesture that was half salute, half waving him off. Delacruz rose and walked toward the lieutenant.

"Your station is over here," he said, gesturing to the second station along the starboard side console ring.

"Aye, sir," Killian replied.

"Mr. Killian," Juliana said. "I know this is your first time as part of an ISG crew and that things were somewhat different in the Merchant Marine, but you can relax. There's no need to be nervous."

She recognized that expression; it was the *Am I that flegging obvious?* expression. She smiled to herself—the ability to keep people guessing and a little off balance was one of the perks of thoroughly studying her bridge crew's personnel records.

She continued, "If you were the kind of person who *should* be nervous stepping onto the bridge of a League starship, you wouldn't be stepping onto the bridge of a League starship."

Killian nodded appreciatively. "Aye, sir," he responded at last, moving to the station Delacruz had indicated.

He took his seat at his station and began reviewing the displays and familiarizing himself with his flexdisplay console.

Sitting behind the captain to her left was a tall, olive-skinned woman with almond eyes, Marissa Flores, the communications officer. She looked up from her console.

"Captain," she began. "Fleet command is hailing us."

"Put them through, Lieutenant," Juliana responded.

"Aye, sir." A moment of silence, then:

"*Deliverance*, this is ISG command."

"This is *Deliverance* actual. We read you, Command."

"*Deliverance*, you are cleared for departure. Godspeed, Captain. Fair winds and following seas."

"Acknowledged, Command. Keep the beacons burning for us." She swiveled to look at Flores. "Lieutenant, patch me in ship-to-ship to the *Brunswick*."

"Aye, sir," Flores answered. Then: "You're on."

"*Brunswick*, this is *Deliverance* actual. We are cleared for departure. Time to set sail, Captain."

"Acknowledged, Captain," came the voice of Captain Brevi. "We're standing by for departure on your mark."

Juliana turned back to the front display. "Mr. Delacruz, stand by to make sail. Lay aloft and loose topgallants; clear away the jib!" She knew she was baffling the newcomers; that always did. But Delacruz, knowing her penchant for arcane naval terminology, just smiled and turned to the helmsman, Ensign Pyotr Thorsten.

"Mr. Thorsten, detach all moorings. Thrusters one quarter. Take us out."

"Aye, sir," came the response in a thick Farmark accent. "One-quarter thrust aft." Thorsten placed his hands on his console—a flexdisplay like the standard readout but with a bio-responsive interface. Thorsten's hands made subtle shifts that communicated his intentions to the *Deliverance's* navigation and maneuvering systems, almost as if he were steering by thinking about it. He eased the ship out of drydock and prepared to leave orbit.

All around Juliana, the bridge crew returned to their duties. She had a feeling that, however busy they might appear to be, they would find it too hard to focus as the ship left drydock. Even after all her years in the service, she'd never gotten over the feeling you get when the thrusters move you out of port into open space. Juliana imagined it was the same for everyone.

"Mr. Hannover," she called to the operations officer. "Switch all bridge displays to a panoramic view for the duration. Departure angle."

"Panoramic view, departure angle, aye." The walls now displayed a panorama view from the perspective of the conning tower, giving the crew the feeling of riding atop the slender projection jutting out from the ship's hull. In the aft view afforded by a departure angle, the dry dock fell away as the thrusters accelerated the vessel forward.

"Gravitic plating off," Delacruz said.

Hannover responded, "Gravitic plating off."

Juliana felt a slight lurch in her stomach as she became appreciably lighter than she had been a few seconds before. She could still feel the downward force of the ship's meager acceleration, but the sudden change was always jarring.

She pressed a button on her chair console. "All hands, prepare for acceleration burn in thirty seconds."

By now, the *Deliverance* was already a couple of kilometers away from drydock, and the *Brunswick* had cleared its moorings and fallen into formation astern starboard. It would be safe to use the fusion engines now, and Juliana wasn't going to waste any time.

"Mr. Thorsten, bring us about to three-one-five mark four-five."

"Coming about, three-one-five mark four-five, aye."

"Mr. Filipov-Ibañez, has the *Brunswick* made its turn as well?"

"Aye, Captain," Filipov-Ibañez, the tactical officer, said. "She has made her turn and is in formation with us."

"Mr. Thorsten, bring the fusion engines online and take us to a cruising acceleration of one gee."

"Aye, Captain. One gee in five, four, three, two, one, engaging."

The crew suddenly felt a *lot* heavier. The weak downward force of the maneuvering thrusters was now replaced by an intense feeling of being pulled downward toward the deck, much more forcefully than gravitic plating usually managed.

Now that the ship was under acceleration, Juliana could feel the rumble of the fusion engines through the bulkheads and deck plating. No matter how often she'd done it, from her earliest experiences in space with her father to the present moment, setting sail was always thrilling. That was especially true on a brand-new naval vessel as it fired up its top-of-the-line fusion engines and got underway. She looked around at her bridge officers—the newer officers in particular—and could tell they agreed with her: thrilling didn't even begin to describe it.

She sank back into her chair and closed her eyes. *This is my ship*, she thought. *And I am her captain.*

AFTER TWO DAYS, the Expedition reached the Sheridan line in the system, the line beyond which the sun's gravity well was shallow enough to risk the hyperdrive. Juliana wasn't about to take any chances by getting too close to a gravity well in hyperspace—bad things could happen to a starship that did that—so she ordered the fleet to travel a whole extra standard day past the Sheridan line just to be safe.

The *Deliverance* and the *Brunswick* reached the jump point, and Juliana could feel the anticipation on the bridge. Everyone here had made a hyperspace jump before, but no one had ever jumped in this direction. The stars they were aiming at weren't the stars of the Roger's Star or Kittim systems. They were the uninhabited stars beyond League space. The stars that would take them to Commonwealth space and their deliverance—or to ruin.

The ship was no longer under acceleration and coasted in null gee at the jump point, the *Brunswick* five kilometers off the starboard bow. The crew was performing the last checks and run-throughs before the jump. The engineers were inspecting the antimatter injector nozzles and the deuterium tanks. Stellar cartography was matching the sky they could see with the star charts the Pioneers had brought with them four centuries ago, checking and rechecking their computations on the direction to Commonwealth space. Killian appeared to be busy assigning his security details to maintain a quiet but watchful presence.

Juliana surveyed her crew and ran through one last checklist of her own. *Time to get to it*, she thought.

"Mr. Hannover, ship status?" she said, her voice cutting through the tension.

"Board is green; clear for jump, Captain," Hannover replied from his station.

"Mr. Thorsten, initiate hyperspace jump on my mark."

"Aye, Captain."

"Mark."

The stars disappeared.

5 | MAKINDI | ON PATROL

THE JOURNEY FROM THE LEAGUE to the Commonwealth reminded Benjamin Makindi of a far more mundane trip he'd once taken. Returning home from a tour of duty, he and a friend decided to take the overland route from Novaroma to Brunswick. In the Corps, they'd both spent a fair amount of time traveling among the worlds of the League but had not seen that much of New Sydney itself.

They rented a ground car and set out on the one highway heading east from Novaroma. Neither had ever seen such staggering expanses of desert such as those in the western hemisphere on New Sydney.

There were times on that drive when they'd be a hundred klicks away from the nearest town. A hundred klicks from the nearest hydrogen station—when they'd be the lone vehicle they could see on what appeared to be an endless stretch of highway going off into the distance. In fact, the only evidence of human civilization had been the road they were driving on.

Benjamin got a similar feeling from the way the *Deliverance* and *Brunswick* were jumping through deep space. When traveling within the boundaries of the League, upon emerging from hyperspace, you began to get telemetry from beacons in the outlying reaches of the system, picked up radio signals, often just stray ones from the planets further in-system, or encountered other immediate and comforting signs of human life. In contrast, on this voyage, the ships would finish their jumps, and there would be nothing. No waiting beacon to align the ship's chronometers. No background radio chatter. No ships waiting to jump out. No handhelds pinging with messages stored in transmission buffers. Nothing. Just the void.

Further, the Expedition's straight-line race to get to Commonwealth space meant that their jump points tended to be in the middle of deep space, light-years away from a star system. Two ships just hanging in the darkness. It was unnerving. And because Captain Kavanagh wasn't about to cut any corners—she made sure that the crews went through the complete series of inspections after a hyperspace jump and before refueling—the time they spent in the emptiness of the void was even longer.

On his overland trip with his friend, Benjamin had been fascinated by the emptiness, by the sense that the planet was indifferent to their presence, even as their vehicle made its way across the trackless waste. He felt the same way about space—the emptiness was a source of fascination, not terror. But he noted with resignation that other people aboard were reacting differently. After years of experience doing everything from security details to crowd control to combat, he could tell when he was in the presence of a mob on the edge.

BENJAMIN LOOKED THROUGH THE daily briefing packet that summarized reports from different shifts. The Security Chief, Killian—one of those hybrid civilian/swabbie officers the fleet thought was such a good idea to recruit—was insistent that everyone be on the lookout for trouble. That made sense, of course; the tedious paperwork and daily incident digests made less. Benjamin knew the crew was on edge; he could *feel* it. One of his earliest tours had been on Iskander, a decade after the rebellion when the moon was still under occupation. The crowds there had the same energy as the crew did here: simmering.

Although Major Li had given him the option to follow a fixed-watch schedule, working the same shift day in and day out, Benjamin preferred the standard one-shift-on-two-shifts-off wartime rhythm. True, it did keep him from settling into a set sleep pattern, but he liked the ability to patrol at different times of the ship's operation.

He knew from experience that wartime was hours of tedium punctuated by moments of terror. And while the *Deliverance* and *Brunswick* weren't in combat, they were still on a wartime mission as far as Benjamin was concerned. This meant that the mission would flow along the same contours—there would be hours of dull, tedious routine—vitally important, but still tedious—followed by the sudden crisis of a fight or public drunkenness. Given that, learning how to stay vigilant amid the monotony was a vital discipline; remaining on a traditional combat watch schedule was what worked for him.

Today, having been on morning watch and off for forenoon and afternoon watches, he was back on for the first dog watch at 1600. He usually focused his patrolling on the messes, both officer and enlisted, since there had been a few fights in the messes in recent days and a lot more drinking going on off-duty. Today, he decided to start at the bow and work his way down before ending up at the enlisted mess.

Benjamin took the lift up to deck one and presented himself before the security system. The system scanned his handprint, retinal pattern, and facial features. A chime sounded, followed by a message: SPEAK YOUR NAME.

"Master Gunnery Sergeant Benjamin Makindi, SN 011-78-04."

The red light over the entry hatch turned green and slid aside. Benjamin stepped over the coaming and onto the engineering deck. Engineering, at the very top of the habitable section of the vessel, was the only department that took up the space of three whole decks. As they almost always were, Benjamin's eyes were drawn to the central power conduit, a ceramo-metallic column about two meters wide in the center of the deck. It glowed with a pulsing blue light, indicating power flowing through it. His eyes followed the column to its top, two decks up, where the cylindrical fusion reactor sat. Engineering officers climbed and descended gangways, tuned instruments, and kept their eye on the container of star fire at the top of the room. Still others monitored the far more dangerous reactor one deck above, where deuterium and anti-deuterium were annihilated to provide the tremendous energies used to power the hyperspace coils in the drive ring.

"She's a beaut, isn't she, Master Gunnery Sergeant?"

Benjamin turned to see Lt. Commander Piter Zhao-McKenzie, the *Deliverance's* chief engineer, beside him.

"That she is, Commander," Benjamin said, returning his gaze to his immediate level.

"On your rounds?" Zhao-McKenzie asked.

"Aye, sir. Anything I should know about?"

"No, everything's quiet. Engine and crew functioning well."

"Any disciplinary problems at all?"

Zhao-McKenzie shook his head. "Surprisingly, no."

"Surprisingly?"

"I mean, this is a deep space mission unlike one that anyone in the fleet has ever undertaken. Even when you sign up for a one-year tour, you can still communicate with your loved ones while you're away. You're still in the League. Here, we're cut off. I'd have thought that'd impact our morale more, but everyone seems to be holding up okay."

"That's good to hear," Benjamin said. "Other departments haven't been as lucky. I'm glad that engineering seems to be immune to whatever is affecting everyone else."

Benjamin was about to take his leave and continue his rounds when Zhao-McKenzie said, "Well, aboard the *Deliverance*, anyway."

"Sir?"

Zhao-McKenzie quickly checked to see if any of his crew were within earshot and then approached Benjamin almost conspiratorially. "I don't want to tell tales out of school or go outside the proper channels, but a day or so ago, when we were stopped for refueling, I had a call with my counterpart on the *Brunswick*, Lt. Commander Abdullah-Mendoza. He told me he'd been stressed out lately and had imagined that his officers were plotting against him."

"Plotting against him?" asked Benjamin, incredulously.

"On some level, he knew he was being ridiculous. What was there to plot? And just because he'd managed to stop some conversations mid-sentence when he approached didn't mean anyone was up to anything. That's often how younger officers act around their superiors, you know? But it was clear to me that the void was getting to him. I don't think he's a risk to the *Brunswick* or anything. I just thought you should know."

"Thank you, Commander. I'll make a note of it. I am sure the Lt. Commander is fine."

"Yeah, me too," Zhao-McKenzie said. "Just thought I should say something, just in case."

"I appreciate that, Commander. Well, I'd best be back about my rounds."

"Come visit again, Master Gunnery Sergeant," said Zhao-McKenzie amiably before returning to his engines. Benjamin took one last look at the source of all that powered the *Deliverance* before exiting through the secured hatch. He was grateful the chief engineer had told him about Abdullah-Mendoza. He wasn't worried that the *Brunswick's* chief engineer was having paranoid delusions; he was worried that the man was right.

From engineering, he went down through the decks of the bow section, first to fabrication, where they took some of the raw power generated one deck above them and used it to manufacture everything from tools to uniforms. Lt. Abbassi looked up from their workstation as Benjamin walked through and waved before turning their head back to the display in front of them. Benjamin smiled; he knew from experience that if Abbassi had anything to report, they'd have done so. He took their immersion in their work as a sign that all was well in fabrication.

Auxiliary control one deck down was quiet. One officer of the watch sat quietly at a systems monitoring board at what would have been the operations station on the main bridge. The officer nodded to Benjamin and returned to her monitoring.

His next stop at life sciences on deck four was likewise routine. Everyone was in good spirits, and the officer of the watch reported no problems or disciplinary issues among the personnel of that department. Benjamin figured it had something to do with them being scientists or, perhaps, because they had so many plants around them. It's not that plants were all that unusual—the starship was full of them, from potted plants in common areas to the walls of greenery in quarters and offices doing double duty as air scrubbers and mood enhancers—but of all the departments aboard, life sciences was the greenest, except for hydroponics on deck twenty-two, of course.

Benjamin moved next to the first of five decks of enlisted quarters. On most naval vessels, the marines were part of the scenery; no one was surprised to see a marine walk across the deck. But that was not the case in the crew quarters, even though the marines were primarily bunked on one of the enlisted decks. It seemed to Benjamin that every time he entered a common area or lounge, conversations became hushed, and glances became furtive. In one case, four crew'men sitting on a pair of neighboring bunks ended their conversation and dispersed as he walked near. Was he imagining it? Had he simply been primed to think this way by Lt. Commander Zhao-McKenzie's report about Abdullah-Mendoza?

He might have written it off altogether as mental priming but for what happened on the last enlisted crew deck. As he emerged from the companionway to deck nine, he heard shouting from the berthing compartment.

"You're flegging nuts, man!" cried one voice.

"You're the one who doesn't see it! You're just buying into what they're selling!" shouted a second.

The first responded, "You've been breathing too deeply when you're in waste recycling. It may explain why you're so full of sh—"

The first speaker stopped shouting as soon as Benjamin entered the berthing compartment.

"Is there some kind of problem here, Crew'man?"

"None, Master Gunnery Sergeant," said the first speaker, a crew'man named Tuckerman. "We were just having a disagreement."

"That true?" said Benjamin to the second voice, a Crew'man Apprentice Whittier.

"Sir, yes, sir," he said as he stiffened. "Just a sailor's argument."

"What about?"

Both crew'men looked sheepish, lacking the fire of conviction they'd displayed only a few moments ago.

Finally, Tuckerman spoke up. "We were just arguing about whether the ISG sent us out here knowing that the Commonwealth was gone."

"You were arguing about whether the ISG sent us on a pointless mission?"

"Yes, sir."

"In my experience, the ISG may send its personnel into near-hopeless missions but never pointless ones," Benjamin responded.

"Aye, sir," Tuckerman and Whittier responded in unison.

"I trust we can keep the discussions to a suitable volume and an appropriate level of shipboard behavior?"

"Sir, yes, sir," they said again in unison.

"Very well. As you were," Benjamin said and continued on his way. *What a stupid thing to argue about*, he thought. There were many missions whose wisdom he and the ISG had disagreed on, but he'd never known the fleet to spend money on a mission that *couldn't* succeed. In his experience, military bureaucracies were reluctant to spend money, materiel, and resources where they couldn't accomplish anything. Still, that argument bore noting; it had stoked some violent passions. Benjamin couldn't have guessed how quickly his impressions would be vindicated.

Descending one last deck to deck ten, he entered the enlisted mess. Various crew'men and petty officers sat at tables, at the bar, or on couches and in chairs along the far bulkhead, whose flexdisplay had been set to a view of a lakefront somewhere on Pherat. For the most part, conversations were subdued, creating a pleasant background din that was perfect for eating and relaxing after shift.

Without warning, a sudden eruption at a table near the lakeside view shattered the low-key din.

"You're a traitor!" shouted a young petty officer, leaping to his feet, knocking the chair he'd been sitting in off its magnetic grips and sending it tumbling over.

A crew'man sitting opposite the petty officer rose, not quite as abruptly but no less angrily. "Traitor? Because I refuse to buy into Parvat-Singh's lies? Because I can see the truth?"

Everyone in the mess fell silent, staring anxiously at the rising confrontation. Benjamin took out his handheld and signaled for backup. This was about to get ugly.

"Truth? Truth?!? How about some made-up horseshite that you're using to try to scare people with!" the petty officer rejoined.

The crew'man was not deterred. "You career ISG think you know better, but that's only because you martinets had free thinking drilled out of you years ago. Whatever they say to do, you do! This whole goddam fleet is run by mindless zombies who just—"

The petty officer's right fist slammed into the crew'man's jaw so forcefully that not only was the latter unable to finish his thought, but he was also unable to retain all of his teeth. Bloodied and wounded, the crew'man turned and flailed at the petty officer, who, being not only a better combatant but still separated by a table from his would-be assailant, managed to dodge out of the way.

Benjamin rushed forward toward the men as bystanders and others at nearby tables ran for the entryway. "Ship's Security! Stand down!" he shouted, but the two men showed no interest in disengaging. *Where's that backup?* Benjamin grumbled to himself.

As he approached the two men, the crew'man leaped over the table toward the petty officer, but he was still outmatched. No sooner had his feet hit the decking than the petty officer hit him with an uppercut that sent him back across the table, reeling.

Benjamin reached the men and grabbed ahold of the petty officer's shoulders to restrain him from further violence. But before he could repeat the words "ship's security," the petty officer wheeled upon his supposed new attacker and threw a punch right at Benjamin's left cheek.

The punch stung like hell, but Benjamin had taken worse. He turned toward the petty officer, whose face now betrayed the look of a man who knew just how badly he'd screwed up. Not only had he just assaulted a marine attempting to perform his official duties, but that marine could take a punch and likely dole out much more. As if to prove correct what he assumed the petty officer to be thinking, Benjamin grabbed him by the tunic and threw him into the bulkhead. The petty officer crumpled into a heap and held up his right arm with his palm open as if shielding himself, signaling his surrender.

Benjamin turned to the crew'man, who was only just getting back to his feet from having been splayed across the table. "Don't," was all he said, and the crew'man dropped to his knees and raised both hands above his head.

Two more marines came rushing in from off the lift, weapons ready. Without turning, Benjamin gestured to the two recent combatants on the floor. "Take them both to the brig. I'll inform Lt. Killian."

"Aye, Master Gunnery Sergeant," they replied, shackling the petty officer and crew'man before removing them from the mess.

Dammit, thought Benjamin. *I hate it when I'm right.*

THE DOOR TO INTERROGATION Room 1 slid open, and Lt. Jareth Killian entered. Benjamin drew himself to attention, and the prisoner seated at the table did likewise.

"At ease," Killian said, looking over the prisoner before turning his gaze to Benjamin. "What can you tell me, Master Gunnery Sergeant?"

"An argument in the enlisted mess, sir. Escalated to throwing punches."

"Which one do we have here—the puncher or the punchee?"

"The puncher, sir. Petty Officer Ando Lee-Chowdhury." At once, Killian turned his head to look at the detainee sitting at the table.

"Sir?" said Benjamin. "Everything alright?"

"Yes, Master Gunnery Sergeant. Yes, thank you," Killian replied as he took a seat opposite Lee-Chowdhury at the table. Benjamin was not convinced—something about this young man had spooked the lieutenant. Killian's reaction might have lasted only a split-second, but Benjamin had caught it.

As Killian pulled out his handheld to review the petty officer's record, Benjamin walked to the corner of the room opposite the door, to the right and behind Lee-Chowdhury. He would typically have stood in the corner that afforded him the best view of the detainee, but today, he was more interested in the lieutenant.

"Petty Officer Ando Lee-Chowdhury," Killian began. "I see the Master Gunnery Sergeant's incident report here. Why don't you tell me why you decided to start a fight in the enlisted mess?"

"Sir, I didn't start it."

"Do you deny that you threw the first punch? And, apparently, the *only* punch that landed?"

"No, sir."

"Do you have a different definition of 'starting a fight' than the rest of us do?"

"No, sir. But if you'd'a been there, you'd'a understood."

"Help me understand, Petty Officer."

"So, this civvy—"

"Civvy?"

"Civvy, yeah, sir. It's just what we call those members of the crew who are civilian fill-ins." Benjamin could see Killian wince a little, but Lee-Chowdhury didn't notice.

"Go on."

"So, this civ—this crew'man, Quan, he's goin' on about how the Chancellor's been lyin' to us, sendin' us off on a doomed mission that's only s'posed to make the folks back home feel better. He says the Commonwealth's gone, and there ain't no one to find, and the Chancellor knows that."

"That sounds like a particularly idiotic theory, I agree," said Killian. "But I don't think stupidity in opinions is justification for a punch in the jaw."

"It weren't his bullsh—, uh, nonsense, sir, that was the problem. Thing is, he starts sayin' that I'm too blind to understand because members of the military have all been brainwashed, and we can't do any thinkin' on our own. He called the ISG leadership 'mindless zombies'! That's an insult to the entire service, Lieutenant! That oughtn't be tolerated!"

"As to the crew'man's statements about the fleet, sir," interjected Benjamin. "I can vouch for the accuracy of the petty officer's summary."

"Thank you, Master Gunnery Sergeant."

Lee-Chowdhury appreciated the validation and leaned forward to make his case. "You're fleet, sir. You understand. We're out here as we always are, puttin' ourselves on the line for the League. Fleet were the first to die when the aliens invaded. Fleet will be there to kick 'em out in the end. To say that we're just playin' at goin' on a mission, well, that's as near treason as far as I can figure."

"It's offensive, for sure," Killian replied. "Even for a 'civvy' like me."

Lee-Chowdhury paled a bit but, to his credit, recovered quickly. "I didn't mean nuthin' by it, sir. Just to provide some context."

"It's alright, Petty Officer."

"May I ask, sir, where did you come from, then? You certainly seem like fleet to me."

"Thank you. I have a security background in private industry and, before that, the Merchant Marine."

"Oh, yeah? Well, the Merch is great. My brother was in the Merch. Died during a pirate raid."

"I'm sorry to hear that," Killian said, but with a tinge of something else. Benjamin looked closely at the lieutenant; the change in his demeanor had been subtle, but Benjamin paid attention to subtle cues. The man was under some kind of stress.

"Maybe that's how I know you," Lee-Chowdhury said. "I was sure you were a fleet man, but maybe I just remember your name from somewhere because of my brother."

"Anything's possible," Killian said. "Though it is a big fleet."

"Aye, that it is."

"Well, Petty Officer Lee-Chowdhury. Is there anything you'd like to add to your statement before we wrap up here today?"

"Only that that fool has been spreading his bullsh—, uh, nonsense around. Could be bad for morale."

"Understood, Petty Officer."

"We'll look into it," Benjamin added before turning to Killian. "I've heard other whispers of this conspiracy theory around the ship, Lieutenant. It bears some further examination."

"Understood, Master Gunnery Sergeant."

Killian rose and walked to the door, and Benjamin followed him out.

"Sir, what do you think?"

Killian was visibly distracted by something; it took him a beat to respond, and even then, something was off.

"Think? Oh, about the Petty Officer?"

"Yes, sir," said Benjamin, trying to keep his confusion at the lieutenant's behavior out of his voice.

"Sailor's fight. I think we can keep this to non-judicial punishment." He paused and seemed lost in thought for a second before snapping back into the moment and continuing. "At least, that's what I'll recommend to the captain. But this odd conspiracy theory—you're right; it does bear looking into."

"Aye, sir. I'll do that."

"Thank you, Master Gunnery Sergeant. You did some excellent work today."

"Thank you, sir," Benjamin replied and saluted.

Killian returned the salute, then turned and strode out of the security compartment toward the main lift.

Benjamin kept his gaze on the departing lieutenant until he disappeared into the corridor. That was odd. There was nothing outwardly wrong about the way Killian had engaged Lee-Chowdhury, but the young petty officer had triggered something in the lieutenant.

At the end of his watch, Benjamin returned to his quarters, one of the few private quarters aboard for enlisted personnel. He sat down at his workstation and turned the interface on.

"Computer, confidential security access, Makindi 327–Bravo-11."

"*Confidential security access granted.*"

"Restrict access records to captain-level security override."

"*Acknowledged. Trace and access records restricted to security levels captain and above.*"

"Display personnel records of Lt. Jareth Killian."

"*Displaying.*"

Benjamin leaned forward and read. He scrolled through Killian's entire service record, recruitment interview notes, and personnel evaluations. Nothing.

"Display all available records of Jareth Killian in the League Merchant Marine."

"*Displaying.*"

Benjamin read the outline of Killian's service record. Young, hard-working, and able. Promoted to security chief after death of previous chief.

Excellent record preventing theft and black market dealing. Two excellent letters of recommendation from Captains Idris Mfese and Josiah Bloch. The service record ended with a brief note: Discharged, 2781-09-17 (STD).

"Computer, display the crew manifests of all the ships Jareth Killian served aboard in the Merchant Marine."

"*Displaying.*"

The crew manifests of two ships, the *Ambivalent Parrot* and the *Cantankerous Vixen*, began to scroll on the screen. Benjamin let the information roll by without interruption until one name scrolled into view: Kian Lee-Chowdhury, cargo mate aboard the *Cantankerous Vixen*. Killian had served with the petty officer's brother. Why didn't he mention that?

Benjamin sat back, considering what he knew: next to nothing. Killian and Lee-Chowdhury's brother had served on the same ship, and for reasons Benjamin had no access to, Killian had failed to mention that he knew him to Lee-Chowdhury when the detainee had brought him up. For all Benjamin knew, the two men hadn't liked each other. Perhaps Kian had treated Killian poorly. Maybe they'd fought over the same woman. Who knew?

He looked at the time—2345. He'd just spent a few hours trying to find anything suspicious in his superior officer's past but found nothing, and midwatch was coming up at 0000 hours. He took a few minutes to wash his face and grab a coffee before heading to the lift and down to deck twenty-four.

Benjamin walked into the security offices and nodded to the officer of the watch. He headed toward the information workstations, where he planned to analyze intracom traffic to learn more about that conspiracy theory. He was about to begin his investigation when he realized that an eyewitness might still be awake. He got up, walked to the brig, turned, and hurried back.

"Where's the detainee in brig cell two?"

"Who?" the watch officer asked.

"Petty Officer Lee-Chowdhury."

"Oh, him. He was released on his own recognizance. But to keep him out of trouble, he was transferred to the *Brunswick*. Left aboard the last shuttle during refueling a couple of hours ago."

"On whose orders?"

"Lt. Killian's."

Now, *that* was suspicious.

6 | KILLIAN | THE VOID

JARETH WAS AT HIS bridge post, conducting his security "rounds," tapping into his security officers' displays and monitoring the same screens they were watching. Everything was routine—painfully routine. He watched a while before he could feel his eyes start to glaze over—he had been on duty for six hours already, when focus started to wane, and the displays became abstract works of art.

Jareth decided to stand up to get some blood circulating again, and as he did, something caught his eye.

"What the hell?" he muttered to himself as he sat back down. One of the shuttles that carried antimatter pods from the *Deliverance* to the *Brunswick* had departed . . . well . . . wrong. He couldn't put his finger on it, but it didn't look right.

"What is it, Killian?" asked Delacruz, walking to Jareth's station.

"There's something not right about that shuttle," he said, running several scans to back up his impression. "I can't put my finger on it. It's—" Suddenly, it occurred to him. "It's not carrying a docking-ring adaptor, Commander."

The *Deliverance* didn't have proper fueling shuttles; only starbases and tanker platforms usually did. To make the Deliverance's shuttles function like fuel transports, they were fitted with a special ring that created a small null-g area between the two docked vessels, allowing for the safe transfer of volatile cargo.

Delacruz spun. "Flores, hail that shuttle."

"Aye, sir." Then: "Shuttle Bravo, this is *Deliverance*, respond. Shuttle Bravo, this is *Deliverance*, respond. Over."

Nothing.

"Commander," Jareth said. "There's something going on. Either that shuttle left without a docking ring and is having radio problems, or that's a pilot with a shuttle full of antimatter who has no intention of off-loading that cargo."

"I think you may be right, Lieutenant," Delacruz said. "We need to secure that shuttle. Flores, find out who's supposed to be on that run. Filipov-Ibañez, suggestions?"

"We could blow it out of the sky, Commander, but we'd be down a shuttle and would likely set a whole shipment of antimatter loose in space that would be hard to corral."

"Agreed," said Delacruz.

"Let me go over to the shuttle," Jareth said.

"What do you mean, Killian?" Delacruz asked. "Take another shuttle with some marines?"

"No, sir. If the pilot sees me coming in another shuttle, that could spook him. I'm thinking of going EVA."

Delacruz looked at him. He'd never shown Jareth any disrespect, but in that moment, Jareth began to feel almost as if the commander now considered him an honest-to-God fleet man. "Flores," Delacruz said, keeping his eyes on his security chief, "get the captain down here."

A few minutes later, Captain Kavanagh walked onto the bridge. Delacruz filled her in on the situation and Jareth's proposal.

"What do you plan on doing once you get over there, Mr. Killian?" she asked.

"Well, that will depend, Captain," he responded. It began to dawn on him what he was volunteering to do. Extravehicular activity is always dicey, and there's something about being in the void with nothing around you but a pressure suit to make you start to lose it. "My plan will be to get onto the shuttle without being noticed. Once I'm inside, I'll assess the situation and go from there."

The captain looked at him. There's a fine line between improvising and pulling a plan out of your arse, and he could tell she knew that he was walking that line.

She nodded and said, "Get to it, mister."

"Aye, Captain." Jareth left the bridge and went down to the starboard docking bays. He suited up in a Mark IX EVA suit, not the heaviest duty or offering the most protection, but it would allow him the most freedom of movement once he got on board the shuttle. The advantage of the Mark IX was that it was somewhat stealthy—a deep gray instead of the usual bright white—and had a helmet with a wide field of vision. It was intended for boarding parties, but needless to say, probably not for this exact use. He checked out a sidearm and secured it to his EVA suit, setting it for the non-lethal setting—he could change that quickly enough if necessary.

Jareth put his com in his ear and activated the circuit. As soon as he did, he heard Flores's voice: "Lieutenant, the shuttle has stopped midway between us and the *Brunswick* and seems to be holding station. The pilot is a Petty Officer Rishard Trayner. No prior disciplinary problems in his file. Was a civilian volunteer from Fairhaven with experience in atmospheric flights primarily."

"Copy that," he responded. "Can you tell me from his personnel file how many hours he had logged in micro-gravity?"

"Before this expedition, he had thirty hours logged. Most of his work was doing in-atmosphere refueling for aircraft."

"Thank you, Lieutenant," he said. The Expedition had taken many civilians on the voyage in an effort to keep as much experienced military talent in the League as possible. Trayner must have been one of those civilians: a man skilled in refueling and docking but not necessarily a space veteran. Jareth could use that.

The docking bays were designed for small personnel shuttles. The four bays were arranged in a ring around the hull—port, starboard, "top," and "bottom"—that all emerged into the common area Jareth now stood in. He turned to the docking bay master standing at the primary control console.

"Chief Ahmadi," he said. "Is there any way to cut all the lights in here? I don't want a bright light to shine right as we're opening the docking port."

"Yes, Lieutenant. I can take care of that," he replied. He pressed a few buttons, and all the lights except those on his console and various wall panels turned off.

"Thank you, Chief." Jareth put his helmet on, stepped up to the starboard docking port, and gripped the handle beside the hatch.

"Ready whenever you are, Lieutenant," Ahmadi said.

"Open the hatch, Chief." The interior hatch on the port rotated away, exposing the inside of the airlock. Jareth paused just a moment and took a breath—going through an airlock was nothing new; people did this all the time. But usually, when the exterior door opened, a ship would be waiting. Not this time.

Jareth stepped into the airlock and attached his tether to a grip inside. "I'm tethered, Chief. Go ahead and finish the cycle."

The interior hatch closed behind him with a *thunk* that communicated an airtight seal, and a hissing noise sounded as the air was removed from the lock. Eventually, the hiss faded into silence, and he stood there in vacuum. The far hatch cycled open, revealing a field of stars and two objects in the distance: the shuttle and a kilometer beyond it, the *Brunswick*. The tether cable he had was a two-kilometer-long microfilament, thinly gauged but extremely strong. *It had better be*, Jareth thought. It was the only thing keeping him from drifting into deep space if he couldn't get into that shuttle. He walked to the edge of the airlock and jumped.

The jump was enough to carry him sufficiently far from the ship's hull before he began firing his suit thrusters. Slowly, he closed the gap between the *Deliverance* and the shuttle, which had positioned itself almost exactly halfway along the two-kilometer separation distance the *Deliverance* and *Brunswick* used during an antimatter transfer.

Jareth began firing the suit thrusters to brake his flight and managed to execute it so that he came to a full relative stop near the rear cargo hatch. He took another tether cord and secured himself to the grips on the shuttle. In his ear over the intervessel comm channel, he could hear Flores repeating the hail to Shuttle Bravo without success. Whatever this Trayner was up to, it wasn't good.

He pressed the private commlink button on his suit. "Killian to *Deliverance*. I'm about to go in."

"Copy," said Flores.

Jareth looked along the perimeter of the docking port. Somewhere, there was a—there it was—a non-descript panel covering an equally non-descript data port. Had he not known it was there, he would never have noticed it. That was precisely the point and one of the reasons that only specific individuals, the chief security officer among them, even knew that such a port existed.

He extended a data cable out of a pocket on his sleeve and fit it into the data port. On his heads-up display in his helmet appeared a command interface for access. He scanned the interface using the helmet's eye-tracking software and entered the code for access. This was tricky—shuttle hatches weren't meant to open in vacuum on their own. They were expected to be fitted to an airlock. On this shuttle module, a small antechamber could serve as an impromptu airlock in an emergency. Still, generally, these had not been set up to do so in the ordinary course of shuttling cargo back and forth between the *Deliverance* and the *Brunswick*. He had to be careful; if he opened up the hatch without taking some precautions, not only was it possible that the contents of the shuttle—including the pilot and the antimatter cargo—would be vented along with the atmosphere into space, but the explosive decompression of the atmosphere would propel the shuttle forward and away from him.

Jareth accessed the hatch control system to see if the antechamber had been sealed. It hadn't, but fortunately, he could do so remotely. He sealed the antechamber, cycled the air out, turned off the motion-sensor lighting, overrode any "hatch open" alarms or indicators, and opened the outer hatch. He heard nothing as the hatch opened, and he worried the mechanism would sound too loud inside. If the ambient noise of the shuttle were loud enough, it was possible Trayner might not hear the hatch open.

Jareth was about to disconnect from the data port when he realized he needed to do one more thing. He accessed the environmental control systems and placed a couple of custom commands geared for voice recognition into the system. *You never know.* He uncoupled the data interface and replaced the panel. He took another moment, another deep breath, and steeled himself. *Let's go. This time, you've actually been trained to do this.*

He detached himself from the *Deliverance*'s tether and stepped inside the lock, and the hatch door cycled closed behind him. In the darkness, he moved up to the small window that looked into the rest of the shuttle. In front of him was the storage compartment with the two tanks of antideuterium to be transferred to the *Brunswick*. He could barely make out the readout indicating that the magnetic bottle inside those tanks was functioning at full strength. *Thank Abe's God for small mercies,* he thought. Beyond that, he saw nothing unusual about the cargo or the cargo room.

Once the antechamber had been repressurized, he stepped through the antechamber door into the cargo section. Jareth made his way through the cargo section as stealthily as possible in an EVA suit, grateful for the Mark IX's freedom of movement. He unholstered his sidearm, double-checked the non-lethal setting, and approached the sliding divider that separated the cargo hold from the flight deck. The divider was partially open, offering a view of the pilot and controls.

Trayner was standing at the fore of the shuttle control deck. Jareth thought at first that the petty officer was staring at the displays but eventually realized that Trayner was just standing there, nearly catatonic. *He's snapped,* Jareth thought, remembering that this sometimes happened, usually among those working in a solar system's outer reaches. It was called the "Lightyear Stare," a condition whereby those who have been in deep space for too long stare off into space and become lost to the outside world.

But Jareth wasn't convinced—what might be a known phenomenon among asteroid miners and deep spacers wasn't common in the kind of work that Trayner was doing. Of course, neither was the work he was being asked to do. After all, Jareth reasoned, Trayner was a flatlander who'd spent more consecutive days in hyperspace and deep space than most experienced ISG personnel; it could happen. The Void was getting to a lot of folks.

Jareth raised the sidearm in his right hand and slid the divider back quickly with his left, pivoting around the sliding panel as it moved and stepping onto the flight deck.

"Rishard," he said firmly—his voice being broadcast by the suit mics, "Put your hands up and stand away from the control panel."

At first, Trayner did nothing. Maybe it was the Lightyear Stare, after all. And then, in an instant, Trayner whirled to face him. Jareth was about to fire when he saw that Trayner was holding a device in his hand—a remote designed to shut down the magnetic containment systems of the cargo pods. Where had Trayner gotten a remote that should only have been available to the maintenance crews who filled those pods? Jareth reminded himself there would be plenty of investigating after this was over. For now, this situation was already moving into backup plan territory. With a quick eye-blink command, he activated the magnetic boot grips on his suit.

"Rishard," he said again, firmly but with as calm a tone as he could muster, given that he was standing in front of two potential antimatter bombs. "Don't do anything rash. Just put the remote down and come with me."

"What's the point?" Trayner asked, surprisingly engaged, given that moments before, he appeared to have gone over into catatonia. "We're out here in the middle of nowhere. Headed nowhere. There's nothing to find. No one out here. We'll travel all those light-years and find nothing but a dead empire with no one to help. And then we'll slink back home to worlds we cannot defend and cannot save. We're a people under a death sentence. I'm just doing the humane thing; I'm giving us a mercy killing."

The Void could get to you, Jareth thought. And this was the way it had gotten to Rishard Trayner.

"Rishard, I know it seems hopeless. But we still have a ways to go. Who knows what we'll find? We could get there and find a Commonwealth teeming with life, ready to help us."

"Then why haven't they come before? Why did they abandon us?" Jareth felt his own bitterness swell; after all, it's the chip all Leaguers carried on their shoulders, the feeling of having been abandoned by the mother who gave them birth. Jareth brushed those thoughts aside to respond with more hope than he might have felt at that moment.

"We'll find out, won't we, Rishard? I'm sure it'll be a simple explanation. But I'm sure they're there. We'll find them, and they'll help us save our worlds. We'll save Fairhaven, I promise."

When Trayner heard the name of his homeworld, he looked up, but Jareth could see that the despair had taken him, perhaps even more than the Void had. Trayner no longer believed that he could save Fairhaven. He looked down at the hand that held the remote and—

"Bounce! Bounce! Bounce!" Jareth said, using one of the custom commands he'd uploaded into the shuttle's computer. The cabin gravity switched off immediately. In response, Trayner behaved precisely like every other newcomer to space flight—he looked immediately for something to hang on to. Even when the fundamental laws of inertia dictated that if he'd remained motionless, he'd stay right where he was, when the inner ear told you you were falling, you lunged out to break your fall. When the gravity turned off, Trayner dropped the remote and lunged for the overhead handholds. Before he could grab onto them, Jareth fired his sidearm; a beanbag projectile launched across the cabin and thudded into Trayner, knocking him into the bulkhead. The force pushed Jareth's upper body back, but the magnetic grips on his EVA suit's boots kept him from flying in the opposite direction into the cargo hold.

Trayner hit the bulkhead and got the wind knocked out of him. Jareth crossed quickly and grabbed the remote, tumbling in free fall. Once he had it secured, he shouted again, "Daisy! Daisy! Daisy!" The gravity came back on—at three gees. Trayner slumped to the ground, immobilized. Jareth turned off the mag grips and made his way over. It was difficult, but between the two of them, he was the one in a tactical EVA suit and expecting this. He reached Trayner and injected him with a sedative. Once Trayner was out, Jareth reset the gravity to one-third gee, picked Trainer's body up, and secured him to a berth in the cargo hold. He'd be out for a while, but Jareth made sure the restraints were secure, nonetheless.

"*Deliverance,*" he radioed. "Trayner is in custody; I have control of the shuttle. I will proceed to *Brunswick* and offload the cargo before returning to *Deliverance*. Please detach the tether on your end."

"Copy that, Lieutenant. The captain conveys her thanks."

Jareth took his position in the pilot's chair and engaged the thrusters, moving the shuttle toward the *Brunswick*. As the shuttle moved toward the starship, Jareth slumped in the pilot's chair, not so much out of exhaustion as out of a sudden deficiency in adrenaline. *All right,* he thought. *You held your own against one unarmed man. Let's hope it doesn't get worse than that.*

BACK ABOARD THE *DELIVERANCE,* Jareth handed Trayner off to his security officers, who escorted him to the brig on the security level. He got out of the EVA suit before following them to security to write up the incident report. Almost immediately after he filed the report, his handheld pinged: he was being called into a meeting on the conference level.

He wrapped up things with his staff and headed down to Briefing Room A. Commander Delacruz was there, and for some reason, the ship's surgeon and Chief Medical Officer, Dr. Lissa Kwok-Tranh, was there, too.

"Have a seat, Mr. Killian," Captain Kavanagh said as he entered.

"Thank you, Captain. I just forwarded my written report to you."

"Yes, I saw that. Thank you," the captain continued. "I want to say right off the bat that I think your conduct aboard the shuttle in securing it without any loss of life or harm to the shuttle was commendable."

"Thank you, Captain," Jareth replied, taking a seat in the chair opposite, feeling perhaps that he could give his imposter syndrome the afternoon off.

"Mr. Killian," Delacruz began. "This incident has raised a number of questions that we'd like your input on as chief of security."

"Of course, Commander."

"In your report, you noted that you thought at first that Trayner was evidencing 'Lightyear Stare.'"

"Yes, sir. I realize upon reflection that that can't have been the case since he had already piloted the shuttle and wouldn't have had enough time to lapse into it."

"Nevertheless," added Dr. Kwok-Tranh, "we think you may be on to something. As I am sure you've noticed in your observations, the crews are on edge. The stresses are rising above the level that the wellness counselors or the therapy dogs can easily alleviate. My staff and I suspect that a syndrome is developing. It's probably a combination of factors, including the trauma we're all still experiencing concerning the devastation of Farmark."

Jareth thought immediately of Chollie in that Novaroma bar and knew that even though he had tried to speak encouragingly to the man, somewhere deep down, he felt he would someday know that same dread or that his loved ones would when he had died in the last lines of defense of the systems.

"There is also the factor to consider that it has been four centuries since anyone spent this many hours in hyperspace and deep space," Kwok-Tranh continued. "The best way I can think to describe it is a low-level but persistent anxiety. Have you or your staff noticed anything like this?"

Jareth's thoughts turned toward Makindi and what he'd shared the day that Ando Lee-Chowdhury had been detained for brawling. "Some of my staff have described a strange conspiracy theory afoot—one that believes the ISG sent us on a mission that couldn't succeed. I thought that it might be a function of being in deep space, so I reviewed the logs from the Pioneer expedition since those journeys were the closest in kind to our mission. I didn't find anything like this."

"There may be a reason those ships didn't experience the same stresses," Kwok-Tranh said, glancing at the captain and first officer. Had they already discussed this? Probably. He was being brought in for a different purpose. She continued.

"We believe the major difference was that those vessels were civilian vessels. While a number of the commanding officers were former Navy or Marine officers, the vessels themselves were organized following civilian codes of conduct rather than military."

She stopped there and paused, waiting for him to catch up. It took him a couple of seconds, but then: "Ah, fraternization."

"Yes, Lieutenant."

"Do you really think that sex kept them from going stir-crazy?"

"It's possible. Many of those who traveled were already in family unit relationships. We know that there were several in-voyage marriages and even pregnancies. It may be that the laxer interpersonal rules kept them from experiencing the brunt of the psychological stresses associated with the long voyage."

Jareth looked from the captain to the exec to Dr. Kwok-Tranh. He wasn't sure what they were asking of him when suddenly he realized: "You're thinking of doing that aboard the *Deliverance* and the *Brunswick*."

"That's correct," Captain Kavanagh responded. "We need your assessment of the security risks."

"Well—it is an extraordinary circumstance. Generally, I wouldn't argue for decreasing discipline. Might I suggest that if you do this, you ensure that no relations are permitted between officers and enlisted or perhaps even among people of differing ranks?"

Delacruz leaned forward. "What's the purpose of that?"

"To create a new rule that replaces the relaxed old rule. Whatever else, the discipline of a ship is the most important antidote to security trouble. I understand the genuine psychological need arising among the crew from this journey, but I think it should be addressed within the context of more rules, not fewer."

That got a surprised reaction from the captain. "Mr. Killian, every day you sound more and more like a career navy man." Jareth thought Captain Kavanagh seemed pleased, even though his proposal had effectively limited her to Captain Brevi on the *Brunswick*. But something told him that the captain was not affected by whatever was going on throughout the fleet. No, she was too driven to let a little thing like the abyss of deep space derail her.

"Well, thank you, Captain," he said. Then, an idea occurred to him. "I know that I am way outside my area of expertise on this, but it strikes me that there are additional things we might do for morale."

"Such as?" asked Dr. Kwok-Tranh.

"It's occurred to me that another thing that the Pioneers had that we don't was a clear sense of purpose."

The captain and the exec looked dubious. "Our purpose is pretty clear, mister," said Delacruz.

"With respect, Commander, our *mission* is clear. Our purpose isn't." The captain's eyes were fixed on Jareth. She nodded, and he continued.

"The Pioneers had a mission, but they also had a *purpose*: to expand the boundaries of human civilization, to carry the human race into the unknown. They were part of something bigger. We have a mission: to contact the Commonwealth and enlist its aid. But what I think is affecting people is that the mission might fail. And the Void doesn't help keep your mood up when you're trying to stay focused. We need to remember that we have a purpose as well as a mission. Captain, you have one; that's why you're not as affected as many of the crew. I'm not saying we shouldn't alter the fraternization rules and add the other rules; I'm saying we need to think about ways to give the crews a sense of purpose, too."

The three of them sat there and looked at Jareth for a while—so long that Jareth thought he might be in trouble.

"Mr. Killian," the captain said at last. "You did not list 'philosopher' on your application to the fleet."

"No, sir, I did not."

"Mr. Delacruz, Dr. Kwok-Tranh, what do you think of the lieutenant's observations?"

Delacruz answered first. "Captain, there's something to that. We're career, and for us, purpose and mission are often intertwined. But many of the people on board our ships are reservists or civilian volunteers. You and I have had our purpose since we entered the Academy, if not before: protect the worlds of the League, whatever it takes. But most of these folks signed on for the mission."

Kwok-Tranh spoke up next. "The lieutenant raises an interesting point, psychologically. Mission goes to task, but purpose goes to the heart of meaning. And out here in the expanse, it can all feel meaningless, especially if the odds of our mission's success seem slim."

Kavanagh considered this. She leaned over and activated a commlink on her handheld.

"Lt. Flores," she said. "Please inform the crew of both vessels that I will be giving a mission update address at 0900 hours tomorrow morning. We're not going to jump today once refueling is complete. Until further notice, the fleet is at Condition Four."

"Aye, Captain," came Flores's response, surprise in her voice. Surprise was evident in the expressions of everyone in the captain's office. Jareth knew the fleet hadn't been at anything lower than Condition Two readiness the entire voyage. He looked at his handheld; it was 1530 hours now—the captain had just given the fleet the night off. Those shifts still on duty would find an atmosphere much more at ease than had been the case for most of the journey.

Despite the day's near-tragedy, Jareth felt hopeful. This was a good idea. The crew would get a break, even if it were a small one, and when it was over, the captain would remind them all why they were out there.

7 | BLACKSTONE | THE BRUNSWICK

"BLACKSTONE!" CALLED KEHLANI ZHAO across the officer's mess.

Rebekah Blackstone looked up to see the wiry ensign bounding through the dining chamber toward her table.

"You'll never guess what we've been seeing in stellar cartography!"

"Well, then, I suppose there's no point in trying," Rebekah replied, returning her attention to the polytool in front of her.

"Will you get your nose out of that thing?" Kehlani continued. "This is some good shite I'm about to tell you!"

Rebekah made a show of relenting to the ensign's persistence, stowed her polytool, and turned to square up to her companion. "Well, okay then. I'm all ears. What are you seeing in stellar cartography?"

"First of all, it's so fantastic that we're getting to rest here for a bit. You can't see shite in hyperspace. I don't even know why they bothered to staff the stellar cartography division on this ship."

"In case we get lost," said Rebekah. "You all are our map home."

"Sure. Sure. Anyway. We're about fifty light-years from a stellar nursery full of molecular clouds! We don't get this kind of opportunity very often! We're getting such good data!"

"I'm glad to hear that," Rebekah said, although without as much conviction as she might have put into saying so.

"Are you?" replied Kehlani, not hiding her skepticism.

"Are you questioning me, Ensign? You realize that that attitude borders on insubordination." She was attempting to be playful, but there was a bit too much truth in her words for it to come across entirely so.

"I'm sorry, *Lieutenant*. Didn't mean to overstep my bounds, *Lieutenant*."

Rebekah dropped her head, breathed, and lifted her head again to look into her companion's eyes. "You know I love you; I've made a lifetime commitment to you and Lyra. Our triad means the world to me. But it's not a legal arrangement yet. And because of that, we can't get shared quarters or do anything that resembles a relationship. No one knows we're together. And when you, an ensign, talk like that to me, a lieutenant, it undermines my authority, which is already in short supply on this ship."

"I thought you said you were going to talk to the captain and tell him about us."

"I did. I talked to Captain Brevi and Commander Sato-Abdullah. They both understand, and we're not going to get in trouble or anything, but because we're not legal yet, the ISG can't grant us the privileges that come with being life-committed."

"So, we can't get into trouble. Then what's the problem?"

"The problem is appearances. The rest of the crew doesn't know we're in a triad. It just looks bad."

"It looks bad for *you*, is what you mean," Kehlani said.

"Look, Kehlani, this isn't about you—"

"It sure feels like it's about me!"

"It's about the fact that I am having a hard enough time justifying my presence on this mission without having to fight for respect as an officer. Having officers of lower rank take liberties with me—even officers I love—doesn't help me maintain any respect aboard." Rebekah knew she was going to lose this argument. Even if she won it, she knew she was hurting Kehlani's feelings. But dammit—why couldn't she understand this?

"If you think that your navy career is going to be tanked because I speak to you like you're my *spouse*, then how exactly does our triad fit into your life?"

"Kehlani, it's not about speaking to me as your spouse when we're alone. Then we're not a lieutenant and an ensign aboard a naval vessel—we're you and me. But where there are crew around—" Rebekah didn't even know if she wanted to continue. She'd been making some version of this point for the last few weeks, and she hadn't stumbled on the right formula of words to help Kehlani see what she was getting at. Maybe there was no magic formula. "It just doesn't help. And I'm already feeling insecure about my status on this ship."

"That's not my fault, Rebekah. I'm sorry—*Lieutenant*. You're the one who wanted to come on this mission to be with *me*. You're the one who talked command into assigning you even though the need for a cryptologist seemed dubious. But you did it because you wanted to be with *me*. And now that you're here, *I'm* the one who's somehow hurting *your* career and making *you* feel like you have no part to play in this mission? Why didn't you just stay home on Fairhaven with Lyra? Why come along only to make both her and me feel abandoned?"

Rebekah could see in her partner's eyes that Kehlani regretted saying those last words, but it was too late. Tears started to well in Rebekah's eyes, and she turned away toward the bulkhead. She simultaneously felt awful about this conversation and worried that other officers would see her and think what a silly girl she must be.

"Rebekah," said Kehlani softly. "I'm sorry. I didn't mean that. I don't feel abandoned. And I'm sure Lyra doesn't either. Remember, she was supportive of us both going. Rebekah?"

Rebekah said nothing and stared at the bulkhead, willing the tears to remain inside, willing herself not to fall apart. But it felt like it was too late for that—she was already being pulled apart. On the one side was her commitment to the ISG, the service that had helped her find her calling as a linguist and a cryptologist and whose traditions and values she, a career fleet woman, had come to accept as her own. On the other side was her family, neither of whom had been in the ISG before the invasion of Farmark, one of whom joined up for the Expedition as a civilian recruit with an astrophysics background. She loved them both, but neither of them really understood what the ISG meant to her, and that disconnect was now causing two of them a great deal of pain. And Abe's God only knew what pain the one at home was going through.

"Rebekah?"

"I think I just need some time. I'm going to go down to communications and finish some projects I've been working on," Rebekah said softly, dabbing the corners of her eyes with her sleeve.

"You know that the fleet has the night off, right? Captain Brevi just shared the news from Captain Kavanagh."

"Yeah, I know," said Rebekah, turning back to face Kehlani. "I just think it would be better for us both if we took a few hours apart. Our feelings are probably a little raw right now."

Kehlani looked pained but nodded. "Okay."

Rebekah took Kehlani's hands and leaned in to kiss her on the forehead. "I love you, you know. You, who get so excited about molecular clouds."

Kehlani raised her hand and caressed Rebekah's tear-stained cheek, tracing her fingers down Rebekah's rich mahogany skin. "I love you too, you total word nerd," she half-spoke and half-laughed, fighting off her own tears.

Rebekah sat upright and straightened her tunic in a half-hearted attempt to make herself look put-together. She knew that she looked anything but. And she knew that despite the polite avoidance the other officers in the lounge were effecting, this incident with Kehlani had had precisely the effect she'd been hoping to prevent. They'd all just seen a lieutenant get all emotional with an ensign—quite against regulations and most unprofessional.

"If you change your mind, I'll be in my quarters, just watching silly vids," Kehlani said.

"Thanks. I'll let you know."

"And at least come by for breakfast if you're not on the forenoon watch. We can watch Kavanagh's address together."

"That would be nice," Rebekah said. She stood up, gathered her things, stopped to touch Kehlani on the shoulder, then turned and walked out of the lounge for the lift.

✦

REBEKAH WOKE UP IN a state of disorientation. *What? Where's my bed? My—Abe's God, don't tell me.*

She looked around and realized that she had fallen asleep at her work-station in a small communications compartment. The night before, she'd worked until nearly 0100, diving headlong into several unfinished projects as if she could overtake the pain of her conversation with Kehlani through sheer industriousness.

Rebekah felt her face and noted the sleep lines in her skin from falling asleep on her arm. She found her reflection in a darkened screen and tried to repair the damage her unscheduled slumber had wrought. *'I'll just lay my head down for a minute,'* she thought. *'Just close my eyes for a moment.' How'd that work out for you?* She pulled her long, black hair back into a ponytail, with some rebellious strands hanging beside her face. *It'll have to do for now.*

She glanced at her handheld. 0905. *Crike,* she thought. She fumbled with her handheld and messaged Kehlani: *I'm on my way!* The message didn't go through. *Kehlani, is everything okay?* Again, the message would not send. What in space was going on?

Now, as her consciousness and senses returned more fully, rousing from her usual morning stupor, she became aware of a commotion outside her small compartment. She grabbed her polytool and opened the door to the rest of the communications suite, only to find utter bedlam. Officers and technicians were running around, trying to resolve some kind of crisis.

"I can't get anything through—I can't tell whether they're not receiving us or we're not broadcasting!"

"We'd have to be—how can all our comms be down? The board reads green!"

"I've lost all control over those systems. Even the Long Radar is offline."

Above all of this din, a voice came over the loudspeaker. Rebekah could barely make sense of what the voice was saying. She didn't recognize the speaker at all—it wasn't Captain Brevi or Commander Sato-Abdullah, and it certainly wasn't Captain Kavanagh. The words were still a fog to her, but the tone was one of strident zeal.

She tried to focus on what was happening in front of her. She made her way to Lt. Commander Amara Petrov-Jones, the officer in charge. "Commander, what's going on? How can I help?"

The frazzled officer turned toward Rebekah, anxiety, frustration, and confusion written across her face.

"Blackstone. See if you can get anything through to the *Deliverance*. There's something seriously wrong with our comms—we haven't been able to get any messages in or out on any standard channel."

"Aye, sir," Rebekah said. Then she pointed to the ceiling at the speakers through which the unknown orator's voice was coming uninterrupted. "What's that?"

"A nightmare," Petrov-Jones replied. "Just see what you can do to get the comms—"

At once, the entire deck was flooded with a red light, and an ear-shattering klaxon sounded, followed by a voice that pierced through the din and oration alike.

"*Fatal environmental failure! All hands, abandon ship! All hands, abandon ship! Fatal environmental failure!*"

Everyone in communications froze and turned toward Petrov-Jones just as she began to scream:

"RUN!"

8 | KILLIAN | THE BREAK

JARETH WENT OFF DUTY at 1600 hours and immediately went to the officer's lounge. He wasn't hungry, but he knew that it was the place where he was likeliest to find the most people. Sure enough, several department heads and various off-duty folks had gathered there, talking, sipping drinks, or eating from trays of snacks and assorted treats prepared by the food services. The atmosphere of the place felt lighter to Jareth than at any time since the Expedition had departed Sharon System.

"Killian," Lt. Aiden Patel-Smith from Environmental Engineering called out. "Come join us," he continued, waving Jareth over. As Jareth approached, Patel-Smith turned to his table mates. "Do you all know Jareth Killian, Chief of Security?"

"Hi. Jareth," Jareth said.

"Killian," Patel-Smith continued, "This is Crew'man Zara Okafur-Brown, Crew'man Mariam Andersson-Li, and Lt. Javier Nguyen. Zara and Mariam work with me in environmental; Javi's in reclamation."

"Good to meet you all," Jareth said. Patel-Smith slid an order pad Jareth's way, and he selected a beer. He realized that he had been so concerned with making the right impression on this mission that he hadn't had so much as a sip of alcohol since Dominic's bar on New Sydney. But there was an air of relaxation now aboard ship, and it felt pleasant to indulge in a bit of rest and recreation.

"How do you all like working in environmental and reclamation?" Jareth asked his new companions.

"It's terrific, right mates?" responded Patel-Smith with a broad grin. "What could compare with the excitement of monitoring humidity levels and temperature? I mean, that's cutting-edge fleet stuff right there!" Patel-Smith and his colleagues all laughed.

"It can't be all that bad, can it?" Jareth asked, a little uncomfortable, not for the first time, with the fact that he had a great job aboard ship.

"Nah, I'm just joshing. It's good work. It doesn't get that exciting, but to be honest, if things were to get exciting in environmental engineering, we'd all be in trouble."

"What do you mean?"

"It's mostly the humidity and temperature stuff, but you'd be surprised how much the right oxygen–nitrogen mix can contribute to better brain function, how the right temps aid in sleep and physical restoration—all of which can be interesting enough. But if things were to get *really* interesting, it'd be because there'd been some kind of contamination in the air or water supply—cesium, uranium, polonium, shite like that."

"Does that happen often?" Jareth asked, incredulous that he'd been aboard a ship that might have been dealing with toxins more than he'd realized.

"Nah, man. Exceedingly rare. And you'd definitely know if it happened. The alarm system would go nuts, and before you knew it, you'd be in an environmental suit running for a life pod or an airlock. So, you can see why we prefer our work to be boring. No need to feel guilty that you're the one with the fancy job and title, hanging around with the captain all day," Patel-Smith said, again grinning widely.

"Are you bridge crew, Jareth?" Okafur-Brown asked in an accent he wouldn't have been able to place but for his encounter with Chollie at Dominic's—one of the Farmark accents.

"Yes. There are four other members of my team who rotate shifts on the bridge."

Nguyen followed up. "What's it like?" Jareth thought this was an odd question for a fleet officer to ask, but then it dawned on him—these were repurposed civilians like him. They must have been experts in various fields and served on this expedition to allow seasoned fleet officers to stay behind in defense of the League.

"It's good. Probably not that much more exciting than any other duty station. It's not like we're encountering anyone out here or having to make any combat decisions."

Patel-Smith chimed in. "I heard you were a part of that business today with the shuttle delivery. Sending the chief of security on a shuttle repair mission seems like overkill. What really happened?"

There wasn't anything classified about what had happened earlier, and certainly, there would be rumors and whispers. Jareth had the facts and the truth of the matter; he could help keep the record straight.

"The Void got to one of our crew. Snapped and decided to take himself out—perhaps along with a good part of the *Brunswick*."

"Abe's God," Patel-Smith responded. "It's as bad as I thought."

"What do you mean?"

Patel-Smith looked around the table before continuing. "We were all just talking about it before you got here. Everyone is stressed out. Mariam was saying how she was surprised that someone hadn't snapped already. I was saying that the ship felt like a powder keg."

"Yeh," said Anderson-Li in a thick southern Fairhaven accent. "We weh juss nai sayeen hai teense uht eez." Jareth's brain took a second to catch up: *We were just now saying how tense it is.* He was reminded of why he always had to put the captions on when he watched movies from Fairhaven.

"Grateful for the break," Nguyen followed. "I think it'll help."

Jareth was pleased to hear that. The captain's plan was working. He was aware that even among these four crewmates, the break was meaningful—a chance to catch your breath, a respite from the relentless drive across an unforgiving and uncaring void of space toward a destination they were not even sure would be worth getting to once they arrived.

A floater drifted over with Jareth's drink in a bulb with a straw, which he took into his hand before uncapping the straw.

"To the captain," he offered, raising his drink.

"The captain!" they all responded, raising their own.

"To Farmark," offered Patel-Smith.

"And to chorging the bastards what did this to it," continued Okafur-Brown.

"Hear, hear!" they all responded in a chorus.

The toasts went on for enough time for everyone to have drained their drinks and require another round. When the floaters arrived with the next round, the conversation became more sober, even if Jareth and his ship-mates were trending in the opposite direction.

"Do you think we'll find anyone?" Anderson-Li asked. Jareth wasn't sure if she was asking the table or just him, but given that it was unlikely she had never talked to her friends about this topic, he decided to answer first, just in case.

"I do," he responded. "It's not possible that a union of nearly two hundred worlds just disappeared. Someone's gotta be there."

"Why haven't they ever come looking for us?"

"I guess we'll find out when we get there," he answered, though that was only half a consolation. Somewhere deep down, he understood that it was wishful thinking. Maybe they were all gone; maybe their Pioneer ancestors had gotten out just in time.

Before the invasion, Jareth had heard reports that some people on Farmark believed that the Commonwealth was a hoax—that it had never existed. They thought that the League's ancestors all had come from Farmark and created the lie of the Commonwealth for some unspecified, nefarious purpose. As ridiculous a conspiracy theory as it had been, it wasn't like the Commonwealth had shown up to disprove it.

"If we get there," Nguyen started, "How far do you think we'll get to go?"

"What do you mean?" asked Patel-Smith.

"Do you think we'll get to go all the way to Earth?" Nguyen continued.

"Nah," responded Patel-Smith. "We probably won't get any farther than Sigma Librae—that was the frontier world closest to us when the colonists left. I imagine we won't even get that far; that's probably a few systems inland now." Patel's use of *inland* made no sense literally, but even after all these centuries in space, no one had ever come up with a better way of describing a system that wasn't on the frontier.

"Plus," Jareth chimed in, "last time anyone checked, Earth is at the center of the Commonwealth—that's a lot of extra traveling we'd have to do. Especially when the Navy will no doubt be able to respond to our request in Sigma Librae. Messenger drones with laser comms can communicate much faster than ships having to travel and refuel along the way."

"I was hoping we'd get to Earth," Nguyen said a little dejectedly.

"How come?" asked Okafur-Brown.

"How come?" Nguyen responded somewhat incredulously. "You don't want to visit the home planet of the human race? To see ancient cities? To see if any of the children's stories about Earth are true?"

"I dunno," responded Okafur-Brown. "I've gone this long without seeing it."

"Spoken like a true Farmarker!" cried Patel-Smith. "We don't need no nothin' what y'all are offerin.' We's doin' just fine on our own."

"Is that supposed to be a Farmark accent, or are you having some kind of stroke, Newby?" Okafur-Brown replied with the somewhat derogatory term for a New Sydney resident.

Patel-Smith laughed, and then Okafur-Brown. And the tone of the evening shifted back from serious to jovial.

The floaters would make a few more visits and serve more drinks before the evening was over. Jareth returned to his cabin, trying to remind himself to drink a lot of water and take some anti-inflammatories before going to sleep. He didn't want to be hungover when the captain gave her address.

But at the moment, even knowing that he'd overdone it a little bit, Jareth was happy. He had had an enjoyable night with some people he had not known before, and the camaraderie was enough to elevate their spirits.

He lay down on his bed, set the wall display to a nighttime view of the Reinmann Forest on New Sydney, and barely managed to whisper, "To the captain!" before passing out completely.

✦

MERCIFULLY, THE WATER AND anti-inflammatories did their trick, and when Jareth's alarm went off the following morning, he felt no worse for wear. He showered, dressed, and ate quickly; he was excited to get to the bridge that morning for his front-row seat to the captain's address.

He walked onto the bridge at 0749 hours and saw Filipov-Ibañez, Flores, Thorsten, and Delacruz already there. He wasn't the only one excited to begin the shift.

Jareth approached Ensign Upshur, the overnight security officer, to relieve him.

"Anything unusual?"

"No, sir. Pretty quiet. We did have some trouble with the SecLink to the *Brunswick*. I made a note in the log and sent a message to their comms officer."

"What trouble?"

"Just some latency issues. Our logs were taking a while to sync. I figured their network was probably overburdened by the extra data from the R&R—videos, music, you know. Plus, I'm sure they were gearing up to make sure the captain's speech would go off without a hitch."

"But the security comms aren't a part of the general network. Overuse of one shouldn't affect the other at all."

"The *Brunswick* is a newer ship but older than we are, sir. We don't know how things might be jerry-rigged over there."

"Yeah—" Jareth said, not entirely convinced. "Anyway, I relieve you."

"I stand relieved," Upshur responded. "Have a good shift, and enjoy the speech, sir."

Jareth nodded in response, but his mind was still on this minor communications issue; something about it just didn't seem right. After every downjump, the *Deliverance* and the *Brunswick* synced their security logs and reports. At most, the info swap took a second. Two kilometers in vacuum might as well be instantaneous at the speed of light—there shouldn't be any latency.

Jareth spent the better part of the next hour trying to figure it out. He started looking through the transmission logs and noticed the same thing over and over—the *Brunswick's* security comms were slow—as if they were being overtaxed with something. He scanned through the logs from the previous day to see if the *Brunswick* had scheduled any repairs or systems maintenance that could account for the delay. Nothing on the schedule. What could they be up to?

"What's that, Lieutenant?" asked Commander Delacruz. Jareth had been thinking out loud again.

"Overnight reported a latency in the communications with the *Brunswick's* security net. I'm having a hard time accounting for it."

Delacruz looked the way Jareth was beginning to feel—concerned but unsure why. He turned to Flores. "Lieutenant, are we performing any maintenance on our end that could account for the latency?"

Flores responded immediately. "No, sir. I ran a full diagnostic suite yesterday before the break. Most of our systems were on standby all night."

"Raise the *Brunswick*, Lieutenant," Delacruz said.

"Aye, sir." Flores began working her magic on her console, but right away, her expression said something was amiss. "Sir, I can't raise them. The open channel doesn't seem to be receiving. I've tried hailing them, but that doesn't seem to be working. I can't tell if they're not receiving us or if they're ignoring us."

"Surely they're not trying to avoid my speech," came the captain's voice from the entry hatch. Captain Kavanagh entered the bridge in a good mood that was instantly derailed by the expressions she saw on the faces of her officers. "Report."

Delacruz stepped toward her. "Lt. Killian investigated a latency reported overnight in the SecLink communications with the *Brunswick*. He has been unable to determine the source. Lt. Flores attempted to raise the *Brunswick* on both the standard open channel and through standard hails and has been unsuccessful."

"What the devil are they up to over there?" Kavanagh responded. "Lt. Flores, keep hailing them."

"Aye, Captain."

"Lt. Killian, can you access any of their security net from here?"

"I can transmit data to a buffer that appears to receive it, but any time I try to handshake with their system, the connection stalls."

"All of these systems are supposed to be redundant," the captain grumbled. "There's no excuse for this. This expedition can't succeed if our tech—"

"Captain!" shouted Flores. "I'm receiving a transmission from the *Brunswick*! It's audio-only."

"On speakers," replied the captain, but before Flores could comply, a static hiss came from every speaker on the bridge.

"Captain, they're broadcasting to the entire ship. They've logged into our comms."

"What the—"

Members of the Doomed Expedition—came a voice over the speakers—*I know you were all expecting to hear from our illustrious fleet captain with words of encouragement for us in this dark time. We have decided to dispense with this charade.*

"Cut that transmission, now!"

"I'm trying, Captain," came Flores's anxious response. "I don't have control over our internal comms. I'm not even sure how they're doing it."

Jareth could see the panic in Flores's eyes: it wasn't just a matter of an unwanted broadcast; it was the hacking of a vital system. He immediately initiated system firewall countermeasures—a specially designed suite of programs that built a cascading firewall so that even if someone had hacked into a vital system, the suite would create a firewall *within* the system to prevent it from being fully compromised. His board lit up with alerts—systems throughout the ship were being hacked. Mercifully, the firewall cascades were sealing off engineering and life-support systems and holding the line in the comms and systems that had already been penetrated.

Members of the Doomed Expedition. Surely, by now, you have realized that our mission is a fraud. We were sent on this mission to give the peoples of the League the illusion of doing something. It is a lie. Nothing can be done. We were never going to find the Commonwealth. The Commonwealth is gone. The League will soon follow in its footsteps.

"Who *is* that?" Kavanagh asked angrily.

"That's Jaxon Kimura-García," Jareth replied, stunned. "That's the *Brunswick's* chief of security."

"Abe's God," muttered Filipov-Ibañez at tactical. "That means . . ."

"That means Mr. Killian's network latency isn't an accident," finished the captain. "Flores, do whatever you can to get through to anyone else on that ship."

Everything we have been told is a lie. Everything we have been asked to do is an act of futility.

Flores turned back to her console, hands flying across the display, desperately trying to get any kind of alternate communications stream going. Filipov-Ibañez, likewise, was hard at work trying to get any information about the *Deliverance's* sister ship from his sensors. Next to Jareth, Hannover ran through his operations overview, checking to see that essential systems were still functioning correctly—many of which were doing so only because of the cascading firewalls.

We refuse to go along with this pointless quest, jumping headlong from one extinction into another. We will be masters of our fate.

"Mr. Thorsten," said Delacruz. "I need you to move us away from that vessel. Full impulse."

"Aye, Commander."

We will not be puppets dancing on the strings of the powerful to mollify the masses.

For his part, Jareth continued trying to log onto the *Brunswick's* security network, though he knew by now that this was fruitless. When the security chief went rogue, the entire security apparatus was lost. No matter what he tried, he couldn't make any headway accessing the *Brunswick's* SecNet.

If death be our fate, then it shall be at our hands, not the consequence of a cruel and uncaring cosmos fed by guileless fools.

"Crike," muttered Hannover. "Who *is* this arsehole?"

"He's about to be a mass murderer," said Filipov-Ibañez. "Captain, I am detecting a surge in neutrino emissions from the *Brunswick's* engine core."

"Good God," said the captain. "They're going to blow the hyperdrive."

"Flores," followed Delacruz, "Any luck getting through to anyone over there?"

"No, Commander," replied a visibly distressed Flores.

"It's okay, Lieutenant," said the captain in the maternal tone she adopted from time to time with the younger officers. "Keep trying."

We will not let the void wear us down through attrition. We make of ourselves an offering of our own free will!

Jareth was having no luck getting access to any of the *Brunswick's* systems, even with his security overrides. All critical systems had been walled off, their command codes rewritten. Then something occurred to him. "I think I have something."

Delacruz came over to his station. "What've you got, Lieutenant?"

"A non-critical system. I can access it. One sec."

"Lieutenant?"

"Stand by." Jareth's hands danced over his console as he identified a system weakness and sought to exploit it. There it was, just as he'd hoped. "Environmental control."

"How are you going to shut down the reactor breach with environmental control?"

"I'm not," Jareth responded dourly. "I'm just going to try to save as many of them as I can." *One in particular,* he thought. Ando Lee-Chowdhury. If he didn't make it off, that blood was going to be on his hands.

Hear us, O Doomed Expedition! Know that your deaths today will save countless years of suffering in the cold, empty loneliness of space! Our futile quest is at an end. Today, we reach our destination.

Jareth found the environmental status interface and entered a few lines of data into the database.

"What are you doing, Lieutenant? Report!" Kavanagh not-quite barked.

"I'm tricking the environmental systems into believing there's been a polonium leak," Jareth said, pressing send.

Though no one aboard the *Deliverance* could hear it, at that moment, all around the *Brunswick*, section bulkheads were slamming closed. Decks were being sealed off. Escape pod moorings were being unlocked, and klaxons were blaring: "*Fatal environmental failure! All hands abandon ship! All hands, abandon ship! Fatal environmental failure!*"

Today, we—what is this? What is this nonsense? Another lie from those who would keep you enslaved for spectacle! This trick will not delay the inevitable—we claim our victory!

The bridge crew watched on the viewscreen as dozens of life pods separated from the *Brunswick*, jetting away from the vessel in all directions.

"Thorsten? Status," said Delacruz, turning toward the helmsman.

"We're ten kilometers away. I don't know if that's far enough to—"

Just then, the screen was filled with a blinding white light. Though the display itself could not emit enough light to harm a viewer, the bridge crew was relieved when the filters cut in and reduced the terrifying glare.

There was no shockwave, no pounding on the hull, except for small pieces of what had once been the Brunswick hull colliding with the ship at high velocity. Everyone sat there stunned as they watched the remnants of a proud League starship break apart.

The captain slumped into her chair. Jareth saw her saying something to herself—like she was reciting a mantra or counting. Then, in a moment, she was back on her feet, entirely in command.

"Filipov-Ibañez, scan that wreckage. Are there any survivors?"

"I am picking up a couple dozen life pods. And there is one section of the *Brunswick* that is more or less intact—decks thirty and aft. The bulkheads appear to be holding."

The captain turned to communications. "Flores, get ahold of those life pods and give them coordinates to rendezvous with us. Mr. Thorsten, move us back to within two klicks of the blast site."

"Aye, sir."

"Aye, Captain."

"Mr. Hannover," the captain continued. "Get every shuttle we've got out there looking for survivors. I also want a search-and-rescue team to board what's left of the *Brunswick* and try to find anyone still aboard."

"Aye, Captain."

"Mr. Killian," she said, turning toward him. "I want you to walk me through your thinking."

"Y-yes, Captain," he stammered. He didn't know why he was more terrified than he had been during the crisis itself. He thought maybe it was just all catching up with him. It had been a miserable two days for everyone— a near suicide with a shipment of antimatter and now a mass suicide and murder by blowing up a starship's matter–antimatter reactor. Maybe it was because even when he didn't fail to act, people still died.

"I had been trying to access every security system I could to initiate an emergency shutdown of the reactors, both fusion and matter–antimatter. Nothing I tried was working. Kimura-García had anticipated almost every avenue that could be used to stop the overload. But once I realized that, I realized there might be something else I could do—if not to save the ship, then to save the people."

"Why did you tell the *Brunswick's* environmental system that it had a polonium leak?"

"I knew that that environmental contaminant would initiate an automatic evacuation and containment order and increase the likelihood of crew members donning spacesuits offering offer radiation protection. Kimura-García and his confederates would have blocked any other attempt to seal the bulkheads or initiate life pod ejection, but I thought this might be a low-level enough system not to have been sabotaged. After all, how much trouble can a bunch of humidity and temperature controls be to your plot to overload the reactors?"

"Good work, Lieutenant," the captain replied. "You continue to impress me with the range of your expertise."

"It's partly your doing, Captain," Jareth responded, and the captain's face screwed up in a puzzled expression. "You gave us the night off yesterday, and I just happened to wind up socializing with a bunch of environmental and reclamation folks last night in the officers' lounge. It's amazing the random bits of knowledge you can get over a few beers."

Kavanagh stared at him for a second, and he could tell she was not entirely sure whether he was putting her on. But then she smiled—a kind of knowing smile that he was not altogether sure was meant for him to understand. "I thank you, anyway, Lieutenant. You helped to save a lot of people."

Over the next several hours, the bridge crew focused on the recovery efforts and tried not to focus on the fact that however many people they had rescued from the catastrophe, the numbers were far too few.

✛

THE AFTERNOON WATCH ENDED at 1600 hours, but there was other business to attend to. Captain Kavanagh summoned Commander Delacruz, Lt. Cmdr. Hannover, Dr. Kwok-Tranh, and Jareth to the main briefing room two decks up.

The main briefing room was the largest on that deck and was outfitted with the same flexdisplay bulkheads the bridge sported. For this meeting, they had been configured to look like the walls of an old library full of leather-bound books. In the center of the room was an oval-shaped conference table with a flexdisplay surface. Most of it was set to display a wood surface, but the section in front of the captain was scrolling tables of data. Judging by the captain's expression, Jareth assumed she was looking at the lists of the dead and missing.

Kavanagh looked up from her display as her officers walked in. There was a running pool aboard ship about the captain's age, no one was ever sure—but however old she was, she looked ten years older than she had that morning. "Please, sit," she said wearily.

They all took their places around the table, and personalized displays appeared on the flexdisplay surfaces in front of them. Each of them had access now to the same scrolling list of names. Jareth scanned down the list of survivors, looking for—hoping for—one name in particular. But the universe was not about to let Jareth Killian off the hook so easily. The name Ando Lee-Chowdhury was not listed among the living.

"Commander Delacruz," the captain said, looking at her first officer. On cue, he began to report.

"We have successfully rescued twenty-eight members of the *Brunswick* crew from life pods and an additional twenty-three from the remaining section of the *Brunswick* itself. That puts the dead and missing at seventy-seven. Most of the refugees have been put in temporary accommodations in the cargo bays. As lacking in creature comforts as the bays are, they allow a large number of *Brunswick* personnel to bunk together—the solidarity and camaraderie may benefit them in this time."

Dr. Kwok-Tranh picked up from Delacruz and continued. "There are about a dozen seriously injured, some with radiation exposure, who have been transported to sickbay for treatment and another two dozen with injuries that my staff are treating on-site in the cargo bay."

"Mr. Killian?" the captain said, turning toward her security chief.

"All access codes to vital systems have been reset and access is being restored to individuals after a vetting process to identify anyone who had been a participant in the conspiracy. We have already identified one individual who helped Rishard Trayner get access to the remote switch for the antimatter containment fields. That individual is presently in the brig. Master Gunnery Sergeant Makindi is heading up a special team to follow up on leads related to the conspiracy theory. We are examining communications logs between the *Brunswick* and the *Deliverance*, especially where such communications involved Lt. Jaxon Kimura-García. Makindi's initial assessment is that the conspiracy did not have anywhere like the same levels of support on the *Deliverance* as it did on the *Brunswick*. But he and his team are continuing to investigate."

"Thank you, Lieutenant," the captain said. "Mr. Hannover?"

"From an operations standpoint, Captain, the destruction of the *Brunswick* has brought us both gains and losses. For one thing, we no longer have to share our antimatter stores with another vessel. If we desire, the antimatter we have in the cargo containers can be used to take us farther into Commonwealth space than we had initially planned. If it should be that the border systems are no longer functioning, that option will allow us to travel farther than would ordinarily be possible."

Discomfort filled the room as everyone sought to reconcile the obvious tension between the loss of so many comrades and the idea that there could be any benefit regarding shared resources. The fact that everyone knew it was true didn't make it any easier. Hannover continued.

"But now we have fifty-one more mouths to feed, fifty-one more people taxing our environmental and life-support systems, and fifty-one more people contributing to the waste heat we'll have to shed. That's a 40 percent increase in personnel for this vessel. I've already spoken to personnel in hydroponics, stores, and environmental. Everyone is optimistic that the *Deliverance* can handle it, but no one could give me a guarantee. But, because the surviving portion of the *Brunswick* comprised life support and ship's stores, we have recovered additional supplies and food stuffs, which should ease some of the burden."

Delacruz added, "In addition to the extra rations we will need, there's also the additional mass of the added crew."

"How much mass?" asked the captain.

Delacruz paused and looked away. "Too little."

Like everyone else, Jareth understood that the greater the number of survivors, the greater the burden it would place on the *Deliverance's* systems.

Yet, in that moment, he would have gladly triple-bunked or hot-bunked if it meant more survivors from the *Brunswick*—one in particular.

Delacruz continued. "But enough that we will have to recalculate our hyperspace routes and, of course, the acceleration and deceleration times for in-system maneuvers."

"How long before we can resume jumps?" the captain followed up.

Hannover responded, "I'd say it's another day at least before we have an accurate inventory, I mean—"

"It's alright, Commander," the captain interjected. "We're all lacking the right words at the moment."

"Speaking of which, Captain," said Kwok-Tranh, "Are you still planning on giving your address?"

"Have you—" the captain began before catching herself—Jareth was pretty sure *lost your mind* would have been the next words out of her mouth. She took a breath. "I would be interested in hearing your thoughts on the subject, Doctor."

If Kwok-Tranh had picked up on the subtext of the captain's question, she didn't let on. She continued without hesitation. "It's important that you do. Obviously, it can't be the same speech, but I think something is required beyond the usual ISG statement of condolence at the loss of a crew member." Jareth was unfamiliar with such a statement but knew it was probably like most institutional statements, full of pleasant-sounding platitudes that don't say anything. "If anything," Kwok-Tranh continued, "now the crew and the survivors of the *Brunswick* need to be reminded of their purpose more than ever. It might be the best way to help them grieve and to provide them with a way to focus that grief."

The captain considered this. She got up and walked to the flexdisplay on the nearest bulkhead. She placed her hand on the surface and said, "Full external." Immediately, the view shifted from the old library shelves to the image of the space surrounding the *Deliverance*. Jareth experienced a moment of vertigo when his brain told him, quite beyond reason, that the conference room had been instantaneously transported into deep space. He looked down at the still-visible deck and conference table to alleviate the mental confusion.

"It's so beautiful, isn't it?" Kavanagh said after a moment or two of staring into the starry depths. "And so deadly at the same time. When someone like Rishard Trayner lets space get to him and tries to blow up a shuttle full of antimatter, we think he's the anomaly. But maybe he's the normal one."

"Captain—" began Kwok-Tranh.

"Lissa, let me finish. I promise—you don't have to worry about me."

Dr. Kwok-Tranh sat back in her chair and nodded. The captain continued.

"We *don't* belong out here. We belong on a planet with plenty of oxygen in the atmosphere, fresh water in the ground, and mass pulling us down toward the surface. Out here, we have to bring all our air and water with us; we have to use acceleration, gravity plating, or mag boots just to stop from drifting into the ceiling. It's not natural that we should be out here. It's understandable that a rational person, exposed to this environment for any period of time, should let it get to them. I sometimes forget that. I've been in space so long that I have to stop and remind myself of its emptiness, its hostility to us."

She turned back to face her officers.

"The ISG was so desperate to launch this expedition and so short-staffed because of the losses at Farmark that we had to fill so many of our positions with civilians. Sometimes"—she turned to Jareth—"we luck out. But we forgot that there's more to being a successful fleet officer than being skilled at your specialization—you have to be able to come to terms with space itself. That's something it takes career personnel years to do. I was shortsighted not to have recognized that it would be so much harder for our civilian recruits. By the time it occurred to me to give a speech to the fleet, it was already too late."

She turned once again and stared at the display. Everyone else sat in silence, pondering what she'd said.

It was Delacruz who broke the silence. "Juliana," he began, exercising that rare privilege that only the closest of first officers can get away with when addressing their commanding officers. "This isn't on you alone. No one in the fleet gave that much thought to it. The ISG screened people for task competency, not long-range mission compatibility. The whole League was—*is*—in crisis mode. Please, don't take this all upon yourself."

Captain Kavanagh turned back toward her officers and paused another moment. She leaned forward and put her hands on the table; when she spoke, she wasn't angry or combative—more resigned. "I'm the captain, Husayn. It's my job to take it upon myself." Then: "I'll give that speech, Doctor. You're right that it can't be the same one. But I think now I know which one it has to be."

She drew herself up and tugged on her tunic, straightening it out. To Jareth, it was as if the captain had exorcised a melancholy demon from herself; an entirely different captain stood before them again.

"Mr. Hannover, I'll expect a supply distribution and resource management report by 0800 tomorrow morning. Mr. Killian, I want a full roster of the complement aboard from the *Brunswick* and a complete list of all civilian recruits among both crews. I'd like you to work with Dr. Kwok-Tranh and the ship's counselors to organize group therapy for our civilian and fleet members. Make sure they understand that it's mandatory."

"Aye, Captain."

"Aye, Captain."

"Mr. Delacruz, inform the crew that their captain will issue an address later this evening. I'll give it in the theater, and attendees are welcome and encouraged, but it'll be broadcast ship-wide, too."

"Aye, Captain."

"Thank you, all, for your work today. This is the darkest day of our expedition, and I am committed to making sure that no other day will be as dark. I am convinced I have the very crew I need to make that happen. Dismissed."

They arose as a body and walked out of the briefing room. As everyone approached the lift, Jareth took Commander Delacruz aside.

"Commander, I need you to help me understand what happened in there. The captain seemed tired, then angry, then lost, then pensive, and then herself again. Despite what she said to Dr. Kwok-Tranh, should we be worried?"

Delacruz smiled and put his hand on Jareth's shoulder, half conspiratorially, half as if he were talking down to a child. "Lieutenant, you had the rare privilege of seeing the captain's humanity on display in a way that most crew never get to see. You should count yourself doubly lucky: lucky that you are considered part of the group that the captain trusts the most to be herself with, and lucky that you have a captain who understands that strength is not in being unaffected by what happens to you, it's in being affected but going forward anyway. I've served with my share of captains, and the ones who like to project the tough-guy-nothing-fazes-me image always break first under pressure. It's the captains like Captain Kavanagh who allow themselves to feel what their crews are feeling but manage to forge ahead anyway—those are the great ones. Those are the captains I'd sail with to the farthest reaches of space." He patted Jareth on the shoulder and walked toward the lift.

Jareth remained a moment longer, thinking about what he'd just heard. For most of the voyage, he had considered himself one who'd adapted to fleet life pretty quickly. But in that moment, he came to understand that there was still so much he had to learn about what it meant to be an officer and what it meant to serve in the ISG.

There was still so much he did not know, but there were some things he now understood with clarity better than he ever had: he was in the right place and with the right crew. The more he considered this, the more he understood Delacruz's statement about good captains.

Jareth snapped out of his reverie and headed for the lift. He, too, would sail with Juliana Kavanagh to the farthest reaches of space, but before that, he had a lot of work to do to make sure they all would get there in one piece.

ISG ARCHIVES

CLASSIFICATION: UNCLASSIFIED

DOCUMENT TITLE: ADDRESS TO EXPEDITION

AUTHOR: JULIANA KAVANAGH

RANK: CAPTAIN, LSS DELIVERANCE

DATE: 23 FEBRUARY 2791 (STANDARD)

LOCATION: LSS DELIVERANCE, IN TRANSIT

RECORD NUMBER: CEF-001-3121-01A27

SUMMARY: Remarks following destruction of the LSS Brunswick

REMARKS:

This morning, I was prepared to give an address to the combined crews of our expeditionary fleet. It was meant to be a mid-journey reminder of the cause that each of us serves by being a part of this critical endeavor. It was intended to infuse us once more with a sense of mission and purpose in what has been a challenging time.

To attempt to give that address now would be folly. But just as foolish would be to try to say anything that could make our present sorrow make sense. I do not even know how to begin to describe the loss we have experienced in our fleet. It is a loss that goes beyond the seventy-seven lives lost.

Those of us who have pledged our lives to the fleet know the risks that come with such a commitment; the dangers of space travel and the challenges of providing security to our systems are full of perils. Every tour might be our last. These are the risks we sign up for. Even those of us on this expedition from the civilian world knew that this voyage might be a one-way trip.

But no one is prepared to face the threats that lurk in the human heart: the fear, the hopelessness, the dread that can make rational people lose all sense of perspective and cause them to collapse inward, often dragging others with them.

Although veterans of space never lose sight of how hostile the cosmos is to us, we learn to live with that horror and manage it over a career in the service. Tonight, we understand in a very real way that we cannot expect those of us who have joined this mission from civilian walks of life to be able to adapt quickly and easily to the demands of a deep-space mission. It is stressful enough for us career spacers; the toll it takes on our civilian crew has been too long overlooked.

Tonight, we face the consequences of that emotional and psychological toll. In the coming days, we will communicate how we as a crew will address that toll and the measures we will take to ensure that no crew member, civilian or fleet, ever has to face the terror of the void alone.

But tonight, I am here to give voice to our grief. To name the loss. To take a stand for the future of this expedition.

I mourn the seventy-seven souls lost: comrades we will never see again, shipmates and fleet mates who will never return to their home port, will never again see their loved ones, will never again gaze upon the stars of home.

I will mourn the brokenness that caused some of our comrades to conspire to inflict death on so many and such suffering on those who survived. But I will not allow myself to hate them--I grieve for them, too.

I grieve for them, but I will not yield to them. I will fight everything they believed in and everything that drove them to commit this heinous act. I will not surrender to their lie: the nihilistic view that our task is meaningless, our chances are nil, our mission a diversion.

Our mission is the most crucial mission the human race has undertaken in centuries. We seek not only to enlist the aid of the Commonwealth in fighting the Invaders who destroyed Farmark and have left our systems in fear--we seek to reunite our two long-separated branches of humanity. We strive to rejoin the greater interstellar society of the human race and reclaim our ancestors' birthright as human beings to that great civilization that shone so brightly into the void.

I do not know whether our mission will succeed; I only know that there can be no doubt that we must try. For to forsake this mission is to forsake humanity's shared future and surrender to the centuries-long silence that we have longed to hear filled with the voices of our cousins from across the void.

So long as I am captain of this vessel, we shall not surrender to despair; we shall not surrender to fear; we shall not surrender to the nihilism that excuses us from carrying out the responsibilities we bear to future generations to provide them with worlds safe, secure, free, and bound together in common purpose.

So long as you are my crew and remain committed to this vision, we shall prevail in this task and bring deliverance to the homes we love.

APPROVALS FOR ARCHIVING:

Nelso Brigantes-Fyfe, Adm., CINCSYD /s/

Turandot Halpern-Shah, Adm., CINCHAV /s/

----

9 | KILLIAN | ETA LUPI

IN THE FOLLOWING DAYS and weeks, the mood aboard ship was complicated, to say the least: grief mixed with a renewed sense of purpose; feelings of loss for those who'd died mixed with feelings of gratitude for those who'd survived. Jareth wasn't sure where he landed on that spectrum. He was grateful that he'd helped to save even those few survivors from the *Brunswick*, but he couldn't process the fact that because of him, one petty officer was dead today who would otherwise have been alive and aboard the *Deliverance*. There were times when he couldn't decide which shame was greater—had the shame of his self-protective act aboard the *Deliverance* been worth it to cover the shame of his failure on the *Vixen*?

Jareth was relieved that the mood aboard ship was mostly quiet. After the drama and the exhaustion of the events surrounding the Break, the crew seemed content to focus on the work—to make sure the Expedition made it to Commonwealth space as quickly and safely as possible.

Jareth tried to follow the same strategy, though it was sometimes tricky. He never felt quite at ease around Makindi. The Master Gunnery Sergeant never said anything, never uttered an insubordinate word or expressed anything but dutiful obedience to his directives. And yet, Jareth felt that the man's assessment of him as an officer had changed. Did he *know*? Did he suspect? Jareth could tell that his feelings were affecting the way he comported himself around the marine. *Crike, you're in danger of becoming a self-fulfilling prophecy. You're so worried that he'll become suspicious that you're going to act in ways that guarantee he will. Just focus on the work like everyone else.*

Jareth was encouraged to see that the crew's dedication to the work of the mission was not an excuse to suppress feelings or bury what had happened; on the contrary, the ship's counselors were working overtime, and the group sessions that he and Dr. Kwok-Tranh had helped to organize were helping crew members to cope and build new community at the same time.

The captain's amnesty for anyone involved in the conspiracy or spreading its message provided they issued a full confession in writing, seemed to offer many crew members a needed reset. Jareth had been reluctant to give any amnesty but came to see the wisdom of not vilifying those who'd succumbed to despair. He also considered that there were only so many brig cells aboard, and he wasn't quite ready to start spacing people just yet.

All the same, Jareth knew he'd be lying if he said that the ship was filled with the same optimistic feeling that the crew had had when they set out nearly two months ago. When he and Dr. Kwok-Tranh had reported as much to the captain, she said, "Perhaps we can do without optimism; it breaks too easily in the face of dire circumstances. Hope, on the other hand—hope endures." Jareth wasn't so sure about that. The Void had taken a lot of people's hopes.

In those quieter days after the Break, Jareth reflected a lot on what Commander Delacruz had said about Captain Kavanagh: that she was one of those great captains who allowed themselves to feel what their crews were feeling but managed to forge ahead anyway. He had to admit that every day, the captain proved the truth of that statement, and every day, her attitude and example spread just a little more throughout the crew. It was almost as if everyone had agreed that although no one knew what lay ahead, they'd face it together.

He began to wonder whether he could bravely face the future when the past terrified him so. There was only one way to find out, he reasoned. Follow the Captain and try to live out the hope she always talked about, the kind of hope that didn't bury the tragedies of life but admitted them, confronted them, and moved on ahead anyway. If he was going to be the kind of officer the ISG had trusted he could become, he had to do at least that much and follow his commanding officer boldly forward.

THE CLOSER THE SHIP got to Commonwealth space, the more the ship's mood turned to anticipation. With every jump, the Expedition was that much closer to the last known borders of that great interstellar civilization. The *Deliverance* was even beginning to arrive in star systems with names— names that had been assigned by astronomers on ancient Earth before space travel was a regular occurrence. The ship approached one such system now: Eta Lupi, the Cerberus system.

The *Deliverance* was still in the hyperspace stream headed toward Cerberus when an alarm went off at tactical.

"Report, Mr. Filipov-Ibañez," said the captain.

"Mass detected at downjump coordinates. Assessing options." Filipov-Ibañez reviewed his sensors to determine whether the object in the way could be pushed aside by the ship's downjump wake in spacetime or whether the emergence coordinates would need to be adjusted. He looked up from his sensors. "It's small, Captain. Less than three meters. We can push it."

"Mr. Thorsten," Captain Kavanagh said, "maintain course and downjump coordinates. Tactical, I want a report as soon as we're clear of the interference."

"Aye, Captain."

The *Deliverance* continued its downward trajectory and finally dropped out of hyperspace into normal space. The interference on the screens eventually abated, and the stars came back into view. Jareth's stomach lurched a little as those stars traced circles in the forward viewer. He knew that from time to time, starships rolled when they came out of hyperspace—it had something to do with suddenly losing an extra dimension to travel in—but it always made him a little queasy. He never understood why some commanders preferred to have the screens on when emerging from hyperspace. Maybe it was because the stars were comforting, even when spinning around.

"Engaging thrusters to counter roll," called Thorsten from the helm. The stars stopped in their dizzying orbits and became a stable star field. One star in the center of the screen was a good deal brighter than the others: Cerberus.

"Thank you, Mr. Thorsten," said Captain Kavanagh. "Mr. Filipov-Ibañez, anything?"

"Aye, Captain. Object coming onto viewer now."

On the main screen was a small metallic canister, three meters long.

"It's a *breadcrumb*," said the captain, sitting forward in her seat. "Small beacons that were meant to point the way from one system to the next. An expeditionary vessel would leave behind a breadcrumb in each system it visited containing an up-to-date copy of the ship's log and coordinates to the next destination."

Delacruz nodded. "One of my ancestors had a company during the Second Expansion, making those for the scout vessels traveling ahead of the colonization fleets."

Kavanagh turned to her first officer. "Well, now we know how the Delacruz family financed their part of the Pioneers' expedition."

"Given the rate of expansion back then, it was a steady income stream," Delacruz said, refusing to take his captain's bait.

"In theory, there should be an entire trail of breadcrumbs all the way from the Commonwealth to Sharon system, but since we've been jumping directly in as straight a line as possible, we haven't been jumping into many systems directly and had the opportunity to run into any before now."

Filipov-Ibañez had his head down over his display. "Passive sensors are picking up trace energy readings. The core is probably still active; they made these things to last a long time."

"Can you interface with it?" the captain asked.

"It's possible, Captain," Filipov-Ibañez replied. "But it might take too long to do it remotely. It'd be easier if we brought it on board."

"Mr. Killian, do you have any objection to bringing it on board?"

"No, Captain," Jareth replied as he scanned the tactical report that Filipov-Ibañez had shared. "The atomic core is a decay core—there's not enough fissionable material on that thing to pose a risk, and we can safely contain whatever stray radiation it might still be emitting. If this is one of the colony expedition's breadcrumbs, it's been out here for four hundred years. I wouldn't think there's much fuel left to worry about."

"Very well," Kavanagh said. "Mr. Filipov-Ibañez, can we mag-grapple that thing into the hold?"

"We could, Captain, but if we're going to try to extract any data from it, I'd recommend against using strong magnetic fields around it."

The captain pressed an intercom button on her chair. "Major Li, take a shuttle to secure that breadcrumb and bring it into the shuttle bay."

"Aye, Captain," the marine's voice called through the bridge intercom.

The *Deliverance* stayed at station while the shuttle flew out alongside the breadcrumb, wrangled it, and brought it back aboard.

"Captain," Major Li's voice finally came through the speaker. "The device is secure in the SB."

"Thank you, Major," the captain replied and turned to Flores. "Lieutenant, alert the crew that we will commence post-hyperspace checks and resupply immediately."

"Aye, Captain."

"Mr. Hannover, whom do you recommend for accessing that thing?"

"Ensign Meera Akintola is the best specialist on board for data access."

"Have her report to the shuttle bay immediately to get whatever information she can from that breadcrumb."

"Aye, Captain." Hannover bent over his console and sent a message to Ensign Akintola.

Jareth had become much more vigilant during these refueling exercises, almost to the point of paranoia. He didn't think there was a risk of someone trying to do what Rishard Trayner had tried, but that experience and the loss of the *Brunswick* had made him wary of letting his guard down. And so, while the resupply shuttle was carrying the antimatter refueling load to the ship's bow and the access port, he kept an eye on the shuttle's systems and the *Deliverance's* comm traffic.

There were the usual kind of messages posted on the ship's intranet—*Please pick up after yourselves after using the common area, Did someone leave their handheld in the shower on deck 7?, We're taking ideas for a movie night tonight*—that kind of thing. Still, Jareth noticed that one keyword was starting to climb in the frequency of mentions: *breadcrumb*.

He immediately pulled up all the related messages containing *breadcrumb* and began reading. A couple were of the *Wow! We found a breadcrumb!* variety. There were a handful of the *Can anyone explain what a breadcrumb is? My searches are only producing recipes* type of messages. But then he saw an enormous thread of messages about the breadcrumb. He opened it, began to read, and burst out laughing.

"Mr. Killian?" said Commander Delacruz, rising and walking toward his station.

"Apologies, Commander," he replied. "I was just monitoring comm traffic on the intranet when I came across a thread about the breadcrumb I wasn't expecting."

"Anything we should worry about?"

"No, sir," Jareth responded with an amused grin. "There's already a betting pool on the breadcrumb."

At this, the captain got up from her command seat and walked over. "A betting pool?! On what?"

"Well, on a lot of things. The odds on whether we'll get it open, whether we'll be able to access it, and whether the data has been corrupted. And then there are the odds about whether anyone's family name will be listed on the recording, with different odds for single and combined family names."

The captain stared at him. "Mr. Killian, are you telling me that the first encounter we have with a relic of the Pioneers' expedition is the subject of an organized gambling ring on my vessel?!?"

The bridge was silent. But before Jareth could respond, the captain continued. "And are you also telling me that I would get a different payout than Mr. Filipov-Ibañez because he's got two names, and I have one?!?"

Jareth smiled. "Yes, Captain. Actually, it looks like your payout would be higher because it's like the lieutenant commander has two tickets in the sweepstakes, and you have only one. So that payout for you would be double."

"Oh," she replied. "Well, that's okay, then." As everyone on the bridge crew laughed, Filipov-Ibañez, most of all, the captain gave him a wink and headed back to her chair. "As you were, Mr. Killian."

In that moment, Jareth saw that Kavanagh understood: the betting pool was healthy—a relatively harmless way for the crew to blow off some steam. He went back to scrolling through the intranet messages and marveled at all the ways the crew had come up with to gamble on this unexpected find.

Sooner than anyone expected, Lt. Flores broke the silence of the crew's routine. "Captain, incoming call from Ensign Akintola."

"Put her through."

"Captain Kavanagh," came the ensign's voice through the intercom. "I have successfully accessed the breadcrumb's data drive and downloaded its log. There is an encoded voice message with it."

"Can you play it for us, Ensign?"

"Aye, Captain. Stand by."

A second or two later, a strange voice came across the speakers—a voice from four hundred years in the past. It had an unusual cadence, pronounced some words oddly, and used an occasional word that the crew didn't recognize, but everyone was paying more attention to what it said rather than how.

To any Commonwealth vessel that comes across this muniment, this is Captain Grigorii Filipov, commanding the colony ship Conestoga. *The date is 23 January 2369 Standard, just over three months from our departure from Terranova. We have marked sundry systems suitable for terraforming and encoded those locations in the accompanying data, but we will not be terraforming any of them. Chancellor Ibañez reports that our colonial synedrion has unanimously decided to press on and search for habitable worlds—the colonists would prefer to get their feet on the ground as soon as possible rather than dwell in orbital habitats for years. And so, we press on. Directional data for our next jump are included in the accompanying dataset, as per standard procedure. We look forward to welcoming you to our colony once it is up and running. Forward the Commonwealth!*

Everyone sat silent for a moment.

"Thank you, Ensign," said the captain at last. "Please prepare a full report for my review."

"Aye, Captain," Akintola said before closing the channel.

"That was . . . extraordinary," Kavanagh continued. "I've heard recordings of Pioneer speeches at the Settlement Museum on New Sydney, but I've never heard ordinary speech like that. A living snapshot of our founding generation."

"And to hear them decide to go the habitable world route rather than the terraforming route as well," added Delacruz. "It's something every schoolchild knows, but to hear a recording from the time when they decided to do it—"

"Still, it makes me sad for a couple of reasons," replied the captain. "First, because it's obvious that we're the first vessel to access that recording. We're not that far from Commonwealth space now, and it's clear that no Commonwealth vessel has even made it this far. That recording means a lot to us, but it was meant for *them*—and they never got it.

"And second," she continued, "I can't believe Filipov-Ibañez won the damned pool! And on an exacta, too!"

10 | KAVANAGH | SIGMA LIBRAE

JULIANA COULDN'T HELP BUT note that the capture of the breadcrumb had improved the mood shipwide. It was almost as if the crew had finally gotten proof that people had once been out this way—that they had come from where the Expedition was going. She found that it made the subsequent days go by more quickly, with the routine becoming a comfortable ritual as the ship made its pilgrimage toward the Commonwealth.

They still had not yet seen any signs of the Commonwealth itself, which was somewhat curious—surely, they had expanded past Sigma Librae and begun colonizing some of the nearby stars. But every system was empty, devoid even of automated pre-colonization probes. It was strange, but it didn't tell Juliana anything; it said nothing about whether the Commonwealth was still alive and well or a smoking ruin. All it told her was that they hadn't come this way.

But the next jump would tell them something—it was to Sigma Librae, the frontier station that the Pioneer expedition had recorded as the last inhabited system of the Commonwealth. If no one was in that system, then fears of a dying Commonwealth might be true after all.

There was excitement onboard about finally reaching Commonwealth space but a little anxiety, too. Juliana could tell that her bridge officers were not immune to the tension. Every one of them had the hyperspace transit countdown displayed on their workstations.

"We're down, Captain," Thorsten said. Juliana looked up from her command display, and sure enough, there were stars again on the forward display. Even someone who'd spent as much time in hyperspace as she had breathed a little easier when she could see the stars. And now that the Expedition was again jumping system to system rather than into deep space, the stars had become comforting again.

"Captain!" called Flores.

"Report, Lieutenant."

"After outburst interference abated, comm sensors recorded a transponder registry ping. Something out there is looking at us."

Juliana turned to Filipov-Ibañez. "Activate our Long Radar, Commander. Let me know what you find."

Unless they had just come across an automated relay, left behind at an abandoned station by a decaying civilization, they had likely just arrived in Commonwealth space. And someone was here. No one said a word. Everyone waited in silence to hear what Filipov-Ibañez would find.

"There is what appears to be an automated shipping-lane transponder-registry station about 250,000 klicks downsystem. And beyond that … ships, Captain! Ships!" The excitement in Filipov-Ibañez's voice was evident. No one minded—everyone, including Juliana, felt it.

"How many, and how far?"

"LR is picking up at least a dozen. They seem to be located primarily between the fourth and sixth planets. There may be others further downsystem, but our range isn't good enough to tell. We're still far out."

"Lt. Flores, how long until we are in communication range?"

"We can send signals now, but there will be a four-hour lag between message and response," Flores replied.

"Mr. Thorsten, how long until we encounter the nearest vessels?"

"At current velocity, Captain, approximately 120 hours—five days, give or take."

"Not so sure about that one, Captain," Filipov-Ibañez interjected from his station. "New bogies on the LR. And they're headed toward us."

"Confirmed," added Thorsten. "I'd say 55 hours at current velocities."

Juliana took a moment. This was it, and they all knew it. "Well, I guess we'd better introduce ourselves."

THIS IS CAPTAIN JULIANA Kavanagh of the Starship Deliverance. *We are on a diplomatic mission on behalf of the League of Four Worlds. Our planets have come under attack from a hostile intelligence, and we are in need of assistance. We stand ready to accept boarders for a security check and to initiate diplomatic relations.*

On Juliana's command, they transmitted that message every five minutes for an hour and then sat back to listen. She cursed the damnable physics that had long allowed people to move matter between places in less time than lightspeed would permit but prevented them from sending information faster than light. Yes, they could send hyperspace drones loaded with messages from one system to another with relative speed and efficiency. Nevertheless, even they still had to transmit with a line-of-sight laser or by good old-fashioned radio. Long Radar was also useless in this regard; it could use perturbations in hyperspace to give a real-time view of matter in the surrounding area. However, it couldn't be modulated to carry information—it could only receive. Juliana found it all so frustrating. Imagine if they'd had FTL communications all this time—they'd never have lost contact with the Commonwealth in the first place. *And so,* she thought, *we are forced to wait to talk to people we can see long beforehand.* The ancient poet was right, she realized. The waiting was the hardest part.

Three and half hours later, an alert went off at communications.

"Receiving transmission via carrier wave," Flores said. "No LOS laser detected."

"Let's hear it," Juliana said.

Flores made some adjustments at her console, and the bridge was filled with an unfamiliar voice and what sounded like three exceptionally long words: *Anononvesso, hivutuanadpiripayaferaboridin. Inaderesebetwivinatusaigos.*

There was a confused, stunned silence on the bridge. Not being able to communicate in a common language was not one of the many contingencies that the command staff had prepared for; after all, the Commonwealth had used standard Anglic as its lingua franca since its inception.

"Flores, check to see if that is in any known language on record. Sounds like the Commonwealth has stopped using Anglic."

"I'm running it through all the translation matrices, Captain," Flores responded. "There's no match with any known language on file."

"Can the ship's computer figure it out?"

"Possibly, but we'd need to get a baseline. Without any frame of reference, it'll be harder for the computer to do that. If we knew they were trying to say 'hello,' that would be one thing."

"Understood. Thank you, Lieutenant. We'll need to get that interpreted. Do we have any linguists on board?"

Hannover turned to his console and began searching through personnel files. "The only linguist I see is a Lt. Blackstone, Rebekah Blackstone, a cryptologist and linguist—aboard the *Brunswick*."

Juliana felt a wave of grief wash over her as the sights and sounds of that horrific day came rushing back. She closed her eyes and gave the grief five seconds to have its way. *Five . . . four . . . three . . . two . . . one . . .*

"Is she one of the ones—did she make it?"

"Cross-referencing, Captain," Hannover replied. "Yes, she's in the temporary quarters in the cargo holds."

"Let's get her up here," Juliana said, feeling some measure of relief. Out of all the death on that day, here was a life saved that could help save them all. "Mr. Killian, please escort Lt. Blackstone to the bridge."

Killian leapt to his feet. "Aye, Captain. Right away."

Juliana smiled to herself. *That is one eager-to-please lieutenant, J.G.,* she thought.

✚

SEVERAL MINUTES LATER, THE hatch to the bridge swung open, and Lieutenants Killian and Blackstone entered.

"Lieutenant," Juliana said without waiting for an introduction. "Please listen to this." Then, turning to Hannover, she said, "Play the recording, Lieutenant Commander."

Hannover pressed a button on his console, and once again, the bridge was full of that alien voice: *Anononvesso, hivutuanadpiripayaferaboridin. Inaderesebetwivinatusaigos.*

Blackstone listened intently and nodded to Hannover as if to say, "Play it again." He did. Juliana watched this young woman in a uniform that showed signs of repeated wear and the consequences of living on a cargo deck, with her hair in a hastily tied ponytail, nevertheless displaying a focus that Juliana found admirable. After Blackstone had heard it several times, Juliana asked her, "Do you know what language that is?"

"It's Anglic," Blackstone said. "Not our Standard Anglic, but it's a kind of Anglic. Commonwealth standard speech has undergone a major shift in the time we've been out of communication."

"That's all we need."

"Languages change, Captain. Sometimes, they change suddenly and drastically for reasons we still don't understand. It's been known to happen. It happened similarly in English, Anglic's ancestor."

Juliana slumped a little. "We've got enough to worry about without having to figure out how to make ourselves understood."

"The situation may not be all that dire, Captain," said Blackstone. "Our language has not changed appreciably since Settlement."

"I guess that's true. We could understand the logs of that breadcrumb easily enough. But shouldn't ours have changed just as much?"

"It's called 'colonial lag,' Captain. It's a long-established phenomenon that colonial languages change much more slowly than the language of the mother country. It's almost as if the colonists attempt to preserve a connection to their homeland through speech. Our dialect of Standard Anglic has changed, but only slightly in a few meaningful ways. When we read things written during Settlement, they are still understandable, even if they sound somewhat quaint or archaic. That's a good thing—it means that while we will have to make ourselves understood, we won't have to start from scratch. The Commonwealthers will just have to adopt an older version of their language to make themselves understood. Hopefully, if they have anyone worth their salt in languages on the other side, they'll recognize our speech for what it is."

"Excellent. In the meantime, Lieutenant, I want you to monitor any radio communications we receive from downsystem—whether civilian or fleet—and see what you can learn about their speech on your own. We can't afford to have any mix-ups due to language. There's too much at stake."

"Of course, Captain."

"Mr. Killian, please escort Lt. Blackstone to communications and have them set her up at a workstation there. Ms. Blackstone, I understand you're in the temporary quarters in cargo deck two. I am going to arrange to have your belongings brought up to senior officers' quarters so that you'll have a workstation in your quarters and slightly more comfortable accommodations."

"That's quite alright, Captain, I should be fine staying—"

"Lieutenant, the success of this mission depends on us being able to communicate our needs and enlist support. It won't do to have my chief interpreter impeded by a lack of a decent night's sleep."

"Yes, sir," Blackstone replied obediently.

"I can stop by the quartermaster on my way back to the bridge and make sure the lieutenant has a proper set of bedding, a fresh uniform, and personal items for the officers' quarters," Killian volunteered.

Juliana turned to Killian and raised an eyebrow. Lt. Blackstone was an attractive woman, and Juliana knew her crew had been in deep space for a long time. Killian blushed upon realizing that he was being so obvious. He was being a little obvious, but it was equally true that Juliana had a knack for reading people well. "Thank you, Mr. Killian. I am sure the lieutenant appreciates the assistance."

Both lieutenants nodded and exited the bridge. Juliana returned to her seat and turned to Delacruz.

"I'm not equipped for this. Just think of how long it took me to understand you and your Fairhaven accent."

"And I'm going easy on you," Delacruz replied. "You should come to dinner at my folks' place. You'd have to bring the lieutenant along with you."

Juliana smiled and turned back to her data terminal to update her log. *This is going to work out*, she thought. *I have one hell of a crew.*

✚

A DAY LATER, FILIPOV-IBAÑEZ confirmed the approaching ships were Commonwealth vessels when long-range scopes could make out the seal of the Commonwealth on their hulls. It was just as everyone had expected it to be: five stars representing the founding worlds, with a planet from which a spiraled swoosh emerged pointing to a sixth star, all bordered by a stylized wreath. It was the Commonwealth, alright; whether they were in anything like good shape was yet to be determined.

Despite Lt. Blackstone's best efforts, the *Deliverance* was still unable to communicate directly with the Commonwealth vessels.

Juliana stared at the three-dee tactical readout projected in the center of the bridge, showing the relative positions of the *Deliverance* and the approaching Commonwealth ships. She turned to her XO, who'd been busy reviewing departmental reports on his console.

"I don't like the idea of taking on boarders without having established some kind of communication. Even when we want the boarders."

Delacruz put a digital bookmark in the reports and turned toward her. "Maybe something simpler? Morse?"

"We have no way of knowing if they can read what we send them."

"It's a pity we can't just pull up next to them and do charades through the window."

Juliana looked at her first officer with a sudden flash of inspiration. "Maybe we can do the next best thing." She got up and turned to her communications officer. "Lt. Flores, are we in an effective line-of-sight visual range of the CSN vessels?"

Flores checked her display. "We are, Captain."

"Initiate a semaphore exchange with them. Hoist some flags, too. See if that works."

"Aye, sir," Flores replied.

"Semaphore?" asked Delacruz as the captain returned to her seat.

"We can't talk with these people just yet. But if my guess is right, the semaphore codes should have remained the same."

"That's a good idea. They survived the transition from sea-going to space-going vessels. The only question I have is: which one of us gets to go out on the hull with the flags?"

"Captain," called Flores from her station. "Semaphore signaling initiated. I am broadcasting our name and registry number. I have also initiated the flag hoists, signaling that we are seeking communication and willing to receive boarders." At that moment, holographic images of brightly colored flags extended from the Sheridan drive to the conning tower as if hanging on a line.

"Mr. Hannover," Juliana said, rising from her seat and walking forward to stand just behind Thorsten at the helm. "Put the lead vessel on the forward viewer, maximum magnification."

"Aye, sir." The lead Commonwealth vessel appeared before them. It had already turned and begun its deceleration burn, backing toward the *Deliverance.*

"Light lag at this range?"

"One hundred twenty-two seconds, Captain. Just over four minutes round trip."

Juliana took out her handheld and started a timer, shifting her gaze back and forth between her handheld screen and the main viewer. Everyone continued with their duties, but she knew it was hard for them not to share in their captain's anticipation as she waited for the display of the approaching vessel to change.

Then: "Aha!" Just after the four-minute mark, the image of the approaching vessel demonstrated a series of brightly colored holographic hoist flags in a similar fashion, hanging virtually from an invisible line extending from their Sheridan drive to their conning tower. Separate projections of semaphore flags were displayed atop the conning tower.

"Message received. Prepare to receive boarders. Twenty-four hours," Juliana read.

"Semaphore relays the name and registry of the vessel as the *Frederick*, CSH-2664," added Flores.

"Thank you, Lieutenant," Juliana said and retook her seat beside Delacruz, grinning.

"Only you would come up with semaphore and hoist flags," Delacruz said as she sat down.

"You would have come up with it eventually."

"Perhaps," he responded. "But of all the Juliana Kavanagh things I have witnessed, that may have been the Juliana Kavanagh-est of them all."

She smiled at her first officer's good-natured ribbing. "Laugh all you want, XO. At least tomorrow's encounter is less likely to resemble an interdiction."

Delacruz smiled in response before turning to Thorsten. "Mr. Thorsten, prepare for turn-and-burn."

"Aye, Commander," the helmsman replied. Everyone strapped in as Flores signaled the ship-wide null-g alert.

"Flip us, Mr. Thorsten."

Thorsten killed the fusion drives, and everyone became weightless as the one-gee acceleration disappeared.

"Engaging maneuvering thrusters," Thorsten reported from his station. Unlike the departure from drydock, he did not pilot the ship directly but entered a series of firing commands into the nav computer. The *Deliverance* spun smoothly on its yaw axis, and the view on the forward display swung away from the oncoming Commonwealth vessels to the space that had previously been astern. "Flip complete. Beginning deceleration in ten seconds."

Flores signaled the gravity alarm, and everyone braced themselves. Even after a short time in null g, the transition to acceleration gravity could still be rough. The engines came back on, and everyone was pulled down into their seats.

"Well done, Mr. Thorsten," Juliana said. "Switch display to ship-aft view. Now, we wait—again."

11 | BLACKSTONE | SIGMA LIBRAE

REBEKAH SAT ON HER bedroll among the cargo crates and storage lockers of cargo hold level two, deck thirty-seven. She held her polytool in her hand and scrolled through its contents, looking for anything that could distract her.

She had hoped against hope that Kehlani had been one of the ones who made it off the *Brunswick* in time. But of all the life pods recovered that awful day, not one of them carried the woman who had been her partner. The woman whom she had quarreled with the night before. The woman whose company she had forsaken to spend more time on her work.

She looked at her polytool and watched as its contents rolled by. She wasn't even reading them at this point; they blurred as she stared at the device itself—a present from Kehlani on Rebekah's last birthday, the only surviving piece of the life she'd had just a couple of weeks ago. She looked around at her fellow shipmates spread around the cargo deck on cots and bedrolls among the containers. Most just sat quietly; some worked on data pads or handhelds. The mood on deck had been one of quiet solidarity for the survivors of the *Brunswick* who hadn't yet been assigned to some better quarters.

The compartment hatch opened, and a tall, fair-complexioned man with somewhat tussled hair got out and approached the duty officer. Rebekah watched as the duty officer turned and pointed in her direction. She turned to look behind her to see who the duty officer might have been pointing at, but no one was there.

The man made his way directly toward her. "Lt. Rebekah Blackstone?"

"Yes?" Rebekah said, turning back toward the visitor.

"I'm Lt. Jareth Killian, Security Chief. I have orders from Captain Kavanagh to escort you to the bridge."

"Of course," she said and began to put down the hand tablet she had been working on.

"Is that a linguistics polytool?" Killian asked.

"Uh, yes," she replied as she stood up, unsure why the lieutenant would be interested in knowing.

"Terrific. Please bring that with you. I'm sure the captain will want you to have whatever tools you usually use." Rebekah looked at him uncertainly—why in space would the captain need a linguist?

"Please follow me," he said. They walked down the corridor to the service lift and took it to the bridge level. As the doors opened, the lieutenant greeted the marines on duty and vouched for her. One of the marines slid the hatch to the side, and the lieutenant gestured for Rebekah to enter. She stepped over the coaming onto the bridge.

"Lieutenant," the captain said without waiting for an introduction. "Please listen to this."

✚

"THANK YOU, MR. KILLIAN. I am sure the lieutenant appreciates the assistance."

Killian and Rebekah nodded and exited the bridge. She was in a daze. Had she really just been summoned to the bridge by the captain and asked to aid the ship's mission with *linguistics*? She half expected to wake up on her bedroll in cargo level two, having dreamt the whole thing. She was awash with feelings, most of them bittersweet—she was finally getting to use her gifts and talents on this mission, but Kehlani wasn't here to see it.

This lieutenant escorting her, Killian, seemed pretty eager. She could guess why. He was cute enough, she supposed, but there was no way she was anywhere near ready to entertain such notions. They rode down the lift to the communications level and got off.

"So," Killian began as they walked down the corridor. "How did you get interested in linguistics and cryptology?"

"I'm from Fairhaven," Rebekah said. "Have you ever been?"

"Yeah. When I was in the Merchant Marine, I went to Fairhaven a lot."

"Well, if you've been to Mesopotamia, you know there are a lot of different language communities there. That's where I grew up. I had friends in school who came from neighborhoods that spoke Russki, Zhongwen, Xhosa, Eridani, and Espanyolic. I picked up their languages pretty easily. When I took my ISG entrance exams, I demonstrated an aptitude for it and have been in linguistics and cryptology ever since. Granted, that's been more cryptology than anything else—it's not like we encounter any new languages in the League."

"Until now, of course."

"Until now," she replied, still half disbelieving.

They reached the communications center, and Killian swiped them through the security door. "I'll encode your ID, so you'll have access to this area," he said to her. "In the meantime, Ensigns Weinrib-Pratt and Živojinović will give you anything you need. I'll be sure to take care of your bedding, toiletries, and uniform request with the quartermaster."

"Thank you, Lieutenant. I do appreciate it." She turned and greeted Weinrib-Pratt and Živojinović, who promptly set her up at the communications log terminal. Killian nodded politely and then ducked out. This communications suite was a brighter, newer version of the one she'd known on the *Brunswick*, and that familiarity helped her feel at home.

Weinrib-Pratt and Živojinović were friendly and responsive to her questions and requests. They gave her access to all the comms recordings and any signal traffic they'd intercepted since downjumping into the Sigma Librae system. Armed with gigabytes of data, Rebekah dived in. She connected her polytool to the network, and it began transcribing the audio of received and intercepted communications into the phonetic alphabet. She listened to the recordings as the transcription flashed across the flexdisplay in front of her. She paused at points to make annotations and scribbled down notes—*vocalic insertion between consonant clusters—rule-based? Voicing and/or forwarding of intervocalic dentals [ð] > [v], [θ] > [f]*. Before long, she worked up an annotated gloss of the audio recordings: *unknown vessel, heave to and prepare for boarding. Intercept within two sikos(?) (poss. 'cycles'? days? sols?)*.

She sat back and smiled. After months on this expedition, having endured feelings of irrelevancy, inadequacy, isolation, and loss, she was finally experiencing a new emotion. She was having fun.

SOMETIME LATER, KILLIAN RETURNED to communications. Rebekah was still sitting at her flex console, scrolling through pages of text and scribbling notes by hand and on her polytool. As he arrived, she pushed back in her chair and rubbed her eyes.

"How's it coming?" Killian asked.

She turned and looked up with a tired smile. "It's coming along—I think I can figure out what's happening in Commonwealth speech. The changes are not that out of the ordinary and seem to happen in regular patterns—which makes everything easier."

"That's great!" he replied. "Wanna take a break? I'd be happy to treat you to a bite in the officers' mess."

She looked over at her console—there was a ton of work to do, and she *enjoyed* doing the ton of work she had. But she had to be honest—even with her new-found enthusiasm, she was flagging a bit.

"Dinner?" she said. "I haven't had a proper sit-down meal since coming over from the *Brunswick*. I guess I've figured if I kept working, I could hold off the grief. But thank you, Lieutenant. I would be happy to join you."

She knew it was no big gesture on his part since the crew didn't have to pay for the food they ate aboard the ship, but she appreciated the opportunity to take a break. They made their way to the officer's mess seventeen decks up and grabbed a table alongside a flexdisplay wall, currently showing a scene from the savannah of eastern New Sydney.

"Do you mind me asking you a question, Lieutenant?" he asked her after they sat down to eat.

"You mean the '*why do we need you?*' question?" she said.

Killian gaped. Plainly, that was the question he had been about to ask.

"I take it you get that question a lot."

"You could say that. Or 'My handheld has translation functionality built-in; what do you do that's so special?'"

"Well . . . yeah," Killian said, shrugging.

"Okay. Let me give you an illustration. How do you understand this statement: *time flies like an arrow; fruit flies like a banana.*"

Killian laughed out loud. "That's funny."

"An ancient bit of humor. But you understood that it was a joke and a play on words."

"Yeah, I mean, it *had* to be. Fruit doesn't fly, so you have to rethink it. The two halves sound like they're saying the same kind of thing, but they're not at all."

"Very good, Lieutenant," Rebekah said. "Yes, on the surface, the structure of the sentences appears identical: noun-verb-adverb-article-noun. But because of context clues—you know that fruit *doesn't fly*—your brain reinterpreted the second as noun-noun-verb-article-noun. Would it surprise you to learn that computers have a tough time figuring that out? Getting computers to translate in those cases rarely yields a satisfactory result."

"So, you have to know that *flies* can mean both 'moves through the air' and 'little insects.'"

"Which computers can know, but what's harder to know is when I mean which. There was a split-second when you thought that *flies* in the second sentence might mean moving through the air—that's how the joke works—but your knowledge about the world forced you to recontextualize and figure out the necessary interpretation."

"So, computers don't know that fruit can't fly?"

"They do if we tell them, but how much information do we have to encode along with every single word that goes into a translation matrix? Do we have to encode its meaning, physical dimensions, likely use, and context? Beyond that, its metaphorical and figurative meanings? I am not even sure that information is encoded in our brains alongside every word. It would be a massive undertaking, and even then, it wouldn't include the most useful skill in working with language: intuition. Of course, there *is* a kind of computer that can use intuition . . ."

She could see him grimace; he'd taken her meaning. AIs could do that. But AIs, while not strictly illegal, were taboo and generally not found in any system that had access to matter–antimatter reactors and nuclear weapons. He nodded. "Yeah, so that's why starships need human interpreters and linguists."

"Right, because they'll never put a machine capable of doing what I do on a starship. For all the obvious reasons."

"Right, no one is going to risk another At-Taqadam," Killian said.

"At-Taqadam?"

"I'm sure you heard this story about how an early-generation AI managed the city of At-Taqadam on New Damascus. The AI was connected to the city's power grid, utilities, and data centers and reviewed them regularly."

"Okay."

"It did a comprehensive review of the history of philosophical thought, had an existential crisis, and in a moment of panic, committed suicide, taking out the entire city with it when the reactor went critical."

"Oh, yeah," Rebekah said. "I have heard about that. I was thinking more about the *Throne of Zeus.*"

"The AI-piloted ship that decided it could take a shortcut through the sun?" Killian laughed. "Yeah, that's another good one."

"Well, if nothing else, the League's aversion to AI in integrated systems provides me with some job security," Rebekah joked. Killian raised his glass, and they toasted in mock celebration.

"How long do you think it'll take for you to crack the Commonwealth speech?"

"Not too long. It's a lot easier knowing that they're speaking a kind of Anglic, even if it's not the kind we speak. Once I finish figuring out the rules, I should be able to generate an algorithm that can translate back and forth. It won't be 100 percent accurate, but for most purposes, it'll do."

"I look forward to using it. It means we'll have made contact."

"Me, too," she said, excited that her work would help facilitate their mission.

"I just can't get over how much their language has changed," Killian said with the astonishment that most non-linguists had when confronted with the things that linguists took for granted.

"Languages change; it's just what they do. And not just theirs; ours, too. For example, did you know that *sir* once was used only with masculine-identifiers?"

"What?" Killian said. "That can't be right. That word was made for Captain Kavanagh. She's the *sir*-est sir I've ever known."

Rebekah laughed and raised her glass again in another mock toast. She was beginning to realize just how much she'd missed this. She'd walled herself off after the *Brunswick* was lost and Kehlani died. Talking with this Killian person was awakening something in her. The crush she was pretty sure he had on her was hopeless. Still, she was enjoying spending time with him—teaching him about language, talking about language, working with language, making morbid jokes about murderous AIs. And to his credit, he seemed sincerely interested in her as a person and laying the groundwork for a genuine friendship. Rebekah was, to her surprise, after only a couple of weeks, finding a home aboard this starship.

12 | KILLIAN | SIGMA LIBRAE

THE FOLLOWING MORNING, BEFORE reporting to the bridge, Jareth went to see the captain in her office. Along the way, he could see the effect the *Frederick's* imminent arrival was having on the crew. *We made it*, he thought. *Now, it's all over, but for the diplomacy.*

He reached the captain's quarters and pressed the door chime.

"Enter," came Captain Kavanagh's voice through an external speaker. The hatch moved inward and slid to one side, and Jareth stepped in. The captain's office was an additional room in her quarters, the largest quarters on the ship. Jareth looked over the office and tried to take it all in. On one bulkhead was a vintage ship's wheel surrounded by nautical charts and framed old maritime maps of seas that Jareth didn't recognize. A free-fall-secure bookshelf was on the far bulkhead full of antique volumes, a sextant, and other objects that Jareth had never seen before. In front of the bookcase, at a desk that had all the appearances of being made out of wood but must have been a flexdisplay, sat his commanding officer. She was looking at a tactical display of the Sigma Librae system projected into the air in front of her. With a swipe of the hand, she returned the projection to the flexdisplay of her desk and looked up.

"What can I do for you, Mr. Killian?"

"I have some security concerns about our contact with the *Frederick* later."

"As you are paid to do, Lieutenant. Go on."

"Instead of the usual couple of security officers, I recommend a marine contingent."

Kavanagh looked at Jareth closely. "Is that necessary?"

"Hopefully not, sir. But I'd feel better if we could establish more in-depth communications than we have been able to. We know what will happen in large measure, but we can't gauge their intentions because we can't talk to them."

"Lt. Blackstone is working as fast as she can, Mr. Killian."

"Yes, sir. I have no complaints about the lieutenant's work. I only note that, whatever the reason, we have not been able to communicate clearly with a vessel from which we are about to receive a boarding party. I would make the same recommendation if we had encountered a League vessel whose comms were not working perfectly and only fragments could get through."

The captain considered this. "Fair enough. This is an extraordinary circumstance. Your request is approved."

"Thank you, sir."

"Just remember, this is, first and foremost, a diplomatic encounter, not a military one."

"Understood, sir."

"Alright. Dismissed."

Jareth made his way back down to the bridge and continued his preparations for receiving the boarding party from the *Frederick*. He selected a small group of marines who had demonstrated experience with boarding parties, both as boarders and repelling them. He wasn't going to take any chances of allowing his shipmates to be harmed by not having done what was necessary. Not again.

A FEW HOURS LATER, a shuttlecraft left the *CSS Frederick* and headed for the *Deliverance's* portside docking port. Scans confirmed that the shuttle's docking ring was compatible with the League's standard. In four hundred years, the League had not changed the standard-sized docking port configuration, which had been a standard configuration for centuries before the League was founded; apparently, the Commonwealth hadn't either.

Jareth and Captain Kavanagh waited with a contingent of marines on the other side of the airlock. They watched the lock cycling on the far side. Through the entrance came an officer and an escort. The inner door to the airlock began to cycle, and it was just then that something in one of the escort personnel's hands caught Jareth's eye. What was that? Were they carrying weapons? Shite. *Not this time*, was all he thought.

For a moment, all he could see was the docking bay corridor of the *Cantankerous Vixen*, with pockmarks from small weapons fire, scorch marks made by concussion grenades, and the crippled body of Kian Lee-Chowdhury lying among the shattered remnants of the hold.

"Stand back, Captain!" Jareth barked and turned to the security detail. "Safeties off, stand ready. Two ranks."

The security detail formed into two ranks in the corridor, with the front rank on a knee, weapons raised but not aimed, fingers near the trigger. "Stand by," he said.

Just before stepping through the now-opening airlock, the Commonwealth officer saw the marines and turned and shouted. His original escort stood to the side to make way. As they did so, Jareth saw what they had been holding in their hands—data devices, handhelds, and other miscellaneous tools. Not a weapon among them.

Commonwealth marines rushed out from the other vessel through the airlock passage. They followed standard boarding party formation, splitting off in twos, one to each side, and forming a protective cordon with weapons raised. The officer walked down the center of the cordon onto the deck.

"Stand down!" Captain Kavanagh ordered the security team, pushing her way past Jareth. The ranks shouldered their weapons, and those kneeling stood up at attention. She walked forward toward the other officer with her arm extended.

"My name is Captain Juliana Kavanagh of the *LSS Deliverance*. On behalf of the League of Four Worlds, it is my privilege to welcome you aboard our vessel."

The officer in charge of the boarding party seemed perplexed. Everything had started out calmly, and then he was in the middle of storming the ship as if he were raiding a pirate vessel. And now he was receiving a formal greeting from uniformed officers and crew.

The visiting officer gave a similar order to his party. He regarded Captain Kavanagh, still standing there with her arm extended. Somewhat awkwardly, he shook her hand and began to speak.

"Lyutenasuzukiodaferederik. Yava ennereddississem widuda perapa teranasaponnasinnacha enavaleishana kommaweffmershaoko, sujjettinyaseoz tasivo fainazanapenodiz. Biyakapatanaodisvesso?"

The captain didn't move from her position and said, "Lt. Blackstone."

"Yes, Captain," Blackstone said and made her way forward. The captain remained facing the officer standing there and smiled. He smiled back but uncomfortably. It was unclear whether he was fazed by the fact that the crew of this strange ship couldn't understand him or the fact that his assessment of the situation had changed so radically in mere seconds.

Lt. Blackstone moved into position beside the captain. She carried with her a pad of paper and a pencil. "Captain," she said.

"Lieutenant, see if you can understand anything this man is saying," Kavanagh instructed. Blackstone then gestured to the visiting officer and invited him to repeat himself. He did. Blackstone scribbled some notes down as he spoke. "I believe, Captain, he's telling us that we're in violation for not having the right transponder code." The look on the captain's face made Jareth think that if the captain had been drinking a beverage, she would have spat it out. As it was, he was sure that her "say what?" expression would live on in the annals of interstellar diplomacy.

"What? Is he going to give us a ticket?"

"He did mention the possibility of fines," Blackstone responded without irony.

"Lieutenant, did you happen to get this man's name?"

"I believe it's Suzuki, and I think he's a lieutenant, though I have to admit I'm relying as much on the stripes on his sleeve."

"Thank God for navy tradition," the captain responded. "See if you can translate this for me: Lt. Suzuki, I apologize that our transponder was not recognized by your vessels. We are not from the Commonwealth. We are from an independent group of worlds known as the League of Four Worlds. We have traveled about seven hundred light-years to ask the Commonwealth for aid." She said most of this slowly and deliberately, the way tourists do in those parts of the League where Anglic is not spoken.

Blackstone did her best to translate. It looked to Jareth like she might be using some version of the algorithm she'd try to program into a translation device. Whether Lt. Suzuki had trouble understanding Blackstone's words or Captain Kavanagh's meaning was unclear. He scrunched up his face in an expression of confusion.

"Alladivesso, nomeddaferumawisha sisetemadeyagama, deyamussahavana perapa teranasaponnasinnacha," was all he said.

"Lieutenant?"

"Captain, I think he's just insisting that we have a proper transponder signature no matter where we're from," Blackstone responded. "I can't tell whether he doesn't understand me or the idea that we're not from the Commonwealth."

"Alright, let's try another tack," the captain said, turning back to Suzuki. "I would like to speak with your commanding officer. We will not be able to pay any fines until I have had an opportunity to speak with the ranking officer in this system."

This time, Blackstone's words were understood better—in particular, "I would like to speak with your commanding officer." But Jareth observed that the overall meaning of what the captain was saying seemed confusing to the officer. It was almost as if the phrase "we are not from the Commonwealth" was nonsensical to the man. Were there no independent systems outside the borders? No colonies yet to be subsumed? Something was off.

Suzuki turned and said something to one of his marines. Captain Kavanagh shot a look at Lt. Blackstone, who responded with a look of her own that meant something like *it's okay—I'll tell you later.* After a brief back-and-forth with the marine, Suzuki turned back toward Blackstone and said a few words. Jareth knew that this was a breach of protocol—you don't address the interpreter; you always address the other party speaking. But perhaps this gaffe was another sign of just how rattled this man was.

Finally, Suzuki turned to the captain and made a gesture that might have been a salute, but the kind of salute given by someone who wasn't sure he was supposed to but was too afraid not to. Then he said, "Kapatana," spun on his heels, and walked back toward his shuttle, his cordon of marines falling in behind him. Jareth turned and dismissed his marines.

When the Commonwealth shuttle disembarked, the captain turned to Blackstone and said, "What do you think?"

Blackstone began shaking her head. "I'm still trying to make sense of it, Captain. This felt like a customs inspection or a highway patrol traffic stop rather than a border crossing. Because I'm still working out the language, I can't be sure where the communications trouble lies, but I don't think they understood what we meant."

"That was my impression, too," Kavanagh said. "I would have expected that the news of visitors arriving from seven hundred light-years away would merit a bigger reaction. It's almost like part of him just *couldn't* understand."

"I had the same feeling," Blackstone replied. "In any event, he said we should go with them to the main fleet station in-system. They'll broadcast coordinates, and he instructed us to fall in formation behind the lead vessel."

"Well, that's something," the captain said. "Maybe by then, you'll have figured out more of their speech. Thank you, Lieutenant. Dismissed." Blackstone nodded and took the lift back down to communications. As soon as the lift doors closed, the captain whirled on Jareth.

"What were you doing back there, Lieutenant?"

"Apologies, Captain," he blurted. "There was a moment when it looked like Lt. Suzuki was bringing an armed party on board."

"Well, he certainly did, but that was only *after* you chose to have your marines form a firing line and raise their weapons."

Jareth had no defense and no excuse. He had overreacted and nearly turned a challenging situation into a disastrous one. In an instant, he was back in Captain Mfese's office aboard the *Cantankerous Vixen*, only this time, he was guilty not of having underreacted but of having overreacted. *Crike, Killian,* he thought, *are you incapable of getting this right? Are your only reactions to freeze or flip out?* There was nothing he could say: if he told her he had overreacted because of what had happened aboard the *Vixen*, it'd be over for him. If he told her any other reason, it'd be a lie. In the end, this was not the time for excuses, anyway. *Own up to it, Killian. It's the only way.*

"It was an error in judgment, Captain. I assumed a more hostile posture than I ought to have and mistakenly identified weapons where there were none. It won't happen again."

"Lieutenant, I know that you security types are trained to see bogeymen behind every tree, but we can't afford any missteps or misunderstandings here. There is too much on the line. I'll expect better from you, or I may be forced to reconsider your appointment on my bridge staff."

"Understood, Captain," he responded as matter-of-factly, albeit contritely, as he could muster, but inside, he was dying a thousand deaths. Jareth knew he had let his captain down again and nearly imperiled his crew.

"Good," she said and stepped into the lift.

"I'll be along in a moment," he said. She nodded, and the lift door closed.

He was just about to double over and grab his knees to catch his breath and tamp down his racing anxiety when he heard another lift car arrive and its doors open. Master Gunnery Sergeant Makindi stepped out.

"Sir," the marine said as he drew up before Jareth.

"What can I do for you, Master Gunnery Sergeant?"

"Sir, I wish to strongly object to the danger you put my marines in during the reception of the *Frederick's* boarding party."

"They were in no danger," Jareth lied. He would own his faults with his captain but not with this jarhead.

"Sir, I do not believe that is an accurate assessment of the situation."

"You weren't there, Master Gunnery Sergeant."

"No, sir. But the reports my marines have given me suggest that they were given orders by a reckless amateur who was out of his league and overreacted."

"Marine, you are bordering on insubordination."

"The lieutenant is welcome to reassign me to the *Brunswick* if he is unsatisfied with my performance."

Jareth paled. *What had he just said? What was he implying? What did he know?* He knew that his expression had already likely given too much away; if it hadn't, the sweat he could feel coming on surely would. He was not nearly as stoic as the master gunnery sergeant he was sparring with. *Retreat* was the only thought that came to mind. He drew himself up and tried to look as officious as possible.

"Your objection is noted, Master Gunnery Sergeant. Dismissed."

Makindi straightened up and saluted. "Sir," he said, and Jareth could feel the contempt with which the word was spoken. The marine turned and left via the companionway to the decks below.

Now, Jareth doubled over and grasped his knees. The gravitic plating was on, but he felt dizzy and in danger of passing out. He drew some deep breaths and walked himself back from the edge of a full-blown panic attack. He would never shake the *Vixen* or the sins that followed in its wake, would he?

When he finally caught his breath, he straightened up and turned toward the lift. He entered the next available car and took it down to the bridge level, praying that he wouldn't look like he'd just gotten mugged when he arrived.

He walked onto the bridge just in time to hear Flores call out. "Captain, we have received what appear to be coordinates from the lead Commonwealth vessel. The numerical string appears to be organized in the standard configuration for a star system's mapping. The coordinates appear to be a location in orbit around a gas giant downsystem."

The captain had been standing near one of the flex displays near tactical, reviewing some of the analyses Filipov-Ibañez had recently conducted. "Thank you, Lieutenant," she replied. "Mr. Thorsten, fall in behind the lead Commonwealth vessel and lay in a course toward those coordinates."

"Aye, Captain."

The captain took her seat next to Commander Delacruz and sank a little more than usual into the chair as if sighing with her whole body.

"I take it our first contact didn't go as well as you hoped?" Delacruz said.

"I don't know what to make of it. Of all the things I was expecting to find when we got to Commonwealth space, nearly being issued a ticket for not having a properly registered vessel was not at all on my list."

"That would be low on mine as well," Delacruz agreed.

"There's more to it. It's expected that they wouldn't know who we were and would be cautious about any requests we might make. But when we tried to explain that we were from outside the Commonwealth, it was almost like what we were saying to him was beyond his comprehension. Like I'd told him I'd come from another dimension or was trying to describe a new color."

"Like Mr. Square in *Flatland*," Delacruz said, "when Lord Sphere visited him from the third dimension."

Kavanagh smiled. "I'm glad to see that some things are still required reading at the academy."

"Of course. Professor Dillane's course in *Command Thinking* wouldn't be the same without it. I guess you'll have to find a way to knock this person into the third dimension so that he can grasp what we're talking about."

The captain chuckled before putting her head back and closing her eyes for a moment. "Steady as she goes, Mr. Thorsten," she said.

Not having been to the academy, Jareth looked up *Flatland* on his data display and read a brief synopsis of the ancient novel about a square who lives in a two-dimensional world. One day, he visits a one-dimensional world where he tries to convince the residents there of the second dimension. Later, he is visited by a sphere who tries to convince him of the existence of a third dimension, something the square initially rejects before the sphere kicks him up into the third dimension. He can look *down* at his entire world, seeing inside people's homes and the people themselves. It was a compelling parable, but, in that moment, Jareth could think of nothing more horrifying than someone having the ability to look inside him from some other dimension.

13 | BLACKSTONE | NEW ST. LOUIS

"ALL HANDS, SECURE FOR PORT."

Commander Delacruz's voice came over the ship-wide comm, and Rebekah knew that was her cue. She grabbed her polytool, a flexpad, and a pad and pencil and stashed them in a shoulder bag. One brief look in the mirror to make sure she looked like she belonged on a diplomatic delegation, and she was off down the lift to the docking port level.

Arriving at the docking bay, Rebekah looked on the screens at the approaching Commonwealth station in orbit around the largest of three gas giants in the system. The station was a familiar design: a cylindrical hub with spokes radiating from the midsection. At the end of each spoke was a docking fixture. The station was spinning, meaning that once docked, the Deliverance would benefit from spin gravity. She watched as the *Deliverance* matched the station's rotational velocity and docked with the station.

A moment later, Captain Kavanagh and Lt. Killian got off the lift and joined her at the entryway of the airlock, waiting for the station crew to cycle it.

"Do you think they'll let us have a look around?" Killian asked the captain.

"Judging from what we have seen so far, I wouldn't get my hopes up, Lieutenant," Kavanagh responded.

Rebekah only half-listened, scrolling through her polytool display, trying to review as much of her data on the Commonwealth language as possible.

After a few minutes, the green light above the airlock door came on, and the lock slid aside. Three armed Commonwealth marines stood inside the airlock.

"It is good to see you, gentlemen," Captain Kavanagh said. Rebekah did her best to approximate Commonwealth speech and make the captain's words understood. She couldn't tell whether she was entirely successful; the guards just grunted, nodded, and gestured for them to enter the airlock chamber. They did so, and the guards fell in behind them.

The airlock turned out to be an elevator that moved up toward the station along the spoke. It opened into a circular corridor that arced away up to the left and the right, following the circumference of the station. On the other side of the airlock was an official who did not appear to be wearing a navy uniform, but neither did he seem to be wearing what Rebekah would have assumed was ordinary civilian clothing. Of course, having been out of the fashion circles of the Commonwealth for four centuries, she couldn't know either way at this point. The man began to speak.

"Wilakama tede Nasena Lusa satesha," the official said. "Yama Korunah Samifa, Kamanadanata adisa satesha."

Everyone turned to look at Rebekah as if to say, *You're up*. She looked down at her polytool and made a couple of marks before looking back up at the officer. "Kamanadanata Samifa," she began—the officer looked somewhat perplexed at how she spoke, almost as if he were trying to place that accent. "Wibi farada Ligaa fo Worodoz. Disaz Kapatana Juliana Kavanagh, kapatana ada setaraship Deliveranasa."

The officer said nothing. In fact, it appeared he was struggling to make sense of not only Rebekah's words but also the situation as a whole.

"What are you saying to each other?" Captain Kavanagh asked.

"I believe he introduced himself as the commandant of this station—Colonel Smith."

"What did you tell him?"

"I think I introduced you as Captain Kavanagh of the starship *Deliverance* from the League of Four Worlds. To be honest, Captain, I don't have enough data. I'm doing a lot of guessing."

The official—Smith?—turned and muttered something unintelligible to a marine nearby, who saluted and bolted down the corridor. Whatever Smith's plan had been for this encounter, it was not working out as he'd expected.

Everyone stared awkwardly at one another, unsure what to say or whether to say anything. Killian kept creeping off to one side, perhaps trying to look around. He made a gesture toward some displays on the wall meant to signal, 'May I take a look?' The official nodded, and Killian walked over to view what looked like travel posters and large photographic displays.

"Rebekah! Uh, Lieutenant, come see this!" he called excitedly.

Rebekah stashed her polytool in her bag and came over, and her mouth dropped. The colors and images of the travel poster were intriguing, but she was stunned by what she read. "Welcome to the New St. Louis Station!"

Next to that display was another that said, "Join the Merchant Marine! A life of adventure awaits ya." Next to that: "New St. Louis: the frontier never looked so beautiful" against a backdrop of a forest with golden-leafed trees and a stunningly beautiful waterfall that dropped off into the mists below.

She turned backward to look at the officer and gestured at the first poster.

"Yah!" he said, smiling. "Wilakama tede Nasena Lusa satesha!"

"Oh my God," Rebekah beamed. "This is going to make everything so much easier."

"How so?" Killian asked. By this time, the captain had come over to see what all the fuss was about.

"Their *pronunciation* has changed, but their spelling hasn't!" Rebekah said almost breathlessly. "That means we can communicate with them without having to learn an entirely new language. There will still be changes, to be sure, but they'll be a lot more manageable!" She grinned from ear to ear.

Before anyone else could say anything, she pulled out a datapad and found an application. She looked at it and said, "Testing. Testing. Testing. Alpha. Bravo. Charlie." On the screen appeared the words TESTING TESTING TESTING ALPHA BRAVO CHARLIE. "Hah!" she shouted and handed the pad to Kavanagh. "Go ahead, Captain. Just hold this in front of you while you speak."

Captain Kavanagh raised an eyebrow but took Rebekah's advice without any questions. The captain took the datapad and walked back over to the officer, who was still wearing a genial, albeit perplexed, expression. She held the datapad in front of her, facing the officer, took a deep breath, and began:

"My name is Juliana Kavanagh, Captain of the starship *Deliverance*, on a mission from the League of Four Worlds to seek the aid of the Commonwealth in repelling invaders who have attacked one of our worlds." As the words flashed across the datapad, Rebekah could see some of the tension the captain had been carrying in her body drain out. She'd traveled hundreds of light-years to be able to bring this message, and now, thanks to Rebekah's quick thinking, she could finally relay it.

Commandant Smith's eyes grew wide as he read the text before him. At that very moment, the marine returned with another officer, likely the one the Commandant had summoned. Smith barked another unintelligible string of words at him, and the man ran off immediately. Smith turned back to the captain and spoke as Rebekah translated, "It is my pleasure to meet you, Captain."

A minute later, the other officer returned holding what looked like a clear piece of glass—another type of datapad. Smith made a few gestures on its surface and pulled up an application of his own. He held it in front of him and began speaking. On the screen before him appeared: I THANK YOU FOR THE IDEA NOW PERHAPS WE CAN BETTER UNDERSTAND ONE ANOTHER PLEASE FOLLOW ME TO THE CONFERENCE ROOM WHERE WE CAN TALK FURTHER.

The captain, Rebekah, and Killian all looked at each other overjoyed. Rebekah was positively beaming. "Aurelius could not have been happier when he decoded Linear A!" she exclaimed.

"If you say so," the captain replied, smiling. Rebekah knew neither Captain Kavanagh nor Lt. Killian likely had any idea what she was talking about, but she was sure they got the gist: this was a big deal. They could talk to their would-be rescuers. Their chances of mission success had just quadrupled, at least.

THE *DELIVERANCE* OFFICERS WERE escorted into a comfortable but unremarkable conference room. It was the kind of room frequently found on older space stations—gunmetal gray walls, a few plants for color and air scrubbing, and institutional furniture. Rebekah noted that the environment aboard the *Deliverance* felt like a luxury liner by comparison.

Commandant Smith waved for them to sit on one side of the oval-shaped table as he and his aide took the opposite side.

Captain Kavanagh sat right in the middle of her side of the table; Rebekah and Killian sat to her left and right, respectively. The captain took Rebekah's datapad and propped it up in front of her. She waited for her Commonwealth counterpart to do the same with his display, which he did. The captain began to speak.

"Thank you for giving us this audience, Commandant Smith. We are grateful for the opportunity to make our case with you."

Smith smiled agreeably enough as he read along on the captain's display.

IT IS A PLEASURE TO MEET YOU CAPTAIN, his display began as he started to speak. CAN YOU PLEASE REPEAT WHAT YOU SAID EARLIER

"Certainly, Commandant. I'm Juliana Kavanagh, captain of the starship *Deliverance*, on a mission from the League of Four Worlds to seek the aid of the Commonwealth in repelling invaders who have attacked one of our worlds." Rebekah noted it was almost word for word what she'd said earlier, testament to the fact that she'd been waiting to say those exact words for a while.

AH YES YES YOU DID SAY THAT YES YES WHAT SYSTEM ARE YOU FROM

"We are from three systems—Sharon, Roger's Star, and Kittim. The Kittim system, home to the planet Farmark, was overrun by invaders."

I SEE I SEE ONE MOMENT. Smith and his aide, who never gave his name, began conferring as they leaned over the aide's datapad. The aide scrolled through pages of text but could not find what he was looking for. After a few moments of this, Smith turned back to Captain Kavanagh.

WHAT ADMINISTRATIVE ZONE ARE THOSE SYSTEMS IN

"We're not in any administrative zone, Commandant."

I SEE I SEE ARE YOUR WORLDS IN A SPECIAL ECONOMIC DE-VELOPMENT ZONE WHO IS YOUR PROVINCIAL GOVERNOR

Rebekah and Killian turned simultaneously to stare at the captain incredulously. Captain Kavanagh was unfazed; she maintained polite eye contact with Commandant Smith, took a breath, and replied.

"Commandant, I believe there has been a misunderstanding. We're not *from* the Commonwealth. We're from the League of Four Worlds, about seven hundred light-years"—she paused to get her bearings and pointed—"*that* way."

Smith conferred with his aide again. They spoke in low whispers, and Rebekah listened intently and tried to record them clandestinely with her handheld.

THIS IS MOST IRREGULAR THERE ARE NO INHABITED SYS-TEMS OUTSIDE COMMONWEALTH SPACE

"With all due respect, Commandant, there are. Four of them. In a league. Founded by pioneers from the Commonwealth four hundred years ago."

WE HAVE NO RECORD OF THE SETTLEMENTS YOU MENTION WE LACK THE ABILITY TO PROCESS YOUR REQUEST AT THIS TIME AND MUST CONFER WITH SUPERIORS IN SECTOR ADMINIS-TRATION WHILE WE DO THAT YOU AND YOUR PEOPLE ARE FREE TO USE THE STATION FOR SHORE LEAVE AND YOU CAN MAKE ARRANGEMENTS FOR GETTING A PROPER TRANSPONDER

"Wait, that's it?!" Killian blurted out. The captain reached out her hand and placed it on his forearm.

The captain continued. "Forgive my security officer's outburst. We have traveled a great distance at much personal cost. We are understandably anxious about being able to fulfill our mission. I certainly understand your need to confer with your superiors, however much we would love to move the process along more quickly."

Smith looked thoughtful. CAPTAIN CAVANAUGH—his pad misspelled the captain's name—WHAT YOU ASK IS NOT SOMETHING WE HAVE PROCEDURES FOR IT WOULD BE UNSEEMLY AND INAPPROPRIATE TO COMMIT TO A CAUSE OF ACTION WITHOUT APPROVAL FROM HIGHER UPS WE WILL KEEP YOU UPDATED AS SOON AS WE HEAR BACK I HOPE YOUR CREW ENJOYS ITS SHORE LEAVE AND PLEASE TELL THEM TO BE RESPECTFUL OF OUR STATION

Captain Kavanagh smiled, nodded to the commandant, and said, "We thank you for your gracious offer. We look forward to hearing from you."

With that, Smith and his aide got up from the table and exited.

"Well, that was—something," Killian said.

"At least I could get some more language data from them. I think I have enough now to construct a translation device," Rebekah added.

"I'm still going to want you along for these meetings, Lieutenant," said the captain. "The pads and devices are nice, but the old-fashioned person-to-person touches will win the day."

"Understood, Captain."

"It was always wishful thinking that we'd be able to accomplish our mission in our first interaction," the captain continued. "I will admit that what has surprised me is not that they have procedures to fulfill and higher-ups to consult, but that there seems to be a fundamental aspect of our claims that they have a hard time getting their heads around."

"That we're from outside the Commonwealth," Rebekah replied.

"Exactly. I keep trying to put myself in their position—what if a strange starship showed up in League space claiming to be from the Confederation of Planets and asked for help?"

"But we know that there are inhabited settlements outside the League," Killian protested.

"Fair enough, Lieutenant. I suppose that discovering that there were people we didn't know about would be surprising, but the underlying concept wouldn't be. These folks don't seem to have even considered the possibility."

"It's almost like they don't even have the words for it," Rebekah said.

Captain Kavanagh turned to look at her interpreter and smiled. "That is an excellent way of putting it, Lt. Blackstone." She drew herself up from the table and turned to her security chief. "Mr. Killian, return to the *Deliverance* and inform them about shore leave. Tell Commander Delacruz to begin organizing shifts for liberty."

"Are you not returning to the ship, Captain?" he asked.

"I will in a bit. Right now, I'm going to take advantage of our access to this station. We've made it to the Commonwealth, Lieutenant. I'm going to look around and see some of it. While the good lieutenant figures out how they talk, I'm going to see if I can get any insights as to how they think."

14 | KAVANAGH | KENMORE

A DAY LATER, THE *DELIVERANCE* received word from the commandant that the League delegation was expected at District Command, two star systems over in the Kenmore system. Their escort was a Commonwealth vessel named the *Babylon*, a modestly sized vessel, much smaller than their cruiser but bristling with weapons. Juliana assumed that meant it was a frigate and that the Commonwealth considered them a risk. Fair enough, she supposed. She would have done the same thing. Besides, she was sure that most of her feelings about the *Babylon* were envy—she would have loved to have had half that ship's weapons complement.

Even though brief, the shore leave had done the crew a world of good. The morning security reports that Killian was filing showed fewer arguments, instances of insubordination, and complaints being logged into the system. The medical and wellness divisions reported a similar decrease in patients and clients. They hadn't finished their mission, but by making contact with the Commonwealth and discovering that it was still in one piece, they'd increased the odds significantly—and that wasn't nothing for a crew that had begun to feel nihilistic and despairing after more than two months in deep space.

The *Deliverance* followed the *Babylon* away from New St. Louis and toward the Sheridan line for transit toward Kenmore. As efficient as the ship's brand-new engines were, they were not as effective as the *Babylon's*, so the *Babylon* had to adjust its jump point accordingly to escort them. After two days, they reached the correct coordinates and jumped toward the Kenmore system.

As the stars disappeared once more from their view screens to be replaced by the eerie otherness of hyperspace, Filipov-Ibañez leaned back from his station and said, "Well, at least we're getting somewhere now! These hyperspace jumps to somewhere are better than the jumps to nowhere."

"I hope you're right, Commander," replied Juliana. "Part of me feels like we're being handed off."

"Handed off?" responded Delacruz. "How so?"

"If you notice, we got no substantive answers to our requests. No indications that the Commonwealth would respond to our pleas, only statements that it would be inappropriate for the officers at a given level to respond one way or another."

"We're all familiar with naval protocols, Captain," said Delacruz.

"Protocol is one thing; passing the buck is another." She turned her seat to face Delacruz more directly. "If you were commandant of a League border station and a ship from the Commonwealth arrived, provided evidence that they were who they said they were, and said that they needed League aid, how would you respond?"

Delacruz looked pensive for a moment. "Well, I'd say that I'd love to help but that I'd need to clear it with my superiors. There's a chain of command."

"Exactly!" Juliana said, pointing at her XO as if to underscore her point. Before he could object that it sounded like she was agreeing with him, she continued, "You'd say you'd love to help *but* . . . We never got the 'we'd love to help'; we only got the 'but.'"

Delacruz considered this. "Now that you mention it, they didn't even give us anything to mollify us. No half-promises or empty phrases that sound good but can't be relied on."

"Precisely. What we got was, 'We don't have procedures for this' and 'You'll have to speak to our superiors.' We didn't even get pretend sympathy for our losses." She swiveled to face Filipov-Ibañez. "And so, Commander, I hope you're right that we're finally getting *somewhere*."

Despite her nagging doubts, Juliana knew their odds of finishing their mission were significantly better than they had been a few days before. But it was just so curious.

"Commander, if I remember correctly, your ancestors are from North America on Earth, right?"

"Yes, well, the Delacruz half. We're not sure about the Fox half."

"How much North American history do you know?"

"Just what I can remember from the Academy and a couple of courses in school. Why?"

"I just keep trying to find analogs to our situation to see if I can make sense of it. There are a couple of scenarios that come to mind. For instance, what if a group of pioneers had struck out from the then United States on its way to Oregon, and then no one ever followed them? What if they had gone back centuries later only to discover that the United States had not expanded across the Mississippi and the people there denied that anyone lived on the other side of the river?"

"That doesn't quite work. Even then, the Americans would have known that there were peoples to their west."

"Yes, of course. As I said, I'm struggling to find a satisfactory parallel."

"Maybe there are none, Captain. Perhaps this is a unique situation, and we should remember to take it as such. Maybe it's a good idea to let go of our expectations and roll with whatever comes our way."

Juliana smiled. "You're right, of course, Commander. It's too bad the ISG doesn't offer bonuses for wisdom." She sat back in her chair. "Steady as she goes, Mr. Thorsten."

"Steady as she goes, Captain."

Several hours later, the *Deliverance* emerged from hyperspace in the Kenmore system.

"We're down, Captain," Thorsten said from the helm. "The *Babylon* is already down and is about five kilometers ahead of us."

"Captain," interjected Filipov-Ibañez. "I'm reading another vessel approaching at an intercept vector."

"Lt. Flores, raise the *Babylon*," Juliana replied as she rose and moved toward the forward display.

"Aye, Captain." Moments later, a chime indicated a secure connection, and Captain Renno Caradif's image appeared in the center of the display.

"Captain Caradif," Juliana began. "Thank you for escorting us this far. Can you identify the vessel on an intercept course with us? Have you not been able to alert the District Command regarding our arrival?"

Caradif looked annoyed, but he remained professional. His reactions lagged slightly as he read the embedded text they sent along with Juliana's transmission.

"Captain Cavanaugh"—the Babylon's text transcription misspelled Juliana's name the same way New St. Louis's datapad had—"we have made a full report to District Command. The approaching vessel is the *Ganges*, which will join us in escorting you to Command."

Juliana gestured to Flores, and Flores muted the connection. She turned to Delacruz. "A second escort? This is feeling less and less like we're guests and more and more like we're detainees."

"Could be standard protocol, for all we know," Delacruz replied. "A lot might have changed in four hundred years. Remember: expectations."

Juliana nodded and made another gesture to Flores; the mic was unmuted. "Thank you, Captain Caradif," she said, turning to the display again. "We appreciate your thoughtfulness and willingness to protect us after such a harrowing journey. Please forward transit coordinates at your convenience."

Caradif nodded and broke the connection; Juliana turned from the forward display and walked to her communications officer's station.

"Transit coordinates received, Captain," Flores said. "Sending to helm."

Thorsten made some adjustments on his display. "Confirm transit coordinates received. Inputting into navicomputer now. The coordinates point to a rocky planet downsystem."

"Thank you, Mr. Thorsten," Juliana said. "Lt. Flores, signal receipt confirmation to the *Babylon* and let them know we are ready to proceed."

"Aye, Captain."

"Mr. Thorsten, as soon as you get the signal from the *Babylon*, move us out, matching course and speed."

"Aye, Captain."

"Excellent. Thank you all," Juliana said, making her way to the hatch. "I will be in my quarters. Mr. Delacruz, you have the conn."

Juliana exited the bridge into the access corridor and acknowledged the on-duty marine keeping watch outside.

The main lift was before her, but she was suddenly seized by the idea of walking. She headed over to the companionway and began to climb. The ship was under one-gee acceleration, so she would get her exercise for sure. But even more than the physical benefits, it gave her a chance to see her ship. A good captain, in her estimation, should always walk the decks of her vessel regularly.

She climbed past operations and the briefing room levels, past the weapons deck with its stores of nuclear missiles and point-defense cannon rounds. Whenever she ran into crew members, she stopped to talk to them, to see how they felt about the mission and how they were holding up after everything they'd been through.

She was feeling good about her captain's tour when she emerged from the companionway onto the tactical and security level. She happened past just as a meeting of some kind was ending. A door slid open, and Lt. Killian strode out, clearly irritated by something. He saw her and offered a brief salute before continuing into the security suite office area.

A few other officers emerged after him, the last of which was Master Gunnery Sergeant Makindi.

"Master Gunnery Sergeant," she called.

He drew up straight and came to attention. "Sir!"

"At ease, Master Gunnery Sergeant," she said as she approached him. The marine adopted a posture that only a marine could consider relaxed.

"It looks like that was some kind of meeting you all just had."

"Just a difference of opinion, sir."

"With whom? Lt. Killian?"

Makindi looked uneasy, but he answered. "Yes, sir. The lieutenant and I do not see eye-to-eye on very many things."

"Anything I should know about?"

"No, sir," Makindi said. Juliana could see that he was itching to complain about his superior officer, but naval propriety and the chain of command would not allow it. Juliana thought about going off-record with him but decided against it; that wouldn't make the marine more comfortable.

"Master Gunnery Sergeant, if my security chief and one of my senior non-commissioned marine officers are unable to work together—"

"Forgive the interruption, sir. We can work together. At this point, my problems with the lieutenant appear to be a conflict of personalities. As of yet, I have no other cause to object to his orders and leadership."

That sounded somewhat provisional to Juliana, as if Makindi were admitting to looking for such a cause.

"If that should change, you'll inform Major Li and bring the matter to my attention."

"Aye, sir."

"In time, Master Gunnery Sergeant, I imagine you'll discover that you and Mr. Killian have more in common than you realize."

"I appreciate your insight, Captain." Juliana was sure that was his deferentially polite way of telling her she was full of it.

"How is your healing coming along?"

"My recovery is coming along nicely. The CMO says that the nano repairs have concluded fully, and the muscle on my right flank is already beginning to develop some tone. My other injuries are almost entirely recovered."

"That's wonderful to hear, Master Gunnery Sergeant, but it's not what I asked. I asked you how your *healing* was coming along."

Makindi stared at his commanding officer with a mix of what Juliana assumed was confusion and dread.

"That, sir," he paused. "That is coming along more slowly than I would like."

"Master Gunny," Juliana said. "If you were able to get through such a loss quickly and easily, you wouldn't be half the leader I know you to be. It is going to take some time because the marines under your command *matter* to you. And there is one thing you will never have to apologize for under my command: allowing those under you to matter to you. I consider it an essential aspect of command character."

Makindi looked at Juliana, and she could tell he was unsure what to make of her. She had no doubts that he'd always respected her and her command, but it was clear that he wasn't used to his commanding officers engaging with him in this fashion. Finally, he said, "Thank you, Captain. I appreciate your words."

Juliana knew that for a man who prided himself on a stoic demeanor, that was about as much of an emotional response as she was likely to get. She reached out and placed her hand on his shoulder. "Of course, Master Gunny. Thank you for your time. As you were."

She dropped her hand from his shoulder, and he saluted once more before turning and going back into the security suite. Juliana made her way back to the companionway to continue her climb. She had ten more decks—and who knows how many more rehabilitation projects—left to go.

SEVERAL DAYS LATER, the *Deliverance* arrived at Kenmore III, a planet the locals called New Hibernia. In orbit was another standard model space station but significantly larger—the sector's administrative headquarters for the Commonwealth Navy.

The *Deliverance* docked, and once again, Juliana, Lt. Blackstone, and Lt. Killian found themselves at another conference table with more naval officials. Opposite them was a thin, lanky woman with a pallid complexion wearing fleet captain's stripes, bearing all the hallmarks of someone who'd grown up in a low-g environment. On either side of her sat various officers, some appearing to be naval personnel, others marines.

The woman opposite them began to speak. As she did, the earpieces that Blackstone had designed to translate Commonwealth speech began to render the fleet captain's speech into something the Leaguers could understand. Even so, the Commonwealthers' accent was quite odd at this port of call. Blackstone's translation device didn't catch every word, but they managed.

"Captain Kavanagh," the officer began. "I am Commodore Tala Segovia, commandant of this station and sector administrator for the Kenmore Sector."

"It is a pleasure to meet you, Commodore Segovia," Juliana said, holding Rebekah's tablet in front of her to transcribe her words. "I am Captain Juliana Kavanagh of the League Starship *Deliverance* on a mission from the League of Four Worlds."

Segovia took a beat before reacting—having to read the subtitles always caused a slight delay. "Captain, I have read the reports from Commandant Smith and have some questions for you."

"We would be happy to provide you with any information you need."

"Excellent. For starters, you claim to be from outside the Commonwealth, but there are no settlements outside Commonwealth space."

This again. "Commodore, the founders of our worlds traveled some distance from Commonwealth space in search of planets that could be settled without terraforming. They traveled so far that light-speed communication was impractical. And lacking the resources needed to make the return trip, no vessel from our League had the means to return to Commonwealth space until the present crisis."

Segovia turned to the aides sitting to either side as they all whispered their impressions in reaction. Presently, Segovia looked back at the captain. "My advisors tell me that it is simply not possible for there to be settled worlds as far out as you say. It is far likelier that you originate from one of the lesser populated sectors of the Commonwealth and have lost your way. In that case, we must identify the proper administrative region for you to pursue your request."

"Excuse me, Commodore. I would be happy to share our well-documented history, star charts, and any other information you need to verify that our claims are true. I think you'll find that our version of events is far more likely than the idea that we constructed a four-hundred-year-old polity of four planets and built a navy, all *within* Commonwealth space without anyone in the Commonwealth even noticing."

Juliana was patient and understood that negotiating with the Commonwealth might take time. She was even working on letting go of her expectations, just as Delacruz had suggested. But this was starting to get annoying. It was one thing to adjust your expectations, but it was becoming clear that the Commonwealth representatives were unwilling to adjust theirs. Why was it so hard for them to conceive of human settlements outside Commonwealth space? That was how the Commonwealth had grown for centuries, expanding and subsuming colonies others had established outside its borders. Juliana regretted allowing some measure of frustration to creep into her voice. Fortunately, if Segovia had noticed Juliana's snark, she didn't let on. Instead, she continued as levelly as she had before.

"Captain, you have to understand how irregular it is to have a vessel appear at one of our customs stations claiming to be from human settlements that no one had any idea existed, reporting an invasion by aliens that no one has ever encountered before, and demanding military assistance.

Would you not explore every remaining possible avenue before accepting such an outlandish claim?"

"Commodore Segovia, I might be suspicious that I was being tricked had my visitors not dropped out of hyperspace in naval vessels that were not locally made, bearing uniforms and insignia of a clearly established military organization, and speaking a dialect I was unfamiliar with. Those factors alone might convince me there was some merit to my visitors' claims."

Segovia again conferred with her staff in whispers too low for Blackstone's earpieces to pick up. One of her advisors repeatedly pointed to something on a data pad in front of him. After a few minutes, Segovia nodded at that officer, sat upright in her chair, and turned back to Juliana and her companions.

"Captain Kavanagh," she began. "It is clear that this is a situation for which we have no existing protocols. We are unable to consider your request for aid without consulting with our superiors. We must reach out to the command apparatus of the Constellation of which this sector is a part and seek counsel. Until we have word from Constellation Command, we are unable to proceed. Your crew is welcome to use this facility for shore leave and may even visit the surface of New Hibernia. If you wish to take advantage of the opportunity to visit the world below, please check in with the customs officer here to receive appropriate travel permits. As a gesture of welcome, we can even arrange for some complimentary marks for your crew. We will be in touch with you at the earliest opportunity."

With that, Segovia rose, and her staff followed suit. They made their way out of the conference room and left the three *Deliverance* officers sitting there in silence.

"Is anyone noticing a pattern here?" Juliana asked.

"What, you mean the part where they don't understand where we're from or the part where they fall back on procedure to kick the can down the road?" Killian responded.

"How far up the ladder will we have to take this?" Juliana replied. "If I may employ another metaphor. It is entirely reasonable that a frontier outpost couldn't make this sort of determination. But, given the size of the Commonwealth, surely a Sector Command is authorized to act locally."

"Maybe we'll have to go all the way to Earth," Killian said.

"Do you think we will?" asked Blackstone excitedly. "I would love to do that! Just the opportunity to catalog their language changes!"

"Ideally, Lieutenant," Juliana replied, "we could accomplish our mission without having to do that. But I'm beginning to think that Lt. Killian may be more correct than he knows—our situation seems so outside of their experience that they don't know how to proceed without getting permission.

Something tells me that's systemic, which means we may not get answers for a while. So, Lt. Blackstone, you may get your chance to sample the linguistic tapestry of Old Earth after all."

15 | BLACKSTONE | NEW HIBERNIA

AFTER THE MEETING, Rebekah, Killian, and the captain headed back to the *Deliverance*. Walking along the station's corridors back toward the docking port, they passed a large window offering a view outside as the station spun slowly for gravity. The planet New Hibernia rotated into view—a blue-green ball with various land masses and biome types. Of course, the *Deliverance's* cameras had been looking at the planet since it docked, but there was always something special about viewing a planet through glass—knowing that the object you're looking at truly is *right there*.

"We've been breathing recycled air for too long," Captain Kavanagh said wistfully. "We should take this opportunity to let our people go planet-side."

"I agree," Killian said. "The crew's mood has improved just by being in Commonwealth space. It might do them good to be under an open sky again, especially the civilian recruits."

"Does that include you, Lieutenant?"

"It might. I got my space legs back faster than I'd expected to. I haven't missed being planet-side as much as I thought I might."

"This work does suit you, Lieutenant," the captain replied. Rebekah saw that Killian looked visibly pleased to hear his captain's words. She had wondered how things were between the two of them after he'd botched the first contact with the *Frederick*.

"I'd love to go down to the planet, Captain," Rebekah said. "It's a change of scenery for sure, but also a whole new pool of linguistic informants."

The captain smiled at Rebekah's enthusiasm for her work. "Then it's settled," she said. She grabbed her handheld and opened the commlink to the ship. "*Deliverance*, this is the captain. Do you read?"

"Aye, Captain. This is *Deliverance*," came Flores's voice.

"Inform Commander Delacruz that we have been granted shore leave both aboard the station and on the planet below. Please instruct him to make arrangements as soon as possible for parties who wish to visit the surface in regular shifts. It looks like we're going to be waiting a bit for the higher-ups' higher-ups to get back to us."

"Acknowledged, Captain."

"Kavanagh out." Then, turning to Rebekah and Killian, she continued: "We passed the customs office on the way from the meeting. Why don't you two skip going back to the ship and head down to the planet now? Beat the rush." She winked at them both and then turned and headed back to the *Deliverance*.

Rebekah and Killian looked at each other, shrugged, and returned to the customs office. The customs officer was surprisingly accommodating and seemed excited to have visitors interested in the planet below.

They underwent the standard bio scans to ensure they weren't carrying any pathogens that would harm the local biome and were cleared for entry.

With transit passes in hand and some complimentary marks for use on the surface, the two made their way to the lower docking ring, where orbital shuttles departed regularly for the surface. They took their places aboard the first available shuttle and strapped in.

The experience was somewhat surreal and reminded Rebekah of the first time she had ever gone off-world on a trip to New Sydney with her parents. Everything on New Sydney had been just slightly different from things on Fairhaven. The public comm stations all had a different design. Their maglev cars were wider. The restaurants served different foods. It was all familiar enough but different at the same time, which made it weirder. It might have been easier to adapt to if it had been entirely different. But it was the subtle differences that caught her by surprise.

That was how this experience felt to her now. She'd been on orbital shuttles many times, but this one felt different. Four hundred years' worth of divergence altered the experience. Little design decisions and technological improvements made it at once familiar and strange.

The two lieutenants tried to look as indifferent as possible to the differences. They were already attracting a lot of attention, with stolen glances and whispers around them. Rebekah could hear people wondering who the people in the strange uniforms were. The two of them whispered as well, lest they draw even more attention to themselves by speaking.

Not long after they boarded, the shuttle dropped from its moorings and made its way to the surface. It was heading to a spaceport in a city called—well, *spelled* Cill Mhantáin—Rebekah wasn't quite sure how that was supposed to be pronounced and didn't want to ask anyone.

After debarking from the shuttle, they exited the spaceport toward the maglev station and found the trains headed downtown. The landscape was a pleasant mix of low hills and broad plains as they passed through rural and suburban regions. In terms of architectural style, the buildings reminded them of some of the buildings on Farmark. The parks were full of activity, with groups of people playing recreational sports or just lounging around and enjoying the beautiful late summer weather.

They arrived in downtown Cill Mhantáin at the central station and walked out into the main hall. It was not as grand as the Bundt Station in New Kalgoorlie or Grand Central Station in Rivendell on Fairhaven, but neither was it utilitarian. Everywhere, people were coming and going, and Rebekah found the feeling of being among an "alien" population exhilarating—but also infuriating. For so long, the peoples of the League had wondered what had become of the Commonwealth, and now here it was—just going about its business. Its citizens getting on with their lives, going to and fro, playing sports, enjoying their leisure time, and talking in weird accents.

Despite their uniforms, the two lieutenants did their best not to stand out, but there was part of Rebekah that wanted to, that wanted the locals to rush over and surround them, saying, "We're so glad you're okay! We've been worried sick about you for four centuries, wondering what became of you." But they were more or less invisible to the locals; they didn't stick out nearly as much as they feared or desired.

They exited the station onto a grand mall: a large reflecting pool lay at the center, with paved tree-lined paths on either side. At the far end was a large official-looking building, perhaps the capitol, perhaps something else. They picked the right-side path and began to walk along at a leisurely pace. People in business suits hurried past as joggers wove their way in and out of the pedestrians. Couples and friend groups sat on the benches lining the path, watching the aquatic fowl on the reflecting pool or looking up into the warm summer sky. *One nice thing about space travel*, Rebekah thought, *is that no matter what the fleet calendar said, the weather and climate were always local phenomena.*

The sunlight and warmth of the day were more invigorating than either of them expected them to be. Rebekah could feel tension ebbing in her muscles and endorphin levels rising through her body. The same thing must have been happening to Killian because, all of a sudden, he decided to take a risk.

"Rebekah," he began. "I've enjoyed getting to know you and working with you."

"Thank you, Lieutenant," she responded. "I have as well." *Here it comes. Here's where I break the poor, crushing lieutenant's heart.*

"Please. Jareth," he replied.

"Okay. Jareth."

"I've been thinking I would like to get to know you better."

She stopped on the path so suddenly that Killian almost walked past her. He stopped and turned. Rebekah's expression was complex; it wasn't annoyance—it was more sorrowful than that.

"I've guessed as much. And knew this conversation was coming sooner or later."

She could see that he was immediately embarrassed, likely at having been so obvious.

"But despite knowing it was coming, I never knew how to respond. I will admit that having noticed your attentions—and don't worry, they haven't been *that* obvious—I have found myself tempted, but it's way too soon. I only just lost Kehlani."

"Kehlani?"

"Of course—there's no reason you would have known. Kehlani was aboard the *Brunswick*; she died during the Break. She and I were two of a triad; our remaining partner, Lyra, is back home on Fairhaven. We are so far out of communication range that I haven't spent any mental energy at all figuring out how I'm going to tell her."

"I'm s-so sorry," Killian stammered. "I had no idea."

"No one did. Our commanding officers knew, but it wasn't a legal arrangement, so it wouldn't be on any of the ISG records you might have seen. And we weren't into the whole wearing the earrings thing."

"I mean, I'm sorry for your loss. Far sorrier about that than for hitting on a triked woman."

Rebekah laughed at that before growing more somber. "I'm just not in a place—"

"Understood," he said, raising his hands as if to say, *say no more.* "And even when you are in that place, our friendship is not dependent on me being first in line for something else. And if there's anything you need . . . ."

She smiled at that. "Thank you, Jareth," she said, reaching a hand to his forearm. "I appreciate you saying that."

Rebekah wasn't sure what had changed within Jareth in the last few moments. He almost seemed *too* accepting of her rejection, even with it being as painless as she could make it. She thought she saw something register on his face when she mentioned the *Brunswick*. It was almost as if the mere mention of the ship killed the mood. What was that about?

After a moment, Jareth said, "I can't imagine how you've been holding up all this time."

"Partially, it's because I'm career ISG. These were the risks I signed up for. But the most helpful thing has been the work. When you came to find me in the cargo bay, I was looking at my polytool, thinking that it was the last piece left of the life I'd known. It was like a miracle that at that very moment, you came to invite me to work that has been incredibly meaningful and has helped me cope with Kehlani's death and the loss of the *Brunswick*. The group therapy has been helpful, too. Of course, part of me is still in shock, I'm sure. When we get back to the League, and I have to tell Lyra what happened—"

"I think many in the crew—not just the former *Brunswick* crew—are carrying around grief that hasn't yet sunk in."

"Yeah. I've noticed that many of my *Brunswick* shipmates have thrown themselves into whatever work they're assigned here. It's almost like they're trying to stay ahead of the grief. At least they're in the group therapy sessions for when that strategy fails."

Around that time, Rebekah became conscious that they had been standing in the middle of this park, yammering away in an odd-sounding foreign language. A handful of people looked at them curiously, including one old man sitting on a nearby bench. His expression made it hard to tell whether he was angry, confused, amazed, or shocked. But as soon as he made eye contact, he rose and came walking over to the two of them.

"Are ye Ter'novans?" the man asked excitedly.

They both reacted in surprise, and Rebekah's eyes grew wide.

"Ter'novans?" she replied.

"Aye, ye seem to ken th'Old Speech from Ter'nova. There aren't so many of us around what can speak that anymore, certainly not so young as ye."

"Terranova!" Rebekah exclaimed. "No, we're not from Terranova, but our ancestors were."

"Ah, I see," the man continued. "What system are ye from? Have ye a Ter'novan community there, too? I was of the opinion that outside of New Hibernia, there weren't many Old Ter'novan fellowships."

"We're from the League of Four Worlds. It's a human settlement seven hundred light-years from here. It was founded by an expedition that set sail from Terranova four centuries ago," Rebekah said to him. Then she turned to Jareth, "This is incredible—it means that League Anglic is likely descended from the Terranovan dialect! There's a paper in this for sure!" Jareth smiled, seemingly with genuine affection for her and her linguistic obsessions.

"But," the old man said, "there are no human settlements outside the Commonwealth. Art thou sure?"

"I am," Rebekah said. "I'm very sure." She recognized the expression on his face now—she thought of it as "Commonwealth befuddlement," the facial expression people made when you told them you were from *outside* Commonwealth space.

"My name is Rebekah Blackstone. My colleague is Jareth Killian. What is your name, sir?"

"Aye, Killian," he responded, looking at Jareth with some satisfaction. "That's a fine Ter'novan name. I'm Ciaran McFarrell. It's a pleasure to meet thee, Rebekah, and thee, Jareth."

"Can we invite you somewhere to dine with us and tell us about your planet and your community?" Rebekah asked.

His eyes lit up with the glow of someone who had much to tell and few opportunities to tell it. "I'd be honored to share a repast with you both."

"Fantastic," replied Rebekah. "Please, lead the way."

Ciaran bowed ever so slightly, then turned and began walking down the path.

Jareth turned to Rebekah as they fell in and began walking after him. "Linguistic opportunities just follow you around, don't they, kid?"

She didn't say anything; she didn't have to: the ear-to-ear grin on her face was response enough.

Hours later, Rebekah and Jareth returned to the Cill Mhantáin spaceport via maglev from downtown. They had spent nearly four hours at dinner with Ciaran, listening to him tell them about how his ancestors had come from Terranova and been among the first to colonize New Hibernia. Terranovans had colonized many of the neighboring star systems, and the Terranovan dialect of Anglic had been the standard speech of the worlds in this Constellation—what the Commonwealthers called the larger administrative subdivisions of space.

Once the worlds out in that region proved to be flourishing, immigration started to bring populations in from the core worlds, who brought with them what Ciaran called "the new talk"—the rising dialect of the older planets that eventually supplanted the local speech, except among some stubborn old timers like Ciaran in some of the smaller towns and villages outside the city centers.

"You really enjoyed that, didn't you?" Jareth asked as they rode back up to the Kenmore III orbital station.

"I did," Rebekah said, grinning. "I got so much data, and I even got Ciaran's comm node address so I can follow up with him if I have any questions."

"Well, I hope that it'll help."

"Oh, it will. I've learned so much from talking to him that my work on the earpiece translator will be greatly improved. I can't wait to start working on it."

"Wait, not *now*? You're not serious, are you? Don't you want to go to sleep? It's 0130 ship time."

Rebekah just grinned an almost maniacal grin.

Once back aboard the *Deliverance*, Jareth said good night and went straight to his quarters; Rebekah went straight to the communications lab to input her new data. Sleep could wait; there was linguistics afoot. She worked through the night and several watches of the following day, hardly aware of the passage of time.

Somewhere toward the end of the forenoon watch, the captain's voice came across the ship-wide comms: "Attention all hands. Sector Command has concluded that they are incapable of determining whether they can offer us assistance and are referring us to Constellation Command at Epsilon Ophiuchi. A shore leave recall order is issued for any personnel still on the planet's surface. We will be departing at 1800 hours ship time. All departments, make ready for orbital departure and hyperspace transit. Kavanagh out." *I guess we're getting kicked down the road again*, Rebekah thought before returning to her data and programming.

She finally went off shift when the *Deliverance* unmoored and set sail for the jump point. She set the walls of her quarters to display the exterior aft view of New Hibernia as the ship headed away from the planet out into the system. Over the next six hours, the view of New Hibernia receded from a disk that filled the entire wall to a speck of light at the center. And just like that, the first non-League world she—or anyone from the League—had ever set foot on faded into the depths of space.

16 | KAVANAGH | PORT VARLEY

THREE DAYS LATER, the *Deliverance* downjumped at Epsilon Ophiuchi and proceeded toward Port Varley, matching accelerations with the escort vessels in the convoy as they made their way downsystem.

"Captain," called Filipov-Ibañez from his station.

"Report."

"I have an unusual reading on the LR. There appears to be some kind of asteroid or something in our general trajectory, but the rest of the ships in our convoy do not seem overly concerned."

"Show me."

Filipov-Ibañez made a dragging gesture across his screen toward the central three-dee holographic display, and the tactical representation from the Long Radar station hung in the air between the helm and the command officers' chairs. The four closest blips were the escort. The large mass further downrange was Port Varley. There was something in the way and it was big.

Juliana rose and inspected the projection before her. "Lt. Flores, signal the *Babylon* and inquire as to the nature of the object on the LR. Use text since there's no point trying to talk to them yet."

"Aye, Captain," Flores responded, then began typing a series of commands into her flex console.

"Mr. Filipov-Ibañez, scan that object with sensors at whatever resolution you can get from this distance," Juliana said before turning toward her exec. "Thoughts?"

"Looks too big to be something they've built—unless they have leaped ahead in technology since colonization," Delacruz said.

"Captain," chimed in Filipov-Ibañez. "Using optical magnification, it appears to be an asteroid, and it's rotating."

Before Juliana could respond, Flores called out from communications. "Receiving a response from the *Babylon*, Captain. That object *is* Port Varley. The planet behind it is Epsilon Ophiuchi IV and is uninhabitable."

"Confirmed, Captain," added Filipov-Ibañez after a moment. "EO4 is a super-terrestrial planet approximately forty-four septillion kilograms in mass with a surface gravity of seven-point-four gees."

"That doesn't sound very habitable," said Juliana.

"The lack of any observable atmosphere would also be something to consider," added Filipov-Ibañez wryly.

Delacruz leaned forward, looking at the tactical projection and rubbing his chin thoughtfully.

"Commander?" Juliana said.

"They needed a station in this system, and instead of building something like New Hibernia Station or New St. Louis, they spun up an asteroid, hollowed it out, and put it at the L2 Lagrange point of a super-terrestrial?"

"So, it seems, Commander. Why?"

"It's a staggering feat of engineering that suggests that whatever the Commonwealth's issues with offering us aid are, they don't have anything to do with resources or technology."

"It certainly doesn't seem so, does it?"

In another half-day, the *Deliverance* reached the "turn and burn" point, flipped, and began its deceleration burn toward the asteroid now looming ever larger in the scans. Two days later, they reached Port Varley.

The asteroid was more enormous than any the crew had ever seen in the three systems of the League. It bristled with lights that were ports or external arrays. The *Deliverance* waited at station as the beast rotated, eventually revealing a series of large docking bays.

"Captain," called Flores. "We are receiving instructions from the *Babylon* to dock in bay four. They have included precise coordinates, which I am relaying to the helm now."

"Received," confirmed Thorsten.

"Mr. Thorsten, match orientation and rotational velocity with docking bay four and take us in."

"Aye, sir."

Thorsten moved the ship into a position just above—or below, depending on your perspective—docking bay four such that the *Deliverance* appeared stationary relative to the bay. In theory, this maneuver was no different from the maneuvers with which he had docked at New Hibernia Station and New St. Louis, except that in those situations, the ship was merely matching velocities with an exterior projection of a spinning drum. Here, it felt to Juliana like they were diving into a giant rock, crashing through the ceiling. Of course, from the perspective of those on the rock, she acknowledged, they would be coming up through the floor.

Thorsten skillfully maneuvered the starship, and before long, it was docked and securely moored to the station. Rotating along with the station provided a downward pull at one-third gee, which Juliana saw as a welcome respite after several days of accelerating and decelerating at one gee.

"Lt. Flores, signal harbor control that we have successfully docked and inquire what shore leave or liberty accommodations exist. Commander," she said, turning to Delacruz, "once that's straightened out, organize shore leave for anyone interested, prioritizing anyone unable to take advantage of doing so at New Hibernia or New St. Louis."

"Aye, Captain."

Juliana pressed a button on her command chair display. "Lt. Blackstone, meet us at the starboard docking port."

"Aye, Captain," came Blackstone's disembodied voice through the bridge speakers.

Juliana stood up. "Mr. Delacruz, you have the conn. Mr. Killian, you're with me."

Juliana and her security chief left the bridge and went to the starboard side docking port, where Blackstone was already waiting.

"Third time's the charm, Captain?" she said, handing them her revised translator earpieces.

"Let's find out!" replied Juliana, marshaling all the good humor she could.

They crossed through the airlock onto the entry deck of Port Varley's docking bay four.

Lt. Blackstone's updates to her translators were indeed improvements, and the deck officer was far more understandable than previous officials had been. He pointed them toward a lift at the end of the deck. A marine waited there and gestured for them to enter the car.

The transparent doors to the lift closed, and the lift began to rise through the rock of Port Varley. After a few moments, the car slowed up before traveling sideways down a perpendicular tunnel. They traveled that way for what felt like kilometers, passing several stops or stations. Not long after that, the car decelerated and began to make its way up again.

The car rose through about ten meters of rock before emerging through the interior surface of the hollowed-out asteroid. Juliana had imagined that there might be some interior spaces in this rock but assumed that most of the station would be concentric decks radiating outward from the center. Instead, she was gazing out on a space that had to be at least ten kilometers from end to end and two kilometers in diameter.

They were now on the exterior lift of a two-hundred-meter-tall tower located at the midway point along the length of the curving interior surface of Port Varley. The surface was covered with vegetation, interrupted by clusters of buildings, walking paths, ponds, waterways, and trams that connected one village cluster to another. Running along the axis of the space was a tube emitting illumination as bright as daylight on most human worlds.

Juliana looked up at the tower they were ascending. The building was triangular at its base, with three sides narrowing toward the top, where a circular series of decks was located. The lift car rose along the tower's exterior before entering the underside of the circular decks at the top. The car stopped at the middle floor of the top section, and the doors opened onto a large concourse. A Commonwealth Navy official bearing commander's stripes was waiting for them.

"Pilizavalami, Kabadana Kavana," he said, Blackstone's earpiece rendering his words as *Please follow me, Captain Kavanagh.*

They followed the officer into a large conference room on the exterior of this level. The far wall of the conference room was glass, affording them a breathtaking view of the asteroid's interior below. The three of them tried to be nonchalant, but it was hard; this was an astonishing feat of engineering, and they were duly impressed.

Opposite them across the table were five naval officers, who rose as Juliana and her officers entered. The officer in the center reached out their hand and shook the captain's hand. "I am Admiral Kim Azikiwe, Commander in Chief for the Ophiuchi Constellation." They turned to their left and indicated the officers standing there. "This is Captain Öztürk of Commonwealth Security and Commodore Requeña of Fleet Intelligence." They turned to their right and continued. "And these are Commodores Babaevsky and Ingraham from Fleet Operations. Please, sit down."

Juliana immediately perceived these officers as heavy hitters. It was clear that communications had gone ahead of them, and they were able to assemble this particular delegation.

Everyone sat, and Juliana took out her display pad. Since it was not known whether the Commonwealth was making any effort to understand League language the way Blackstone had been to understand theirs, Juliana opted to ensure she was as clearly understood as possible.

"Thank you, Admiral," she began. "I am Captain Juliana Kavanagh of the League Starship *Deliverance,* and this is my security chief, Lt. Jareth Killian, and my interpreter and linguist, Lt. Rebekah Blackstone."

The Commonwealth officers read Juliana's datapad carefully but were also intentional about making frequent eye contact with her as she spoke. She could tell they were well-versed in protocol and diplomacy, unlike the officers they'd encountered in previous meetings. That felt promising—maybe these people could do something about the League's requests.

"Thank you, Captain," responded Admiral Azikiwe cordially. "We have read the reports from New St. Louis and New Hibernia and the communications you shared with those commands. We would like to hear your story directly from you, Captain, if it would not be too much trouble."

Juliana was not at all annoyed at having to repeat herself yet again; she was always appreciative of any opportunity to make the League's case and, in this instance, especially appreciative of the chance to make her pitch before senior Navy brass. And so, she began with a description of the founding colonists and their decisions to travel deeper and deeper into uncharted space. She talked about the early lean years of the League and the resources dedicated just to surviving. She spoke about the attack on Farmark and the devastation that attack had had not just on Farmark and the ISG but on the psyches of all citizens of the League. She talked about the hope that so many in the League had felt when the Expedition was announced, the challenges that the Expedition had faced, the Void, the Break, and the loss of the *Brunswick*. She described the experience of finally having arrived in Commonwealth space to find herself perplexed by what appeared to be a systemic indifference to the plight of the League and its peoples. Juliana spoke clearly, without undue emotion but with considerable passion, befitting an ISG officer entrusted with rescuing her people from destruction. The Commonwealth Navy officers hung on every word and listened thoughtfully, sometimes interrupting for a clarifying question, but never incredulously or impatiently.

After Juliana finished speaking, Admiral Azikiwe leaned back and rubbed the bridge of their nose. "Captain, I thank you for sharing your story and the story of your people. You have helped to provide a much more comprehensive picture for us than we could glean from fleet reports and ship communications. Would you and your officers excuse us for a few minutes while my staff and I have the opportunity to discuss what you have said?"

Juliana replied as warmly as ever, "We would be happy to. Thank you." The three League officers rose, exited the conference room, and returned to the concourse.

When the door closed behind them and the transparent walls fogged over, Juliana turned to the two lieutenants. "Well? Impressions?"

"From where I was sitting," began Blackstone, "I believe they were sincere in wanting to hear what you said. They were attentive and thoughtful."

"I agree," Killian said. "They didn't have the same bureaucratic attitude I could feel in those other meetings."

Before Juliana could respond, the wall behind them unfogged, and the conference room door opened. Captain Öztürk stood in the doorway. "Please come back in, Captain."

The three of them shared a half-expectant look and re-entered the conference room. After they took their seats, Admiral Azikiwe began to speak.

"Captain, Lieutenants, we are grateful to you for taking the time to explain your request for assistance clearly. We can only imagine what you have been through in the wake of this attack and the subsequent journey to Commonwealth space. It is a truly compelling story, and your plight arouses the greatest sympathy."

Uh oh, thought Juliana. She could feel the next word coming.

"However," continued the admiral, "we cannot make any commitments to aid you in your struggle. Unfortunately, we are limited by existing protocols and legislative frameworks that cannot be overridden at this command level."

Juliana took a beat, took a deep breath, and exhaled slowly.

"Thank you, Admiral," she began calmly. "Can you advise us on our next step? To whom do we make our appeal? Who has the authority to grant our request?"

"Fleet Command is your ultimate recourse," replied the admiral.

Commodore Ingraham from Fleet Operations leaned forward and raised her hand as if she were in class. With a nod from Admiral Azikiwe, she added, "And the fact that you've taken this request up the chain of command will work in your favor. You shouldn't have any trouble raising this issue with Fleet Command."

"Thank you, Commodore," Juliana said. "How do we go about filing this request with Fleet Command?"

"In person would be the most effective way. It minimizes the delays that might be caused by back-and-forth communications via hyperdrone relay."

"In person?"

"Yes. On Earth."

17 | KILLIAN | SOL

THE FOLLOWING MORNING, the crew of the *Deliverance* made ready for departure. Jareth was dealing with a torrent of thoughts. It had never really occurred to him that the Expedition might make it to Earth. The mission parameters had anticipated a resolution to their request at or near the Commonwealth border. But here they were—left with but one option: to visit the homeworld of the human race. He had to admit that whatever frustration he felt about jumping through Commonwealth hoops, he also felt tremendous excitement about the journey ahead. He was sure many of his shipmates felt that way.

He knew that Rebekah felt the same way. On the lift ride back to docking bay four the day before, as they stood in silence as the captain processed what had happened in the meeting, Rebekah caught his eye and mouthed the word *Earth!* to him. He knew that there was no way to mouth an exclamation point, but it was there; he was sure of it.

As the crew continued making its preparations, Captain Kavanagh received a multi-party communication from the captains of the *Babylon* and *Ganges* to discuss the journey's particulars. They identified particular hyperspace routes they would take and what systems they would pass through. Jareth was pleased to note that Rebekah's translation software was up and running, providing near real-time subtitle translation of the Commonwealth captains' speech.

"With all due respect, Captains," Captain Kavanagh said, "We prefer to go straight."

"Straight?" the *Ganges's* captain asked. "That means we'll be jumping into deep space without fuel stations or fleet bases."

"Don't worry about that. We've got plenty of fuel for all of us, and we're experts in deep-space refueling and navigation. We'll get you through it." The entire bridge crew stifled a laugh, and Jareth could well imagine the satisfaction the captain was getting from offering her expertise to their Commonwealth guides.

The *Deliverance* detached its moorings and was ejected at one-third gee from Port Varley. Ensign Thorsten used the maneuvering thrusters to spin the ship toward the Sheridan line and the jump point out of the system. The *Babylon* and the *Ganges* likewise disembarked from the station and fell into formation on either side.

Epsilon Ophiuchi was about one hundred light-years from the Sol System, home to Planet Earth, the capital of the Commonwealth and humanity's homeworld. It would take at least nine hyperspace jumps and the rest of the *Deliverance*'s antimatter stores to reach the Sol System.

A day and a half after leaving Port Varley, the convoy reached the Sheridan line and prepared to jump out. Jareth knew that, technically speaking, the star at the heart of the Sol system was already visible to them on the screen, but the reality was that it was indistinguishable from the tens of thousands of other stars on the display. Nevertheless, Thorsten aimed at that star, entered the rendezvous coordinates into the hypernav computer and began the jump process.

"Board is green; clear for jump, Captain," Hannover called from his station.

"Mr. Thorsten, initiate hyperspace jump on my mark."

"Aye, aye."

"Mark."

Once more, the tens of thousands of stars on the screen—including the star that shone its life-giving light on the Earth—disappeared.

Nine days later, the convoy emerged from its final jump—the first time in as many days that they would emerge in an actual system.

"We're down, Captain," Thorsten said from the helm.

"Mr. Filipov-Ibañez," the captain began, "are the other vessels down with us?"

Filipov-Ibañez checked his sensors. "Downjump interference abated. Scanning . . . Our Commonwealth escort is still in hyper—no, wait—they're down, too."

"Ms. Flores, signal the *Babylon* that we're ready to follow their lead in-system."

"Aye, Captain. Convoy telemetry is coming in. Should be appearing at helm," Flores reported.

"Roger that, Captain," said Thorsten. "I have the convoy protocols at my station. Ready to execute on your order."

"Make it so, Mr. Thorsten."

"Aye, Captain." The ship turned and fell into formation to head down-system to Earth. The *Babylon* led, with the *Deliverance* next, followed by the *Ganges*. Jareth noted that it was almost like the Commonwealth didn't trust them. Almost.

"Mr. Delacruz," Captain Kavanagh continued, directing her attention to the first officer. "We're going to be in orbit around Earth for a while. I'd like you to come up with a schedule for the crew for some shore leave."

"Are you sure that's a good idea, Captain?" the exec asked. "We've got a lot to do, and assuming things go well, we'll need a full complement for any refits or weapons installations."

"Commander, we've just spent the last few months in a perpetual hyperspace drill. There's going to be a fair amount of diplomacy that needs to happen, but only a small number of us are going to get to do that. While we're waiting for the Commonwealth to figure out how to help us, there's going to be a lot of downtime. Besides, given the harrowing voyage we've just completed, the crew has earned it."

"Of course, Captain," the exec said and left the bridge.

The captain turned back to Ensign Thorsten. "Steady as she goes, Mr. Thorsten."

"Aye, Captain. Steady as she goes."

By now, Jareth had gotten used to the captain's fondness for archaic naval sayings and realized with some fascination that most of them went back to the days of wooden sailing ships on the planet they were now headed for.

Jareth spent his time at his console reviewing security logs, cross-checking weapons inventory with weapons use logs, and reading reports on those crew members detained in the brig. Now that the Expedition had been in Commonwealth space for a while, the incidents of disorderliness had declined and were nothing like what they had been in the Void. But people were still knuckleheads, and something was always going on. It was routine, but given the extraordinary events likely to take place soon, he relished a few hours of routine. A couple of hours in, his review was cut off by a shout from Thorsten at the helm.

"Captain!" All heads on the bridge turned to look. Thorsten was pointing excitedly at the forward display.

"What *is* that?" asked Flores.

"It's magnificent," gasped Filipov-Ibañez.

"It's called 'Saturn,'" the captain said. "A jewel of the Sol system." Everyone gazed in awe. There were gas giants in the systems of the League, even a couple of ringed planets—but nothing like this.

"Does 'Saturn' mean something?"

"It's the name of a god of the ancient Romans, the father of the sky god Jupiter," the captain replied.

"That name seems about right," replied Filipov-Ibañez. "Father of the sky indeed."

The captain ordered the flex displays to show a 360-degree view, and it was as if the bridge were suddenly hanging in space with that monster of a planet and its stunning rings taking up most of the starboard sky.

However, the view of the Sol System was only the second most surprising thing Jareth found about being at the heart of the Commonwealth; the most surprising thing was just how *inhabited* this system was. It seemed as though every rock in the system had a human operation on it—a mining station, a research outpost, a city. There were full-fledged colonies on Saturn's moons under enormous domes and habitats that floated in Saturn's orbit. The forward display placed ID boxes around every object with a transponder within a light hour, and the sheer number of vessels plying the space between the worlds of this system was breathtaking. After over two months in transit, most of which had been in the soul-crushing emptiness of the void between stars, the space of the Sol system was downright crowded.

Jareth reflected that even the Sharon system back home, with its two inhabited worlds, New Sydney and Pherat, couldn't hold a candle to the sheer volume of humanity that lived on and among the worlds of Sol. Flores and Filipov-Ibañez had all they could do to track the comms and ship traffic they were sailing through. Even Thorsten looked a little overwhelmed at constantly double-checking the ship's course to ensure they wouldn't collide with a local freighter, transport, or orbital habitat.

At the end of his shift, Jareth took a walking tour of the ship—part security inspection, part method to burn off a little nervousness and excitement.

Everywhere, people had set their wall screens to the external view. Both the enlisted and officers' messes had set their 360 displays to the external view. Crew members sat in small groups to share a meal or a drink and gestured excitedly at the objects in view. Even the theater on deck sixteen was showing documentary features on the planets of the Sol system. The specialists in navigation on deck thirty were busy developing high-precision charts of the system, mapping gravity wells, hyperspace lane exits, and solar wind patterns. The science officers a deck below in astrophysics were busily taking measurements and making observations. Jareth was fascinated to see how everyone's excitement about being in the mother system of humanity was being expressed. When he got down to communications on deck thirty-two, it was hardly a surprise to find Rebekah poring over a text about the most common languages spoken on Earth.

She looked up as he walked in. "Patrolling the perimeter?"

"Something like that. Just burning off some nervous energy."

"I know what you mean. I've been doing crash courses on Neo-Mandarin, Espanyolic, and Z'lu as if I'm going to need to speak all of these languages when we arrive on Earth."

"As if learning their version of Anglic wasn't enough!"

"Yeah," she admitted sheepishly. "I was prepared to meet with Commonwealth officials and negotiate our rescue. I don't think I was ever mentally prepared for the idea of coming to the cradle of human civilization and having to function on the largest stage possible. It feels like being summoned before the emperor. I'm just anxious about missing something."

"Well," Jareth offered unhelpfully, "unless things have changed here, I don't think there will be an actual emperor you'll have to report to."

She gave him a look that was a combination of an eyeroll and a smile, simultaneously acknowledging the dopiness of his answer and the fact that she appreciated the stupid joke, nonetheless. But it was also a look that Jareth understood to mean that the two of them had become genuine friends. For a fleeting moment, he wondered if she would still be his friend if she knew everything there was to know about him, but he cast that thought aside. *Try to enjoy the moment.*

"You wanna grab some dinner in the officer's lounge? They've got the walls set to a view of the system. Apparently, there's another gas giant on our way to Earth that's supposed to be even bigger than the ringed one."

Rebekah looked at her polytool and the Earth languages displayed on it before taking a deep breath. "Neo-Mandarin can wait," she said at last. "Da wi go na ida s'ma fuda."

"What?"

"That's Commonwealth for 'Let's go and eat some food'—I think."

"You're not gonna talk like that all night, are you?"

"Not unless you're going to make some more helpful observations about Commonwealth governance," she said with a wry look.

"I think I can agree to a moratorium under those terms," Jareth responded. With that, they made their way up to the officer's lounge for a meal of traditional New Sydney fare and stunningly gorgeous gas giants.

At the end of the meal, despite his frustration during previous encounters with Commonwealth officials, he was beginning to feel ever more optimistic, not just about the mission's chances but about his own. Not with Rebekah—that was a non-starter—but with himself. Maybe, just maybe, being a part of this mission would help him to find his own redemption from the sins of his past. If he could help the League secure its deliverance with the Commonwealth's help, perhaps his account sheet would finally be balanced.

✛

A FEW DAYS LATER, having traversed the asteroid belt and the orbit of Mars, the convoy neared Earth. As the *Deliverance* approached Earth orbit, you could hear a pin drop on the bridge.

They approached the planet from the side facing away from the sun, and the globe they could see was covered in night. Thousands of cities gleamed out of the blackness, and their coastal settlements enabled the crew to make out the contours of continents and landmasses.

Jareth was in awe again. The League had done a thorough job of colonizing the four worlds over the last four centuries. There were still some vast stretches of wild land, but their worlds did not resemble those of the early days of settlement: a single colony surrounded by a vast wilderness. The League's planets were thoroughly populated—but not like this.

The cities of Earth were so many and so large that it was hard to tell where one might end and another begin. Their placement struck Jareth as less planned out than the League's settlements. These had the feeling of organic growth, not the managed development that governed the League's colony worlds. The nightscape of Earth reminded Jareth of the chaotic nature of human civilization in its natural environment.

Suddenly, Jareth began to feel a measure of inadequacy. Everything about this *one* system of the Commonwealth put the entire League to shame—who were they to persuade this mighty empire of anything? And who was he, some rube from a backwater planet, thinking he could contribute anything meaningful to this effort? He looked down at his console and caught a trace of his reflection in the flexdisplay surface. He noted the single silver bar on each lapel of his uniform collar. *You're an officer in the Interstellar Guard of the League of Four Worlds; get it together.* He looked around; no one else seemed to be descending into an existential crisis. They all seemed to be entranced by the vision of the world beneath them.

"Entering Earth orbit," Thorsten said, almost reluctantly, as if he didn't want to spoil the moment of silent wonder.

"Standard orbit, helm," the captain replied.

"Standard orbit, aye."

The *Deliverance* entered orbit as the braking jets fired to reduce its speed to the preferred orbital velocity at the preferred orbital distance.

"All hands, stand by for null-g."

Hannover relayed the order throughout the ship. "All hands, deceleration to zero gees in ten seconds." A signal beeped, counting down. The crew clicked on their magnetic boots.

The countdown stopped, and so did any forward motion as the vessel entered the free-fall of orbit.

"Zero acceleration. Null g," Thorsten reported.

Jareth's stomach lurched. Every time that happened, he had to remind himself that even seasoned space veterans felt some disorientation when the gravity suddenly disappeared. But if the crew's inner ears were causing them trouble, those senses yielded in their efforts to the astonishment in their eyes as the ship came around the planet and into the daylight side.

"Good God," said Filipov-Ibañez. "That's . . . "

" . . . the most beautiful planet I've ever seen," finished Thorsten.

There was silence on the bridge as everyone gazed down at a stunning blue and white marble. Jareth gaped. The League's worlds were earth-like—they had oxygen–nitrogen atmospheres, plenty of surface water, mixed biomes, and so on. But there was just something about the color of all those things on Earth. Even the blue sky, seen as a sliver sideways through the atmosphere, seemed more powerfully blue than the corresponding atmospheres of the worlds he knew.

Even the captain was nonplussed.

"I guess," she began, "this is your reaction when you see the world your species evolved on. Perhaps Earth couldn't help but look perfect to us."

"All the same," Jareth said. "Damn . . . "

It was at least a minute before anyone realized they had forgotten to turn on the gravitic plating. Only when his coffee bulb came floating into his view of Earth did Commander Delacruz give the order to turn it on. The crew's stomachs and inner ears returned to the comfort levels associated with a sense of "down," but it didn't matter. Their attention was fixated on the beautiful blue and white marble in the center of the forward display.

"Captain," said Filipov-Ibañez after another minute or two of awed silence. "Should I adjust ship's chronometers to local cycles in case we need to acclimatize for shore parties?"

"No need, Mr. Filipov-Ibañez," the captain replied. "Standard Fleet Time is already based on Earth's 24-hour time cycle. Just synchronize the ship clock with the correct minute of Earth's standard mean time. You should be able to find the frequency in the ship's archives. We'll worry about the difference in hours later. We may wind up time-lagged when we visit certain parts of the planet, but at least we've been living on their cycle for months already."

"Aye, sir."

Jareth slapped his forehead so loud that the captain and Commander Delacruz turned to look in his direction.

"Mr. Killian?" Delacruz asked.

"Sorry, sir," he replied sheepishly. "I had always wondered why the standard fleet day was twenty-four hours long, given that none of our worlds has that as a rotational cycle. I feel like such an idiot; of course, it's based on Earth."

Delacruz chuckled, and Jareth could tell from a quick scan of the other faces on the bridge that he differed from his colleagues only by the fact that he had publicly admitted to his ignorance.

"Don't worry about it, Mr. Killian," said the captain, smirking a little. "We've been on our own for such a long time that it's hardly surprising that we wouldn't assume that Earth had anything to do with how we do things. We had a whole lecture in my fleet history courses at the academy that explained the origins of things like the 24-hour clock, the 365-day year, the 360-degree circle, and so on. My fellow cadets and I were all surprised. We'd all assumed these numbers were some kind of mathematical compromise among the worlds of the League."

"Exactly!" Jareth exclaimed. "Uh, sir," he added quickly.

Filipov-Ibañez looked up from his console. "We're about seventeen minutes off their standard hour, Captain."

"Seventeen minutes—that's not bad for four hundred years of separation and sub-luminal time-dilation," said the captain. Filipov-Ibañez was about to say something, perhaps that there was no way of knowing how many hours or even weeks they were out of sync on top of the minutes when he saw the twinkle in the captain's eye that suggested she was making a joke.

"Yes, sir," he smiled back.

"Captain?" Jareth asked tentatively.

"Yes, Mr. Killian?" responded a visibly amused commanding officer.

"The gravity on Earth, is it—"

"It's one *gee*, Lieutenant," she said, grinning. Jareth slumped. *Abe's God, what an idiot I am*, he thought.

Visiting the United Nations of Earth
Commonwealth Bureau of Commerce
and Tourism

OVERVIEW

Planet Earth (a.k.a. Terra, Sol III) is humanity's homeworld and the birthplace of human interstellar civilization. It has been under the governance of the United Nations of Earth since 2074, the end of the Terran Third World War. The UNE was one of the founding worlds of the Commonwealth of Humanity and hosts the Commonwealth's capital in the ancient Terran city of Jerusalem.

With recorded history dating back nearly 6,000 years before the present and civilization extending back more than 11,000 years, the historical and cultural richness of Earth's legacy cannot be underestimated. Visitors to Earth may be initially overwhelmed by the diversity of cultures, languages, religions, and traditions. UN Tourism offices in most cities can help off-world visitors get acclimated.

Excepting Venusians, visitors to Earth from elsewhere in the Sol system may find Earth's constant one gravity exhausting. Low-gravity orbital habitat residents and Belters should consult a physician before making any travel arrangements. Lunans and Martians should also factor frequent rest into their itineraries. Extra-Solar visitors should consult the recommendations of their local departments of health.

Travelers to the UNE must demonstrate proof of vaccination for Schedule A diseases. Visitors with neural implants must provide evidence of phage immunization or purge.

Visitors are required to follow all local regulations and environmental warnings and must avoid areas indicated with radiation markers and sea-level flooding warnings.

UNE QUICK FACTS

Source: *Galactic Factbook*, Commonwealth Information Service

Flag

Seal/Coat of arms

Motto	"One World, Many Peoples"
Other traditional mottos	"Pax, Dignitas, Aequalitas" (Latin) "Peace, Dignity, Equality"
Anthem	"The Home of All" Duration: 1 minute and 18 seconds. 1:18
Orthographic map of the UNE in Sol system	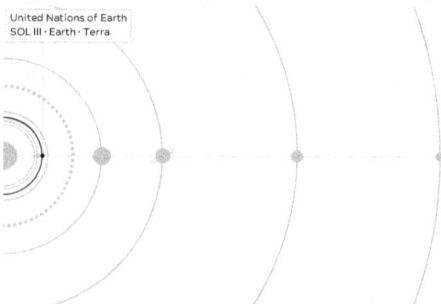
Capital city	New York City, 40°43′N 74°0′W

Largest city	Lagos, 6°27′N 3°23′E
Official languages	Anglic, Arabi, Espanyolic, Fransi, Lang Belta, Lunar Creole, Neo-Mandarin, Russki, English (legacy)
Demonym(s)	Terran, Earther
Government	Federal republic
Executive	The Secretariat • Secretary-General • Undersecretary-General
Legislative	World Parliament • Upper house: Security Council • Lower house: General Assembly
Judicial	International Court of Justice • President of the Court
Initial Formation (International Agency)	Multinational Charter, 24 October 1945
Reconstitution (Planetary Government)	Confederation, 24 October 2074
Constitution Ratified	14 July 2075 (Last Amendment, 29 September 2777)
Area	Total area, 510,072,000 km2 Water (%), 70.8 Land area, 148,940,000 km2
Population	16,235,986,429 (2790 Census)
Density	31.8/km2
Currency	Commonwealth Mark (CHM) ₡
Net affix	.une

18 | KAVANAGH | IN HIGH COUNCIL

THE FOLLOWING MORNING, AS Juliana made her way to the bridge, it seemed that, as with Saturn, every display aboard ship showed the planet beneath. As wowed as the crew had been by the ringed gas giant, they were absolutely transfixed by Earth. Perhaps she was right—maybe you couldn't help but feel this way about the planet your species evolved on. Juliana had heard that some of the most moving images in human history had been images of the Earth from space; she could see why—such images were clearly moving her crew. In at least one instance, she saw a crew member staring at that cerulean orb in the viewer with tears streaming down their face.

She was sure that part of that was not just that the Earth was beautiful but what it represented—they'd made it. They were at the heart of the Commonwealth—all their hopes that someone was at the end of their long road were vindicated. The Commonwealth was still here. Earth was still here. Hope was still here. *You got them here; now, bring this home.*

She entered the bridge and saw Lt. Blackstone standing near a data readout along the portside bulkhead flexdisplay.

"Captain on the bridge," called Hannover, and Blackstone turned and drew up to attention.

"As you were," Juliana said. "Lt. Blackstone. To what do I owe the pleasure?"

"Good morning, Captain. I wanted to discuss protocol, given that the CSN plans to provide its own interpreter."

"That's not unusual in diplomacy, Lieutenant. You will translate for me; their interpreter will translate for them. Of course, I still expect you to tell me if that person gets anything wrong. I don't care who they trot out; you're the greatest Commonwealth–League Anglic expert in the galaxy."

Blackstone smiled. "Thank you, sir."

"No need to thank me. You've been a blessing to us on this mission. Sometimes, I am pained to recall just how close we came to losing you."

Juliana could see that her praise was received by the young lieutenant with mixed emotions. She knew that so many of the *Brunswick* survivors were continuing to process the losses they had endured.

"It's okay, Lieutenant. We are allowed to be happy and grieve at the same time. Two things can be true at once." There was an expression like gratitude on Blackstone's face as she nodded her assent.

The bridge hatch slid aside, and Juliana turned to see her security chief entering.

"Oh, good, Mr. Killian. You're here. We've just received word from the *Babylon* that Commonwealth Fleet Command will receive our delegation at 1400 Terran Standard. That's 1100 ship time. Lt. Blackstone and I were discussing how we might go about communications protocols for this meeting. Apparently, the CSN will have its own interpreter."

"That seems like a bad idea," he said. "Who's got more experience navigating the differences between League speech and Commonwealth speech than Rebekah, uh, Lt. Blackstone?"

"I agree. But this is a protocol matter. Each side brings its own interpreter."

"Captain Kavanagh is right," added Blackstone. "But aside from protocol, having more than one person trying to bridge the communications gap can only be a good thing."

"I'll want you, Major Li, and Master Gunnery Sergeant Makindi along," continued Juliana. "If they are going to go full diplomatic, then let's show them just how seriously they should take us. I'm still not convinced that they accept us as a full-fledged polity, and I keep expecting them to issue us that ticket for not having a registered transponder in Sigma Librae."

Blackstone and Killian laughed, but Juliana knew they needed to be convincing and present as legitimate a face as possible. For reasons she still could not figure out, the Commonwealthers they encountered seemed to have so much trouble with the *idea* of the League—that any human settlement could exist outside the boundaries of the Commonwealth. Until she got them to embrace that idea wholly, the League couldn't afford to be seen as anything other than fully serious. It was the primary reason she requested the shore party dress in their Class-A uniforms for this mission. She wanted everyone to look as naval as possible.

Blackstone took her leave, Killian took his station, and Juliana took her seat. Before heading down to the planet, everyone still had some routine work. But Juliana's thoughts weren't on her work. She did something for those two hours or so, but she would have been hard-pressed to say what it was. Her thoughts were dominated by the reality that she was about to set foot on Earth—the single grandest stage in human civilization. *Well, Jules*, she thought, *here's where we find out whether you can fill the Old Admiral's shoes. Whether you're more than just a name the fleet brass wanted to advertise on this mission.*

Even when she could return to her work, she kept stealing glances at that blue wonder on the displays and getting lost in thought. To her relief, she wasn't alone—she noticed Hannover, Flores, Killian, and Filipov-Ibañez doing the same thing from time to time.

Before long, it was time. She switched off her panel and stood.

"Mr. Filipov-Ibañez, Mr. Killian, you're with me. Lt. Flores, signal Lt. Blackstone to have her join us in the shuttle bay. Commander Delacruz, you have the conn."

"Aye, Captain," Delacruz responded. "We'll take good care of her. Good luck."

"Thank you, Commander. Let's hope we won't need luck."

She, Filipov-Ibañez, and Killian made their way off the bridge and down ten decks to the shuttle bay. Lt. Blackstone was already there, along with two marines, Major Li and Master Gunnery Sergeant Makindi. Both snapped to attention as Juliana walked in.

"At ease," she said. "Please take your seats aboard."

They strapped themselves in as the shuttle pilot made their preparations. For some reason, Juliana was feeling far more anxiety than she usually would for a shuttle landing. She looked around, and it seemed like she was not alone. Killian had an odd expression on his face, Filipov-Ibañez looked like he was on his way to the principal's office, and Blackstone looked like she was suppressing the urge to throw up. They were still in the shuttle bay, and the ship's gravitic plating was still on, so it wasn't space sickness. It was the moment.

The docking bay crane picked up the shuttle and moved it to the center of the bay, suspended over the hangar bay doors beneath them.

"Shuttle Charlie," came Chief Ahmadi's voice over the intercom. "This is *Deliverance*. Stand by for depressurization and hangar door separation."

"*Deliverance*, this is Shuttle Charlie," the pilot, Petty Officer Santos-Wang, responded. "We copy and are standing by."

The sounds of machinery and miscellaneous ship functions outside the shuttle slowly faded into silence as the air was pumped out of the shuttle bay. Beneath them, the enormous hangar doors parted, and with them, their gravitic plating and any sense of down. Grappled as they were by the docking bay crane, they suddenly felt like they were falling even though the shuttle wasn't moving at all relative to the crane and the ship.

"Shuttle Charlie, you are cleared for departure."

"This is Charlie. We copy, *Deliverance*. You may release the docking clamps."

"Docking clamps releasing in three, two, one. Release."

Nothing happened. The conservation of momentum preserved the shuttle's relative position in free fall with the ship as it fell around the planet, and the shuttle floated right where it had been in the hangar bay, eerily suspended over the void of stars to the aft of the ship.

"*Deliverance*, this is Shuttle Charlie. Engaging maneuvering thrusters now."

"Copy, Charlie. Smooth sailing and safe passage."

"Roger that, *Deliverance*. Keep the home fires burning. Out."

With that, Santos-Wang engaged the thrusters, and the shuttle gently fell out of the hangar bay. As it cleared the bay, the hangar doors silently closed above them, and the pilot started to turn the shuttle toward the planet below. They engaged the engines, pushing the passengers back into their seats.

At their present point in orbit, they were on the night side of the planet, and the place they were traveling to was in the middle of the day side. Santos-Wang accelerated the shuttle away from the *Deliverance* and westward around the planet. The shuttle crossed the terminator from night into day and descended into the atmosphere, flying over a massive ocean unlike any in the League.

"Do you see that?" Killian asked his companions as they fell through the layers of Earth's atmosphere. "It's enormous."

"It takes up almost one entire hemisphere of the planet," Juliana said. "There's another one, not quite as large on the far side." Such staggering amounts of water were difficult for Leaguers to imagine. Their planets had plenty of water, but their seas were smaller and more evenly spaced.

Before they knew it, the shuttle was no longer above the ocean and cruised over an enormous landmass that seemed to go on forever. At last, the massive continent ended, and another ocean appeared. Just off the northwestern shores of the continent were two big islands—one larger than the other. The pilot set their course for the larger of the two.

Santos-Wang's console beeped, and a message flashed in text on their heads-up display. "They're giving us coordinates to land on a particular landing pad in the spaceport below," they said.

"Take us in," Juliana answered.

Having shed most of its velocity coming through the atmosphere, the shuttle nosed down and made for the coastal city ahead of them. They skimmed over the sea that separated this island from the smaller island to the west, and everyone was transfixed. No one bothered looking ahead at the spaceport—they were too busy staring out at the seas of Earth. Juliana assumed that somewhere deep in their minds was the knowledge that they had all come from these seas; they were home in ways that, before this moment, had been primarily intellectual. There was nothing intellectual about this now; this wasn't New Sydney, Pherat, Fairhaven, or Farmark. This planet was the origin of every single one of them.

Juliana looked at her companions and, not for the first time that day, saw tears on their cheeks as they looked out at the churning waves.

Well, all except the marines, who had fallen asleep as soon as the shuttle had departed the *Deliverance* and slept the entire way down.

The shuttle set down on an airfield in the city of Bristol on the island of Great Britain. Juliana smiled, remembering Lt. Blackstone's excitement when she'd learned that the part of Britain they were visiting was called "England," where English had come from. Juliana reflected wryly that that fact didn't guarantee that anyone there would understand them.

The Commonwealth fleet offices were bright and modern, but they were housed in a building unbelievably old, dating back to the beginning of the Space Age.

"I can't fathom a building that is eight hundred years old," Killian said.

"We'll encounter buildings even older," said Filipov-Ibañez. "There are buildings in London, about 190 klicks from here, that are older still."

Killian's face betrayed his disbelief.

"Mr. Killian," Juliana interjected. "There are structures on Earth that are almost *six thousand years* old."

She understood why the lieutenant had such a hard time with the idea. After all, when you lived on a planet where nothing was older than four hundred years, that kind of antiquity was mind-boggling. When everything on a planet was so new to you, it was hard to grasp that it was so old. Even she had to admit that that was how everything on Earth felt: really new and really, really *old*.

As their delegation moved through the corridors of the fleet high command, they could tell they were drawing attention. Some people were polite, but others outright stared. Who could blame them? The Leaguers were tempted to stare back—four hundred years of isolation had made for enough changes in fashion and styles that each appeared strange to the other. Besides, the lighter gravity on the League worlds meant that the *Deliverance* crew members were generally taller than everyone else.

Their Commonwealth escort took them at last to a conference room that was remarkable in terms of its ordinariness—a rectangular-shaped room with simple white walls and ceiling and a large wooden table in the middle with about twenty chairs around it. Juliana, Killian, Blackstone, and Filipov-Ibañez took their seats around the table as the two marines stood along the wall behind them. The petty officer who had led them in turned, said something unintelligible, and left the room. A short woman with a medium-dark complexion introduced herself as Dr. Kapoor and translated, "The admiral will be with you in a moment." Blackstone caught Juliana's eye and nodded subtly—she had understood the same thing.

Juliana poured herself a glass of water from the pitcher in the middle of the table. Killian tried to figure out where the light was coming from; no fixtures were in the ceiling or walls.

After about a minute, a side door opened, and a diminutive man walked in, flanked by adjutants. There was nothing impressive about him in stature, but he had an almost regal bearing. Juliana rose, and her officers followed her lead. The admiral waved them to sit and took his seat at the head of the table, with his adjutants taking their places to either side. He said something that sounded like *Haiz urana netepereda?*, and Dr. Kapoor answered and identified herself. Juliana's handheld pinged with a text message from Rebekah: *she's a professor of English literature.* The admiral began to speak again as Dr. Kapoor interpreted.

"I am Admiral Samal Mbenga. On behalf of the Commonwealth Star Navy, it is my privilege to welcome you to Earth and to our headquarters. As ye must by now understand, your presence hath caused something of a sensation here. We were unaware of your existence until ye did arrive. It is without need to say, we have had to rethink many things. We have ne'er engaged with any beyond the Commonwealth's bound. And now, lo, we do discover thence that not only human settlements lie outside our realm, but e'en alien invaders do threaten those settlements. Prithee, pardon our astonishment at such tidings, for they come upon us in swift succession."

Juliana leaned forward, "Admiral," she began. "Thank you for your hospitality and for taking the time to meet with us today. We are honored to be here at the headquarters of the CSN and privileged to be standing on the soil of Mother Earth."

Admiral Mbenga nodded his acknowledgment of her gracious words. Juliana continued.

"We also understand your astonishment at the news we bring. However, it strikes us that whether you were aware of us or not, surely the Navy is prepared to respond to external threats, is it not? At least that part of the situation must be something you can respond to. That is all the help we need." Blackstone translated Juliana's words so expertly and fluently that Dr. Kapoor was taken somewhat aback. She looked at the lieutenant with an expression that suggested she thought Blackstone had to be an Earther who had somehow learned Commonwealth speech better than she had. Juliana took that as a moment of pride for her staff—no rubes, they.

"Captain Kavanagh," Mbenga continued via Dr. Kapoor, "the Commonwealth Navy hath ne'er faced an external menace. Truly, aught beyond our borders hath ever sought our shores. In the days of Expansion, no foreign host or peril crossed our path. The Navy hath stood to safeguard civil tranquility, pursue scientific inquiry, extend aid in times of need, and purge the space lanes of dread pirates. Yet, forsooth, the means be ours to counter any external peril that may upon our shores do call."

"Admiral, one has called. The loss of Farmark is testament to that." Juliana's tone was level but tinged with frustration. It was unclear whether Dr. Kapoor picked up on it and, if she did, whether she attempted to give the admiral some indication of it, but Juliana was growing exasperated. She had been nothing but patient and accommodating. She had given the Commonwealth the benefit of the doubt at every turn, even when her officers reacted with frustration and indignation. But now, what had been a curiosity at first was becoming a pathology. First on New St. Louis, then on New Hibernia, then again at Port Varley, and now at last here on Earth—they kept getting stonewalled. It was almost as if they didn't want to be bothered helping the League. But no, that wasn't quite it—it was almost as if they were afraid to try. But Juliana didn't think they were fearful of the enemy, *per se*. It was something else.

"With all due deference, Captain, Farmark and thy–'League'? Prithee, have I that correct?—thy League of Worlds falleth not under the Commonwealth's charge. As thou hast relayed to our forces, yon foes lack light-speed travel. By thine own account of their pace, they pose no immediate threat, not for three and two-score hundred years, if thine intelligence holdeth true."

Captain Kavanagh's mouth hung open. "Not your responsibility? Are you not the Commonwealth of *Humanity*? Are we not human worlds under attack?"

Admiral Mbenga was beginning to look perturbed. "Verily, mere semantics. Until most recently, nary a whisper did speak of humanity beyond the confines of the Commonwealth. Nonetheless, a moniker cannot forge legal responsibility."

"*Legal responsibility?*" Juliana said, looking to Rebekah to see if she'd understood correctly. She turned to her officers and, in a hushed tone just loud enough so they could hear but not loud enough so that Kapoor could, said, "Does he think we're going to sue the Commonwealth? In what court?"

Not perceiving Juliana's growing frustration, Admiral Mbenga continued. "Indeed, legal responsibility, should ye seek redress in the courts." So, there it was. He did think they were going to sue.

Juliana could feel everything falling apart. They had come all this way—the void hadn't stopped them, the violence wrought by human despair hadn't stopped them. They had made it. The Commonwealth was still here, alive and thriving. Why couldn't she get through? Why was she failing at this? What was she not communicating? What was she missing? She gave herself another five seconds to wallow, then gathered herself together and pursued another tactic. "May I ask, Admiral, what do you recommend we do?"

Mbenga nodded to one of his adjutants, who leaned forward and began to speak. "Verily, we have regarded your circumstance, and there do exist various and sundry alternatives ye might pursue." He never identified himself, but his name tag and rank insignia identified him as Captain Fitzgerald.

"Please continue," Captain Kavanagh said.

"The Navy might release unto you certain proprietary information as pertains to weapons and shield design that ye might manufacture for to assist your fleet. Mayhaps also, ye might treat direct-like with our artisans of weapons systems for to arrange the purchase of sundry systems that Naval Command may determine proper for you to have and which shall not compromise our security."

"Compromise *your* security?" Killian asked. All the heads in the room turned toward the lieutenant as Blackstone interpreted. "If we had an arms capability that could threaten your security, we wouldn't be having this conversation. We'd be back home, celebrating a victory over an invading enemy."

"So I understand, Lieutenant," Fitzgerald said. "But were ye to possess certain of our technology, ye could conceivably become a threat."

Killian began to answer, but Juliana cut him off. "Certainly, Captain. We don't wish to compromise the security of the Commonwealth. I wonder whether you might have any other suggestions beyond the acquisition of weaponry."

"What meanst thou?" Mbenga interjected.

"How we might appeal the apparent decision that the Commonwealth Navy had already made prior to this meeting not to provide direct military assistance to the League of Four Worlds." That time, the irritation in her voice did not escape Dr. Kapoor's notice, and it registered on the faces of the admiral and his staff long before Blackstone's translation was finished.

Mbenga seemed unfazed; if anything, he was more indifferent. "If ye were citizens of the Commonwealth, I should advise you to write your elected representatives in Jerusalem."

UNITED COMMONWEALTH NEWS SERVICE

DATE: 10 APRIL 2791 (CS) 15:00 GMT

LOCATION: COMMONWEALTH NAVAL COMMAND, BRISTOL, ENGLAND, EUROPEAN UNION, EARTH (SOL III)

SPEAKERS: CAPTAIN SUNIL CRITTENDEN, CSN PUBLIC RELA-
            TIONS; CAPTAIN JULIANA KAVANAGH, LEAGUE OF
            FOUR WORLDS

SUBJECT: ANNOUNCEMENT OF VISITORS FROM LOST COLONY

CRITTENDEN: Good afternoon. This is an announcement un-like any other that the Commonwealth Star Navy has ever made. Today, we welcome a very special delegation of visitors to Naval Command. I am pleased to welcome Captain Juliana Kavanagh, Captain of the League Starship *Deliverance*, a vessel from the League of Four Worlds, a small planetary union some seven hundred light years beyond the boundaries of the Commonwealth. Captain Kavanagh and her vessel arrived at the outpost station at New St. Louis several weeks ago. They have been making their way to the heart of the Commonwealth to meet with senior navy leadership and governmental officials. We are very happy to host Captain Kavanagh and her crew and welcome them to the homeworld of humanity.

We will take your questions. Due to changes in our language over the last several centuries, Captain Kavanagh will speak through an interpreter, Dr. Gita Kapoor.

QUESTION: Captain Crittenden, how long have you been aware of the existence of our visitors' planetary union?

CRITTENDEN: We first learned of the existence of these settlements when Captain Kavanagh and her vessel arrived at New St. Louis a few weeks ago.

QUESTION: Does the Commonwealth plan to incorporate these settlements as it did other colonies?

CRITTENDEN: That is a political and legal question that the CSN is unable to address.

QUESTION: Captain Kavanagh, how long did it take you to reach the Commonwealth?

KAVANAGH [translated]: Nearly three months from our departure from our worlds.

QUESTION: Was the journey difficult?

KAVANAGH [translated]: It was. Voyaging through deep space without support and into uncharted territory is challenging. And we suffered a tragedy en route when our sister ship, the *Brunswick*, was destroyed.

QUESTION: Captain Kavanagh, after such a difficult journey, what does it mean to you to be on Earth?

KAVANAGH [translated]: It is a great day for us and for our League to be here on Earth. [Possible additional words left untranslated.]

QUESTION: What are your impressions of Earth?

KAVANAGH [translated]: It's beautiful and lives up to its reputation in our legends.

QUESTION: What are you planning to do while here on Earth?

KAVANAGH [translated]: We hope to meet with governmental officials to discuss aid for our league.

QUESTION: What kind of aid are you seeking?

CRITTENDEN: Unfortunately, the captain's schedule is quite busy, and she and her crew have had a long journey, so we need to wrap this up. Thank you all for coming, and stay tuned for additional announcements and information on our visitors. Thank you all for your time. And to the people of Earth, thank you for your hospitality toward our guests.

FURTHER INFORMATION:

Commonwealth Star Navy Office of Public Affairs

pa@csn.mil.une

Infonode: 19.66.17.01.csn.mil.une

168

19 | KILLIAN | REGROUPING

THE *DELIVERANCE'S* DELEGATION WAS afforded accommodations at an ancient hotel not far from Fleet Command. Since the CSN high command had no intention of discussing the matter further beyond the parameters that Captain Fitzgerald had laid out, these accommodations felt to Jareth and the others more like a door prize rather than a commitment. It felt like it was the Commonwealth's way of saying, "We're sorry we can't help you with any ships, but here's a comfortable bed to sleep in tonight in a fancy hotel." Having said that, Jareth wouldn't lie—moving around constantly under one gee was a little exhausting. It was nice to have somewhere nearby where they could sleep in comfort.

The Commonwealth was a post-scarcity economy, so food, housing, education, healthcare, and essential clothing were provided for every citizen. But money was still used for things beyond basic need—and the *Deliverance* crew didn't have any. Having no diplomatic relations with the League, the Commonwealth was not in a position to exchange League credits for Commonwealth marks, but Fleet Command gave them a few hundred marks to use for any expenses. None of them had any idea whether that was a lot of money or not.

That night, the four of them met in the tavern of their hotel to debrief. They invited the two marines to join them, but Li and Makindi politely demurred and said they preferred to stand back and keep an eye on things. The rest tried to be inconspicuous, but it didn't work. Everyone continued to stare at them, a behavior that had only increased with the broadcasting of several stories on the local media feeds about the visitors from a "lost colony."

"To the captain!" Filipov-Ibañez said, raising his glass.

Kavanagh nodded in appreciation but was quick to decline the honor. "I haven't accomplished anything yet. My diplomacy doesn't seem to be working."

"Their behavior is a riddle, sure," continued Filipov-Ibañez. "But you need to think about this tactically, sir. If I may give my captain some advice."

Kavanagh nodded. "We're in a bar, Lt. Commander. I think 'speak freely' is implied."

"Good, good, good. Imagine the Commonwealth is a fortress. You come up to the gate with a battering ram, but it is not strong enough. So, you go and get a larger battering ram, but that, too, is not strong enough. Finally, you go and get the largest battering ram the world has ever seen, and even that is not strong enough. What do you do?"

Kavanagh stared forward for a moment before turning to her tactical officer. "You look for another way in."

"You look for another way in. Precisely. It is not that your tactics and approach aren't good ones—they just don't work at this gate."

Kavanagh took out her handheld and checked a readout. "Good, they're in range," she said and hailed the ship.

"*Deliverance*. We're receiving you," came Flores's voice.

"Lt. Flores, this is Captain Kavanagh. I need you to contact any members of the Commonwealth Parliament and see if you can get us a meeting as soon as possible."

"Captain, my records show there are over four hundred members of the Parliament. Any I should focus on?"

"Stand by." Kavanagh turned toward the rest of them. "Any ideas?"

"Terranova," offered Rebekah. "It's where the KGM Expedition left from."

"Maybe New Hibernia?" offered Jareth. "It was the first Commonwealth world we had contact with."

"Earth," said Filipov-Ibañez matter-of-factly. "We're here."

Kavanagh turned back to her handheld. "Lieutenant, start with the Parliamentary delegations of Terranova, New Hibernia, and Earth. Keep me apprised of any responses."

"Will do, Captain. Just for your information, the Commonwealth has limited our access to their comms and information nets, so it may take some doing."

"Do what you can, Lieutenant. Kavanagh out." The captain put her handheld away and picked up her glass. "To looking for another way in."

"To looking for another way in!" the rest responded and downed their drinks. They sat for a moment, quietly enjoying the tastes of Earth's libations before Jareth broke the silence.

"You guys ever watch *Captain Defender*?" he asked.

"I did," Filipov-Ibañez said. "One of the reasons I'm in the fleet."

"Yes," said the captain. "Loved that stuff."

"My fathers loved to watch it together," Rebekah said. "It was never my thing, but believe me, I'm familiar."

"I met him once," Jareth continued.

"Jory Kelman?" Kavanagh asked. "When?"

"This was years after the show went off the air, of course. My family and I were traveling on vacation somewhere around Playadoro. Anyway, we were in this restaurant and there was Kelman at the bar. I was thrilled. I kept asking my parents all through dinner if I could go up and get his autograph. They kept insisting that Mr. Kelman was entitled to a vacation of his own, too. Well, I must have worn them down because they finally let me go over. As I'm walking up to him, a man at the bar bumps into him, and Kelman spills his drink all over the guy. The guy becomes real belligerent. 'What the fleg are you doing, punk?' and all that. And Kelman starts groveling. 'So sorry, so sorry. It's a mistake, it's a mistake. There's no need for violence. Here's some money for a new shirt.' He was a complete yert—nothing like Captain Defender at all. Captain Defender would have smacked the guy across the room for the injustice of attacking someone over an innocent mistake. I just turned around and went back to my parents and finished my dinner."

"Wow, Killian," Filipov-Ibañez said. "That's quite a story."

"Indeed," said the captain. "What made you think of that?"

"Because I hadn't had that feeling since that time—until we arrived in the Commonwealth, anyway. I'm afraid, Captain, that we came looking for Captain Defender, but we found Jory Kelman instead." Jareth hadn't intended to kill the conversation at the table, but he did. They all drank the remainder of their drinks in silence.

Eventually, the gathering broke up. They didn't have much else to discuss until they heard back from the *Deliverance*. Rebekah left for her room first to watch local media broadcasts and see if she could understand the language. The captain was next, followed not long thereafter by Filipov-Ibañez. Jareth nodded to the two marines who had been keeping an only mildly inconspicuous watch nearby. "You're dismissed. Go get some rest. I'll be fine." Li and Makindi both nodded and left the lounge. Jareth knew that Li would trust him to take care of himself and that Makindi likely wouldn't care if he came to some tragic end.

He sat for a while staring out the window. Craft of various sizes were coming in and out of the Bristol spaceport. There was just so much going on here on Earth. It's not that League spaceports weren't busy; Earth's were just busier. League cities were crowded; Earth's were more crowded. Jareth found it all a bit overwhelming. It was hard not to feel like a yokel here on Earth, and he had to remember not to gawk whenever he saw anything new.

A waiter came up. Jareth was about to brace himself for another round of trying to overcome the language barrier, especially with Rebekah having gone for the evening, when the man pointed at the drink on his tray, pointed at Jareth, and then pointed at a woman sitting at the end of the bar. Jareth had never learned any sign language, but that he understood. He took the drink and raised the glass to the woman at the end of the bar.

She got up, walked over to his table, and gestured at an empty chair. "Please, sit," he said. She nodded, either because she understood his words or his intention.

She extended her hand. "Lira," she said.

"Jareth," he said, taking it.

"Thou art from new planet?"

"Yes," Jareth said, raising an eyebrow. "From new planet: New Sydney."

"I had studied English on university. It did come to my ear that ye could comprehend thereof. Thus spake they on . . . *terayavid*." That last word wasn't in Anglic or English, but he understood her meaning.

"Yes, we can. How many years did you study English?"

"Forgiveness, sir. I came not hither language to talk about." With that, she reached out and squeezed his hand in a particular manner that made her intentions unambiguous. Jareth looked her over. She was short, like all Earthers, with long dark hair and a darker shade of the olive skin color the majority of people on the planet had. But it was the deep brown eyes that he was a sucker for. And she was looking right into his with hers.

"Hast thou a chamber for thyself?" she asked.

"I do."

She stood up and made a gesture that meant something like *well then?* Jareth downed the remainder of his drink. He got up, took her hand, and led her back to his room to engage in an activity that did not require any grammar. *The things I do for interstellar relations*, he thought.

JARETH WAS AWOKEN BY a knock at his door. "Killian, wake up!" came Filipov-Ibañez's voice. He looked over to his left, but the bed was empty; Lira must have left while he was still sleeping. He got up and padded over to the door.

"What is it, Miguel?" he said, opening it.

"Captain wants to see us in the lounge in thirty minutes," Filipov-Ibañez replied, looking Jareth over. "What's with you? Did you not sleep well?"

"Oh, I slept well, just not enough."

Whether Filipov-Ibañez didn't get Jareth's meaning or chose not to, he said, "Alright, well, I hope that's enough time for you," and was off.

Jareth closed the door and went back into his room. A clean dress uniform hung in his closet courtesy of the hotel valet. He showered, dressed, and headed downstairs to the lobby. The captain and the rest of the party were already there.

"Mr. Killian," the captain said. "Are you recovered from your diplomatic mission?" *Abe's God, did this woman know everything?* Jareth marveled.

"Yes, Captain," he said somewhat more timidly than he'd planned.

"Good," the captain replied—was that a wink? No one else seemed to understand the captain's question or its implications. Was this an actual *moment* between the two of them?

A long black ground car pulled up to the front of the hotel. Their CSN hosts/escorts/guards gestured toward the door and the car beyond.

They took their seats in the vehicle, and it moved effortlessly along the winding streets of the ancient city and across the Avon River, which, for some reason, had Rebekah giddy with excitement to see. Eventually, they took the Coronation Road toward the Bristol Spaceport, which was not in Bristol or the old seaports at the river's mouth but in the countryside outside somewhere called Abbots Leigh. Everyone sat and stared at the alien yet also somehow familiar scenery.

"Why did they put the CSN headquarters here, of all places?" Filipov-Ibañez asked.

"Bristol has an ancient maritime heritage, being a major shipbuilding center and a center of logistics and supply for the British Navy," Captain Kavanagh replied. "When the United Nations Navy was established, Bristol was chosen as naval headquarters. When the Commonwealth was founded, the UNN was subsumed into the Commonwealth Star Navy, and its headquarters became the CSN headquarters. It made sense to build a spaceport nearby."

"But," Jareth began, wrinkling up his face in confusion, "when they founded the UNN, they had the whole planet to pick from. Why not put the headquarters somewhere more central and not in need of enormous sea retaining walls?"

The captain laughed. "A true Son of the Pioneers—pragmatic to the last. For us Leaguers, practical considerations were always more important than symbolic or traditional ones. Earthers aren't like that. Tradition and symbol are far more important here."

Jareth felt there was so much to process about this place. Ever since their delegation had landed, he could feel his body react to the particular gravity, the scent of the atmosphere, and the spectrum of the sunlight. It was no surprise that the planet *felt* right. But boy, was this place weird. Physiology might be one thing, but culture was something else altogether.

They were soon at the spaceport and were ushered toward a suborbital shuttle for the trip from Bristol to Jerusalem.

"Anyone know why they picked this Jerusalem place as the Commonwealth capital?" Jareth asked as they were strapping in for launch.

"It's completely obvious," Filipov-Ibañez replied. "It is in the middle of this world, right where three giant landmasses come together. Perfectly logical and appropriate."

"Continental location hardly makes a difference to our interstellar delegations," one of their Commonwealth guides interjected, with Rebekah's help. "New York City is the planetary capital, and it's not in a central location. The story of how Jerusalem was chosen is long and complex and has more to do with sentimental reasons relating to religion and history."

"Sure, sure. That makes for a good story," Filipov-Ibañez replied. "But having a central location is how all the League's capitals are placed. It makes sense."

The Commonwealth guide shrugged and turned back to his handheld.

The suborbital launch was not dissimilar from the one Jareth had taken from New Kalgoorlie to Novaroma, but if anything, the Commonwealth's mag accelerator was even more powerful. In no time, they were arcing over the planet and turning back toward the surface. As the suborbital came in, they saw a vast blue sea.

"What is that?" Filipov-Ibañez asked.

"That is the Mediterranean Sea," their guide replied.

"Mediterranean? What does that mean?"

The guide thought for a minute. He looked lost in thought, but then it became apparent he was accessing some kind of data implant. "It is from an old Earth language called Latin, and it means 'middle of the earth.'"

"I told you so," Filipov-Ibañez said, folding his arms with a gesture of triumphant vindication.

Jerusalem was older than anything any of them had ever seen before. They rode from the spaceport in a long ground vehicle in a motorcade and proceeded to the Parliament building along streets lined with buildings of ancient stone. Their guide, a Yonatan Abu-Sharif, was from this region and pointed out various landmarks along the way—the Mount with its three holy structures atop it, the Old City, the Ancient City, the different planetary embassies, and various ancient quarters. Rebekah and the captain were the most interested in the history and architecture of the place; Jareth mostly stared out the window and marveled.

The streets were full of different processions that Jareth assumed were religious but had no way of knowing. Crowds in brightly colored clothing carried leafy branches along; others blew strangely shaped horns that didn't look like they'd been manufactured but found. Jareth marveled at the diversity in costume, language, and appearance of the Commonwealth's capital city. Not only were the crowds representative of Earth's tremendous diversity but also of the diversity of the entire Commonwealth. Squat stocky visitors from high-gee environments moved in and among taller lither visitors from low-gee planets, some of whom were borne along in robot-pulled carts or moving with the aid of walking suits.

The motorcade moved past the Mount and on toward an enormous structure on a neighboring hill, reportedly three-quarters of a millennium old but visibly less ancient than the surrounding city. The Parliament building was a heptagon, from each corner of which came a raised spine that ascended toward the center and converged with the others, arcing upward into a massive spire. A great ring of windows made its way around the heptagonal base, and the spire glittered with even more windows. There was a flame atop the spire, but it was hard for Jareth to tell whether it was a real flame (which seemed unlikely) or a statue glittering in the sun. The entire building was a work of art. *Unlike our dull, functional buildings*, Jareth thought.

The motorcade turned and headed directly toward one of the spines. As it approached, doors at the end opened, and the vehicles entered the structure, descending along a ramp until they deposited the *Deliverance* crew at a receiving area where a delegation was waiting.

The woman at the head of the delegation came forward, holding out her hand to the captain. "Nara Simonov," she said through her interpreter. "Senator Isfahani sent me to welcome thee and to guide thee to his office."

"Captain Juliana Kavanagh. Thank you for your welcome," Rebekah was quick to translate.

The other delegation members said nothing, but their uniform dress and stern demeanor indicated they were security. Jareth wondered whether that was for his party's protection or theirs.

They walked through the doorway in the receiving area and into a corridor with banks of elevators. The door of an elevator opened, and Ms. Simonov gestured for them to get in as the security detail stood outside. They entered the circular elevator and were followed by the security agents, one of whom placed his hand on a panel and closed the doors. The elevator began to rise, at first straight up, then at an angle. Suddenly, the elevator walls became transparent, and the car ascended one of the seven spines of the building until it was traveling up the central spire. Jareth and his crew mates were given a magnificent view of Jerusalem as they ascended and were mesmerized.

"Have you ever seen anything like that, Captain?" asked Filipov-Ibañez.

"No, Commander. New Kalgoorlie is big enough, but I've never seen anything that old before. It boggles the mind. Of course, the cities of Earth are ancient, but until you've seen them . . . "

Ms. Simonov smiled at their conversation—indeed, all the Earthers they met were amused by their awe at the age of Earth's cities. "There is a city twenty kilometers from here—Jericho—that is 11,000 years old."

She seemed to anticipate the next question when she said, "There aren't any buildings there that old. It's just been a place of human habitation for that long." Even so, Jareth was impressed. It was hard for him to be on Earth and not feel like a rookie at the whole civilization thing.

The elevator came to a stop, and the walls once again became opaque. The lift moved sideways for a moment and then rotated so that it faced the interior of the spire. The doors opened, and a circular hallway stood before them. Their guides ushered them along the hallway until they arrived at a pair of heavy wooden doors. Simonov placed her hand upon the panel to the side of the doors, and they opened. She nodded to the security agents, who turned back down the hallway as she ushered the landing party into the office. Inside was a receiving area with a couple of couches and a desk with a staffer, who nodded to Simonov and then stared at them as we walked past. *Why does everyone have to do that?* Jareth wondered. *Surely, they've seen off-worlders before. Well, okay, not off-worlders from a "lost colony," I suppose.*

Simonov led them through the outer receiving area into a spacious office with a wall of windows and a breathtaking view.

A tall, dark, and bearded man in flowing robes stood off to the left side of the office by a large wooden desk. The interpreter who had come with Simonov moved to stand by his side, and he began to speak. "Most senators prefer a view of the Old City—I like having this view. I can imagine that I can see my hometown."

He walked forward, smiling, with his arm extended. "Reza Isfahani, Senator to the Commonwealth representing the United Nations of Earth. Welcome, welcome." Even though he spoke that strange version of Anglic they had come to expect here in the Commonwealth, Jareth thought he was speaking it with some kind of accent on top of that. When he turned to look at Rebekah, it was clear that she had noticed his accent as well, and Jareth could see her scribbling notes in her polytool.

The captain took Isfahani's proffered hand. "Juliana Kavanagh, Captain of the LSS *Deliverance*, representing the League of Four Worlds. Thank you for your hospitality, Senator Isfahani. This is Lt. Commander Miguel Filipov-Ibañez, my tactical officer, Lt. Jareth Killian, my security chief, Lt. Rebekah Blackstone, linguistics, and Major Suleiman Li and Master Gunnery Sergeant Benjamin Makindi of the League Marine Corps."

"Welcome to all of you," Senator Isfahani said, smiling warmly at all of them. He gestured to some low cushions arranged in a semi-circle facing the window. "We could sit in chairs and couches if you like, but let us not be bound by protocol—especially in higher gravity. Let us be comfortable." The Leaguers walked over to the cushions and followed their host's example, reclining on the cushions and gazing out the windows at the view.

"Do you live near here, Senator?" Captain Kavanagh asked.

"Oh, no. Well, unless you mean relatively speaking. My home is in Iran, at least a thousand kilometers away. This view keeps me grounded. It helps me not to get too swept away with my position. I had that trouble when I was at the General Assembly. It is all too easy to get distracted by New York. In any event, how are you enjoying Earth?"

As he spoke, an aide came by with a tray containing a teapot, some cups, and a small bowl full of white cubes. Jareth watched as the senator poured himself a cup of tea and then, taking one of the white cubes and placing it between his teeth, began to drink the tea. Sugar, Jareth realized. *Do all Earthers drink tea like that? How do they have any teeth?*

"The planet is lovely, Senator. I wish I could say the same for the results we've been getting." Even Jareth was surprised by the captain's skipping right over the small talk and getting down to business. But he could tell that recently, she was becoming more and more affected by their lack of success. Almost as if she feared something slipping away.

Isfahani smiled and seemed to appreciate Captain Kavanagh's get-to-the-point approach. "I had gathered as much from your request to meet with me, Captain. I understand you have had little success in enlisting the Navy to help in your cause."

"Senator, allow me to be as direct and to the point as I can be. One of our worlds came under attack by an alien force completely unknown to us and against whom we are defenseless. We lost thousands of people in a failed effort to defend Farmark and its system. Subsequent attempts to rescue survivors from the planet's surface proved unsuccessful and resulted in great losses of life. Our own Master Gunnery Sergeant is a witness to the Invaders' devastation of Farmark and the threat they represent." The captain turned to look at the marine and nodded.

Makindi sat up and told his story. Although the captain had certainly known the details of his squad's failed mission on Farmark, it became clear that no one else in the room had. Jareth could barely believe the horror that the man had been through and he noted that even Major Li did not appear unaffected by the tale. Makindi told his tale with an outwardly stoic demeanor, but Jareth could see that there was turmoil beneath the surface. It was no wonder; traumas like that are not easily vanquished and lie just beneath the surface in wait. When Makindi had finished relaying the events of his mission, Captain Kavanagh took a few seconds to allow the room to settle before continuing.

"We have hundreds of thousands of refugees, many of whom are traveling by slowboat to Fairhaven. If we are unable to stop this threat, in a matter of a few years, our entire civilization could be destroyed. There is no situation we can contemplate that is direr. And yet, every time we have tried to present our case and plead for aid, we have come up against roadblocks. We spared no expense in funding this expedition to return to Commonwealth space, depriving our systems of necessary materiel, people, and antimatter in order to enlist the Commonwealth's aid. We have even lost one of our vessels and seventy-seven comrades along the way, and it has all thus far been for naught. We cannot comprehend the lack of willingness to come to our aid in a clear case of dire need. All we keep hearing are rules, regulations, statutes, and laws. We had expected better of the Commonwealth. Given that, all the natural wonder in the universe would not improve my mood or my experience of Earth so far."

Isfahani put down his cup and looked down pensively for a moment.

"Captain, I am afraid that you are up against forces greater than you realize. I mean nothing insidious by that; there is no cabal seeking to stop you. But there is enormous pressure to do nothing to assist you."

"Pressure?" said the captain. "What kind of pressure?"

"The institutional cultures of the Navy and the Department of Colonization have been stuck for the last several centuries in a maintenance mode, Captain. That is, they are most comfortable maintaining the status quo rather than in exploration or expansion."

"Why is that?" Jareth asked, rather out of turn.

Isfahani turned toward him, and Jareth half expected a rebuke, but he said, "Mr. Killian, the causes for the current stagnation are many and varied. Suffice it to say that the average citizen of the Commonwealth does not look to expand or to go beyond our current borders even to explore. It is a centuries-long predisposition of our populace. And the institutions that safeguard that philosophical orientation—the Navy and the DOC—are the same institutions that one might otherwise expect to challenge those assumptions. Alas, both are paragons of conservatism in this regard."

The captain sat for a few moments, staring out the window at the view, wheels turning.

"Senator," she began. "I can appreciate a cultural predisposition against inaction in the abstract, but here we are. We have come with a specific, dire need. Surely that would arouse sympathy in these institutions and certainly in the government to do something, would it not?"

"Captain," Isfahani began gently, "you are assuming that anyone knows about your situation."

"Are you saying—"

"Captain," interjected Rebekah. "I have been monitoring their broadcast media to learn the language, as you know. There are plenty of stories about the 'Lost Colonies' and the expedition that has come back to Earth. But so far, I have not heard a single word about the invasion or the crisis that brought us here."

The captain turned to Isfahani with an expression that demanded an answer.

"It is true, Captain. There has been a news blackout as to the reasons for your arrival. It has been classified as a state secret in the interests of security. I am privileged to know about this because I serve on the Select Committee for Interstellar Security—it's the primary reason why *I* could meet with you, but the delegations from Terranova and New Hibernia could not. And I am bound by law not to reveal classified information. I am sympathetic, Captain, and will do what I can to get you aid, but you should know that the obstacles to generating political will are extremely high." He put down his cup and stood up. Isfahani was cordial and sympathetic, but the meeting was over.

"Until the matter is declassified," he continued, "my efforts will largely be limited to persuading my fellow committee members to champion some kind of action for you. I can't make any promises, of course."

"Of course, Senator. We appreciate any help you can give us."

Jareth could feel the captain's disappointment; he felt it, too. They had made their case directly to the Commonwealth's frontier security, to their naval high command, to their government representatives, and to their legislature. And in every case, they had come up short. *Perhaps there was nothing else to be done*, he thought.

Perhaps the Commonwealth was Jory Kelman, after all.

20 | KAVANAGH | FAMILY HISTORY

"SO, MR. KILLIAN," SENATOR ISFAHANI said as the Leaguers were leaving his office. "Are you and the captain planning on visiting Ireland while you're here?"

Killian looked at Juliana and the others. No one else seemed to know what he was talking about either. "What's Ireland?"

"Ireland is one of the British Isles; you were not far from it when you were at Bristol. It's lovely there."

"I'm sure, but why are you asking about me and the captain in particular?"

"Because you and Captain Kavanagh have Irish names. I thought you'd want to look up any ancestors. Many off-worlders do that when they come to Earth. The Genealogical Database Centers in most cities are favorite tourist destinations. You should see if you can find any living relatives. They'd be quite distant, of course. But I am sure you'd find many Killians and Kavanaghs on Eire."

Juliana and Killian looked at each other. She had no idea the two of them were from a common ancient tribe. After a moment, she said, "We might as well. Until we have some idea of whether the Parliament is going to do anything for us, we're just waiting around. It's a big planet. We might as well see some of it."

"Splendid," Isfahani said. "I will contact you as soon as there is any news to report, Captain."

"Thank you again, Senator," Juliana replied. "We appreciate whatever help you can give us."

They left the senator's office and followed Simonov and the security escorts back toward the elevators. The interpreter did not accompany them, which Juliana immediately seized upon.

"What was that you were saying about looking for another way in, Mr. Filipov-Ibañez?"

"This is the wrong gate, too, I think," he replied.

"So the military is an impenetrable gate, and the political branches are, too. We're going to have to find another way in."

"So, we're not going to this . . . Ireland?" Killian asked.

"Oh no, we're going. I have no real inclination to sightsee or to look up old relatives, but if it convinces the authorities here that we're being good little tourists, then maybe we can figure something out."

"What do you have in mind?" Filipov-Ibañez asked.

The captain looked around. There was no interpreter, and Simonov didn't appear to have any real idea what they were talking about, but one never knew where a listening device might be. Juliana gave her tactical officer a look, and Filipov-Ibañez caught on.

"Got it."

Once aboard their suborbital returning to Bristol, Juliana turned to her officers.

"Alright, I don't think there's anyone listening here. But we have to figure out a way to get our story out there. Options?"

"We could broadcast something ourselves from orbit," Filipov-Ibañez offered. "Though that would probably be a violation of Earth broadcasting regulations or something, and we'd get fined."

Juliana smiled at the joke, but he was right. Violating their hosts' laws was not likely to win them any sympathy.

"If we could access the net, we could post something," suggested Blackstone. "The problem is, even if I could write something in fluent Commonwealth speech, I have no idea where to send it. I've only been able to access their broadcasts–I've got no access to any of their forums, online communities, or anything."

Filipov-Ibañez leaned in. "And they've been particularly stingy about allowing us access to their net—you've noticed, yes? I ask for access to their networks; they tell me, 'We'll get back to you,' or they pretend not to understand me. All my comms I do through the *Deliverance's* systems—not efficient at all."

"I have noticed that, Mr. Filipov-Ibañez," Juliana replied. "They don't want us to have unfiltered access to their media."

"Yeah, I'd noticed that, too," Killian said. "All of our press conferences have been short and through their interpreters, not ours, who is undoubtedly far more competent."

Blackstone's expression was half modest and half saying, *Right?*

"They're managing us," Juliana said. "They're afraid that if the truth of our situation were known, it would change the dynamic, and they don't want that."

"But why is this?" asked Filipov-Ibañez. "I see no reason why helping us is frightening to them, yes? They have the resources, they have the people, they have the technology."

"It's not that," replied Juliana. "It's not the helping us that's the problem. It's something else."

"Any ideas what?"

"No, but we need to work around it, whatever it is. So, here's what I'm thinking: follow Mr. Filipov-Ibañez's advice and look for another way in. They have us on a tight leash, but if they're convinced that we're just sightseeing, they might let their guard down. Let us talk to someone."

"Who?" Killian asked.

"Well, that's the challenge, isn't it, Mr. Killian? It can't be anyone they would see as a threat—journalists, community leaders, that kind of thing. We'll have to keep our eyes open for anyone who could give us access to their net or to others who are sympathetic."

"Captain," Blackstone interjected. "Most of the people on this planet can't talk to us. The further away we get from the kind of people the Commonwealth would be worried about, the further away we get from the type of people we might be able to talk to in the first place."

"Yeah, I doubt some shopkeeper in this Ireland place is connected to a major social movement and happens to have studied English in college," said Filipov-Ibañez, not entirely unhelpfully.

"Until we can figure out what our real obstacle is and what we're up against," Juliana replied, "I don't know that we've got another choice."

JULIANA REGARDED HER BREAKFAST on the table at the sidewalk cafe just outside their Bristol hotel. The food was tasty enough, and even though she was a coffee person, the tea was rather good. Most of all, she enjoyed the morning light and soft spring breeze that blew through the streets. *If only we could bottle this and bring it aboard the ship.*

Their mission was by no means fulfilled, but Juliana appreciated the opportunity for rest and quiet. The deep mattress of her room certainly had helped relieve some of the exhaustion of the travel and moving under a constant one gee.

Across the street, she saw Killian and Blackstone walking in her direction. "Out enjoying the spring weather?" she asked as they approached her table.

"We found one of those Genealogical Database Centers that Senator Isfahani had mentioned," Killian replied. "With Rebekah along as my interpreter, I managed to get a genetic scan and a report as to where my closest living relatives might be. It looks like my best bet is in a town called Bally-na-may-awg?"

"Where?!" said Juliana, laughing.

Killian pointed at the document and the town name on it: *Ballynameagh*. "I'm not sure how it's pronounced, but it's this town in Ireland."

Blackstone chimed in, "I'm pretty sure the clerk pronounced it Bal-yih-nuh-MEE."

"Earth doesn't make any damned sense," Killian added.

Juliana picked up her handheld and called Filipov-Ibañez.

"Commander, the lieutenants are back, and they have our destination. Join us out front when you can."

"Roger, Captain. On my way."

Juliana closed the channel and turned back to Killian. "I have arranged for an air car to take us, so however you pronounce it, as long as you have the name and the coordinates, we should be good to go. I've also given our Marine escort some liberty. Taking armed guards along with us doesn't exactly convey the image of well-behaved tourists exploring their ancient heritage." Juliana could see Killian visibly relax at that news. *Interesting*, she thought. That would bear further investigation, but not now.

A few minutes later, just as Filipov-Ibañez made his way outside, an air car parked in front of the hotel, and the driver got out. Blackstone spoke with the driver and gave him the name of the town. He nodded before opening the rear doors for the four of them to enter. They climbed into the back area, which consisted of two rows of seats facing each other. Blackstone and Killian sat on the backward-facing bench, and Juliana and Filipov-Ibañez sat in the forward-facing one.

"I feel a little odd without our marine escort," said Filipov-Ibañez. "Not that it's unsafe where we're going. I just got used to them."

"If you'll notice," responded Juliana conspiratorially, "that's not the only escort we don't have today." No Commonwealth representative or government functionary traveled with them today. After all, they were just going sightseeing and ancestor-hunting in a small town away from the centers of power.

The car eased away from the hotel and headed out of town on a main avenue. When it reached a sufficient distance from the city it leapt up from the ground and took to the air.

"That was smooth," said Filipov-Ibañez, marveling.

"You're right, Commander," Juliana replied. "This car is using something other than thrusters and aeronautics to fly. Repulsors, maybe?"

"If they are repulsors," Killian said, "they've figured out a way to make them a lot more effective than our gravitic plating."

"Yet another piece of the puzzle," Juliana said. "The Commonwealth isn't reluctant to get involved because they are at a technological disadvantage."

The car skimmed over the countryside before crossing a channel at the wide mouth of a river. Juliana followed along on her handheld's navigation application. She watched as they crossed a region labeled "Wales" before crossing over a larger body of water called the "Irish Sea." Before too long, they were back over land again—Ireland. Green fields, farms, and charming hamlets all rolled by below them.

"There's so many people," Blackstone said.

"It looks kind of empty down there," Juliana replied.

"I don't mean it that way. Every hectare is farmed, built on, or otherwise bears the marks of human civilization."

"Humanity has had a long time to develop this planet. There are few 'wildernesses' left—most of them are just large parks of one kind or another."

They flew past a fairly large city—her handheld identified it as Dublin, the capital of Ireland. Not long after that, the car began its descent. Along a country road, the driver eased the car down toward the surface and drove the remaining distance on the ground toward Ballynameagh.

Juliana scrolled through the information on their destination that she could find on the portion of Earth's information networks available to them. The town of Ballynameagh had existed as a township for centuries, but after World War III, it had seen an influx of refugees from around Ireland and the British Isles. Many such refugees built new towns in rural areas, away from where the fighting had been, as havens and chances to start anew. Juliana watched as artificially ancient-looking architecture built of more modern materials raced by the windows.

The driver pulled over alongside a building marked as a tourist information center. He got out and opened the doors before turning to talk to Blackstone.

"He said we can find a tour guide here to show us around," Blackstone relayed. "He asked if we were planning on staying the night."

"We'll have to play it by ear," Juliana said. Blackstone turned back to the driver, and he nodded and got back in his vehicle.

"He gave me his comm node address. We can signal him with whatever we decide."

"Excellent," Juliana said and gestured to the tourist center. "I take it this is where we start."

They walked into the tourist center, and Blackstone approached the main counter to inquire about finding a guide. Killian, Filipov-Ibañez, and Juliana stayed off to one side and talked about the experience of the flight over. As they did so, a man came straight at them out of the back room.

"Pardon me, fair friends," he said in a lilting but understandable voice. "Where might ye be come from tha' ye do still speak in the Old Way? Are ye Northerners?"

"We are not, friend," responded Juliana genially. "We are from offworld. From the League of Four Worlds." She said that last part slowly and clearly, unsure whether it would register. His eyes widened; it registered.

"Are ye? What brings ye to our fair city?"

Juliana tilted her head in Killian's direction. "It seems this one has traced his ancestry to this town."

"Aye? Welcome, welcome!" the man said, practically beaming. "My name is Tiernan O'Malley; I'd be honored to be your guide here."

Juliana looked up and called to Blackstone. "Lt. Blackstone, I think we've found our guide."

After making all the official arrangements, they departed the tourist center. They walked along the main thoroughfare of charming little shops, cafes, and beautifully designed residences that struck a seemingly ideal balance. Along the way, O'Malley told them about the history of the buildings they walked past, the urban design that went into building the community, and the particular style of architecture the town chose.

They walked down the main street into the town square, and Killian froze.

"Lieutenant?" Juliana said to her security chief. He just pointed.

Right before them was a statue of a tall man dressed in some kind of military uniform, pointing out toward the sky. There was a plaque on the statue. Juliana couldn't read what the text said, but the name on the statue was clear: Padraig Killian.

"It's . . . Padraig Killian," he stammered.

"Friend of yours?" Filipov-Ibañez asked.

"That's my family's pioneer ancestor," Killian replied, dumbfounded. "I had no idea he was from Earth. The pioneers had all left from Terranova in the Wolf system. I had assumed he was from there."

"Can you translate this for us?" Juliana asked O'Malley.

"In troth, I can," he said. "'Tis written in Gaelic. This is what is written hereon:

Dedicated to the Memory of Padraig Killian, Commander in the Commonwealth Star Navy, Astrogeologist, Businessman, and a Leader of the Lost Expedition. Born, 9 May 2315, Presumed Dead, 2369.

"What does that mean, 'Lost Expedition'?" Killian asked O'Malley.

"Aye, 'tis a famous tale. Padraig Killian was one of the leaders of the last colonial expedition of the Commonwealth. They departed from the Wolf system and were never heard from again."

"Didn't anyone look for them?"

"In troth, they did. They sent probes to all the systems along their trajectory, but there was no sign of them."

Juliana couldn't believe what she was hearing. "That was it? They didn't look any further?"

"They knew not whither they might have gone. If they be not in the systems nearest the frontier, there was no means by which we might have found their new location. Many believed they would signal upon their arrival, wherever they might have gone, but that signal never did come."

"It's still on its way," Juliana said.

O'Malley looked perplexed and a little upset. "I do not understand."

"The 'Lost Expedition' wasn't lost. They were looking for habitable worlds and wound up jumping seven hundred light-years before they found four worlds they could colonize. They sent a signal as soon as they arrived— it just won't be here for another three hundred years."

"But they all died," O'Malley insisted, somewhat weakly.

"No, they didn't. Padraig Killian was my ancestor," Killian said, pointing to the name badge on his uniform. "They made it, and they founded our worlds. You all just gave up on them."

"That's a little unfair, Lieutenant," Juliana interjected.

"Okay, fair enough," Killian replied before turning back to O'Malley. "We Leaguers take this kind of thing personally. We have always felt abandoned by the Commonwealth."

"How could they have lost track of the expedition?" Juliana asked. "The Pioneers left breadcrumbs."

"It wouldn't take much, "Filipov-Ibañez said. "All kinds of things can go wrong—power failures, meteorites, who knows? If the first one fails, there's a bubble of, on average, sixty-four potential destinations within a twelve-light-year sphere to search. That's difficult enough. But if the second breadcrumb fails, now you're talking upwards of four thousand possible destinations before picking up another breadcrumb. The trail would go cold."

Throughout this, O'Malley was straining to understand, but he began to look more and more concerned.

"Is something the matter, Mister O'Malley?" Juliana asked. "You look upset."

O'Malley shifted. "The Lost Expedition is why we no longer colonize."

"What!?" Juliana and Killian exclaimed simultaneously.

"The expedition was lost. It was a story that captivated the population for months. Some pleaded that we should keep looking. Alas, in the end, even those who'd funded the expedition began to consider it a loss. And by the end, most believed that the Commonwealth had, in troth, become too vast. The frontier was too large an expanse—we could not search it well enough. Our leaders began to believe that the Commonwealth had reached as far as it could. If 'twere to expand beyond the present frontier, it could not be maintained. In the wise of Ancient Rome, 'twould become more unstable. And the Parliament did enact the Frontier Act."

"So that's it," Juliana said. "They got scared of how big the universe was."

THE FOUR OF THEM decided to extend their stay in Ballynameagh to process what they had learned and to see what else they might find out. Their tour guide showed them around the rest of the town, including a small museum about the Lost Expedition. Juliana found the exhibit's tone strange: at once praising the courage and daring of Padraig Killian and the Pioneers while arguing that the lesson to be learned from their expedition was how foolish it was to keep going out into space forever. Two different ideas were at war within the same narrative.

After leaving the museum, they passed by a small clothes shop, and Blackstone turned to go inside.

"Anyone else tired of sticking out like a sore thumb?" she said. The rest of them followed her inside. Despite the tremendous variety in Terran fashion, they had noticed a basic everyday outfit wherever they'd been—a tunic just above the knee, pants to the ankle, and a wrap over one shoulder. They all found passable Earther outfits made out of smart cloth that allowed them to change the colors and patterns of the fabric.

Juliana messaged the air car driver and told him they would stay over. After a few minutes, he replied that he had arranged for everyone to be accommodated at a local hotel. When she and the rest had finished their shopping excursion, they headed over to the hotel the driver had indicated.

It was a pleasant hotel right on the city square, each of their rooms with a balcony facing the square. From the balcony in her room, Juliana stared out at the town below and watched its people walking to and fro without a care—and briefly resented them for it. The peoples of her home were not living such carefree lives. But that was unfair, she realized. They have no idea what's happening in the League. That's got to change.

She took out her handheld and messaged the rest of her team. "Dinner in the hotel tavern, 1900 local."

At 1900 hours, Juliana found a table in a quiet corner of the hotel tavern just as Filipov-Ibañez and Blackstone arrived. Killian was the straggler and showed up ten minutes later in his new Earth clothing.

"Looking sharp, Killian," said Filipov-Ibañez as he walked up.

"Thanks," he replied. "Thought I'd go with earth tones tonight. Seemed appropriate."

Blackstone asked the servers for their recommendations on the best local specialties, and they were presented with a flavorful mix of local offerings. But no one was interested in the cuisine. Juliana decided to get things going.

"What do we do with what we've learned?" she asked.

"Obviously, we have to get the word out about us," responded Filipov-Ibañez.

"But that part is already out there," Blackstone replied. "I've been reading their communications—they already know we're from outside the Commonwealth. Some have even mentioned that we are the descendants of an expedition previously believed to have been lost."

"The way I see it," Killian began, "we're stuck. Our existence as a surviving colony of a lost expedition is a positive because it shows that exploration isn't futile. But our actual plight . . . ."

"Our actual plight," continued Juliana, "shows that space is every bit as dangerous as they feared it was when they closed the frontier."

"Exactly," Killian said. "The part they know about helps us the best, but it doesn't seem to be helping us at all. And the part that might create a sense of urgency would only reinforce their inclination not to get involved."

"But that's so shortsighted!" Blackstone objected. "Even if we didn't exist, there might be threats to the Commonwealth from outside their border that could come calling."

Filipov-Ibañez began laughing. "You know the kik-kik bird on Southland on New Sydney, yes? Sometimes, when it's being chased, it sticks its head in the ground; it believes that if it can't see the predator, the predator can't see it."

"That's gotta be a myth!" cried Blackstone. "How would that trait get passed down? I imagine the birds that do that get eaten."

"Maybe so. But maybe they get eaten at a lower rate than the birds that try some other strategy. Maybe the Commonwealth thinks it'll work for them."

They continued their conversation and their meal, enjoying some of the local beers, ales, and whiskeys, which they were told originated on this island. Before too long, it was obvious that the day's events had worn everyone out. They paid for their meal and made their separate ways back to their rooms.

Juliana fell into a fitful sleep. She dreamed she'd been hauled before the Admiralty and court-martialed for failing such an easy mission. She tried in vain to explain the obstacles they'd faced, but the more she talked, the less they listened. Then Admiral Turner-Li leaned forward and wagged a finger at her. "We sent the wrong damned Kavanagh!"

Her eyes snapped open, and she stared at the hotel ceiling. *Look for another way in*, she thought. *What would the Old Admiral do in this situation? What had he done to defeat the Red Blade?* Her eyes widened, and in the dim light, she felt she could see clearly. Gaius Kavanagh had hacked the pirate network, causing their sensors to relay false data. He lured the pirates away from their base with those false readings. When his fleet attacked the base, it was defenseless.

We're the false readings, she thought. *The* Deliverance *is the threat they're not ready for.*

She got out of bed and threw on her uniform jacket. She only needed to look presentable from the waist up. She grabbed her handheld and had it project a keyboard interface on the desk in her room and a holo display in the air in front of her. She initiated a connection with the *Deliverance*. It was in the middle of the evening watch on board, and the communications officer on duty was surprised to see his commanding officer on the other end of the call.

"Captain," the petty officer answered. "What do you need, sir?"

"I need you to conference me in with Commander Delacruz and Lt. Flores on a secure and encrypted channel."

"Aye, sir," said the flustered officer. "Standby."

After a few moments, the border of her comm window changed to a bright red color, indicating a secure link. In another few moments, the faces of Commander Delacruz and Lt. Flores appeared on a split screen.

"Captain?" Delacruz asked. "Is everything okay?"

"Just a moment, Commander. I forgot someone." She pulled up her comm menu and clicked on an address. A new pane opened, and Rebekah Blackstone's visibly recently awakened visage appeared.

"Captain?" she said with perhaps even more confusion than Delacruz had.

"I apologize for the interruption, all. I know that it's late by ship time, too. I need your help persuading the Commonwealth to come to our aid."

"I've read your reports, Captain," Delacruz said. "I see that our luck hasn't changed."

"It's about to, Commander. We're going to hack the Commonwealth infonets and get our story out there. We'll use the government channels— those will most likely get picked up by news media."

Delacruz didn't look happy. "Are you sure that's wise, Captain? Hacking a government communications network isn't likely to win us any sympathy and may result in some of us being incarcerated."

"I've considered that," Juliana lied. She was operating out of frustration and desperation to avoid letting this mission's success slip through her fingers. "If I have to spend the rest of my life in a Commonwealth penal colony to save the League, I'll do it." She hoped she would be half as brave if that time should come as she was pretending to be now.

"That's noble of you, Captain," Delacruz replied. "But if we lose you and the chance to succeed at our mission—"

"Commander, I appreciate your thoughts on this," Juliana interrupted. "But we lack any access to the levers of power in this society. We don't have unmonitored access to their information nets. Most people don't understand us. And the invasion of the League has been classified as a state secret. Something bolder than politely or insistently asking is required." *Besides, it's what the Old Admiral would do.*

"Understood, Captain." He still looked unhappy, but she knew he was dutiful and loyal. He would not object again—not with others present, anyway.

"Lt. Blackstone, in addition to being our most excellent linguist, you are also a cryptologist."

"I am, sir."

"I want you to work with Lt. Flores on accessing Commonwealth information distribution systems."

"Aye, Captain. What in particular should we prepare to distribute?"

"Multimedia dossier. I will record a short statement and embed supporting materials—star charts, battle reports, whatever else I can think of."

"Understood, Captain."

"Lt. Flores."

"Captain?"

"I take it you have been assessing the relative accessibility of their comms net."

"I have, sir."

"Excellent. Please review the best options for accessing their systems and provide that information to Lt. Blackstone as soon as you can. If at all possible, I would like to release this information tomorrow."

"Understood, sir."

"Thank you all. Hopefully, this will be the way in we've been looking for. Kavanagh out."

She closed the link, sat back, and took a breath. *All right—time to write that statement.*

JULIANA HEARD A BELL chiming in the distance. There were several houses of worship nearby, but this one was ringing actual bells rather than simulated or synth ones. She took a moment to enjoy the peals as they drifted in through her open balcony door.

She had worked through the night, compiling the digital dossier she would send through the Commonwealth's information nets. She had kept Flores and Blackstone up through the night, but it would be worth it. They would finally be able to put their case before the entirety of the Commonwealth and turn up the pressure.

She looked at the folder of files she would enclose—fleet reports, star charts, casualty reports, and digital images of the Invaders salvaged from Makindi's body cam. *Show them the aliens early,* she thought as she ordered the files. *Let them know what they should be afraid of right at the beginning.* She organized the files and indexed them in a directory file. All that was left was to record the message.

She got up and walked over to the wall mirror in her room. She had put on her Class A uniform and made sure every medal was visible, every button polished. She pulled her hair back and put it up in a bun. *The more serious looking, the better.* She tried to think of the expression her father would have adopted for such a statement; she didn't have to think very long: stern and forceful.

She walked back to the desk, picked up her handheld, and propped it up on a shelf in the room. Briefly, she looked for a good backdrop for the recording before remembering she could digitally insert any background she liked. Her handheld chimed, and she made a gesture so that it would project its notification into the air in front of her. It was a message from Lt.

Blackstone: *Captain, here is the translated text of your speech. I have tagged the data with anchors for both our Anglic and theirs, so your handheld should be able to match it to your spoken words easily.*

Excellent work, Lieutenant, she thought. Blackstone had outdone her already stellar reputation with Juliana by helping Flores gain access to the Commonwealth's information systems. Now, with her translation captions, nothing was preventing them from getting their message out.

She stood before her handheld, straightened her uniform and hair one last time, and spoke: "Cue speech text at start. Begin recording and auto-scrolling after a three-second countdown."

A small red light blinked for three seconds and then was steady. The text of her remarks was projected into the air in front of her. She began.

"Peoples of the Commonwealth of Humanity. I am Juliana Kavanagh, Captain of the starship *Deliverance* from the League of Four Worlds. No doubt you have heard that visitors from a 'lost colony' have come to Commonwealth space in recent days. I am one of those visitors and am here to tell you the truth of our story.

"Just over six standard months ago, one of our worlds was attacked by an alien intelligence and destroyed. The bulk of our star fleet, thousands of naval officers, marines, and untold numbers of civilians died in this attack. Our ships' hulls were insufficient to prevent destruction, and our best weapons proved inadequate. In contrast, the alien vessels' hulls were impregnable and their weapons devastating. Our navy's only advantage was its hyperspace drives, which the aliens showed no evidence of having. But our League is small, and their sublight drives are more than enough to put them in our next closest system in five years. There is simply no way that our League, poor as it is, can advance enough in that time to defeat them.

"As a desperate act with no other real options, we came to you, the peoples of the Commonwealth of Humanity. Although we have been out of contact for four centuries, we have always been inspired by the power and the history of the Commonwealth. And though we had long ago stopped hoping that you would follow after us, we never stopped believing in you and what you represent.

"However, our experience with Commonwealth officials has not vindicated our hopes. The CSN has repeatedly deferred and deflected our requests for aid. Government officials have told us that long-standing policies stand in the way of any meaningful aid. They have denied us access to the very channels that we could use to reach out to you.

"The irony is that those policies were enacted because our ancestors went missing. But the Lost Expedition, whose loss gave rise to the Frontier Act, did survive. Those on that expedition found their way to our homeworlds, and now their descendants are the ones who stand in danger of being lost. Please do not allow this to happen. Do not let the children of our Pioneer ancestors perish.

"In this message, I am embedding star charts, tactical reports, first-person accounts from one of our marines, his suit-cam footage, and other materials to help you understand the foe we're facing.

"We pray that you, peoples of the Commonwealth, can come to our aid before it's too late."

She paused for a couple of seconds. "End recording." The red light went off.

She sat back down at the desk and began assembling the video message. Blackstone's caption file synced automatically with her performance. The rest of the file preparation was easy enough, and her handheld took care of everything that wasn't. Nothing would stand in the way of getting her message through now. She established a link with the *Deliverance,* and Delacruz answered from the office in his quarters.

"Captain."

"Commander, is the downlink ready? I have my dossier package queued to transmit."

"It is, Captain." He paused and looked down for a moment before raising his face again. "Look, Juliana. This isn't the way. I know it feels desperate, and there's no reason to think that we won't continue to get rebuffed, but engaging in a serious technology crime that shows the Commonwealth that we cannot, in fact, be trusted is not the way to go."

"Husayn, I understand that. But these are desperate times. We need to break in where they're weakest and exploit whatever advantage we can get."

"Juliana, the Commonwealth isn't a pirate base. They may be misguided and in a state of cultural arrest, but they're not operating outside the law."

"It's the Kavanagh way."

"It's not the *Juliana* Kavanagh way. When I was first appointed to serve as your executive officer, I'll admit, I was nervous—nervous because I didn't want to serve with a Gaius Kavanagh clone. I'd always thought the fleet made too big a deal about the Old Admiral and thought he was the beneficiary of luck as much as he was of thoughtful strategy."

Juliana sat still as her first officer spouted heresies about her esteemed father.

"I was grateful then to learn and remain grateful that you are nothing like him. You're more thoughtful, diplomatic, caring, and—I'll say it—a better captain than he could ever be, especially when it comes to looking out for your crew. I don't want anything to happen to that Juliana Kavanagh. She's the only Kavanagh in this fleet that I admire."

She could feel the tears welling up in her eyes. "There's a cook on the *Essex* who would probably be upset to hear that," she joked in an attempt to deflect. She suddenly felt lost. She needed to do something. She needed to act—if not something bold and decisive, then what?

She looked at the screen hovering in front of her—a red transmit icon floated in the air just to the side of the face of her loyal first officer. Her hand lingered in mid-air as if it, not she, were deciding whether to reach out and press the button.

"Captain! Captain!" came a loud voice at her door, accompanied by thunderous knocking. "Captain! Captain!"

Juliana jumped back with a start.

"What in space is that?" asked Delacruz.

"Just a sec—I'll find out." Juliana got up and opened her door. There, panting almost as if he'd run from somewhere kilometers away, was Jareth Killian.

"Captain!" he said, breathing heavily. "You're not gonna believe this!"

21 | KILLIAN | PROVIDENCE

JARETH RETURNED TO HIS room after dinner with his crewmates in the hotel tavern. He tried to think of a different "way in," as the captain had said, but he was too spent to give it much thought. He hung up his new Earth outfit and was gratified that it was self-cleaning, so it'd be fresh and ready to wear the following morning.

He collapsed on the bed and allowed Earth's one gee to pull him down into the mattress. Before too long, he was sound asleep.

The following day, he got up and walked out onto the balcony of his hotel room. The view over the town was pleasant, and as he took in the landscape, he felt a certain familiarity with this land. Perhaps some cultural element of this Ireland place had survived the transmission over the centuries into his family. Perhaps racial memory. Perhaps it was the odd familiarity, mixed with the strangeness, that many of his crewmates had felt since they had arrived on Earth. After all, their species had evolved on this planet; maybe their bodies knew they were home. Or maybe it was transferred homesickness.

Jareth hadn't considered how homesick he'd been getting. The League seemed so far away. Further now than the Commonwealth had seemed back before they'd left. Their stars could not even be seen in Earth's night sky.

As he looked out over the town, one building in particular caught his eye: a church. It looked vaguely Abrahamic but somehow different. Jareth's parents belonged to an Abrahamic congregation, but he wasn't particularly religious and had never been a regular attendee. Whether it was homesickness or because it was a reminder of his parents, he decided to get dressed and head on over to the church.

He showered and dressed in his new, less conspicuous clothing. Exiting the hotel, he made his way toward the steeple he'd seen. Along the way, people still stared—so, even without the clothing, his off-worlder height still made him stick out in a town that likely didn't see its share of visitors from other planets. He reached the front of the church and read the sign near the entrance: the St. James Tiberius Neo-Christian Church of Ballynameagh. Somewhere in his mind was the knowledge that "Christian" was an old kind of Abrahamic, so it was close enough.

He walked into the sanctuary, filled with flowers of all different kinds, including some fragrant, bright white trumpet-shaped flowers. A service was taking place, so he ducked into a back pew and tried not to look too out of place. He realized that he'd forgotten Rebekah's earbud device—perhaps he'd gotten too used to her doing all the interpreting—and there was little he could understand. But he didn't care; the priest, minister, rabbi, imam, or whatever the person at the front was called had a great energy to her. He liked the way she talked, even if it sounded like gibberish. He could almost meditate while she spoke or the congregation read responses, their strange, incomprehensible language becoming like background noise.

All the feelings he'd been sitting on started to well up in those moments. The grief, the pain, the guilt. He hung his head and felt the tears run down his cheeks and fall to the ancient stone floor below.

Suddenly, words he could actually understand dragged his mind back into active listening. The congregation was reciting an old prayer or liturgy, and he could swear it was in English. He managed to make out a few words: "... *strange new worlds* ... *new life* ... *boldly go where* ... *Amen.*"

Just as soon as it started, his moment of comprehension ended. The remainder of the service was not understandable except for what must have been another ancient prayer that sounded like one from his parents' church. The "holy be your name" language was familiar to him, at any rate.

When the service was over, he got up, feeling slightly more at peace, probably due to the aesthetics of the place. The round-shaped sanctuary reminded him of the Abrahamic churches on New Sydney, and its layout was similar, with its central pulpit and table, the location of the screen at the front, and the semi-circular pews. However, the Abrahamic star was absent—in its familiar place was a vaguely arrowhead shape at the center of which was the T-shaped symbol he recognized from the Abrahamic churches. Even so, it was familiar enough to be comforting.

Members of the congregation exited the main doors, shaking the hand of the pastor as they went. Jareth noticed that most were smiling and nodding, so he adopted that tactic and smiled pleasantly as he gripped the pastor's hand. It spared him having to remember any of the Commonwealth speech Rebekah had tried to teach him.

It was a beautiful day, warm despite the latitude and the early spring date, and it was a pleasant part of town. He spied out a park bench across the street and sat down. Jareth had always loved people-watching back in New Kalgoorlie, and doing it here on a strange planet surrounded by strange people was too much to resist. He had no plans for that day, and they weren't catching their ride back to Bristol until later that evening. His crewmates would be fine without him for a bit.

He watched the people come and go. They moved effortlessly in the higher gravity, though they didn't look graceful—they were too short for that. He tried to imagine where they might be going to or coming from on this sleepy Sunday, trying to imagine a back story for a people he barely knew or understood when a voice over his shoulder knocked him out of his reverie.

"You know, we've been waiting for you a long time, Mr. Killian."

He looked up, and standing next to him was the pastor. "Pardon me?"

She gestured at the park bench, and Jareth nodded, sliding over to make room for her as she sat down.

"Not *you* specifically," she continued, "But one of your number." He was stunned, both at what she was saying and how she was saying it. Her Anglic was exceptional; somehow, she avoided most of the English archaisms that the other interpreters had used, though she spoke with a fascinating, lilting accent.

"I studied English in the seminary so that I could read the scriptures in the original," she said as if anticipating the reasons for his surprise. "And when we learned of your presence on Earth, we made sure that we could talk with you."

"Who's 'we'?" Jareth asked.

"The NCC," she said. "The Neo-Christian Church. I'm sorry; I thought you knew who we were, given that you were in our worship service this morning."

"No—the church just reminded me of my folks' back on New Sydney."

She smiled. "Providence, then." When it was clear he didn't catch her meaning, she waved her hand and continued to explain.

"Ours is a religious communion that believes that God intended for us to explore the universe to its fullest. We believe that our nature is fully known only when we explore and that we are called to the stars. This ridiculous policy of the Commonwealth to close the frontier is against our nature. It is against what we believe God wills for us, and it is killing us."

"Killing you?"

"It is widely known that the Commonwealth's population is shrinking, especially in the core worlds. Earth's population is only sixteen billion."

Only! Jareth marveled. That was twice the population of the entire League!

She continued: "We believe that we are meant to move forward and that failing to do so is causing a stagnation that is sapping our vitality, killing our spirit."

"But what does that have to do with us?"

"We long suspected that the leaders of the Lost Expedition had traveled farther than we went looking. We suspected that they were made of more adventurous, more courageous stuff than most people assumed. We had faith that you were out there somewhere. And that one day, you'd come back and save us."

"Save *you*? We came here hoping you could save *us!*"

She paused a moment and looked at him with surprise. "And what exactly do you need saving from, Mr. Killian?"

And so, he told her. About Farmark, about the refugees traveling by slowboat, about the fear and desperation gripping their systems, about the League's desperate gamble in sending the Expedition back to the Commonwealth, about Trayner's attempt to blow up a shuttle and the conspiracy that destroyed the *Brunswick*, about the League's feelings of abandonment by the Commonwealth and how those feelings had only gotten worse since he and his shipmates had arrived here.

The pastor sat there listening to every word. At times, she stared off as if the information Jareth was dumping on her was too much. When he was done, he sat back and took a few deep breaths as if he had exerted himself in the telling.

"Mr. Killian, you may have come here intending to deliver yourselves by enlisting the might of the Commonwealth—and it is my fervent prayer that you can do just that. But it may turn out that you will end up delivering us in a much more profound way—that you will help to remind us of our fundamental nature and rescue us from our decline. You will help us to reclaim what we were made to be—explorers of the Creation."

Jareth didn't go in much for religious talk, but something about this woman spoke to him. Maybe it was because she was the first Earther who talked like the kind of people they'd come looking for—brave, adventurous, the kind of people they'd given up hope of finding.

"I'm sorry," she said, seeing the expression on his face. "I get excited about this, and preaching is an occupational hazard."

"Believe me, pastor, I understand. I've been hoping to meet someone—anyone—on this planet who felt this way."

"There are many of us who feel that way, Mr. Killian. Not just the NCC, either. Many of us have been waiting for something to organize around. The plight of your League is precisely the kind of thing that may be the catalyst. I belong to an activist network trying to change things, and many leaders in our network will no doubt find this the opportunity to mobilize. I can help you connect with them and get things moving. I think our government will be surprised to discover how many people want things to change."

He shook his head in amazement. How had this happened?

"But if I may say, Mr. Killian," she continued. "It seems you have more on your mind than successfully completing your mission. Forgive me for saying so, but people don't generally weep in my sanctuary over failing to meet mission goals."

That comment stopped Jareth cold. He thought of that square from *Flatland,* who could see his neighbors' insides when kicked up into the third dimension, and Jareth had the chilling thought that to this woman, he was just like those neighbors. But since he was apparently see-through anyway, he might as well come out with it. And so, he told her everything: about the *Cantankerous Vixen,* about the years of listlessness and self-medication, about Ando Lee-Chowdhury, about the overreaction in Sigma Librae, about Makindi's suspicions, about all of it. "I can't shake the sins of my past; all I seem to do is compound them. I thought perhaps I'd get some measure of redemption by being a part of this expedition, but even that is turning out to be a failure. Do you think it's still possible, pastor?"

"From *me*? I can't offer you that. If you want absolution, there's a Catholic church just down the lane."

"No, I mean—" he stopped. He didn't know what he meant.

"Mr. Killian, the only way to find redemption is to lean into the places where you're broken. But you've done nothing but run away from any opportunity for redemption."

Jareth sat up—startled and beginning to take umbrage. "Excuse me? I wouldn't call joining up for a possible one-way trip to nowhere, running away from any opportunity for redemption. It's the whole reason I volunteered for this mission!"

"Mr. Killian, the only way to overcome your past sins is to atone for them by making sure they don't happen again. You were in a situation where your crewmates' lives were in danger in a life-or-death struggle, and you did nothing to help. And so, instead of facing that situation again, you got on a ship and sailed to Tarshish."

Jareth was confused. "Sailed to where?"

"You sailed *nine hundred light-years* away from where you'd experienced a loss. You messed up, Mr. Killian. But then, rather than face that, you ran away. At first, it was into a bottle, then all the way here. You picked a mission that you knew—or *hoped*—wouldn't place you at risk of reliving that mistake: a diplomatic mission where the biggest trouble you might have would be some unruly shipmates and the occasional missing piece of equipment. You experienced something frightening, a terror you hadn't expected, and your inclination was to pull away rather than face it in all its messy complexity." She paused a moment and then burst out laughing. "Oh my God! You're just like—" And then she was lost in a fit of laughter.

At that moment, Jareth didn't know whether to be outraged or dumbstruck. How dare this woman attempt to analyze his motivations and his character after barely an hour's conversation? At the same time, that energy and that quality that he had found so appealing in the first place disarmed him. He beheld this petite red-headed woman in her clergy attire, doubling over with laughter, seemingly free of malice. He began to laugh, too.

He laughed with her at the absurdity; he laughed at his own foolishness. Dammit—this is what his father had meant when he'd said, "Rethink the direction your life is going," hadn't he? He hadn't meant a metaphorical direction, well, not a metaphorical direction *only*. He'd been telling Jareth that he was running away from his problems, and Jareth had been too dense to understand.

Slowly, his laughter changed to weeping, and he broke down. The pastor inched closer and put her arm around him as he began to convulse from his sobs. She held him tightly as every muscle in his body surrendered to the grief of realizing the futility of his actions. All this time, he'd convinced himself he was daring, an explorer, a *pioneer* when he'd really been a fugitive.

He took a deep breath and straightened up.

"I, uh, wasn't expecting that," he said, wiping stray tears from his cheeks.

"Self-awareness can have that effect on us."

"I'm such a fool."

"Fer lovin' ter yerself!?" the pastor cried, her enchanting accent growing alongside her incredulity. "Mr. Killian, welcome to Earth—the homeworld of the human race! Come join us in being human!"

Jareth turned to stare at her. "Pastor, how is it that I should find my way back to my ancestral home, a small town in the middle of an island I'd never even heard of, and find the one person who can help our League—and maybe even me—completely by accident?"

She said nothing but smiled a knowing and patient smile.

"I'm sorry, pastor—I never even got your name," he said at last.

"It's Myra. Myra Killian. I'm guessing we're thirteenth cousins."

"YOU'RE KIDDING ME," Captain Kavanagh said to Jareth once he'd explained why he'd banged so loudly on her room door. "What are the odds?"

"I know," he said. There are so many people on this planet—I never thought I'd run into someone I was related to."

"Do you think she'll be able to do anything?"

Jareth didn't know what to say. It all seemed so unlikely. They had all come to the Commonwealth, imagining that as soon as contact had been made, the CSN would muster to their aid, and ships would be summoned from far and wide from all over human space to respond to their distress. And then reality came crashing in. The ones they imagined would rise to the occasion seemed the most reluctant to get involved. And then here, in the middle of this out-of-the-way town, was a woman committed to doing whatever it took to ensure their people were helped. His cousin Myra. What was he to think of that?

"I don't know, Captain," he replied at last. "I understand these people so little. Myra is the first one we've met who sounded like the kind of people we'd gone looking for. Perhaps it's too much to hope that she can help us do anything."

"No," the captain said. "I don't think it's too much to hope. Hope is a more powerful ally than we sometimes give it credit for being." She paused and turned, looking back into her room and calling out in the direction of her handheld. "Commander Delacruz, I have decided to take your recommendation. You can sever the downlink at any time."

"Understood, Captain," came Delacruz's voice from within the room. "I am gratified to hear that, and I look forward to getting a debrief later. Delacruz out."

When the captain turned back toward Jareth, he gave her an inquisitive look.

"Is everything okay, Captain?"

"Everything is just perfect, Lieutenant."

A FEW DAYS LATER, after returning to Bristol, Jareth and Captain Kavanagh met with Myra for an update. She listed some groups that had already responded to a summons for action. Jareth was stunned to discover that Myra had not been kidding when she said a whole network of people was sympathetic to the League's cause—groups from around the planet, around the system, and ultimately around the Commonwealth were lending their support.

"Well, of course, our denomination—the NCC—is on board, as it is a central tenet of our faith. But we've also got the Unitarian Universalists, the

New Mission Church, the Union of Israelite Congregations, the ibn-Rushd Islamic Union, the Ethical Union, and, of course, the Methodists."

Jareth and the captain exchanged a look—neither of them got the significance of that.

"There is some encouraging news from the Vatican and from Tibet, too, so we'll probably be getting messages from those faiths as well. But we've also gotten statements from the British Academy, the Moscow Aerospace Consortium, the National Geographic Society, and several other organizations as well. In addition, some of the more local political entities have already begun taking positions on the matter. The European Consuls have issued a statement calling on the Parliament and the Navy to act. The North American President has made a similar statement, as has the South Asian Prime Minister, the East Asian Chair'man, and the Arabian Ra'is. The Martian Congress and the Belters Union will likely pass support resolutions sometime this week. Word is only just now beginning to come in from some of the neighboring systems, but it appears that the Colonial League of New Damascus and the New Parisian Confederation may be instructing their representatives in the Parliament to sponsor enabling legislation to provide for your relief. As systems at the forefront of human settlement beyond Sol, their opinions carry a lot of weight. It's an important symbolic statement. The politics are a little more complex on Earth itself, but I expect the United Nations will also instruct Senator Isfahani to co-sponsor such a measure."

"Reverend Killian," the captain began.

"Myra."

"Myra—we don't know what to say. When our chancellor sent us to find you, we had in mind the vaunted Navy about which we had read so much in our histories. When that approach seemed to fail, we could not imagine how else we might get help. I don't know how to begin to thank you."

"Captain Kavanagh, our Navy is following long-established policies that date back centuries. On some level, the Navy had little choice but to respond as they did. But I think you underestimate just how much our people have been longing for something to call us outside ourselves. For something to awaken that spirit that had once made us great. From time to time, someone would propose lifting the ban and beginning explorations—probes to the core, to the Magellanic Clouds, or something. And every time, someone would object: it's too expensive, it's not worth the effort, we have problems at home, and so on. And every time, a little part of us died. We were being boxed in by our own fear. However, eventually, it becomes exhausting to live in fear, looking only inward, never outward. People weary of fear. After a while, courage can become a much sought-after commodity."

At last, Jareth understood just how weary he'd become of his own fear. Before too long, he would have to do something about it.

22 | KAVANAGH | DELIVERING THE COMMONWEALTH

JULIANA STOOD IN THE observation deck atop the sensor tower projecting from the "top" or "skyward" side of the ship aft. It was the only place on the vessel with genuine windows. The deck was often used for ceremonial or recreational functions since the transparent ceramic of the walls gave attendees a breathtaking view of the cosmos.

She stood on the observation deck alone, gazing at the blue and white marble turning slowly beneath them. She knew that despite the planet's pacific appearance from orbit, it was a hive of intense activity and action to a degree that had stunned her and exceeded even her wildest dreams.

Killian's cousin Myra's hope turned out to be more than just wishful thinking. By the end of the following week, practically every major political subdivision on Earth and each of the five founding worlds of the Commonwealth had lent their support to providing military, technological, and economic aid to the League. Senator Isfahani introduced the Rescue and Assistance Act to the Commonwealth Parliament, and it was passed without delay. A week later, he would introduce a measure to repeal the Frontier Act. It was hard to process just how much had changed—how drastically their failure had turned into success.

Perhaps the strangest of all was how much the Commonwealth itself seemed to have changed. In demeanor, institutional culture, and attitude, everything seemed to shift all at once. It struck her that it was like young people at a school dance; they all wanted to dance, but everyone was afraid to be the first out on the floor. It always took a critical mass of the willing before the party would truly get started.

It had never occurred to her that she and her crew, as broken and hurting as they were, could ever have served as the means of deliverance for anyone else. And yet, somehow, their crippled, bleeding League had become the spark that had reinvigorated the mighty Commonwealth.

She heard footsteps on the decking behind her.

"Yes, Commander? What can I do for you?"

"How did you know it was me?" Delacruz asked.

"You're the only one with the guts to interrupt me when I'm in my stargazing time," Juliana said, turning to her first officer.

"It's beautiful, isn't it?" he said, nodding toward the planet below.

Juliana turned back to the window. "Gets more beautiful all the time."

Delacruz stood alongside her and joined in the quiet appreciation of the view. They stood for a moment in companionable silence before Juliana spoke again.

"I'm gratified that everything has worked out, but I can't help but feel I was just a spectator to it all. I am sure Command will be happy with the result, but it's hard to say I had anything to do with it. It feels an awful lot like dumb luck."

Delacruz turned sharply to look at his commanding officer.

"It was nothing of the kind, Juliana," he said with enough scolding in his voice that Juliana turned with astonishment to face her XO. He shook his head with exaggerated frustration and continued.

"*You* put this crew together. You got them through the catastrophe of the *Brunswick's* doom and turned a survivor of that tragedy into one of the most valuable members of our team. And yes, I am sure that Flores could have figured out a way to communicate—hell, *you* came up with the semaphore and hoist flag ideas—but *you* tapped the person who made it possible to *talk* with the Commonwealth.

"*You* made Killian your security chief, and *you* gave the crew the evening off that gave him the opportunity to learn how to save some of the crew of the *Brunswick*—including Lt. Blackstone. *You* included him in your shore parties, and it wound up being the personal connection that he made that led to everything that's happened since. But most of all, *you* didn't give up, and you inspired your crew not to either. That had *everything* to do with you, Juliana. *That's* the *Kavanagh way.*"

She looked over this man she'd known for so many years and remembered why she'd picked him as her number one. He was the only one in her interviews who'd told her the truth and hadn't been dazzled by the glory by association her last name offered. She shook her head slowly, marveling that she should have lucked out to have such a first officer. But then again, *she* picked him, didn't she?

"Did you come up here for any other reason than to offer a needed corrective to your commanding officer?" she said at last.

"Yes, Captain. We've received orders to report to the San Francisco Navy Yards in high Earth orbit for refits and upgrades. They're going to give us advanced Long Radar systems, upgrades to the hyperdrive, and higher-yield torpedoes, among some other tweaks."

"Well then, Commander. We should get a move on," she said, placing her hand on her exec's shoulder and guiding them toward the passageway to the rest of the ship. "We definitely don't want to be late for that."

Over the coming weeks, both ship and crew received restoration and renewal. The news of the Commonwealth rallying to the League's side caused waves of euphoria to pass through the crew, and many took the opportunity to celebrate with their long-lost Commonwealth cousins.

Wherever *Deliverance* personnel went on Earth for shore leave, they were welcomed, celebrated, and fêted as much as they could take. They had gone from being a curiosity or a cause for suspicion to a *cause célèbre*. Juliana was invited to meet with presidents and prime ministers, the UN Secretary-General, UN General Assembly and Commonwealth Parliament members, and the Presiding Chancellor of the Commonwealth itself. She and Killian even received honorary Irish citizenship from the Irish Taoiseach.

Some of the crew reveled in it—Juliana didn't think there was a microphone put in front of Filipov-Ibañez that he didn't gladly talk into. Others retreated after a few days to the quiet of their hotel or quarters aboard ship. Some got inebriated and caused some trouble on the surface, but the local authorities had generally been forgiving. All the same, Juliana made sure that Lt. Killian had all their names for his records.

After a month, the *Deliverance* had received its upgrades, the Commonwealth Star Navy had begun to muster ships to gather at New St. Louis, and the crew had had their fill of rest and recuperation on Earth; they were itching to get home and fight for Farmark.

BEFORE THEY KNEW IT, the *Deliverance* and its Commonwealth escort were back in the Sharon system. The return voyage had flown by, buoyed by a resurgence in hope and the company of their new allies. The Commonwealth had sent a dozen of its warships on the expedition, along with supply ships, cargo ships, and construction ships whose mission it was to build space stations along the way so that future trips between the Commonwealth and the League wouldn't have to go through such desolate regions without the possibility of aid.

When the combined fleet's vessels neared New Sydney orbit, they saw that a flotilla of ISG and civilian craft had come out to welcome them.

Their comms traffic was overwhelmed by messages of greeting and celebration, along with messages of condolence for their lost colleagues on the *Brunswick*.

If Juliana had wanted to, she doubted she could have overestimated the impact their arrival had on the people of the League. Satellite and perimeter station images of CSN vessels dropping out of hyperspace alongside the *Deliverance* had gone viral throughout the worlds of the League. The lead story that day for one prominent news feed was simply an image of the fleet with a headline that read, "YES!!!"

As the *Deliverance* entered orbit, a hail came in from ISG command. "*Deliverance,* this is ISG command; come in."

"ISG Command, this is *Deliverance* actual," Juliana responded. "We read you."

"Welcome home, Captain. We are so glad to see you—and your new friends."

"We are happy to be home, Command. It's been a long road, with a fair amount of loss."

"Understood, *Deliverance*. The Chancellor would like to meet with you and your officers at your earliest possibility."

"Copy that, Command. We will prepare to be planetside within the hour. *Deliverance* actual, out."

Juliana rose from her seat. "Shall we? Mr. Hannover, you have the conn."

Commander Delacruz, Lt. Commander Filipov-Ibañez, and Lt. Killian rose to follow her out. They met up with Lt. Blackstone and Master Gunnery Sergeant Makindi in the shuttle bay and headed to the planet below.

Juliana and her landing party arrived at the Chancellery and were directed to the Chancellor's office suite. Once there, an aide took them into an adjacent conference room. Chancellor Parvat-Singh sat at the end of a long conference table, wearing the colorful wrap-around clothing traditional to Farmark. As the *Deliverance* crew walked into the room, she stood to greet them.

"Captain Kavanagh, please, you and your crew, do come in," the Chancellor said.

The six of them entered the room and took seats along the table, Juliana sitting opposite the Chancellor, who continued: "I cannot begin to describe the debt the citizens of the League owe you and your crew, Captain. What you have done . . . ."

"What we have done, Madame Chancellor, was only our duty. In many ways, we failed to do what we had set out to do. Our initial strategies did not bear fruit; it was the people of the Commonwealth who rose to our aid and obliterated the roadblocks the Commonwealth government had put up."

"A warning for anyone in office, eh?" said the Chancellor, smiling. "But I am afraid your modesty cannot hide the fact that your advocacy for the people of the League was unfailing. You may not have felt yourself effective, but I can tell you that what you did made a difference. I have read your reports and listened to the accounts of the Commonwealth diplomats who followed you here. They paint a formidable portrait of you, Captain. And of your crew." She nodded to the rest of them.

"Thank you, Madame Chancellor. I was surrounded by excellent people who worked hard, made our case well, and were tireless in resolving the situation. And we had a fair amount of luck, all things told."

"Yes, so I read! Your encounter with your distant relative, Mr. Killian, was a wonderful stroke of luck that turned the tide."

Killian smiled and nodded, looking a little overwhelmed—perhaps by the fact that the Chancellor had known his name. "Yes, Madame Chancellor," was all he said in the end.

The Chancellor continued. "Of course, the only difference between luck and fate is the interpretation you put on the story. Perhaps, Captain, it was your destiny to lead this mission."

Juliana was more inclined to believe in chance than destiny, but she had to admit that it was difficult to distinguish between chance and fate when all you had was the view behind you.

"In any event, Captain Kavanagh, in recognition of your actions in service of the League, in bringing us our cousins from the Commonwealth, giving us not only the best chance we have to defend our worlds but the hope that we can do just that—I am awarding you and the crew of the *Deliverance* the Three Stars. Captain Brevi and the crew of the *Brunswick* will be awarded the same honor posthumously."

It was not the highest military honor, but it was a high honor and certainly more than any of them had expected. Juliana opened her mouth to speak, but the chancellor cut her off.

"Wait a moment, Captain. Before you say anything, there is more. I am promoting you to the rank of rear admiral. You shall have the honor of commanding the fleet that will liberate the Kittim system and retake Farmark."

"Madame Chancellor . . . I don't know what to say."

"Your service to the League has already spoken more than enough, Admiral. Commander Delacruz," she said, turning to her first officer.

"Yes, Madame Chancellor," he replied, now more than a little flustered at what might be in store for him.

"Commander Delacruz, I am promoting you captain of the *Deliverance*, which, I assume, Admiral Kavanagh, will be where you'll want to place your flag."

Juliana turned to look at the man who had, until just moments before, been her executive officer and second-in-command. They shared a brief look, the kind that two people so used to working with each other can share, communicating volumes of information in a split second. She turned back toward the chancellor. "Madame Chancellor, I can think of no ship more appropriate for my flag than the *Deliverance*, no captain whom I'd rather have as her master than Captain Delacruz."

"Then it's settled," said the Chancellor proudly. "Congratulations to both of you." She rose from the table, and they all did likewise. She walked to their side of the room and extended her hand first to Juliana and then to Captain Delacruz, each of whom received her hand gladly.

"Admiral Kavanagh, I leave it to you to pick which of our ISG ships will be a part of your task force and to coordinate with the Commonwealth Navy vessels. I hope you appreciate just how much confidence I have in your leadership. Whatever the result, I know we will have put our best and brightest where they were needed most."

It was unlike Juliana Kavanagh to be speechless or at a loss for words. But she discovered that when the leader of your civilization showered you with praise, it was hard not to be taken somewhat off guard by it.

THE SIX CREWMATES WERE shown to a small side room where some food and drink had been set aside for them. The chancellor's staff seemed to understand that they might all need somewhere to process what had just happened before returning to the busyness of starship life. Juliana, for one, was happy for the opportunity and, given that she never could eat before an important meeting, was famished.

"Congratulations, Captain, I mean, *Admiral*," Killian said.

"Thank you, Lieutenant," Juliana replied. "That's going to take some getting used to."

"Well, it suits you, sir," he said and turned to join Blackstone in conversation.

"He's right," said Delacruz, walking up with two flutes of sparkling wine in his hand; he handed her one.

She gratefully took the glass from him, clinked his, and took a long, slow sip. "Oh, that's nice."

"The best that Fairhaven has to offer."

She looked around at the officers and the marine who'd been the core of her landing parties and diplomatic efforts. They all seemed to enjoy the spread the chancellor's office had put out for them. Even Makindi seemed relaxed—well, relaxed for Makindi. "I'm glad they are getting to share in this moment, too."

"You put together a good crew, Juliana. You should be proud."

She downed the rest of her sparkling wine and put her small plate of hors d'oeuvres down on a nearby table. "Come with me, Captain. There's one last piece of business to do."

She walked toward the other crew members. "Everyone, if I could have a couple minutes of your time."

The four of them stopped and turned toward her.

"Admiral," Filipov-Ibañez said, nodding as the rest of them burst into applause.

"Thank you. I mean it. Thank you. Each of you had a role to play in bringing us to this day. And though there remains a lot of work to be done before our goal of liberating Farmark is achieved, it is appropriate that we mark this moment, and I share with you just how grateful I am."

There was a murmur of gratitude and mutual appreciation for her.

"One of the privileges of being a flag officer, especially in wartime, is that I can make field promotions. Lt. Commander Filipov-Ibañez, I am hereby promoting you to commander. For the help you gave to me—and the brilliant idea you had when we were working out battle plans with our Commonwealth allies—you have more than earned the rank of commander. Congratulations."

Filipov-Ibañez was visibly stunned—Juliana didn't remember ever having seen him at a loss for words. He became even more flummoxed when Captain Delacruz stepped forward. "And while we'll need you at tactical for the coming engagement, I intend you to be in that position as my first officer."

Killian, Blackstone, and Makindi joined Juliana and Delacruz in applauding Filipov-Ibañez's promotion as he reddened thoroughly.

Juliana promoted Blackstone to lieutenant commander and Killian to lieutenant, senior grade. When she got to Makindi, he cut her off.

"Captain, I am grateful for the sentiment, but I am already at the highest enlisted rank in the Corps. If you were to promote me, then I would be an officer, and well, sir—I'm used to working for a living."

Juliana burst out laughing, and everyone else laughed, too. Even Makindi allowed a small expression of amusement to cross his face.

"There's one more thing," Juliana added. "I am not sure the recipient will be as grateful to receive this as the last award. Lt. Killian, I am going to assign you command of the boarding action against the alien flagship during the execution of our battle plan."

Killian looked visibly stunned, and—Juliana noted—Makindi did not look pleased, casting a sidelong glance at the newly promoted lieutenant. *Still need to sort that one out, I guess.*

"Thank you, Admiral. It is an honor," Killian said, though she could tell he was receiving this news with mixed emotions.

"Excellent. Thank you all again. Feel free to linger here as long as you like. In fact, I'm giving you liberty for the next two days. Do with it as you will. Captain Delacruz, shall we return to our ship?"

"We shall, Admiral."

Juliana and Delacruz left the room to return to the *Deliverance,* but not before she noted that Lt. Killian said a hasty goodbye to Lt. Commander Blackstone before ducking out of the room via a side door. *Ball's in your court, Lieutenant.*

THE FOLLOWING MONTHS WERE spent in rigorous training, fleet exercises, and integrating various command and control structures. The League's Commonwealth cousins graciously allowed Juliana to set the tone and help shape the strategy. While she assumed they did so because the League was the Admiral's home turf, many of her officers suspected it was because the Commonwealth had had so little experience in being daring that they were happy to receive tutelage from their frontier colleagues.

One of the great conveniences of placing her flag on the *Deliverance* was that she didn't have to move. The walls of her office in her quarters were familiar to her, providing much-needed continuity at a time when everything was changing. Now, at the close of all the fleet's preparations, it was her sanctuary—a place where she could review battle plans, requisition reports, personnel rosters, and spy-drone sensor data in relative quiet compared to the fleet offices in the Novaroma Orbital Facility.

The door to the office chimed. Juliana smiled; she had a pretty good idea who this was going to be.

"Enter."

The hatch slid open to reveal Killian and Makindi standing outside. *Well, now. Both of them.*

"Come in, Lieutenant. Master Gunnery Sergeant."

The two men entered together, betraying the deep unease that each had with the other. *So, they hadn't decided to come together—they'd happened to show up at the same time. This should be interesting.*

"Admiral," Killian began and then immediately turned toward Makindi. "Don't worry, Master Gunnery Sergeant. I have a feeling that what I am here to talk about will cover your concerns as well." Makindi gave Killian a curious look, bordering on surprise. But given the marine's customary stoic expression, such signs were always subtle.

Killian turned back toward Juliana and continued.

"I wish to discuss Petty Officer Ando Lee-Chowdhury."

"What about him, Lt. Killian?"

"I am responsible for his death. Had I not sent him to the *Brunswick,* he would be alive today."

"You didn't send him to the *Brunswick*, Lieutenant. I did."

"Yes, Admiral. But I made the recommendation."

"A recommendation that I didn't even have time to offer the poor petty officer before he *asked* to be transferred."

Killian's eyes grew wide. "What? How—"

Juliana raised a hand to cut him off. "I saw your recommendation. I hadn't made up my mind about whether I would offer it to Mr. Lee-Chowdhury as part of his NJD. But when I interviewed him, he was the one who offered it as a condition he would be willing to accept. He thought too many conspiracy theories were running rampant on the *Deliverance* and had lost respect for several of his crewmates. Poor kid jumped from the frying pan right into the fire."

Killian looked flummoxed—a mix of relief and something else, consternation? Makindi was eyeing the lieutenant carefully as if to see where he would go next.

Killian straightened himself up. "Nevertheless, Admiral. My motivations were not honorable. I feared the petty officer would figure out my connection to his brother's death aboard the *Cantankerous Vixen*." Now Killian really had Makindi's attention, and the marine narrowed his eyes as he considered his superior officer.

"When I was serving as Security Chief aboard the *Vixen*, we were raided by pirates—Red Blade, the same faction your father destroyed. I heard the pirates come into the hold, tossing things around, destroying property, seizing cargo, and terrorizing the crew. I was in an adjoining compartment the entire time, and I froze. I did nothing. The pirates made off with millions of credits worth of cargo and left Kian Lee-Chowdhury—Petty Officer Lee-Chowdhury's brother—so badly injured that he later died of those injuries." He paused a moment to gather himself. His expression bore all the hallmarks of the simultaneous pain and relief of catharsis.

"I was so desperate to cover this shame that I tried to move Lee-Chowdhury to another ship so that he couldn't expose me as the fraud and coward that I was." He wiped a tear from his cheek. "I am extremely grateful that you have tapped me to lead the boarding action in the upcoming battle, but I am not worthy of the assignment. I'm sorry."

Juliana noticed that the look on Makindi's face had changed altogether. Where it had once borne suspicion and distrust, it now reflected only understanding and compassion.

She turned and looked intently at her security chief, and a smile began to creep across her face.

"Lieutenant, may I ask you a question?"

"Yes, Admiral."

"Do you genuinely think I would have approved you for the position of Chief of Security if I had not thoroughly checked your background and learned everything there was to know about you?"

She could tell that Killian was floored. That was good—having her officers think she was omniscient only worked to instill her authority and make the present conversation easier.

"But," he stammered. "It's not in the records. I—"

"You're right. It's not in the records. The records are never a complete reflection of the individual. That's why I called Captains Mfese and Bloch myself. Mfese—who's quite fond of you—told me all about what happened on the *Vixen*. He told me why he filed the report the way he did—he saw potential in you, not just for the Merchant Marine but for the ISG. He told me that, but for that incident and the politics involved, you might have your own command by now."

Killian was speechless. She got up from behind her desk and walked over to where the dumbfounded lieutenant was standing. He was still in stunned disbelief; she could tell it was a mix of shame that he'd been hiding something from her she'd known the whole time and relief that it was finally out in the open. She put a hand on his shoulder and bade him look her in the eyes.

"I know you thought you could work yourself out of your past. I am sure you thought that if you just did everything right on this mission, that would somehow make up for the mistakes you made before. But that's not how it works. If you want absolution, you'll have to start by forgiving yourself, Lieutenant. It's not going to come from any other quarter."

"Yes, sir," was all he could manage.

"I agreed to your appointment aboard the *Deliverance* not because I thought you were perfect, but because I like taking on rehabilitation projects, and I thought you were *perfectible*. But that perfectibility could not be attained by trying to outdo your mistakes. Stopping Rishard Trayner, triggering the *Brunswick's* evacuation alarm, even finding your cousin Myra can't erase your past. You could only begin to move down the road toward becoming better by owning your past and living with your mistakes. And in my estimation, coming in here to self-report when doing so might have cost you everything—well, I think that's a good start."

She patted Killian on the shoulder and turned back to her desk, retaking her seat. "So, tell me, Lieutenant—do you still want command of the Farmark boarding action?"

"Sir! Yes, sir!" Killian replied, snapping to attention with what appeared to be a growing sense of relief.

"Master Gunnery Sergeant, are you comfortable with Lt. Killian's command in the coming operation?"

Makindi regarded Killian, and Juliana could tell that the man was looking at his superior officer differently than he had even a few minutes ago. "Aye, Admiral," he replied. "I can serve with an officer who's messed up. I can't serve with an officer who's messed up and won't admit it. We all make mistakes, we all have losses we regret, we all have names of fallen comrades on our watch that come to us in the night. We can't let that stop us. If the lieutenant is comfortable with me as his senior enlisted leader with my record, I have no problems with the lieutenant as my commanding officer."

Makindi turned, faced Killian, and extended his hand. Killian took Makindi's hand and shook it firmly. As he did so, he reached out with his left hand to the marine's upper arm in a further embrace and nodded his appreciation and respect.

"Excellent!" Juliana said. She rose from behind her desk, and the two men came to attention. "I am grateful to you both. You represent the best of what the ISG aspires to be."

"Thank you, Admiral," they both said.

"Now, gentlemen, what do you say? Shall we get about the work of liberating the Kittim system?"

"Sir! Yes, sir!" they responded again in unison.

"Then get to it."

Both Killian and Makindi saluted and then turned and exited.

Juliana watched the hatch shut behind them and smiled to herself. *Let's see the Old Admiral do that.*

She sat back down at her desk and keyed a button on her flexdisplay. Lt. Flores's voice came through the speaker: "Admiral?"

"Send a notification out fleet-wide. The task force will muster at the Sharon–Kittim jump point in 72 hours. It's time to go liberate Farmark."

23 | KAVANAGH | FARMARK

THE FLEET JUMPED OUT of hyperspace as close to Farmark as possible, and Juliana breathed a sigh of relief. Leaguers weren't used to jumping in so far downsystem, but using some of the Commonwealth's technology had paid off.

"Filipov-Ibañez, anything on the LR?" Captain Delacruz asked.

"Scanning—Yes, there are seven bogies in orbit around Farmark. Hull configuration matches earlier tactical reports of Invader vessels. They appear to be the only other vessels in the system." They had hoped as much. Reports from the first battle of Farmark had indicated seven ships, and everyone was glad to see no others had joined them in the interim.

"Any signals from Farmark?" Juliana asked.

"None, Admiral," Flores responded.

Captain Delacruz turned to his tactical officer. "Mr. Filipov-Ibañez, sit rep."

"Aye, Captain," he responded. "All twenty-one vessels have down-jumped. Interference has abated, and telemetry is coming in. Ship transponders are online, and all vessels are in formation. Weapons are coming online; backup generators are on standby. We are at condition red, battle stations."

Juliana rose from her chair and turned to face her former first officer. "Captain, with your permission," she said.

"Of course, Admiral."

She turned to the communications officer. "Lt. Flores, signal the *Excalibur* to begin her approach. Second-rank vessels begin creating a perimeter; we don't want these bastards to get away. All other vessels into formation Alpha."

"Aye, Admiral."

Upon the admiral's signal, the task force began its maneuvers. The *Excalibur* fired up its fusion engines and accelerated toward Farmark as the rest of the fleet fell into formation. Everyone watched on the LR as the *Excalibur* picked up velocity. It did not appear that the Invader vessels had even noticed its approach or that of the fleet, for that matter.

"Doesn't look like they have LR," Delacruz said.

"If they don't have hyperspace engines, chances of that are good," Juliana replied.

"The light lag is still significant; they might not even have seen us yet," Delacruz said. As the Excalibur neared its target, the LR began to show movement among the alien vessels.

"Bogies are breaking formation and moving to engage, Admiral," Filipov-Ibañez reported. The shapes on the LR screen showed two vessels heading to intercept the *Excalibur* while the remainder began to fan out behind.

"Flores," Juliana said, "Put fleet-wide comm on speaker."

"Aye, Captain. FleetCom on speaker." The overhead speakers began to relay the signals from the *Excalibur's* bridge.

At once, Captain Mehta-Valdez's voice filled the bridge. *"Helm, hard to port, increase to point five, fire starboard batteries."* The blip on the screen veered to the left. The two bogeys remained in pursuit.

"Fleet, this is *Excalibur*. Nuclear and particle weapons show no effect as predicted. Increasing speed to point seven. Alien vessels in pursuit."

"Flores, signal the *Zamyatin* and the *Niven* to begin their approaches." On the screen, the next two League ships began to engage. They employed the same tactic, flying in on a parabolic curve, banking hard—this time to starboard—and unleashing their port-side batteries. Everyone watched as three alien vessels began to pursue the two League ships.

"Admiral," called Filipov-Ibañez. "Two alien vessels remain in orbit, one on the far side of the planet and the one from the nearside that did not engage the *Zamyatin* and *Niven*."

"Are you thinking that our straggler is the command ship?"

"Yes, Admiral, that was my thinking."

"Only one way to find out. Flores, signal the *Čapek* to begin her run." The fourth League vessel began to make her way downsystem. It angled around Farmark and went toward the one vessel on the far side of the planet. The *Čapek* attacked and veered, and the sixth vessel pursued. There was one vessel left in orbit.

"I think you're right, Mr. Filipov-Ibañez. That's our target. Fleet-wide channel, Ms. Flores."

"Fleet-wide channel, Admiral."

"This is Admiral Kavanagh to all vessels in the fleet: synchronize ships' chronometers using time stamp embedded in this message and adjusting for relativistic distortions. At T-plus 90, initiate attack pattern Echo-1-3. Mark."

The chronometer ticked down toward the execution time, and everyone on the bridge held their breaths. Nothing like this had ever been tried in the history of space warfare. The fact that the Commonwealth had sworn by the technology that made it possible did nothing to ease anyone's nerves. The jump this far downsystem had already been harrowing enough.

Juliana stood up, and Captain Delacruz followed. "Give me a three-dee tactical," she called out. The computer moved the flat tactical display from the forward bulkhead flexdisplay to a holo-projected image floating at the center of the bridge. In the center of the display was a sphere representing Farmark, surrounded by tiny representations of each vessel. Each vessel trailed a line showing its flight path and followed a dotted line emerging from its bow, indicating its computed trajectory. Commonwealth and League vessels were coded blue, and alien vessels were coded red.

The countdown clock neared zero: *five, four, three, two, one*—then, in an instant, the blips of light that had represented the *Riyadh, Berlin, Babylon, Al-Wadi, Tianjin, Beijing,* and *Jakarta* all disappeared. Just as suddenly, those blips reappeared in the projection *behind* the pursuing alien vessels. Juliana knew that jumping this close to a planetary body was theoretically possible, but she couldn't have believed it was achievable with such precision. She was gratified to see the Commonwealthers had been right about what their ships could do; their ships had performed admirably. But that was just the first stage: the next part was the part they were risking everything on.

BEFORE THE FLEET LEFT Commonwealth space, *Deliverance* personnel met with Commonwealth Navy officials to devise a strategy for engaging the aliens at Farmark. These meetings were made easier by Lt. Commander Blackstone's translation earpieces, which had become all the rage. The CSN machine shops produced as many of them as needed. Juliana was proud to own a pair of "first edition" earpieces, even if they didn't look as stylish as the ones the CSN was churning out.

The CSN had been willing to offer many defensive technologies and several improvements to drive efficiency. But all the intel the ISG had received from the first battle of Farmark had shown how impenetrable the alien hulls had been. As the *Deliverance* personnel reminded their CSN hosts, it wasn't defensive technology that was their greatest need—it was offense. Nuclear, particle, and laser weapons had all failed to make a dent. League scientists had speculated the alien hulls were made of some kind of neutronium—incredibly thin but incredibly dense, and their Commonwealth counterparts tended to agree.

In one such strategy meeting, Killian and Filipov-Ibañez had been pressing the matter of offensive weapons when the point about neutronium was raised again.

Finally, Filipov-Ibañez said, "It's still matter. And matter doesn't get along with antimatter."

"A matter–antimatter warhead isn't likely to make much more of a dent, Commander," replied Admiral Xu of the Commonwealth Navy and director of Naval Weapons Research. "Given the density of neutronium, most of the blast will bounce off the vessel. A blast might *push* the alien vessel to one side, but the chances of it penetrating the hull are next to zero. We've discussed this before, if you'll recall."

"No, I mean, what if we just fired raw antimatter at them? I don't care what their ships are made of—if it's matter, it's going to react with antimatter, yes?"

Everyone was in disbelief. No one had ever thought of hurling raw antimatter at an enemy—it was just too volatile and, for the League, too valuable. Juliana was confident the League would never have devised this idea as a practical strategy, maybe not even as a desperate one. Perhaps Filipov-Ibañez could conceive of it only after seeing how antimatter-rich the Commonwealth had been.

Xu had been dubious. "Son, there are several problems with that idea. What kind of delivery mechanism would we use? How would we prevent stray chunks of antimatter from hitting friendly vessels? Or, for that matter, falling into Farmark and reacting with the atmosphere or the surface, releasing deadly gamma rays with every reaction?"

Filipov-Ibañez was unfazed. He sat for a moment and then said, "Why don't we use something like the mag accelerators for a suborbital? Hold the antimatter in magnetic suspension—we do that all the time—and then fire it out of a magnetic gun—antimatter bullets. What if the mechanism we used to extract it just accelerated it away from the storage container?"

Juliana leaned in. "And we do so at point-blank range."

Admiral Xu frowned. "Point-blank? I don't understand—what are you proposing?"

Juliana continued. "In the first battle of Farmark, the opposing fleets barely came into visual contact. That was hardly surprising: modern space battles are complex mathematical computations of enemy ship vectors and missile trajectories. Particle and energy beams are targeted where the enemy vessel *will* be, as opposed to where it is. But remember your naval history, Admiral—it hasn't always been that way. In the naval battles of Old Earth, ships would pull up alongside one another and fire their primitive gunpowder cannons right into the enemy vessel's sides."

Killian began to laugh.

"Lieutenant?" Juliana said, turning to look at her security chief.

"Begging your pardon, Captain. It's just that your interest in ancient naval history has predisposed you to think about this as a military solution. I can say with certainty that it would never have occurred to the rest of us."

Juliana shrugged, smiled, and turned back to the admiral.

"A broadside, Admiral. Pull right up alongside the enemy vessels and let them have it from all batteries."

"A point-blank broadside," Admiral Xu considered, albeit skeptically. "From what you've said, your ships didn't last very long even at standard engagement range. How do you expect to get close enough to even begin to use this weapon—assuming we build it?"

Commander Nina Hjálmarsdottir of the Commonwealth Naval Engineers spoke up. "Micro-jumps. Jump into the system and assess the tactical situation. Then jump into close proximity using micro-jumps."

"Our ships aren't capable of micro-jumps, even with the technology upgrades you'll give us," Juliana replied.

"But some of ours are, Captain," Commander Hjálmarsdottir offered. "And we have shielding that can withstand the gamma-ray bursts. Use your ships to draw the aliens out. Launch a conventional barrage. Get them to pursue you away from the planet. Then, have our ships jump in behind them and unleash the antimatter barrage. This will also prevent the planet from getting caught in the crossfire."

They all sat back, considering this. After a few moments, they looked around the room at one another and nodded. The task force fleet had its plan. It would require a lot of careful planning and training, but it would be a good one.

✚

THE COMMONWEALTH VESSELS FLASHED into existence right alongside the pursuing alien vessels. As soon as they did so, the League ships the Invaders had been pursuing banked at right angles away from the plane of fire. The Commonwealth vessels began their barrage.

"*Targeting complete*," spoke a voice over the FleetCom—it was Captain Caradif of the *CSS Babylon*. "*All FI batteries fire!*" Filipov-Ibañez reddened slightly at the last command; he hadn't expected the Commonwealthers to name the weapon after him.

The *Babylon* unleashed its barrage against Invader 7, pursuing the *Čapek* from barely half a kilometer away. A seam of blinding white light erupted along the starboard side of the alien vessel—the matter in the superdense hull annihilated as it came into contact with the antimatter of the barrage. Once holes in the hull formed, subsequent waves went directly into the superstructure, reacting with the matter inside. Without warning, something inside went critical. It was unclear whether the engines had been hit or overloaded or whether the structural collapse of the neutronium hull had caused a system failure. The innards of the alien ship erupted in a blue-white flash of light that vented out the ruptured starboard side into space. The hull careened against the direction of the blast; the vessel was destroyed.

A cry went up from the bridge—perhaps from FleetCom, too—because it sounded to Juliana like everyone in the fleet had shouted simultaneously. But just as quickly, the cries of triumph were overwhelmed by screams of terror.

The *Riyadh* had emerged from hyperspace, rolling to starboard. As its FI batteries fired, its salvos overshot its target vessel, Invader 1. That one miss was all the time the Invader needed. At once, its particle beam weapons lanced out and destroyed the *Riyadh's* drive ring and two of its four point-defense cannons. The next salvo pierced the main hull and began cutting through the *Riyadh,* slicing the ship in half from port to starboard. Venting pockets of atmosphere pushed the two halves away from one another and into a pair of degrading orbits. Shuttlecraft and escape pods were picked off as the surviving crew attempted to flee the wreckage.

"Fleet, this is Kavanagh," Juliana spoke into the air to the FleetCom channel. "Continue to press attack. *Berlin,* jump out of there! *Riyadh's* attack on Invader 1 has failed; you're about to be flanked! Retreat to fallback coordinates behind Edgekeep."

The *Berlin* had successfully incapacitated its target vessel, Invader 2, but it was slow to react to the *Riyadh's* unfortunate fate. The moments that it took to reset its short-range hyperdrive proved fatal. Even with faster fusion engines than its enemy had, it could not outrun or outmaneuver the Invader's deadly particle beam. The *Berlin* began to come apart as if split lengthwise like a piece of firewood at the hands of a lumberjack and his maul.

"*Babylon*, the *Berlin* is down. Jump out of there!"

"Aye, Admiral," came Captain Caradif's voice, "Jumping now." The blip representing the *Babylon* disappeared and reappeared on the far side of Edgekeep, the farther of Farmark's two moons. Juliana could see everyone, herself included, breathe a sigh of relief. The *Babylon* had so long accompanied the *Deliverance* that they'd practically become family.

Before their relief could become too firmly established, another alarm went off, and the holo display ringed one of the objects in a rotating orange ring with yellow arrows pointing inward. *Atmospheric entry imminent*, the alert sounded. The two halves of the *Riyadh* were falling from orbit to the planet below.

"Mr. Filipov-Ibañez, target missiles on the bow section of the *Riyadh*," called Delacruz.

"Belay, that," Juliana said. "Even if you succeed in detonating the core, it's too low in orbit. The radiation will sterilize the entire hemisphere."

"You're right, of course. I just couldn't—"

"I know."

"Mr. Filipov-Ibañez, what are the predicted impact zones on Farmark?" Delacruz said.

"The stern will land in the southern Abyssinian Ocean; the drive section will hit central Abyssinia, about two hundred klicks north of New Debre Tabor."

"What are the chances the drive section's containment holds?"

"Less than 10 percent, Captain."

Juliana and Delacruz watched the dashed line in front of the pieces of the *Riyadh* arc into the planet below, the two halves of the starship following them down the gravity well. The forward flexdisplay wall had returned to a view of the entire theater of operations with Farmark in the center. On the surface of the beleaguered planet flared a piercingly bright light that eclipsed the entire nighttime surface of the planet as the *Riyadh's* antimatter containment fields collapsed upon impact and the entirety of its engine core annihilated itself. When the light faded, a kilometers-wide fireball stood in its place before darkening into a mushroom cloud that reached up into the upper atmosphere.

"Good God," Juliana said. "I suppose it's a blessing in disguise that so much of the planet had already been devastated and its people gone."

Before the crew could register the scale of the devastation, another alarm sounded, and their attention was drawn to the other side of the holographic display.

On the "east" side of the battle theater, the *Tianjin*, *Al-Wadi*, and *Jakarta* were engaging their targets. The *Al-Wadi* and *Jakarta* had successfully neutralized Invaders 4 and 5, respectively. The *Jakarta* was moving toward the *Beijing* for the anticipated conclusion to the operation, but the *Tianjin* was not as successful. It, too, had rolled, and its opening salvo had gone wide of the mark. Invader 3 destroyed the *Tianjin's* drive ring, and as the vessel floated disabled at null-g, the alien vessel finished the ship off, slicing it neatly into pieces. Invader 3 turned its sights on the *Al-Wadi*.

"*Beijing* and *Jakarta*," called Juliana. "Use intel from the *Babylon*, *Al-Wadi*, and *Jakarta's* sensors to target Invader 6's engines and weapons systems alone. I want her disabled but not destroyed. All other ships engage at will." The ships signaled their acknowledgment. "We have to press our advantage now," she said to Delacruz. "Time is not on our side when surprise is our major leg up."

The *Beijing* and *Jakarta* micro-jumped into positions a kilometer above and to the planet-facing side of Invader 6. Each fired a salvo of targeted antimatter bullets with their FI batteries, taking out those surface protrusions they had identified as drives and weapons.

"Invader 6 incapacitated," came the voice of the *Beijing's* skipper, Captain Khan.

"Acknowledged, Captain. Watch your flank; Invader 1 is moving toward your position. *Bismarck, Roosevelt, Mansa*—it's time for you to tag in."

The *Roosevelt* and the *Mansa* disappeared from view and reappeared below and to the planetside of Invader 1. But the element of surprise that accompanied this tactic had been lost—Invader 1's batteries fired immediately at the Commonwealth vessels as they flicked into existence alongside. Like the *Riyadh*, the *Roosevelt* had rolled upon hyperspace emergence but rolled to port, and its sensor tower and observation deck took the brunt of the enemy's weapons fire. The alien vessel then trained its weapons on the *Mansa* as it began to fire its FI batteries. Each vessel inflicted heavy damage on the other, but the *Mansa* appeared worse for wear. Its drive ring was compromised, and fires raged in its engineering section. If those fires were not contained, the entire drive section would have to be jettisoned, leaving the ship stranded and dead in space.

The *Roosevelt* appeared to be listing but was still rolling to port. As it continued to roll, its starboard FI guns came to bear on the alien's keel, and the entire battery unleashed a broadside on the Intruder vessel, forging a white-hot seam along the length of the ship. A blue-white light erupted from the Invader craft, which belched white fire and rocketed upward away from the *Roosevelt*. It left behind a trail of glowing hot detritus as it careened out of the ecliptic.

"*Abu-Bakr*, provide coverage to the *Roosevelt* and *Mansa*. *Scimitar* and *Rapier*, assist in recovery and evacuation operations as directed by *Abu-Bakr*."

"Aye, sir!" the two League starships responded. Lacking the *Deliverance's* upgrades, most of the League's fleet would have to perform mop-up operations after the Commonwealth vessels had landed the initial blows.

But Juliana knew that there wasn't a Leaguer who wasn't anxious to do their part, and she felt enormous pride in the enthusiasm of her ISG comrades.

The *Al-Wadi* was still fighting for its life. Its drive ring was out—a hyperspace jump was impossible—but its fusion drive was still functioning. Its helm officer was either a genius or a lunatic and had reduced most of its attacker's shots to glancing blows rather than hull-shattering strikes. But how long could that last?

The *Bismarck* jumped in behind Invader 3 and hastily fired a salvo from its FI batteries that glanced off the alien vessel's hull, even as the rounds that did make contact released bright flashes of annihilating energy. Invader 3 turned its weapons on the *Bismarck* and tore a hole through its midsection. An all too familiar nightmare image was replayed on the *Deliverance* bridge display as crew and equipment were vented out into the vacuum.

The *Bismarck* listed, and much to everyone's surprise, the Invader vessel returned to its pursuit of the *Al-Wadi*.

"What is that ship doing?" Juliana wondered.

"I think we just learned that the aliens can be irritated—they want to finish the *Al-Wadi* off," Delacruz said.

The *Al-Wadi* went into a high-gee burn even as it took evasive maneuvers and fired off every missile and PDC round it could at the pursuing vessel. The wounded Commonwealth vessel moved toward Reach, the closer in of Farmark's two moons.

"They're going to try to put the moon between themselves and the Invader," Delacruz said.

"I don't think they'll make it without pulling some major, and likely deadly, gees," Juliana said. She surveyed the battle zone. The *Roosevelt* and *Mansa* were alive but not in combat shape. The *Beijing* and *Jakarta* had Invader 6 pinned down. The *Bismarck* had taken heavy damage and had been immobilized. The *Abu-Bakr* was securing the area around the *Roosevelt* and *Mansa*, and the LSS *Scimitar* and LSS *Rapier* were on site conducting relief operations. The CSS *Sun Tzu*, LSS *Sabre*, and LSS *Katana* would be needed for the same thing with the *Bismarck* and *Al-Wadi*, if the latter survived. They were running out of ships with FI cannons. "I think it will have to be us, Captain."

"Understood, Admiral," Delacruz said. "Mr. Thorsten, lay in an intercept course with the *Al-Wadi*. We're going to engage in a maximum burn. If we time this right, we can unload a salvo at the Invader vessel while moving too fast for them to get a lock."

"Aye, sir," Thorsten said. "Computing trajectory and acceleration curve now."

"I guess we'd better strap in," Delacruz said to Juliana. She nodded and was about to head to her chair when she noticed something about the tactical display.

"Where the hell is the *Babylon*?" she said. The ship's icon had disappeared from behind Edgekeep but was nowhere on the board. She scanned the battlefield in vain for the missing vessel as the icon for the *Al-Wadi* passed behind Reach with Invader 3 in hot pursuit.

Suddenly, on the display, another icon appeared behind Reach—the *Babylon*. Somehow, the Commonwealth starship had already attained an acceleration vector of six gees right out of hyperspace as it headed toward the Invader vessel. It vaulted past the *Al-Wadi* and began unleashing its FI barrage before reaching the alien ship. The starship's trajectory imparted a forward momentum to its laterally moving salvo, which, combined with the alien vessel's forward motion, struck Invader 3 head-on at extremely high velocity. Those rounds took a particularly destructive angular path through the alien ship, which split lengthwise along the axis of fire, with blue-white light and radiation erupting from the breach points. Some of the rounds that missed the vessel landed on the moon's surface, producing a pyrotechnic display that felt to Juliana like the cosmos itself was celebrating the *Babylon's* maneuver.

Juliana and her former first officer looked at each other in astonishment. She made a swiping gesture with her hand, and the three-dee display moved back to one of the flexdisplays as a two-dee tactical map.

"Lt. Flores," she said. "Signal the *Sun Tzu*, *Sabre*, and *Katana* to secure the battle zone around the *Bismarck* and *Al-Wadi* and begin conducting recovery and repair operations. And get me Captain Caradif."

"Aye, sir!"

A few moments later, Captain Renno Caradif's face appeared on the forward display. His face was ruddy with excitement, and there was a good deal of shouting and revelry on his bridge.

"Admiral Kavanagh, to what do I owe the pleasure?" he said through the newly installed translation matrix.

"I want to commend you for a brilliant action, Captain. But I confess, I am at a loss to understand how you did it."

"Well, Admiral," he said, smiling. "There are some things about navigating close to gravity wells in hyperspace that they don't teach you at the academy. Our helms'man, Ensign Farragut"—he gestured to the young woman seated in front of him—"used the gravity wells of Edgekeep, Farmark, and Reach to, uh, build up a little momentum, you might say." His bridge crew roared in celebration behind him.

"I look forward to your report, Captain," Juliana said. "Well done. Thank you."

Caradif saluted and closed the connection, but not before his bridge crew could be heard beginning another round of cheering.

Delacruz started to chuckle. "I guess we really woke up their risk-taking side."

"This is not the Commonwealth we met a few months ago," Juliana said, sitting in her chair and shaking her head in disbelief. "That's not even the Renno Caradif we met a few months ago! In any event, it's time to begin your approach, Captain."

Delacruz turned to his helms'man. "Mr. Thorsten, take us in toward that sixth vessel."

When the *Deliverance* arrived alongside what they had identified as the command vessel, they saw that the *Beijing* and *Jakarta* had not only disabled and neutralized the ship, but they'd also managed to punch several holes in its hull.

Captain Delacruz looked over the tactical display before turning back to Ensign Thorsten. "Helm, bring us alongside that vessel. Lt. Flores, signal the *Beijing* and *Jakarta* to provide covering fire if necessary and take out anything that pops up as a threat."

Juliana stood up and turned toward the *Deliverance's* security chief.

"Mr. Killian, you're up."

24 | KILLIAN | FARMARK

"AYE, CAPTAIN."

Jareth left the bridge and headed down to the shuttle bay, where a squad of marines was waiting. Already in pressure combat suits, they were outside an Inter-vessel Attack Craft. "Standing by awaiting your orders, Lieutenant," Gunnery Sergeant Makindi said as he walked in.

"Get your men on the shuttle, Master Gunnery Sergeant. I'll be aboard in a second." Jareth put on his combat suit and boarded the shuttle, taking his seat just behind the pilot, a young ensign named Dupont. "As soon as you get the word from the bridge, Ensign, take us out."

"Aye, sir," she responded.

The vibration through the deck plating told him the *Deliverance's* fusion engines were firing—the ship was pulling alongside the alien craft. The vibration ceased, and the pulse of maneuvering thrusters could be felt—a green light flashed on the command console.

"That's our cue," he said. The pilot lifted the shuttle off the deck, signaled the door control, and flew out into the gap between the two vessels. As they neared the alien ship, Jareth could see it beginning to list. The alien ships were huge and cigar-shaped with a few protrusions on the hull, likely the exhaust for its drive systems, outlets for waste heat, or other necessary externalities that would not function behind a layer of neutronium. The starboard side of this vessel was venting atmosphere and flame in the aft section and at a couple of points closer to the bow.

"Ensign," Jareth said to Dupont. "Is there a breach hole large enough for us to board?"

"Scanning, Lieutenant." She looked at the tactical readout on her heads-up display. "No, sir. I am afraid that the larger breaches are venting flame. Probably their drive section."

"Thank you, Ensign." He touched the com unit on his helmet. "*Deliverance*, this is IVAC-1, requesting targeted firing starboard amidships of the alien vessel to create a breach point."

"Message received, IVAC-1. Stand by," came Flores's voice in his ear. Then: "*Deliverance* to *Beijing*, target concentrated ten-meter burst at intruder vessel using targeting provided by IVAC-1."

"Ensign," Jareth said to the pilot. "Paint a place you'd like to land."

"Aye, sir," she smiled and fired up the targeting laser, illuminating a spot on the hull about a third of the way back from the bow.

"Stand clear, IVAC-1," came a voice over FleetCom from the *Beijing's* communications officer. The *Beijing* fired a concentrated burst, and a ten-meter ring of white light appeared on the side of the alien craft's hull.

"Report."

"The *Beijing* has opened up a sufficient breach in the vessel's side, Lieutenant. It's venting atmosphere, so the ride may be a little bumpy."

"Take us in and let me know if you get a spectral reading on that venting atmosphere."

"Aye, sir." She maneuvered the craft toward the breach and flew the IVAC in. It was buffeted by atmosphere, but not by objects, which was fortunate, though Jareth was sure the marines would gladly have seen an alien or two tumbling out into vacuum. Who was he kidding? *He* would have liked to have seen that. Everyone remembered the size of the holes in the ISG ships' hulls when they returned from the first battle in Kittim. They'd all seen more holes in more League and Commonwealth starships today. Everyone understood how many lives those holes had represented.

"Spectral analysis of the atmosphere is complete. The LZ is depressurized, but I was able to get a reading on the atmo as it was venting. It's oxygen/nitrogen, but I wouldn't recommend removing your helmets without further analysis."

"Thank you, Ensign."

"I'm also getting a slight gravity reading," she continued. "It looks like the gravity vector is down from the center of the vessel toward the outer hull. The ship isn't spinning for spin-gravity, so it may be that the neutronium hull exerts a small gravitic effect. Either way, 'out' is 'down'—bear that in mind." She piloted the shuttle in and identified a point in the superstructure to settle on. The decks, such as they were, seemed to run in concentric circles along the axis of the vessel. The ensign moved the IVAC to a deck visible through the breach hole. The IVAC extended its grappling clamps and secured itself to the deck.

"Helmets on. Safeties off," Jareth said to the marines before turning to the pilot. "Open the hatch, Ensign."

"Aye, sir." And with that, the starboard hatch flew wide open.

"Move! Move! Move!" shouted Makindi, and the marines rushed out of the hatch in parallel formation onto the deck.

Jareth turned to the pilot, "Keep the light on for us. Don't hesitate to frag anything that doesn't look human coming your way."

"You can count on it, Lieutenant."

He hopped onto the deck where the marines had formed a protective cordon, securing the area. As Ensign Dupont had said, there was a slight pull toward the deck, but their magboots gave them the most stability. Master Gunnery Sergeant Makindi came running up. "The LZ is secured, Lieutenant. There are energy readings and possible life signs on the other side of that bulkhead. We're unsure if that's just a panel or some kind of door, but we're about to blow it either way."

"Proceed, Master Gunnery Sergeant." Jareth watched as Makindi returned to the marines and began giving orders. Jareth looked past him to the bulkhead in question. On the wall was an asymmetrically shaped panel, vaguely resembling an ear. Was it a door? He looked around, and for the first time, it sank in that this was an alien ship. There were no recognizable elements of their surroundings beyond the deck flooring and the bulkheads, though even they seemed . . . different, somehow.

"Fire in the hole!" he heard through his commlink. They took cover as a corporal touched off a switch to blow the panel. There was a bright flash and a burst of flame, quickly blown out by the rush of air coming from the breached, rapidly decompressing chamber.

The corporal who had triggered the blast stood up to peer at his work. He turned toward the rest of the boarding party. "It looks like we're through, Master Gunnery Sergeant. The char—" He never finished his thought. Instead, his head exploded, and his now headless body fell to its knees in the low gravity before slumping over in a kind of macabre slow motion.

"Hostiles!" shouted Makindi. "Open fire!" The marines began to pour fire into the breach as whatever was there also returned fire.

"Master Gunnery Sergeant," Jareth called over his comm. "Can you make out anything beyond that breach?"

"No, sir," came the reply. "Switching to IR." Jareth followed Makindi's lead and adjusted a control on his helmet—his visor heads-up display began to show an infrared overlay on his visual field. Something was moving beyond that breach, and his first instinct was to recoil in horror. Whatever it was, it was not human—really not human. Jareth had seen images of the aliens before, but something about seeing them in person filled him with dread.

Makindi's voice came over the com: "Juarez, RPGs!" One of the marines, crouching behind a projection in the opposite bulkhead, reset the settings on his XR-90, took aim, and fired a rocket-propelled grenade through the breach as the remaining marines continued to fire through the opening.

As the grenade hit its target, a green-white flash of light came from beyond the breached bulkhead. "Cease fire! Cease fire!" came Makindi's voice over the com. They waited a few moments; nothing seemed to be moving beyond the breach, and no fire was being returned.

"Master Gunnery Sergeant," Jareth said to Makindi. "Secure that room."

"Aye, sir," he replied. "Juarez. Al-Khwarizmi. McKenzie. Through the hole." The three marines went through the breach into the compartment beyond.

A few moments later, Juarez's voice came over the com. "Clear!"

They got up from their positions and headed into the next compartment. Strewn across the floor were different pieces of the alien.

"Where's the rest of 'im, Master Gunny?" Juarez asked.

"That's all they are: legs," he said. The five limbs of more or less equivalent size strewn about the compartment looked exactly like Makindi had described them months ago: a horrifying combination of a cricket leg with an octopus's tentacle. The upper limb was long, insect-like, but muscular. Past the knee joint, the lower limb was thinner but no less physically powerful. The leg ended in an eight-tentacled foot or hand. The tentacles appeared to be capable of fine motor work; indeed, one of the feet/hands was holding a weapon—probably the same thing that had killed their poor corporal.

"They could be like starfish," Jareth continued. "Well, like huge, cricket, octopus starfish. Their brains may lie in the nexus of their limbs or may be shared among the limbs. I can't figure out whether that makes them easier or harder to kill."

"Harder, Lieutenant," said Makindi. "Trust me on that."

"Lieutenant, take a look at this," said the marine called Al-Khwarizmi.

"What is it, Specialist?"

"There is another hatch in this room, but it's above us on the ceiling." He gestured up at an ear-shaped hatch on the surface above them, toward the ship's center.

"How the hell would they get to that?" asked McKenzie.

"They probably just stretch themselves right up to it. Balance on three limbs, open with two," Makindi said. "That's also how they fight. Those things move a lot differently than we do as bipeds. Remember that."

"Thank you, Master Gunnery Sergeant," Jareth added. "Boarding party, if that's the door out of here, that's where we're going."

Makindi pointed to two of the marines. "Use magboots to get up there and blow that hatch. Juarez, Al-Khwarizmi, I want concussion grenades through that hatch as soon as it's opened. McKenzie, cover the breach with a portable airlock. I don't want to be fighting outrushing atmo every time we breach another room. Peters, pick up that alien weapon. I don't want that lying around where anyone else can come pick that up and blow our heads off. Besides, I am sure that plenty of folks back home would want to take a look."

The marines scattered to affix the charges and set up a firing perimeter, including guarding the way the boarding party had come in case they should be greeted unexpectedly from behind.

Some climbed up the walls using magboots and placed charges around the hatch. Juarez and Al-Khwarizmi stood below, just to either side of the hatch. "Fire in the hole!" shouted a marine as he detonated the charges. The hatch blew backward into the space beyond as Juarez and Al-Khwarizmi fired concussion grenades into the hole. Green flashes of light burst out of the hatch in rapid succession as the grenades went off. They waited—and nothing. One marine, Lance Corporal Stark, still clinging to the "ceiling," extended a mirror to peer around the corner into the space beyond the hatch.

"It's all clear," she said. "Just an empty access tube."

"Let's get up there, Master Gunnery Sergeant," Jareth said to Makindi.

"Aye, aye, sir." He began barking orders to the marines, who started moving up the tube. The footholds were spaced further apart than was ideal, but the marines could make their way up the seventy-five-meter-high tube. Jareth thought this had to be a back door into the inner reaches of the vessel. Ensign Dupont had fortuitously selected a great breach point and landing zone.

"I wonder why there aren't more defensive systems, alarms, that kind of thing," a marine named Tranh said.

Stark replied, "Probably never counted on anyone getting through that hull in the first place."

"Cut the chatter, you two," said Makindi. "Keep your eyes on that hatch above. I don't want any surprises." The marines arranged a cascading cycle in which one marine would climb, focus their weapon on the hatch while others climbed past, and then repeat. Before long, the boarding party had reached the top of the tube.

"Gravity's even lighter this close to the center, but watch your grips; you could still get hurt from a fall like that," Makindi warned.

Unlike the hatch below, this one had some kind of access panel visible. Stark tried to use her fingers to manipulate the controls unsuccessfully. "I can't tell whether my fingers are just the wrong shape or if there's some trick to this, but I can't do it."

"Deploy torches," Makindi said. Stark and Juarez each grabbed a small pistol-shaped object from their belts. Flicking a switch, each ignited a torch and began to cut through the hinges and lock of the hatch. After a few minutes, they were through. The hatch fell forward but slowly in the lower gravity. Stark and Juarez caught it and passed it along to those below them, who ultimately let it fall down the shaft.

Makindi turned to Jareth: "Sir?"

"Proceed, Master Gunnery Sergeant."

Makindi turned again to Stark and Juarez. "Fragmentation grenades." Stark and Juarez hurled two egg-shaped grenades through the hatchway.

"Fire in the hole!" called out Stark seconds before the grenades flashed. Ricochets and the sounds of shrapnel clanged off the interior of the chamber but not much else.

"All right, Marines," Makindi continued. "Gravity is going to be pretty light in there; we're going to breach on the fly. Stark, you up for this?"

Stark looked at Makindi with a massive grin on her face. "You know it, Master Gunny." She positioned herself astride the access tube, one hand on the grip, the other bracing against the opposite bulkhead. Juarez and Al-Khwarizmi positioned themselves just beneath her. Suddenly, Stark let go and dropped downward; Juarez and Al-Khwarizmi each caught a foot, and then, as Stark crouched, they vaulted her through the hatch. Stark flew into the open space, tucked into a ball, and then flipped around to land on the far side of the chamber. She clicked her mag boots on and crouched with her weapon raised, sweeping the room from her upside-down-to-them position. At last, she stood up and raised her head to look back down.

"It's all clear, Master Gunny," she said. "And Lieutenant, you're gonna wanna see this."

"Peters," called Makindi. "You're our rear guard. Get back down to the previous chamber. Keep a watch on the access to this tube. I don't want anything coming up behind us and catching us unawares."

"Aye," Peters replied and drifted back down the tube, using the footholds to brake his descent.

"The rest of you, through the breach!" The marines propelled themselves through the hatch and took station. They had reached the center of the alien starship—a large cylindrical room. As Jareth floated through the breached hatch into the chamber, he saw what Stark had wanted him to see. Covering the floor/ceiling/walls of this room were hundreds of metallic, coffin-shaped devices spaced evenly along the surface. He looked up at the surface opposite where Stark was standing and could see that the top of each device was semi-transparent. Inside each one was an alien creature in what appeared to be suspended animation.

"Abe's God. Are they colonists or reserves?" Jareth said to no one in particular.

McKenzie came alongside and looked at the creature in the pod closest to them. "If you ask me, sir, this looks more like a troop transport than a colony ship. Besides, colonists usually come after the invasion is done."

Jareth nodded thoughtfully. His first instinct was to shoot every single one of these aliens as they slept. But another idea started to well up in his imagination.

The rest of the marines surveyed the room and gawked at the frozen army of Invaders. Makindi had been standing with them, equally entranced, until a sudden epiphany jarred him out of his complacency. "Attention on deck!" Every marine stopped what they were doing and turned toward him.

He pointed toward the hatch they'd just come out of. "That is south," he said. Then he pointed to where Stark was. "That is north. That is east, and that is west," he finished, pointing to either end of the giant cylindrical chamber. I want every access point to this chamber mined. If this is their troop transport, it's only a matter of time before they come to defend it."

Jareth and Makindi watched together as the marines sprang into action, identifying every possible access port, vent, or hatch to the chamber they could find, and placed explosive charges at each one.

"What are your orders now, Lieutenant?" Makindi said to Jareth.

"We came here for information, didn't we?" Jareth said, staring ahead at the closest pod to him. In that device was a creature who'd come to help evict the people of Farmark from their homes, whose comrades had destroyed most of the League's fleet and killed tens of thousands, if not more. The idea that had been floating up through his subconscious broke the surface into conscious thought: "We're taking one of those pods."

Makindi turned to his marines, "You heard the lieutenant; we're taking one of these bastards with us. McKenzie, figure out where they draw their power from and how much. Juarez, figure out how to detach it. Gómez-Lim, work with McKenzie once he's identified the power needs and rig up a battery pack to power this thing. Al-Khwarizmi, look for the best way to get this thing out of here. Stark, you blast anything that so much as pokes its head—uh—knee into this room."

"Aye, Master Gunnery Sergeant," they all responded at once and immediately got to their work.

Jareth pulled a scanning drone out of his armor, tossed it up into the chamber above him, and watched as the drone began to scan the chamber, recording every detail it could of the space. "I'm going to check in with the *Deliverance*."

"Copy that, sir," replied Makindi.

"*Deliverance*, this is Killian. Do you copy? *Deliverance*, come in."

"Try the IVAC, sir. It can relay you to the *Deliverance*."

"Good idea," Jareth replied and adjusted the channel. "Ensign Dupont, do you read? This is Killian. Dupont, come in." He turned to Makindi and shrugged. "There must be some interference from the pods or something. I'm going to go down into that shaft and see if it's any better there. Continue your operations here, Master Gunnery Sergeant."

"Aye, sir," said Makindi, straightening and saluting. He turned to his marines and urged them to pick up their pace. Jareth could feel the anxiety growing in the marine, even through their two armored combat vacuum suits. It had been quiet since they boarded the alien vessel—that couldn't last.

Jareth returned to the "south" hatch and dropped a third of the way down the shaft. He keyed his helmet mic again. "IVAC-1, this is Killian. Do you read?"

"I read you, Lieutenant," came Dupont's voice through his earpieces, though the signal was weak and staticky. "I've been picking up increased electromagnetic interference. I don't know whether they're jamming us or if that's the by-product of something else."

"Understood. I need you to relay a message to the *Deliverance*. We have found what appears to be a holding chamber for hundreds of colonists or troops in suspended animation. We are attempting to extract one and bring it back with us. Got that?"

"Roger, Lieutenant, will do. Anything else?"

"Is the LZ still secure?"

"The LZ is still secure for the time being. No one has come to investigate this breach. All defensive systems are still armed, so be sure to announce yourselves before coming back into firing range."

"Understood," Jareth said. "That may change once they realize we're here. They may start to look for how we got here. Contact us if there's any change. Killian out."

"Wilco," she responded. "Out."

Jareth switched the com channel back to the boarding party's coms, only to be greeted by shouts from frightened marines.

"Hostiles! West!" Makindi shouted into the channel. The air around him erupted with sounds of gunfire and a much slower *thunk* that always seemed to be followed by another marine screaming in pain.

"Lieutenant! This is Makindi—there are breaches in the western and eastern walls. The aliens are coming out of passages we couldn't even see and haven't mined—passages far narrower than we thought they could fit through. I have good coverage of our western flank, but the east is exposed. Lieutenant, do you read me? Lieutenant?"

Jareth was no longer aboard the alien vessel—he was in a storage room aboard the *Cantankerous Vixen*. The marines' shouts sounded like the muffled shouts of his crewmates on the other side of the cargo hold bulkhead. His vision started to narrow, the peripheries turning dark and contracting into a circle. He could feel his extremities go numb, his muscles locking up, and his body slowly drifting downward into the abyss.

He retained enough conscious awareness to realize he was slowly falling down the access tube toward the chamber off the breach site. If he did nothing, physics would pull him away from the nightmare above. He could find Private Peters and take off with Ensign Dupont. *I'm sorry. I'm sorry. I'm sorry.*

Everything went silent. The din of shouts and gunfire was gone, and a sudden stillness overtook his senses. Just as suddenly, he heard a loud *thwoop* sound—the sound of a communications direct-channel override, and Makindi's voice was seemingly all around him.

"Look up at me, Lieutenant."

Jareth willed his eyes to look back up the tube, and there was Makindi, lying across the entrance with his arm extended downward, reaching toward his lieutenant.

"You've got this, LT. And I've got you. Everything else is in the past."

Jareth was stunned to discover that he'd stopped falling and even more stunned to discover that his hands had reached out and grabbed the footholds along the sides of the access tube to stop him.

"You've got this, LT. And I've got you. Everything else is in the past," the marine repeated.

"Everything else is in the past," Jareth echoed. His vision cleared, and his senses returned. He took a deep breath. "I think I should pay Lance Corporal Stark a visit."

"I think that is an excellent idea, LT. And I will help you along."

Jareth unslung his XR-90, switched it to its RPG setting, and slung the rifle back over his shoulder. He placed two hands on the nearest foothold and vaulted himself upward, using other handholds to propel himself ever faster. When he reached Makindi, the marine grabbed him beneath the arms and hurled him upward toward the opposite side of the chamber. Jareth tucked and turned, unslung his rifle, and fired all three RPG rounds into the eastern bulkhead, where he could see the creatures emerging from a small, previously unnoticed panel. One of the rounds struck near the aliens' exit point, but he couldn't see what happened to the others because he untucked at the wrong time to aim his feet toward the opposing bulkhead and slammed into the decking in a whole-body back flop.

"Cheeses, LT," said Stark. "You all right?"

Jareth started drifting up from the decking after bouncing off it when Stark stepped on him and pushed him back toward the surface. "You might wanna turn your magboots on, LT," she said before turning back and continuing to pour fire toward the aliens breaching from the west.

"Did I get any of them?" he wheezed, trying to recover from getting the wind knocked out of him.

"Sure as shite did, LT. Whole eastern wall's on fire. It's definitely slowed them coming that way."

She continued to fire at the aliens to the west, but the creatures were hard to hit because they were taking cover and could either spread themselves out or contract themselves as needed. Stark fired a rocket-propelled grenade into the passageway they were coming out of, and the hatch belched flame when the RPG detonated within. But as soon as she took some satisfaction from that victory, panel doors began sliding around them.

"We're surrounded!" shouted Makindi, who was in a low crouch, pivoting and spraying fire in different directions.

Jareth clicked on his magboots and pulled himself into a low crouch near Stark. He swept the room with his eyes, looking for anywhere that was defensible, but a cylinder doesn't give you many places to hide. But there, not far from where Stark was positioned firing explosive charges into any breach she could see, was what appeared to be a console—semi-circular and about four meters in diameter. *It'll provide some cover, at any rate,* he thought.

"Boarding party," he called into his helmet's commlink. "Rally to Stark. We'll take position using that semi-circular console as a defilade."

The marines fell back in cascading stages around the perimeter of the cylinder until they reached the rally point, with Stark providing suppressing fire to cover their movements. They took up position in the "foxhole," which had good coverage on three sides and reasonable visibility of what might be above them.

Makindi waddled over to Jareth in a crouch, taking care to make sure his boots stayed planted on the deck. "It's good to see you here with us, LT. Any thoughts on where we go next?"

"Considering that our way out is basically up there," Jareth said, pointing up/down toward the hatch they had come from, "It's gonna be a challenge getting back to the IVAC without any cover."

"Agreed," he responded.

Jareth switched his channel to contact the IVAC. "Dupont, come in. This is Killian, over." There was no response. "I still can't get through whatever interference is blocking us here."

"You could make contact from that access tube, right, LT?"

"Yes, why?"

"I'll go. I'll jump over there and contact the IVAC."

"Master Gunny, there's no one left on that side to give you any covering fire. I can't let you do that."

"Do you know of any other way to get a message broadcast from that tube, sir?"

Jareth thought for a moment. "As a matter of fact, I do." He pulled another sensor drone out of his suit and turned it on. He turned the visual sensor toward himself.

"Ensign Dupont. We're pinned down. We've got some cover—such as it is—for now, but hostiles have been steadily coming into the chamber faster than we can repel them. We're holed up behind a semicircular structure almost directly opposite the passage we used to come up here. We could use some help getting out of here. Relay a call to the *Deliverance*. The second and third waves should be available." He turned the sensor drone away and connected to its command interface with his helmet coms. He selected "Auto Return to Base" from its menu options and threw it as hard as he could toward the access tube.

Incoming fire forced him to take cover before he could see whether he'd managed to get it anywhere near the access tube entrance.

"Master Gunny," Stark called out. "I'm getting low on ammo."

"I am, too," said McKenzie.

Makindi thought for a moment. "Suppressing fire doesn't make any sense with creatures who seem pretty resilient to gunfire in the first place. Save your ammo. Choose your shots carefully—remember your training; they're weakest at the nexus of their legs on their underside."

One of the aliens on the far side of the chamber reared up on three legs, holding its weapon with the remaining two. Makindi fired an RPG round right at the part of the creature where its legs came together, and the creature came apart.

"Follow Master Gunny's lead!" cried Stark. "Wait until they rear up and then plug them."

With the cessation of suppressing fire, the aliens began to move relentlessly through the chamber, converging on a spot right near the access tube the boarding party had used to enter. Juarez poured fire at the aliens and emptied his magazine.

"Private!" shouted Makindi. "Conserve your ammo!"

Juarez shrugged and reached for another magazine, but before he could swap it in, a slug from the alien's weapon tore through the top of his helmet and out through his thigh. The marine was dead, but the low gravity robbed him of the dignity of slumping to the ground, and his body continued to crouch there on the decking, rocking back and forth.

More and more of the creatures converged on the spot opposite the boarding party's "foxhole." Stark reared up to throw a fragmentation grenade, but as she threw it, one of the alien rounds took off her right arm, and the grenade drifted only a few meters above their position.

"Cover!" Makindi shouted just before the grenade went off, showering them with shrapnel.

"I'm hit!" McKenzie shouted. One of the pieces of shrapnel had torn a tube going to his air supply.

"Don't panic," Makindi shouted. "There's still air. You're okay. Dupont said it was okay to breathe." But the now terrified marine was losing what remained of his wits. He frantically tried to patch the hole in the air tube and was reaching for a patch kid from his utility pack when a slug entered him just below the shoulder and passed through the left flank of his body, killing him instantly.

More aliens were taking a position right above/below them. Jareth and the seven marines still in the fight continued to fire, but the aliens were not making themselves vulnerable to attack. Makindi fired his second RPG round just beneath one of the Invaders—the explosion blew the creature's leg off but did not kill it. Al-Khwarizmi had only one RPG round left, Gómez-Lim one, and Jareth had spent all of his on his flight across the chamber.

"I need you all to take cover," Makindi said. "And keep Stark out of the line of fire. I'll be damned if I'm going to be the sole survivor of my squad again."

"I'm sorry, Master Gunny," Jareth said, staying at the marine's side. "But I outrank you on this mission, and I'm staying right here."

"My coms are out, Master Gunny," Al-Khwarizmi said. "I couldn't make out what you said."

Makindi only grunted before continuing to fire at the aliens opposite them.

Jareth looked across the cylinder at the alien soldiers gathering and saw that they had come together into a formation and were lifting their weapons toward them. One alien fired, and the commlink was filled with Al-Khwarizmi's screams as an alien projectile smashed through his crouched knee.

Al-Khwarizmi's armor sealed off the site of the wound, and he crumpled to the deck. Jareth looked over at Stark; her armor had sealed her wound and staunched the blood, but he could see on his team readout that her vitals were flagging. She was going into shock. *Perhaps that's a kindness,* he thought. *We're all about to die anyway.*

Suddenly, everyone's suit alarm went off, and red lettering appeared at the top of their heads-up displays: NULL-G WARNING. ACTIVATE MAGNETIC BOOTS. SECURE ALL PERSONNEL.

"What the hell?" said Gómez-Lim. "There's already no gravity. How are we—"

"Do it!" shouted Makindi. "Set to maximum!" At once, everyone in the boarding party set their magboots to maximum. Gómez-Lim reached over to set Al-Khwarizmi's boots as his comrade writhed in pain. One of the other marines secured Stark to the decking.

Just then, the deck opposite exploded in a ring of fire right beneath the alien soldiers. The surviving members of the boarding party crouched in their defilade as shrapnel clanged off of the surrounding deck and pelted their armor. As quickly as the flames had appeared, they disappeared, snuffed out by the torrential winds flowing out of the breach. Those aliens who had not been taken out by the initial explosion were blown right out into the rupture.

As the smoke and fire cleared, the boarding party could see a clear channel out into space, and keeping station right in the center of the channel, holding its own against the venting air, was their IVAC. Ensign Dupont's voice came over the broad channel.

"Good afternoon, comrades. Anyone need a ride?"

DUPONT PILOTED THE IVAC into the chamber and set it down in a broad area near the original breach point. The marines rushed Stark and Al-Khwarizmi into the shuttle and got them connected to the autodocs as quickly as possible. Other marines, not as severely wounded, connected themselves to the remaining autodocs.

Peters came up through the access passage, carrying with him the body of Corporal Emil Kimura-Anders—the one who'd been killed in the initial assault. His body was placed in the shuttle next to those of Juarez, McKenzie, and the others killed in the engagement.

Makindi and Gómez-Lim detached the now alternatively powered suspended animation pod and stowed it in the back of the IVAC. After ensuring that the area was secure, the remaining marines fell in and boarded the craft.

Jareth strapped himself in again behind Dupont, and once everyone was secure, she took the shuttle out. She maneuvered the IVAC back through the breach, through the superstructure, and then out of the initial breach hole.

"*Deliverance*, this is IVAC-1. Over."

"We read you, IVAC-1."

"Prepare the shuttle bay for our return. We've got several wounded and six dead. And a prisoner."

"Roger that, IVAC-1. Main shuttle bay is ready for your arrival. Out."

Jareth removed his helmet and breathed deeply of the copious air of the IVAC.

"How did—"

"How did I do it?" interrupted Dupont without taking her eyes off the shuttle controls.

"Yeah."

"Easy. While you were off exploring, I scanned the surrounding area. It was remarkably ordinary—ordinary metals, composites, and alloys. Their main advantage seemed to be that hull."

"They have some pretty devastating weapons."

"True enough. But I began to think that that hull must be incredibly expensive to manufacture. I guessed that they wouldn't see the need to make the entire ship as indestructible as the hull. Depleted uranium shells and shape charges turned out to be quite effective at clearing a hole all the way through."

"That was quick thinking, Ensign. Commendable, in fact. Literally."

She never took her eyes off her display or the controls as she piloted them into the shuttle bay, but Jareth could see in the reflection of the forward screens that she was smiling.

The IVAC entered the shuttle bay, and the grappling clamps took hold of it as the bay doors closed. After a minute, they could hear sounds outside the vessel as the bay pressurized. A rush of crew'men, medics, technicians, and security officers greeted the boarding party as they exited the shuttle.

Jareth spoke to the security officers first. "There is a suspended animation pod on an independent power source in the IVAC. It's got an alien prisoner in it. Grab some techs and make sure its power supply is secure and that it is stored in a secure location. And keep an eye on it. These aliens are not to be trifled with."

"Aye, sir," responded the team leader. "The admiral has asked you to report to the bridge as soon as possible, Lieutenant."

Jareth nodded his acknowledgment, made his way to the lift, and rode up the ten decks to the bridge. As he approached the hatch, the two marines on duty—who had always been polite and respectful—nodded at him in a way that felt very insider, as though they recognized him now not just as an officer but as a combat veteran. Until that moment, it had not occurred to him that that's what he was.

"Lt. Killian," said Admiral Kavanagh, turning and rising from her chair. "Am I to understand that your mission was a success?" He could feel all the eyes on the bridge staring at him, waiting to hear his report.

"Aye, Admiral. We took some significant losses: six dead and several wounded. In the end, we couldn't secure much in the way of data, as we were under fire for a substantial period, but we got some high-res scans and captured a prisoner."

"So I saw in the communications. How did you manage that?"

"The entire center of their ship was a cryo-ward, with alien reservists in suspended animation. My team figured out how to separate the pod from the ship and how to give it a temporary power supply for transit. I hope that we can get some information out of the individual when we wake it up. As I said, I didn't get as much data information as I would have liked."

"That's alright," Captain Delacruz added. "Something tells me that the insights we'll get from that prisoner will go a long way toward figuring out our foe."

"Understood," Jareth said.

"There remains one final duty," the admiral followed. "The fate of that vessel." She pointed to the center screen display, which showed a profile image of the vessel to their port side, mostly in one piece with enormous holes in the hull, some of which still had materiel occasionally falling out of them. "Its orbit is decaying. I cannot imagine that a neutronium hull impacting the planet's surface at terminal velocity would be good for recovery efforts or any survivors on the surface."

"I'm guessing the task force didn't bring any mass drivers with us," Jareth said and received nods from the captain and admiral. "Then, can we nuke it?"

"That hull is still neutronium, Lieutenant, there's—"

"Forgive me, Admiral. I meant from the inside. The explosion will vent out the holes facing toward the planet and propel the ship in the opposite direction."

The admiral looked thoughtfully for a moment and shared a look with Captain Delacruz, who turned to the tactical officer. "Mr. Filipov-Ibañez, compute the trajectory that vessel would take in the event of a thermonu-clear explosion in the interior, assuming that the hull holds and the current breach points remain as they are."

Filipov-Ibañez moved his fingers across his console, running simula-tions and calculating probabilities.

"Yes, Captain," he said after a few moments. "There is a 91 percent probability that a thermonuclear blast placed amidships will cause a jet that will propel that vessel out of its current orbital decline into either a higher, more stable orbit or out of orbit altogether."

"Make it so," Delacruz replied.

"Aye, Captain," Filipov-Ibañez responded.

"Mr. Thorsten, move the ship, Z plus 50 klicks. Ms. Flores, signal the fleet and alert them to our plans. Mr. Hannover, alert the crew to stand by for missile launch and to take potential radiation precautions."

"Aye, Captain," the three of them said simultaneously.

As the Deliverance moved fifty kilometers away from the alien vessel's orbital plane, Captain Delacruz turned to Jareth again and said, "Mr. Killian, this was your idea. Would you like the honors?"

"It would be my privilege, Captain," he replied. "Commander Filipov-Ibañez, status."

"Mark V torpedo armed, targeted, and awaiting your order."

Well, Chollie, this one's for you, Jareth thought. Then: "Fire!"

The Deliverance's hull echoed with the thud of a missile launch from its portside missile tubes. Everyone turned toward the forward view screen, which tracked the missile's flight into the breach on the alien vessel's star-board side before disappearing within. A split second later, the alien craft's breaches lit up with blue light, and the ship began moving away from the planet.

"Excellent," said Captain Delacruz. "At the very least, we've bought ourselves some time to get some mass drivers in-system, and we've taken out whatever might have been left in that vessel. Mr. Killian, why don't you get out of that battle armor, get cleaned up, and report back here when you're ready?"

"Thank you, Captain," he said, leaving the bridge for the shuttle bay to drop off the combat armor before making his way up to his quarters.

✛

HE TOOK A LONG shower, standing for a while as the hot water ran over him. With the grime and sweat that washed off of him came the stress and tension he'd been carrying around with him for a long time—ever since those first images of Farmark appeared on the viewscreens at the *Infanta de Castilla* all those months ago.

He stood there sobbing as the adrenaline that he'd been living off of for so long ebbed, and all the feelings of grief, sorrow, despair, and fear that he'd been repressing came flooding out. At times, he cried out of relief that they had been able to do what they had set out to do. At times, he cried out of loss—for those who'd died in the invasion, those who died on the Expedition, those who had been killed in this battle, for Master Gunnery Sergeant Makindi's Echo Squadron, for Kian and Ando Lee-Chowdhury. He wept that their first contact with non-human intelligent life had been so costly, and he wondered whether their prisoner would help the League understand these creatures, what they wanted, and whether humanity would have to live in fear of them forever.

After about twenty minutes, he felt all cried out. It wouldn't be the last time, for sure. But it was at least a sign that the healing process from everything he'd been through was beginning.

Jareth dried off and got dressed. He caught himself in the mirror and remembered all those months ago when he'd first put on the uniform and thought that he looked the part. He still looked the part, but now he felt the part, too. That would be a feeling he would have to process in the coming weeks. He'd never thought about what lay beyond this mission, and supposed none of them had felt they had the luxury of planning a future until they could ensure that there would be one.

He returned to the bridge and began writing up his mission report. Command would have much to sift through as it assessed this battle and the risks going forward.

His colleagues on the bridge were busy with all manner of post-combat operations. Filipov-Ibañez was scanning the planet's surface for signs of surviving human life. Flores was encoding messages to transmit back to the rest of the League on hyperspace drones. Hannover was already organizing landing parties to survey the system and track down any life signs that Filipov-Ibañez might find. The admiral and captain were having numerous conversations with their counterparts on other vessels. The ship, which had been on a wartime footing for so long, began to feel like a ship at peace.

THAT NIGHT AFTER SHIFT, Jareth and Rebekah grabbed dinner in the officer's lounge. The atmosphere of celebration was in the air, but it was a quiet celebration—more relief than jubilation. It seemed that many of his shipmates had been having similar reactions to the day. Everyone was happy it was over, but out-and-out revelry was still not where anyone was emotionally.

"So, are you looking forward to going back to Fairhaven?" he asked in between bites.

"Yeah," she responded. "It'll be nice to be home. I'm not sure how long I'll stay, but some familiar environments will do me good. Lyra and I have a lot of reconnecting to do and a lot of grieving, too. You? You headed back to New Sydney?"

"For a time," he said. "I want to see my folks. I didn't exactly leave them on good terms, and it's time to work through all that. I don't feel nearly like the same person I was when we left."

"I'm pretty sure that's true for all of us," Rebekah replied. "If you came out of this the same as you went into it, you missed something along the way."

"Yeah, I guess that's true. Except for the admiral, of course. I'm positive that woman was born in command."

They spent the rest of the evening talking about Rebekah's updated translation matrices and her new earbud interpreters, drinking their share of beer and wine, and reminiscing about their adventures on Earth and the other worlds of the Commonwealth they'd seen.

Jareth knew their lives would change soon enough: in a few days, the *Deliverance* would head out of the system to return to New Sydney, where the crew would be debriefed and interviewed. Some would move on to new assignments, and many would disembark and return to civilian life. Jareth considered that for the rest of their lives, those who'd been on the Expedition or participated in the battle would only be understood by fellow veterans of the voyage. They had been from the farthest reaches of human civilization to its ancient homeland. They had withstood so much along the way. It would be hard to reintegrate with populations that couldn't understand what they had been through.

But all that was still in the future—and knowing that there would be a future was good enough for now.

EPILOG

Return-Path: killian.j.09287@fl.op.isg.01
Authentication-Results: isg.01; auth=cleared; class=unclassified
Content-Type: text, non-encrypted
Delivered-Via: ISG FleetNet, New Sydney Node
Delivered-To: killian.aidan@cv.nk.ns, heike.killian@1132.2298.
nk.ns
Subject Header: Updates
Date: 2792-04-08 21:39 (STD)

Dear Mom and Dad,

I'm sorry I haven't written in a bit—it's been pretty busy on this end. But I thought you'd enjoy hearing about the event tonight.

It took place in the reviewing gallery of the New Sydney Harbor dry-dock, high in orbit. We got to see the newest ship of the line. It's the first ship built by the Commonwealth–League Exploratory Cooperative, and it has a Mark III Sheridan Drive, a next-generation hyperspatial rudder, and a couple of FI antimatter cannons for good measure.

The crowd was mostly fleet officials, but there was also a fair number of civilians. I have no idea how much money they had to pay to take a trip up to the harbor for this occasion. There was plenty of press, too, so this will probably be in the news feeds tomorrow morning.

Admiral Kavanagh was there with a combined delegation of brass from the ISG and the Commonwealth Navy. The Navy Band even played marches. Chancellor Parvat-Singh and Commonwealth Ambassador Isfahani were there as well and made speeches. The usual "Citizens of the Commonwealth and of the League, this is a great day" kind of stuff.

And, of course, Cousin Myra was there. I'm so glad you got to go to her installation as Bishop of New Sydney and Pherat for the NCC. Don't you think she looks a little like Dad's sister Keira? Anyway, you would've liked it—she read from some scriptures about the "glory of God in the heavens" or something and said some nice prayers remembering those who'd died and the promise this new ship represented.

Then, the Chancellor christened the ship by launching an actual bottle of Earth champagne at it. By the way, did you know that Champagne was a place? It's now on my list of places to visit if I ever get back to Earth.

They named the ship *Enterprise*—it's a name that has a lot of meaning to Myra's church. Because of the role they played in getting the Commonwealth to help us, no one was going to say no when they suggested it.

I got a chance to talk to Myra afterward, and she was excited about the new ship—it's the first one in a long time built to go beyond the boundaries of known space and explore. She said the Invaders had come from somewhere, and we needed to find where that was and why they'd done what they'd done. "We need to find out whether we have permanent enemies or future friends." That seemed like a stretch, but she's not wrong—it's something we need to know. And there's so much else to explore, too.

They announced that Admiral Kavanagh would be staying in the League to help develop the Joint Exploration Fleet, and Captain Delacruz was awarded command of the *Enterprise*. That made me really happy to hear.

I also got to see my friend Rebekah there. We shared a glass of champagne—something called *Dom Perignon* from Earth—it was outstanding. Rebekah told me all about her work trying to decipher the Invaders' language—she's one of only fourteen people in the entire League who've been allowed into the presence of the alien! But it was hard to tell whether she was more excited about that work or her new gig at the Academy teaching "Contemporary Commonwealth Language and Literature." It was great to see her. I gave her your contact information for when she's in New Kalgoorlie on business.

Anyway, I just wanted to drop you a quick note to say hello and that I miss you both. I'm glad we got to work through things last summer. It feels good not having to hide anything from you anymore. Or from myself, for that matter.

I should probably wrap this up and get going. The *Enterprise* is setting sail for the unknown reaches—and I am due aboard.

Yours,
Jareth

Lt. Cmdr. Jareth Killian
Chief of Security
CLS *Enterprise*
killian.j.09287@fl.op.isg.01
Science Division
Sharon Central Command, Intersystem Guard
Ut fortiter ire

ACKNOWLEDGMENTS

NO BOOK IS WRITTEN in true isolation, even when we've locked ourselves away to focus (something that never works for me in any event—I'm far more productive in noisy coffee shops). A book is the result of the author's imagination and experiences, and those experiences always involve other people. It's only just that those people be thanked.

Of the Wipf & Stock staff, I would like to thank Matthew Wimer for his continued support of my work, both fiction and nonfiction, and George Callihan for all his help during the submission and publishing process. Thanks, too, to Kate Koppy for beta reading and suggesting I reach out to Wipf & Stock to explore the possibility of publishing with them again. And very special thanks to the Incomparable Robert Berg for his beta reading and savage critique of the first draft, which helped me rework, rewrite, and recreate the narrative in a much better form.

I also would like to thank the aforementioned noisy coffee shops— Soho Tea & Coffee, the Hoosick Street Starbucks, Uncommon Grounds, and Stacks Coffee, where most of the writing took place.

In many ways, this book is an homage to science fiction, a genre that helps us to explore our world through the lens of the possible. Because of that, this book is written with sincere appreciation for the work of Gene Roddenberry, Larry Niven, Isaac Asimov, Margaret Atwood, Gregory Benford, James Blish, Orson Scott Card, James S.A. Corey, Philip K. Dick, Robert Heinlein, Frank Herbert, Cixin Liu, Walter Miller, Sean McMullen, Elizabeth Moon, Mary Doria Russell, Fred Saberhagen, John Scalzi, Neal Stephenson, Harry Turtledove, John Varley, Vernor Vinge, David Weber, Andy Weir, H.G. Wells, Evgenii Zamiatin, and countless others who have stretched the limits of human imagination and inspired me to do the same.

I use several sci-fi tropes throughout the book and do so intentionally. There are clichés and patterns (e.g., the two past, one future series: "the

Roman legions, the Allied forces, or the Belt Rangers") and other inside jokes that are meant for the appreciation of sci-fi fans ("required reading at the academy"). These are also done to show my gratitude for all the great authors and producers of the science fiction that I have so loved and enjoyed.

Mark Schaefer
Troy, New York